HEARTS RISING

PENELOPE BELL

Jacqueline,
Always rise above
and beyond!

A Bell

Penelope

Library of Congress Cataloging-in-Publication Data

Paperback ISBN: 978-17337099-0-3

Hearts Rising | Copyright © 2019 by Penelope Bell | Pending

Cover design Copyright © 2019 by Antonette Santillo, Dragonfly Ink Publishing
Edited by Sandra Ebel, Dragonfly Ink Publishing
www.dragonflyinkpublishing.com

"The phoenix hope, can wing her way through the desert skies, and still defying fortune's spite; revive from ashes and rise."
– Miguel de Cervantes

DEDICATION... the word itself encompasses the very reason why I must dedicate this book to my mother "Ellie."

Her unconditional love, support, compassion, sacrifice, and guidance was truly inspiring, not only for me but family and friends alike. If it wasn't for her consistent urging, this book would never have been written. Even in her darkest and last days on earth, she was more concerned about me publishing my writings than caring about herself.

I know she is looking over me right now and smiling, giving me the "thumbs up" and nudging me to get the next one done.

Thank you, Mom, for giving me the heart to carry through with the promise I made to you and myself.

With love,
"Peanut"

PROLOGUE

There are events and times in our lives that make us stronger. When it happens, we may not recognize it or even understand it. Later, we are tested to see whether those taxing periods did indeed give us the strength to carry on, move forward and rise above.

Such is the circumstance of Victoria Hart, a petite and demure young woman who mentally and emotionally battled against the onslaughts of bullies while growing up. She was part of a group deemed a target for bullying, a group of students who had taken their studies seriously and endeavored to rise above the cruelty they faced almost on a daily basis. During those instances, Victoria fought back the urges to retaliate in kind. She was raised better than that. Fervently hoping, once she was free of the environment appearing to foster the unkind behavior from some classmates, she would be able to put the past behind her. She wasn't going to allow them to burn out her desire to achieve her dreams.

But in this crazy, messy world we all live in, bullies come in all kinds of disguises, all genders, all ages, and at all times, not just when we are young—sometimes unrecognizable until it may be too late. It's when they are unmasked, Victoria is given the opportunity to brandish her honed resolve, and akin to the Phoenix, rises from the ashes.

CHAPTER 1

PAST TIMES
Victoria and Brandon

Brandon Barkley literally swept the petite Victoria Hart off her feet.

"I really am so sorry. I somehow lost control coming over the hill and didn't see you until it was too late," he apologized. "Are you alright?"

Victoria felt like she had been hit by a freight train and gasped for air, having her breath knocked out of her.

"Yes... I'm pretty sure nothing is broken since I can stand up on my own," she said caustically, flashing her exasperated hazel-green eyes and nodding to his hand which was still holding onto her arm. Still somewhat shaken, Victoria removed her snow- and ice-covered goggles, availing herself to see what the talking brick wall looked like.

Brandon continued apologizing profusely as he was getting up. He had reached for her hand to help her up, using his other hand to remove his reflective ski goggles. Victoria immediately caught a whiff of alcohol and figured he had been drinking prior to his downhill escapade.

He pulled away brusquely. "Sorry, again," he responded.

Victoria was on a weekend ski trip with her college roommates at Snowbowl, about fifteen miles from where they attended NAU in

Flagstaff, Arizona. She had learned to ski two years prior during her first year at the university. She loved the exhilaration of gliding down the slopes, and with a headband protecting her ears from the cold, her ski goggles in place, and her long blonde hair tied back in a ponytail whipping around, she felt like she was taking flight as she traversed effortlessly down the hills and moguls.

Victoria was coming down such a slope when she was blindsided by Brandon who was skiing recklessly, showing off for his buddies. The two of them tumbled downhill along the slope and ended up in a mound of snow with him winding up on top of her, the back of her head mere inches from the trunk of a large ponderosa pine tree.

As Victoria was brushing the snow and ice from her sky-blue ski jacket and pants, her long blonde hair had come undone and was cascading down her back. She swept it to the side to shake the ice crystals out.

Her friends had seen what happened and skied over to where Brandon and Victoria were now standing.

"You okay, Victoria?" one asked.

"I'm good, but I think I should head to the chalet to have my equipment checked out and possibly readjusted," Victoria responded.

Brandon's friends had arrived on the scene as well, and Brandon piped up, "Hey, how about we all head up to the Lodge and have some refreshments on me to make up for this?"

Victoria was hesitant at first, but her dorm mates pressed the issue, saying it was a "peace offering" for ruining her run down the slope. Within a short while, they were all sitting around a blazing fireplace in the lodge, drinking Hot Toddies and Rum Chatas.

Without the knit ski hat and ski jacket, Victoria could get a better look at her downhill marauder—dark blonde hair, short on the sides and longer on top which looked as if he spiked it with his fingers, gray-blue eyes, and a pretty fair athletic physique at six feet tall. Names were exchanged, and small talk included where each was from, and once it was determined they all were attending NAU, what courses they were taking.

Victoria was surprised to find out Brandon was aiming for the same accounting degree and found it hard to believe they actually had one class together. Although sitting in a class of about one hundred students could explain that.

Within a couple of weeks, Brandon had Victoria tutoring him with his accounting courses, and she found it somewhat flattering someone like Brandon would even take notice of her.

Because of the bullying she endured, particularly in high school, she had developed a shell around her only classmates who were of her same demeanor would be able to penetrate. Her self-esteem would only appear when she was with her like-minded friends. Victoria didn't date much while in high school, her first real date her Senior Prom, accompanied by a boy who was part of her "nerd herd" realm. Any boys she associated with were only friends or members of the same clubs. One of her best friends in school, Robyn Green, the computer science guru in the group, had a saying when it came to dating. "Romance, no chance." Like Victoria, Robyn had her goals set for a degree, and nothing and no one was going to stand in the way of getting it... especially a guy.

Brandon's attention threw her for a loop. Her lack of experience made her vulnerable. When Brandon was around, he made her feel special. No boy had made her feel that way before.

Eventually, over the semester, Brandon and Victoria became an item. Before Brandon, Victoria hadn't had any serious relationships while in college.

Unlike Victoria, Brandon didn't really seem to be into studying, and Victoria found herself tutoring him more and more so he could at least get passing grades.

Victoria worked hard in high school back in Illinois to get her scholarship and was excited when she received her acceptance letter from NAU. Not only would her scholarship cover her tuition, book fees, and housing, she would also be studying in a completely different atmosphere —mountains, forests, skiing, The Grand Canyon, etc. Phoenix was only a little over two hours away by car down I-17 and offered plenty of venues for entertainment such as theaters, music, museums, and professional sports.

The monetary part of the tuition would also alleviate any need for her parents to have the financial burden of her college education. Victoria's mom, Marya, was a registered nurse, and her father, Ben, had a small accounting firm in a suburb on the outskirts of Chicago. Victoria was all too happy they wouldn't have to dig into their savings to supplement her education expense.

Victoria and her parents lived a comfortable but never extravagant life. She appreciated everything they did have and felt she never needed more.

Brandon, on the other hand, came from wealth and was "overindulged" by his parents. It bothered Victoria, at times, he was so nonchalant about it. He always seemed to take it for granted his family would always pay his way, no matter what, when, or why. He was basically raised by nannies and live-in housekeepers and totally clueless how to handle responsibilities, from picking up after himself to being accountable for his actions. Victoria hoped his cavalier irresponsibility would dissipate as he matured.

Brandon grew up in the Phoenix area and was resolute about making several trips a month to visit family but usually ended up spending more time with his friends. He would frequently leave the university right after his classes on Friday, driving the two-and-a-half hours down to Phoenix either by himself or with a couple of his college buddies. Victoria actually welcomed the time alone and either studied, hiked, or visited the various historical points of interest within an hour's drive of the university. She had several friends who enjoyed the same things, and there was always transportation available.

Brandon was constantly trying to get Victoria to become intimate with him, but she kept putting him off. She wanted to get her degree first and foremost, and hopefully, garner a CPA status a few years after graduating. A deeper relationship would entail taking time away from her studies. She didn't want to throw away all those years of studying and her scholarship. Plus, there was his irresponsibility issue she continued to find troubling.

She knew she was making it difficult for Brandon and told him if they were meant to be, it would happen. She used one of her mother's favorite lines, "Timing is everything."

The summer break before her last year at the university was a busy one. Victoria worked as an intern for one of the accounting offices of the university, gaining experience, and her housing was subsidized for her work. She went back to Illinois that July for four weeks to visit with her parents, then headed back to the university to continue working in the university's accounting office, gaining more accounting experience and knowledge. Her relationship with Brandon was on hold during this time.

Brandon and several of his friends had taken off for Mexico and the Caribbean for their summer break, leaving shortly after classes ended at the beginning of June and didn't return to the campus until late August, just in time to pick up class schedules, books, and get their fraternity housing in order.

During her senior year at NAU, her father's car was hit by a drunk driver, and her father died instantly. Victoria was shaken to her core. It was just before Christmas and the winter break, and she had been planning to fly home for the holidays. Instead, she was back home, grieving with her mother, Marya and offering to move back home and take courses at a college nearby to finish her degree.

"No, Victoria." Her mother was adamant and wouldn't hear of it. "You stay at NAU and get your degree. It's what your father would have wanted, and it's what I want you to do. Make us proud."

Brandon didn't go with her when she went back home to help with her father's funeral arrangements and services. He almost seemed relieved, in fact, when she said he didn't have to attend. His behavior was somewhat callous about it all. She assumed it was because of the strained relationship he had with his own father.

After the winter break, Victoria returned to NAU and went about making sure she graduated with honors. Brandon, on the other hand, appeared to enjoy more and more of the social aspects of college, instead of the academic. Victoria still hoped he would change once he was out in the business world.

Brandon's father already had a job for him at his very well-known and lucrative accounting firm in Phoenix. Ross Barkley was a founding partner of the firm and was held in high esteem by the movers and shakers in the Phoenix, Paradise Valley, and the Scottsdale area.

CHAPTER 2

Graduation finally rolled around, and Victoria did indeed graduate with high honors. Brandon, however, barely made it, and without the help and guidance of Victoria, he wouldn't have graduated at all. His heart just wasn't in it.

Whenever Victoria approached Brandon about his lack of interest and drive, he would just shrug, which was worrisome at best. She felt their relationship needed a solid footing and his laissez-faire attitude was unsettling.

Victoria's mother, Marya, flew in for the graduation, and her hazel eyes were filled with tears as she watched her daughter walk across the dais to receive her degree.

"I am so proud of you, and I know your father is so proud too." Victoria was speechless. It meant so much to hear those words. Her mother always referred to her father in the present tense as if he was an angel, ever present and watching over them.

Brandon had been applying more pressure on Victoria regarding their relationship, and at the graduation celebration held at his parent's home in Paradise Valley, Arizona, he made an elaborate scene, proposing to her in front of everyone. Victoria felt cornered and accepted his proposal while he placed an obscenely large diamond engagement ring on her finger—knowing Brandon probably got the money for it from his parents. It was totally not her style. Victoria liked traditional with a bit of simplicity, and only one word came to mind as she looked down at the ring—garish.

"Victoria, are you sure about this?" her mother asked, pointing to the ring when they walked out to the garden.

"Mom, I'm just as surprised as you. Yes, we've been dating, but I had no idea he was going to pull this, we hadn't discussed marriage. I really wished he wouldn't have proposed so publicly. It should have been a private moment with just the two of us. I do care about him, and when we're together, he makes me feel special, but..."

Just then, one of the Barkley's servants came out to the garden and told them Mr. Barkley requested their presence in the main hall. Victoria and her mother looked at each other.

"Now what," they said simultaneously.

Guests had gathered around, and Ross Barkley stepped out of his library with his son, Brandon, trailing behind him.

Ross, being the egomaniac he was, loudly cleared his throat to get everyone's attention. A hush fell over the room, and the guests all turned in his direction.

"It's my pleasure to announce since Brandon and Victoria are now engaged and each with their accounting degrees in hand, both Brandon and Victoria will have positions at my firm." Applause broke out.

Victoria was flabbergasted. Neither Brandon nor his father had ever made mention of a possible position at the firm for her. Victoria had been sending out her resumes to accounting firms, both in the Chicago and Phoenix areas.

"Hold tight to your dreams, and remember I will always be there for you... your Dad too," Marya whispered, putting her arm around Victoria.

Blindsided, Victoria was too numb to respond. Everything was moving too quickly. Little did she know, it was going to get even more so.

Brandon was still pressuring Victoria to consummate their relationship. He had purchased a high-end condo in Scottsdale—of course—with his parent's money and wanted Victoria to move in with him. She again rebuffed him.

She obtained a six-month lease with an extension option on a small two-bedroom condo in Central Phoenix and was quite happy with the area and the accommodations. Brandon was antagonistic about it.

"I don't know why you won't move in with me. After all, we're engaged to be married. What difference does it make? Besides, it would save on expenses. Then maybe you'll realize just what you've been missing... particularly in the bedroom."

"I had hoped you would understand, Brandon," Victoria shook off his last comment and responded as calmly as she could. "I want to wait until we're married. This is all new to me... a new place to live, a new job, and now, a wedding to plan. The fact you never mentioned anything about an engagement and the position at your father's firm has really thrown me for a loop. I want my own place until we're married."

Brandon was behaving like a child who couldn't have what he wanted when he wanted it. Victoria stood firm. She felt she'd been bullied enough by him and his father, and she wasn't about to be bullied about her living arrangements. Victoria's salary at the firm was quite enough to cover her rent, her car lease, and living expenses with a little to put aside in a savings account.

Victoria felt ramrodded into the engagement, the position at the Barkley firm, then the wedding. Brandon's parents pushed for the wedding to take place that very fall at their country club, and Brandon's mother, Claudine, took control of the wedding arrangements—except for one thing Victoria insisted on. Victoria flew her mother into Phoenix to help her find a wedding dress.

Brandon was relentless until their wedding day, causing Victoria to add to the mental list of doubts she had about the marriage. But she'd committed, and it was too late now—or so she thought at the time.

It was her wedding day, and Victoria should have been happy, but her father wasn't there to walk down the aisle and give her away. And seeing her "husband" playing the fool for his friends left a bitter taste in her mouth. The ceremony seemed so surreal when Victoria and Brandon said their vows, Brandon's ringing with a lack of sincerity as he appeared to snicker his way through them, rolling his eyes.

Victoria had one of her college roommates who lived in the area as her maid of honor, and Brandon had one of his college buddies as his best man. Brandon's mother, the social maven, was disappointed there weren't more bridesmaids and groomsmen and voiced her disapproval. The haughty Claudine Barkley was all about "show" and expressed her displeasure the wedding wasn't elaborate enough and about the small number of invited guests. Although at the wedding and reception, the boisterous chaos which ensued gave a clear indication many of Brandon's college and work buddies were present.

In college, Victoria had spent most of her nights studying while Brandon, on the other hand, spent his nights out with his friends. She could now see firsthand what they were like when they were out those nights. They acted like juveniles, rather than the college graduates they all were, trying to out-drink each other and making vulgar remarks.

"Remember what I said, Honey," Victoria's mother said softly, concerned, putting her arm around her. "I'll always be there for you. And remember what Grandma would say…"

Marya didn't have to say the words, Victoria knew her little Italian grandmother's words and had it marked indelibly in her mind.

"Non fidarti della tua camicia da notte." Don't trust your own nightgown.

On their wedding night, Brandon had booked the Bridal Suite at the Ritz Carlton. A driver was hired to take them to the hotel, and once checked in and escorted to their suite, Brandon passed out cold on the bed.

Some wedding night this is.

He reeked of alcohol, tobacco, and something pungently sweet. The next morning, Brandon looked like hell, was sick as all get out, and proceeded to spend most of the day either in the bathroom or sleeping it off in bed.

Brandon's parents had made arrangements for them to spend a week up in Sedona at a resort, but they ended up canceling due to Brandon's condition. It was well over three days before he was actually coherent and could walk on his own without bumping into something or knocking something over. But his eyes were sunken, red-rimmed, with dark circles.

After another day, their marriage was finally consummated and could only be summed up in one word—disappointing. Brandon seemed to think it was only for his pleasure. His roughness and vulgar comments weren't at all what Victoria had expected or wanted, and she felt an emptiness she never thought she would at a time meant to be special.

Victoria spent the "honeymoon" time off from work moving her things into Brandon's condo, opening wedding gifts, and sending out thank you cards. Her mother stayed at Victoria's apartment in town to help with the wedding, the move, the thank you responses, and anything else Victoria needed. Her mother also needed to talk to Victoria about something very important and waited for the right opportunity which presented itself one afternoon while they were packing moving boxes.

"Victoria, we need to talk," her mother stated seriously as she took her daughter's hand and motioned her to sit down.

"What is it, Mom? Are you okay?" Victoria asked with a bit of dread in her voice, placing her hand on her mother's shoulder. She'd lost her father and couldn't bear anything happening to her mom.

"Oh, Honey, I'm fine. Better than fine if things go the way I'm planning. But I wanted to tell you about it first and hope you'll be okay with it," Marya said, ending her comment with questioning side look.

"And... go ahead, Mom," Victoria said, hesitation in her voice.

"Well, your father and I had many fabulous years together. We had you for a wonderful daughter, and you are all I really have left. Oh, I have some friends back in Illinois I'm fond of, but my world really isn't there anymore. It's lonely living in a big house by myself. Since retiring recently, I try to fill my time with volunteer work, but it just isn't as fulfilling as I wish it would be. My years as a nurse made me truly believe you have to keep moving or you become a victim of loneliness and create your own cage. I want to fly. I want to grow wings and fly," Marya said emphatically, throwing her arms out wide and spinning around.

"Mom, just what are you saying?" Victoria was flabbergasted, looking at her mother like she had grown a third eye. "You want to take a trip... go skydiving... become a pilot?" Victoria asked hesitantly, trying to sound flippant.

"No, no, no. I'm going to sell the big ol' house back in Illinois, pack only what I need and cherish, buy a place in Arizona, and hopefully, be able to do volunteer nurse work with the local VA Rehabilitation Hospital and Clinics here. I've already looked into it, and they really do need the help. I have the right credentials and certainly don't need the income. Your father had all of our finances in order, so I'm positive it will work out. I don't want you to think I'll be infringing on your life and marriage. I just want to be there for you if and when you ever need me,"

Marya responded, holding in check those intuitive feelings mothers tend to get.

"Mom, I'll always need you," Victoria responded with tears in her eyes. "If this is really what you want to do, I'm all for it. I worried about you back there in Illinois alone. Besides, if and when Brandon and I have children, it would be wonderful they have a grandmother as wonderful as you close by."

Soon after their talk, Marya made contact with some friends who had a real estate brokerage near her home and started the ball rolling. She hoped within the next six months, she would have sold her home in Illinois, find a new home in Arizona, get moved in, and begin anew.

After her mom flew back to Illinois to get her house ready to put on the market—deciding what to keep, what to sell, and what to donate—Victoria put her nose to the grindstone at the accounting firm. She rarely saw Brandon during the course of the day since they worked in different divisions.

Victoria was given the choice of changing her last name to Barkley but opted to keep her maiden name for the time being. She didn't like the fact she might be treated differently if she was tagged with the Barkley name, wanting to make a name for herself in the firm. The firm's offices were located on the top three floors of a commercial high rise in the Biltmore area of 24th Street and Camelback Road. Brandon's office was on the top floor, and Victoria's was two floors below. Because Brandon and Victoria's schedule seemed to always conflict, they opted to drive separately to and from the office.

For the first couple of months, Brandon invited Victoria to his client dinners, but then those stopped, and Victoria found herself alone at home most evenings. Occasionally, they would attend social events with Brandon's parents.

A college classmate of Victoria's came to town, and Victoria mentioned going out for a "Girl's Night Out," but Brandon would hear none of it. Victoria opted instead to meet her friend for lunch.

There were some other gals at the firm who invited Victoria to join them to see a musical production at the ASU Gammage Theater. Brandon told her they were going to dinner with clients that evening, then canceled on her when it was too late to go out with her office friends. Victoria realized he lied to her to make sure she didn't go out. He was alienating her from her friends.

When he was home, he was becoming increasingly surlier and verbally abusive, sometimes getting rough with her—grabbing her arm or pinning her against a wall—each time increasingly hurtful than the last. No matter what she did, he found fault with it. Yet at the same time, he was becoming more and more possessive—questioning who she was talking to on the phone, what time she left the office, who she was working with. Victoria felt like she was always being interrogated. He was becoming more and more paranoid. There was an uneasiness building up inside her, causing her to feel frightened when he was around.

The office rumor mill was in overdrive. Victoria caught wind Brandon was running with a pretty fast crowd in the evenings. The group was known for their drinking, drugs, and wild parties.

CHAPTER 3

The accounting firm held their annual holiday party in early December. Victoria was looking forward to getting dressed up and enjoying time with her co-workers. She purposely bought a red, off-the-shoulder dress for the occasion, had her hair done, and got a manicure and pedicure. Feeling very special, she was taken aback by the surly comments from Brandon, suggesting she looked like she was "trolling."

"Brandon, we're going to a holiday event for the company. An event given by your parents where they will be in attendance as well. Sometimes I don't understand how you can come up with these ridiculous thoughts. You know very well, I'm not the kind to go out looking like a tramp or looking for a hookup. I've always been faithful to you. If nothing else, I saved myself for you. Now, I'm wondering why I did if that's all you think of me."

No sooner had she said the words when she was grabbed by the arm, slammed against the wall, and slapped hard on the side of her face. His other hand gripped her neck with such force, she was sure his prints would leave marks. She gasped for air. Just when she thought she was going to pass out, the phone rang.

Brandon jumped back, releasing Victoria as she slid to the floor, sucking in air.

Brandon answered the phone, and Victoria could hear the

conversation. It was Brandon's father. Ross and Claudine Barkley were in a limousine, heading over to pick Brandon and Victoria up for the party. Victoria could see Brandon swallowing hard, a worried look on his now ashen face.

After he hung up, he looked over at Victoria and got down on his knees in front of her. She flinched as he lifted his hand to gently caress her reddened cheek. He looked scared.

"Victoria, I am so sorry," he pathetically whispered. "I don't know what came over me. I've been under so much pressure at work, and it's just getting to me. Please forgive me. I promise it won't happen again."

Victoria knew deep down she couldn't trust him to keep his promise. She also knew the phone call from his father was what saved her. He was asking for her to forgive him—she couldn't.

She rose on shaky legs, ignoring his effort to help her and went into the bathroom. She ran cool water over her hands and looked into the mirror. Staring back was a woman with a haunted look, anger and fear in her eyes. She ran a washcloth under the cool water and raised it to her cheek, then to her neck. Telltale marks from Brandon's fingers were already beginning to reveal themselves on her neck.

"Truly, Victoria, I am so sorry." Brandon stood near the doorway to the bathroom.

"It will never happen again. I promise you. Please say something."

Victoria couldn't look at him or say anything. She needed time to think and time to plan. She had already approached Brandon about counseling, but he blew her off, saying if word got out, it would be detrimental to him, his parents, and the firm.

She went into her walk-in closet and went to the jewelry armoire, rummaging through a drawer, eventually pulling out a large choker necklace. She put it on and looked in a mirror on the armoire. It covered most of the marks on her neck—she hoped no one noticed.

She went back to the bathroom and put the damp washcloth back to her cheek, then patted it dry and dabbed some makeup on her inflamed cheek to tone down the redness. She added a touch more blush to her other cheek to match.

"Victoria..." Brandon said, reaching out to take her arm. Victoria quickly moved out of his reach.

"Don't. Touch. Me... ever again!" she gritted out, her hazel eyes filled with green fire. Brandon stepped back and was visibly shaken by her response.

The phone rang, and as Brandon answered it, she heard his father announcing they were downstairs, waiting in the limo for them. Victoria grabbed her clutch purse and a black velvet wrap and opened their condo door, Brandon trailing sheepishly behind her.

The limo driver had the doors open and assisted Victoria into the car, Brandon entering next, sitting next to Victoria.

The Barkley's, Ross and Claudine, greeted them, seemingly oblivious to the tension between Brandon and Victoria although Brandon's mother did look like she was scrutinizing Victoria's neck.

There was minimal talk between on the ride to the event. Ross Barkley mentioned some high-profile clients who would be in attendance, wanting to make sure Brandon paid special attention to them. Brandon assured his father he would.

The rest of the evening went smoothly. Victoria knew Brandon had to be on his best behavior, especially since his parents were there. Any questionable conduct would cause disfavor with his father and mean severe repercussions.

Victoria received an abundance of compliments from co-workers and clients alike, both on her attire and her work product. Brandon stood to her side without saying a word, just nodding, but nervous—very, very nervous.

A band was performing the old Christmas favorites and some new ones during and after the dinner. At one point, Brandon asked Victoria to dance, but she declined, saying her ankle was bothering her, suggesting he ask his mother to dance. His father seemed busy rubbing elbows with the firm's elite clients. Brandon turned and walked sullenly to where his mother was sitting and invited her to dance. Victoria was relieved, the last thing she wanted was to have Brandon's arms around her while dancing or at any time, for that matter. Even the thought made her cringe.

Her co-worker, Diana Foster, a slender blonde with an abundance of naturally curly blonde hair and enormous blue eyes, sat beside her.

"Victoria, you truly look lovely this evening."

"Diana, thank you! And you as well," Victoria responded as Diana took her hand and squeezed it gently.

"That's a beautiful choker you're wearing," Diana whispered.

Victoria's hand automatically went to her neck, an apprehensive look crossing her face.

Diana leaned into Victoria. "If you ever need anything, don't hesitate to call me. Understand? I can help."

Victoria nodded.

Diana looked up and noticed Brandon watching them, and the look he gave Diana was what you could only call as demonic. Diana rose from the chair and headed off in the direction of some of their co-workers. Victoria and Diana had been working closely together for the past six months. She knew enough about Diana and felt she was trustworthy. Victoria was also privy to some personal matters Diana had to face.

After excusing himself from his mother after the dance, Brandon returned to Victoria at their table.

"So what were you and Diana Foster discussing?" he asked snidely, leaning close, malevolence in his eyes.

Victoria was taken aback at his tone and his look since a short while before he was begging for forgiveness. Now he was in attack mode.

"Nothing of importance to you. Diana was very complimentary of my attire. It was nice to hear," Victoria responded, looking directly at Brandon. His uneasiness showed, and he got up and joined his friends at the bar for another drink.

A short while later, Ross Barkley walked to the microphone near the band and thanked those who attended for jobs well done, and as a show of gratitude, announced they would be receiving their year-end bonus checks the following Monday.

Victoria already knew what she would do with hers. She had kept her checking and savings accounts separate from her joint account with Brandon and had her salary deposited directly into her own account. She hadn't changed any of her beneficiary information. Victoria's mother remained as beneficiary on all her accounts, including her 401k and life insurance.

An hour after Ross Barkley's announcement, they were headed back to their respective homes in the limousine.

Victoria entered their condo, walked directly to the master bathroom, and closed the door, snapping the lock closed. Removing her choker, she was shocked at the bruising which was now quite evident.

Her cheek still seemed inflamed, and she wasn't sure if it would bruise as well.

She removed her high heels and dress, put her robe on, and walked out of the bathroom and bedroom, heading to the kitchen to make herself a cup of hot tea. As she passed the living room, she noticed Brandon sitting on the sofa with his head buried in his hands. No words passed between them the rest of the evening.

It was around midnight. Victoria was in bed and reached over to turn the lamp off. She laid there in the dark, dreading his coming to bed, but it was for naught. She heard the front door of the condo opening and closing. A short time later, she got up and looked out the window and saw him driving his car out of the underground parking garage.

Her sleep was fitful. She wasn't sure if he would be coming back, and if so, in what condition he would be in and in what temperament. She couldn't go on living like this.

She must have finally fallen into a deep sleep somewhere around dawn. The sound of a dog barking outside woke her. She peeked at the clock on the nightstand and saw it was almost nine a.m. Slowly turning her head, she noticed she was alone in the bed. Breathing a sigh of relief, she got out of bed and went into the bathroom. Her stylist had done her hair in an upswept style for the party. Normally, she would have brushed it out before going to bed, but after the events of last night, she had decided to forego her normal ablutions. From all appearances, her night of restlessness created a look of a mad woman, smeared eye-makeup giving her a haunted look, her tresses askew.

After washing up, she left the master suite and headed to the kitchen. Just as she was entering the kitchen, Brandon walked into the condo. She froze.

He walked with his head down toward the bedroom. She could tell by how he looked, he had been out drinking with his friends and heaven knows what else they did.

She decided to ignore him as best she could and make herself breakfast. It was Sunday, and the weather was gorgeous, so she decided to go out after breakfast for a walk through the nearby park. She needed the fresh air if for nothing else but to clear her mind.

After breakfast, she walked into the bedroom only to find Brandon not there. She heard snoring and walked down the hall to the guest room. He was sprawled across the bed. Visions of their wedding night flashed in her mind. She stood shaking her head, then walked back to the master bedroom to take a shower—again locking the bathroom door behind her. Victoria managed to get ready and leave the condo in record time. Brandon hadn't come out of the guest room, and she was glad.

Victoria walked through the park, noticing the families who were enjoying the amenities, the couples either walking or jogging together, and those out walking their dogs. It was a clear, sunny December day, and the temperature was a pleasant seventy-two degrees.

A wistful look came upon her as she watched children interacting with their parents, their laughter bringing her both joy and sadness. After being diagnosed with one of her ovaries being underdeveloped and her gynecologist alternating her medications to regulate her cycle, there was a possibility she might not be able to conceive. Her monthly cycle was a continuing issue even with the constant medication changes.

When she had told Brandon before they married, he just shrugged. It dawned on her now, having a child with Brandon would certainly take attention from him, and he wouldn't like sharing the spotlight he always craved even if it was with his own child.

She so wished Brandon had just once joined her on her walks in the park, but he always came up with an excuse why he couldn't go. He'd rather spend his free time with his boozing buddies at one of their bachelor pads or at a sports bar. She was feeling pangs of jealousy as she watched couples walking together, either holding hands or with arms around each other. Her heart ached for someone to hold her, someone to love her the way a man should.

Her mobile phone rang, startling her. Looking down at the caller ID she smiled. It was Diana, her co-worker from work.

"Hi, Diana!"

"Hi, yourself. Just calling to check up on you."

"I'm okay. Just sitting in the park near the condo, enjoying the weather and people watching."

"You had me worried last evening. Do you remember what I told you?"

"Yes, and I appreciate your concern... and if and when I ever need you, I will call you. Right now, I have some decisions to make and need my head clear to make them."

"I understand. Been there. Done that. You are a bright, beautiful woman, Victoria. You'll make the right decision."

"Thanks, Diana. I needed to hear it. I'll see you at the office tomorrow."

"Okay, Victoria, see you then."

After disconnecting the call, Victoria took a deep cleansing breath and closed her eyes. An hour later, she returned to the condo, only to find Brandon was still out cold in the guest bedroom.

The condo phone rang. It was Clayton, one of Brandon's buddies.

"Hey, Victoria, just checking on Brandon."

"Why?" she asked coldly.

"Well, he wasn't feeling well last evening, so we put him in an Uber and sent him home. His car is... well, somewhere in Old Town Scottsdale near the 'District.'"

Victoria rolled her eyes. She knew about the area, and its nightlife draw for freewheeling clientele.

"Brandon has been in bed since he got home and is still out cold." There was a long pause, waiting for a response from his friend.

"Um... do you want to pick up his car? I can come get you and drive you there... but I don't know exactly where..."

"No. Don't bother. Brandon is going to have to retrieve his own car when he wakes up. I'm not his 'clean up' crew." Victoria was sure the caller had a look of shock on his face.

"Well, um... okay. Just have him call me when he can."

Victoria hung up the phone to cut off any further discussion.

It was early evening when Brandon finally zombie-walked out of the guest room.

"Your friend Clayton called. He said they put you in an Uber last evening to get you home. Your car is somewhere in Old Town Scottsdale in the bar district. He wanted you to call him back. His number is on the caller ID."

Victoria walked into the kitchen and made herself a salad with grilled chicken, totally ignoring Brandon. While eating her salad, she heard Brandon on the phone with his friend. Then he went into the master bedroom and came out ten minutes later, still looking like he had been run down by a Mack truck.

"Just so you know, I'm getting a ride to my car. Hell, I have no idea where it is or if it's been towed." He looked over at Victoria and noticed her lack of response. Victoria didn't look up until she heard the condo door close, breathing a heavy sigh of relief.

The Monday following the holiday party, two dozen long-stemmed red roses were delivered to Victoria at the office from Brandon. Instead of putting them in her own office, she parceled them out to the staff.

The holidays were upon them, and the tension between Victoria and Brandon was at an all-time high. Victoria spoke to Brandon only when necessary and vice versa. He attempted to engage her in conversation several times, but she refused to participate.

Marya, Victoria's mother, came to town for Christmas but opted to stay at one of the resorts nearby. She told Victoria she didn't want to intrude on her and Brandon and considered the stay at the resort a Christmas present to herself. She told Victoria she had been so busy with her relocation to Arizona, she needed some pampering and invited Victoria to join her at the resort spa.

She wasn't sure if her mother's intuition had picked up on Victoria's anxiety. She hadn't wanted to burden her mother with the Brandon issues—at least not yet. She knew she would eventually have to talk with her mother about it.

Victoria felt like she was wearing a mask most of the time, pretending everything was hunky dory, especially around the Barkley's. It was as if she was walking through a minefield, never knowing if Brandon was going to lose it again.

Victoria enjoyed her time with her mom and was ecstatic she would soon be moving to Arizona. She'd missed her. Even though all through college she talked with her on the phone or through emails and texts, she missed actually sitting down and talking with her. The time at the spa did both of them a world of good. Victoria couldn't remember the last time she laughed so hard at some of the stories they shared.

Every once in a while, Victoria would drift off in her thoughts about the issues with Brandon and would catch her mother's look of concern.

The day before New Year's Eve Day, Victoria drove her mom to the airport.

"Victoria, you take care of yourself. Remember, I'm only a phone call away, and soon, I'll be back here in Arizona for good."

Victoria had a lump in her throat and tears burning the backs of her eyes. "Oh, Mom, you have no idea how much I am looking forward to it."

Hugs followed, and Victoria watched as her mother went through the TSA security checkpoint in the terminal, waving as she passed through the last security gate. Tears rolled down Victoria's cheeks nonstop. She walked back to the parking garage and got into her car, sitting there sobbing, waiting for the tears to stop and her vision clear to drive. It took a while.

CHAPTER 4

It was New Year's Eve. Brandon and Victoria had been invited to several parties, including the one at his parent's home. Brandon declined his parent's invitation, stating they had already accepted an invitation from one of his top clients. Ross Barkley was thrilled and told Brandon he totally understood, the client's party and any contacts he would meet there would be beneficial to him and the firm.

Unfortunately, Brandon neglected to tell his father he was planning on just attending the party for a short time, then would bugger out to be with his friends. Brandon also didn't include Victoria in his RSVP to the invitation. When Victoria confronted Brandon about his deception, he just shrugged. Brandon left for the evening around six p.m., dressed to the nines in "black tie" attire. He ordered up an Uber instead of taking his car—the same car that had been towed in Scottsdale a couple of weeks prior, been impounded, and cost him two hundred dollars to get back. Victoria guessed it was the one and only lesson he learned that night.

Victoria was relieved she wouldn't be spending the night celebrating the New Year with Brandon. The old wives' tale, *How you spend the New Year's would dictate how the rest of the New Year would go for you* hit solidly in her mind.

She relished the alone time, the quiet time.

Her mobile phone rang. It was her old high school friend, Robyn, according to the caller ID.

"Hi, is this Robyn?" Victoria asked.

"Ah... let me check... yeah, it's me! Hey, Victoria, how are you! Ready to welcome in the New Year?"

"No, not yet. It's still hours away. Where are you?"

"In Washington, just outside Seattle. You've been on my mind, and what better time to call than New Year's Eve to wish you a Happy New Year!"

"Oh, thanks, Robyn. Same to you."

"Hey, are you and Brandon headed out for the festivities?"

A long pause.

"Victoria... what's up?"

"Robyn, did you ever feel like you want a 'do over,' and the mistakes you made could be erased..."

"Oh, Victoria, something tells me things aren't going well. What's going on?"

"Robyn, it's a long story to go into now. Just know, Brandon isn't the man I thought he was... or maybe I was too blind and too inexperienced to see his faults. His irresponsibility is mindboggling. I saw it in college but had hoped once he was out in the business world, he would mature and accept accountability for his actions. He has issues with drinking, and I suspect drugs are also involved. He hangs with a group of guys who are serious contenders for the arrested development we learned about in psych class."

"How's he treating you? How's his demeanor?" Robyn asked with profound concern. After another long pause, she asked again, "Victoria, has he been physical with you?"

Victoria took a deep breath. "Yes. If it weren't for a phone call interrupting..."

"Oh, Victoria! You can't live in that kind of relationship... you can't survive in it."

"I know. I'm trying to come to terms with what I have to do. I know I won't put myself in a similar position again."

"Sweetie, all you have to do is pick up the phone, and I'll be there, and if need be, I can do some incredible damage to someone's kneecaps with all the classes I've taken in tactical defense."

Visions of Robyn cutting down Brandon with a kickboxing blow to his knees came to her.

"Always my protector, just like in high school."

"You got that right. Seriously, Victoria, you know you can always count on me. Just say the word."

"Okay. Enough about me. What's happening in your world? Hooked up with anyone yet?"

"Changing subjects, huh? Okay. No one on the romance horizon. Heck, I think this flaming red-haired, horny Amazon scares them off."

"You are not an Amazon, you're only 5'9". I'm a munchkin at 5'3". What a pair we made in high school!"

"We've come a long way, haven't we?"

"Yes, we have, Robyn. But my gut tells me we have a lot more ahead of us, and hopefully, it will be all good."

"I hear you, Victoria. Better go now. Happy New Year, Munchkin."

"Happy New Year, Amazon Woman! Love you!"

"Love you back, Victoria!"

Victoria held the phone to her chest. Just what the doctor ordered... a call from a dear friend to remind her she was thought about and cared for.

She settled in on the sofa and turned on the TV. Not wanting to watch all the New Year's celebrations, she got up and slipped in a DVD, then ran into the kitchen. She came back out and positioned herself to watch the romance movie and eat ice cream right out of the container. Best New Year's ever!

At midnight, her mobile phone beeped, indicating she had a text message... then it beeped again... then again.

She picked up her phone and read the messages. The first one was from her mom. *Happy New Year, Sweetheart. I love you!* The next one was from her friend Diana. *Happy New Year, Victoria! Wishing you a wonderful year ahead! Love, Diana.* And the last one was from Robyn. *Had to wish you a Happy New Year again! Love and Hugs, Big Red!*

Victoria thought to herself... yes, she was indeed loved. She responded to them individually with best wishes for the New Year and sent her love as well.

Victoria looked down at the container of ice cream—the empty container. Oh my, she was going have to do extra reps at the gym next week.

She welcomed climbing into bed and sliding between the sheets. Her thoughts alternated between pleasant ones involving her mom and her friends and troubling ones regarding Brandon. Eventually, exhaustion took over, and she fell asleep.

It was well after eight a.m. on New Year's Day when she awoke. She stretched out her arm to make sure Brandon wasn't there and let out a sigh of relief. He had been sleeping in the guest room since the holiday party incident.

Getting up, she walked quietly into the hallway. No sounds came from the guest room, not even snoring. The door was ajar, and looking in, it was quite evident Brandon wasn't there.

Good. Knowing him, if he came home now, he'd just go to bed and sleep away the day, leaving her alone.

Victoria made herself breakfast and after cleaning up, left the condo for a walk. She stopped on her way back to the condo at a coffee shop and got herself a mocha coffee and a bear claw pastry, sitting at one of the tables outside the shop. *"People watching is highly underrated. You can learn so much.*

She noticed a poster in the shop window, advertising an art walk just around the corner. Another fun thing she was sure she would never get Brandon to join her in doing. The art walk covered both sides of the street for three city blocks. Art galleries located within those blocks offered refreshments along the way.

Quite a few local artists had their creations on display. Victoria was amazed at the beautiful works in bronze, the colorful pottery, the impressionist watercolors, intricately loomed blankets, and unique handmade jewelry. A pair of hammered copper, silver, and turquoise earrings caught her eye, marveling at the workmanship. Her mother would love them. On impulse, purchased them for her.

She had come full circle on her tour of the works of art and made a stop at her favorite book store, purchasing a newly released novel she had been waiting for. Book in hand, she ordered her favorite chai drink, and once it was ready, nestled in a cushy chair in a quiet corner. She was so engrossed in her reading, she hadn't noticed how time flew by. Glancing at her watch, she resigned herself to returning to the condo.

Victoria stopped at an open café and ordered a "to go" box of their special lasagna dish she'd enjoyed on previous occasions.

Arriving back at the condo, she noticed Brandon still hadn't returned. She threw a salad together, heated up the lasagna, and settled in for yet another quiet evening all to herself—she hoped.

It was well after eleven p.m. when she heard the condo door open. She was already in bed, and all the lights in the condo were turned off. She heard Brandon let out a yelp when he bumped his knee into something. She wondered if she should have locked the bedroom door. She didn't need fear; he moved down the hallway and went into the guest room. She knew he wouldn't be in very good shape the next morning for work.

When her alarm went off at six a.m., she hurried into the bathroom to shower, locking the bathroom door behind her. A little over an hour later, she was showered, dressed in a navy-blue pencil skirt with a matching jacket and an ivory silk blouse, hair styled in an "updo", makeup on, ready to whip up a protein drink in the kitchen before she left for the office.

Still no sign of Brandon, but sounds of snoring echoed down the hallway. She thought about rousing him, but there was no telling what kind of mood he would be in. No sense in waking a sleeping bear.

She finished her drink and rinsed the blender jar and drinking glass, setting them on the side of the sink. Retrieving her briefcase and purse from the bedroom, she headed out to her car, wondering if and when Brandon would show up at the office.

At lunch, her friend Diana mentioned to her Brandon hadn't come into work. He had missed some important meetings, and his father was on a warpath.

As weeks went by, Brandon continued his partying in the evenings. He no longer was quiet and sullen around her at home. Instead, he was becoming more and more verbally abusive.

Then one night, actually at three a.m., Brandon was again brought home by an Uber. Victoria was startled when Brandon crashed through their bedroom door and pinned her down on the bed. He reeked of booze, nauseating perfume, and something else. She didn't want to know what it was. Prior to the holiday party, they hadn't been intimate in months because of his inebriated states, and when he was sober, which was a rarity, he wasn't able to function, making him all the more angry and aggressive. While he had her restrained, he kneed her in the groin to spread her legs, causing her to scream in pain.

Victoria had enough. She couldn't deal with it any longer. With angry determination, she shoved him off her, making him fall backward, landing on his back on the floor next to the bed. She scurried off the bed on the other side and tried to run across and out of the bedroom, but his hand reached out as she ran by and grabbed her by the ankle, causing her to fall, hitting her head. He grabbed her hair and twisted it tightly around his fist, causing her to cry out in pain.

"Shut up, bitch," he slurred and punched her on the side of her head with a closed fist. She dug her nails in his face. He let go and touched his face, shocked to see blood on his fingers. He lost his balance and fell backward. Victoria was able to get back up, grabbed her mobile phone off the night table, and ran into the bathroom. Locking the door, she dialed 911, her fingers shaking, her whole body trembling, and her head throbbing.

"911. What's your emergency?" a voice answered.

Victoria was breathless. She feared for her life. In a shaky voice, she told the operator her name and address, that her husband was drunk and had violently attacked her. The operator could hear Brandon yelling manically in the background, pounding on the bathroom door, calling Victoria names, telling her what he was going to do to her. The operator told Victoria the police were already on their way, for her to stay put, don't unlock the bathroom door, and stay on the line. The operator asked if there were any guns or other weapons in the residence. Victoria said she didn't know, she had never seen any.

Brandon kept pounding on the door, then took a bedroom chair and tried to break down the door. Victoria cowered in the corner of the bathroom with her mobile phone held tightly, listening to the operator's calming words. A few minutes later, a loud crash was heard, then voices indicating the police had arrived. The officers announced themselves and told Brandon why they were there. There was a scuffle, and they soon had Brandon in cuffs, advising him of his rights.

An officer went over to the bathroom door and told Victoria it was safe to come out, her husband was being taken down to a Squad car. The operator heard the officer, confirming to Victoria she was safe now.

Victoria slowly opened the door, still visibly shaking, so the officer had her sit down. A team of paramedics had also been alerted, and with Victoria's permission, took her vitals, taking note of the red marks on her head, face, and body and the bruising on her ankle. She had a buzzing in her ear, and the paramedics thought she might have damage to her eardrum. The paramedics told her she really needed to be checked out at the hospital.

On the ride in the ambulance, a female police officer, compassion in her eyes, rode along and asked her questions which Victoria answered as best she could. The officer asked if there was anyone she wished to be contacted. Victoria shook her head. Marya, Victoria's mother, was actually moving to Arizona in a couple of weeks, and Victoria didn't want her mother upset. She would tell her what happened when she arrived.

At the hospital, Victoria was ushered into a trauma center treatment room where the doctors and nurses checked her vitals again and examined her physical injuries, including her head injury, and a head scan was ordered. There was blood seeping from her ear— definitely a concussion and trauma to her eardrum. A specialist, called in for further examination, informed her it would take a while to determine the extent of the damage to her hearing, hoping in time, there would be sufficient healing and surgery would not be needed. There was really no way to know how much hearing loss there would be.

A short while later, another police officer introduced himself and advised Victoria her husband was booked on domestic violence and resisting arrest and taken downtown to the central jail. A restraining order would be processed with her approval.

Victoria closed her eyes and cringed at the thought of Brandon's parents getting a call in the middle of the night, informing them their son was in jail, looking to get bailed out. There wasn't anything Victoria could do about it. They created this monster, let them deal him. She was fed up.

The hospital kept Victoria overnight for observation, particularly because of the head injury. As she was waiting to be released the next morning, a very pompous and blustering Ross Barkley entered her hospital room.

"What kind of wife are you! Why can't you handle your husband?" he asked loudly, red in the face.

A nurse was checking Victoria's vitals and told him to settle down and leave. Mr. Barkley just waved her off.

Victoria pressed her hands to the sides of her head, looked scathingly at Ross Barkley.

"Why didn't you handle your son when you had the chance? He never had to work for anything in his life. He never had any responsibilities. You gave him everything. And now this monster you created is embarrassing the shit out of you, isn't he? You asked me what kind of wife I am. I ask you what kind of father have you been all these years? I'm the woman who tutored your son through college so he could graduate without bringing shame on you. I'm the wife who saved herself for a man who never knew how to be a real man. Did you at any time try to find out who his friends were, what they do till all hours of the night, what his work ethic is? God knows what he and his friends have been doing. No, you handed him a job he couldn't care less about.

"Look at me, Ross Barkley, just look at me and tell me this is my fault," Victoria cried out, exposing the bruises and marks on her body.

Ross Barkley stood frozen from her onslaught of words. Looking beaten, he turned on his heel and walked out of the door, just as a security officer was rushing in. Evidently, the nurse had pressed a code on the panel to summon security. When he asked if everything was okay, the nurse looked over at Victoria, and she nodded. The security officer left the room but made a point of saying he would be close by if anything was needed.

Victoria was soon to be released and was asked if she had a ride home. The only person she thought of was her friend at work, Diana who she had gotten close to over the past two months. She briefly told Diana she had to be taken to the hospital the day before, didn't have a car there, and asked if she would be able to drive her home. Diana immediately said yes and told Victoria she was on her way—no questions asked.

Within an hour, Victoria had signed her release papers, received referral and appointment information for the otologist for the damage to her hearing, and was in Diana's VW Bug headed home.

The look on Diana's face when she saw Victoria spoke volumes. Even though Victoria and Diana had only become close over a short time, Victoria knew she had dealt with domestic violence in her past and realized Diana knew the telltale signs.

After stopping at the pharmacy to pick up a prescription ordered by the hospital, they arrived at the condo, Diana insisting on going in with her. The police had given Victoria her purse containing her driver's license, medical cards, and keys when the ambulance had arrived at the hospital. As she opened the door to the condo, you could see through to the bedroom and the mess—a broken lamp, a smashed chair, and blood-stained carpeting. Victoria shivered, and Diana put her arm around her.

"Victoria, are you going to stay here?" Diana asked.

"Yes, for now, but I'm getting the locks changed and changing the code on the security alarm until I can make other arrangements. I definitely can't stay here for any length of time."

Diana looked straight into Victoria's eyes. "I know a group which can help you if need be. What about your position at the accounting firm?"

"I don't know. Deep down, I know I can't stay there. I've been approached by other accounting firms but never gave it a second thought... looks like I need to now," Victoria answered somewhat dejectedly. She really loved her work and her staff, but circumstances being what they were, she knew she couldn't stay.

"I understand. But truly, wherever you end up, I'll be around to share a quart of ice cream and a Hallmark movie with you," Diana said, trying to bring a little lightheartedness into the conversation. Victoria responded with a smile.

"What you really need now, Victoria, is a hot shower or bath."

Victoria agreed and tried to shoo Diana out, telling her she had better get back to work.

"I took some vacation hours for the rest of the day. You're not getting rid of me that easily, Victoria Hart."

Victoria smiled and headed to the bathroom.

After a long hot shower to ease the soreness in her muscles, she threw on her robe, wrapped her hair in a towel, and exited the bathroom. Everything was picked up, the bed linens stripped and replaced with fresh ones, and Victoria could hear the washer running in the laundry room. She found Diana sitting at the kitchen counter, trying to glue the base back on the broken lamp, the broken chair sadly lying on the floor near the door, hopeless beyond repair. Diana gazed up at Victoria and held up the lamp.

"Really, it may not look like it, but it is fixable. It might become the 'Leaning Lamp of Victoria!'" They both laughed.

Victoria walked over to the refrigerator and opened the freezer, set down a container of salted caramel ice cream on the counter, and pulled two spoons out of the drawer. More smiles. Victoria knew the frivolity was just a respite from the events of the past twenty-four hours, hoping any move she made in the future would be smooth.

CHAPTER 5

On Valentine's Day, a little over three weeks later on a Saturday, Victoria's mother, Marya Hart arrived in Arizona, phoning Victoria when she was an hour outside the Phoenix metropolitan area. She surprised Victoria, telling her she had a new car, an SUV, and extolled the fact it got great mileage traveling from DuPage County, Illinois all the way to Phoenix. She had the car packed solid with items she didn't want the movers to handle. The moving truck was scheduled to arrive in two days, and Marya wanted to get into her new home in the Desert Ridge area of North Phoenix as soon as possible.

When Marya arrived at the condo and saw Victoria, she noticed right away the faded bruising and gave her a hug with a deeply concerned look.

"Oh, Victoria, why didn't you tell me? What happened? I knew something was wrong when you didn't call me, and when we did speak, you were hesitant and avoided my questions. I didn't want to pry, but I had no idea it was this bad."

"Mom, the past weeks have been topsy-turvy in more ways than one. Sit down, and I'll tell you all about it. Just know, I'm alright, and things are going to be okay. No doubt about it. There are going to be changes but all for the better. Trust me on this."

Marya's worried face still remained so. Victoria launched into what had transpired over the past months and the climatic events of the weeks prior to her mother's arrival. As she related the happenings, Marya's expression alternated between worried to disbelief and quite a bit of anger.

"Maybe if Brandon and I had lived together before we got married, I would have seen him for what he was."

"Victoria, you can't go back and second guess yourself. It won't change anything. You need to move forward," Marya replied, reaching for Victoria's hands, holding them in her own.

Marya asked Victoria about the status of her marriage and her position with the firm. Victoria told her once she returned from the hospital, she placed a call to an attorney referred to her by her friend Diana. She was able to meet with the attorney immediately, signed divorce documents, and had Brandon served—all within twenty-four hours.

She had then called an accounting firm which had been trying to recruit her and made an appointment for a meeting. Evidently, she had made an impression with her work product. She was offered a position on the spot and asked if she could start the first of the following month, less than three weeks away.

When she gave her notice at Barkley's firm, it was obvious Ross Barkley was notified right away because Victoria received a message she was free to leave immediately if she wished. She would receive two months' salary as "goodwill" compensation, and her health insurance would be covered for ninety days. It appeared Ross Barkley and his legal team were trying to do damage control. She signed off on the employment separation, packed up her personal items in her office, and walked out with her head held high.

Just over a week later, the proverbial shit hit the fan at her old accounting firm. Victoria described the events of that particular week to Marya. Her friend Diana had called her at home, sounding all excited.

"What is it, Diana?"

"Victoria, you are not going to believe this... but maybe you will," she said cryptically.

Victoria knew it had something to do with Brandon. They hadn't spoken or seen one another, and he was honoring the restraining order. His parents had paid his bail, and he was back to work at his father's accounting firm. Diana told her federal investigators had come into the office, and a short while later, they were walking Brandon out in handcuffs. It was discovered he had been embezzling funds from multiple client accounts, big clients who were given to him by his father. They had traced the funds to a money laundering account set up by Brandon, the funds used for illegal ventures, including drugs. While Brandon had been incarcerated for the domestic violence, he was quite vocal about work-related things to other prisoners and the guards, then his lab tests came back, indicating illegal substances. Since he worked at an accounting firm handling government securities accounts, an investigation was authorized, and it opened a Pandora's Box. Three other accountants were also cuffed and escorted out to police cars. Holy hell broke out throughout the firm. A board meeting was held later, and heads were rolling, and Ross Barkley's would, sure enough, be one of them.

The wheels were set in motion. New Beginnings. She felt like the weight of the world was lifted off her shoulders. She felt like she could fly.

Marya shook her blonde head, her eyes glistening with tears as she listened to Victoria recounting her past weeks' ordeals. She was in shock about everything that happened. The fact Victoria handled it the way she had made her think of Victoria's father, Ben. He would be so proud. Victoria had her father's fortitude and determination. Marya would do everything she could to help Victoria fulfill her dreams and put the past behind her.

Victoria would be starting her position with the new accounting firm soon, but she had time to help her mom with the move into her new home. It was a one-story with a split layout, the master on one side and two guest suites on the other. Her mom decided to use one of the guest suites as an office or den. The kitchen was spacious and airy with two islands and lots of cabinets and counter space. There was no formal living room. Instead, it had a large family room with a fireplace, open to the kitchen and a dining area. From the kitchen, there was a formal dining room a short way down the hall with a concealed butler's pantry across from the entryway to the dining room. The pantry could be accessed by pulling an ornate lever on a hinged bookcase functioning as a doorway. Victoria marveled at it when she saw Marya open it. A small wine cooler sat in a corner of the pantry.

While unpacking boxes and putting things away, Marya broached the subject of where Victoria was going to live since the divorce was fast-tracked, and she would need to find a place soon. Brandon had already signed all the papers with no contest, and from what Victoria's attorney told her, the condo was held in the name of a revocable trust with Brandon's parents as the trustees and Brandon the beneficiary. Victoria didn't want the condo, regardless—too many bad memories. Her new office was in North Central Phoenix, and she had been scouting out the housing within a thirty- to forty-minute drive to the office.

As they were putting things away after emptying several boxes, Victoria noticed her mother wasn't putting anything other than linens in the larger of the guest suites.

"Mom, what gives? What's with the guest suite? Are you planning on turning it into a sewing or crafts room? Maybe even a meditation room?" Victoria sat down on the floor and went into a lotus position and started chanting. Her mother busted out laughing.

"No, silly. I was hoping you would consider moving in with me for a little while until you get situated in your new job. That way, you can take your time, and there won't be as much pressure on you. There's plenty of room here, and you'll have use of the den down the hall if you need to do any office work. Plus, I hear there is a mighty fine chef on the premises," her mother added with a twinkle in her eyes.

"Let me sleep on it, Mom. Although I will tell you, it sounds like a great idea."

Later, Victoria drove back to the condo. Turning into the complex and entering the underground garage, she looked around and was totally turned off by the surroundings—cold, sterile, bounded by cement. The only greenery found was in planters and pots, mostly fake. Entering the condo, memories flashed of the arguments, the belittling, and the smell of drunkenness. She was grateful a servant from Brandon's parents' household had called a week prior and made an appointment to pick up Brandon's clothes and personal belongings. At least that part of him was out of her life. There were only a few pieces of furniture and kitchen items Victoria had brought with her when she moved in after the wedding. She nodded her head. Yep, it wouldn't take much for her to move out—the sooner, the better.

The next morning, she called her mom and told her. Marya was ecstatic, and they set a date for the move, making arrangements to rent a small moving van. Two days later, Victoria was unpacked and resting on the bed she had growing up back in Illinois and safely under her mother's roof in Phoenix. She looked out the window and saw a cardinal sitting on a tree branch just outside.

"Hi, Dad! Here I am again," she whispered.

It didn't take long for Victoria and her mom to settle into a routine. Victoria made sure she was helping with the expenses and was still able to put money away in the hopes of buying a place of her own. Her mom told her there was no hurry, to just concentrate on getting her CPA, which Victoria really was driven to achieve.

Victoria had started her new job, and it didn't long for the executives of the firm to notice how well she did and how well-liked by her clients. Her referrals kept adding to the firm's list of clients. At twenty-three years of age, she was on track to get her CPA designation and a partnership in the firm.

Her mom had made many friends through the community association, and her contact at the VA Rehabilitation Hospital and Clinic had proven to be worthwhile. She volunteered three days a week and helped with special events on the weekends. The influx of patients dealing with injuries sustained in the Middle East wars had increased, and Marya felt her time with the Vets was well spent.

All was well in the Hart household.

CHAPTER 6

THE 10 YEAR REUNION
Victoria and Drew

Shortly after her twenty-eighth birthday in the month of July, Victoria received an invitation to her ten-year high school class reunion in Illinois at the end of September. She was about to toss it in the trash when her mom noticed the bold high school imprint on the envelope and invitation.

As promised, her mom was not one to pry, but something triggered in her mind, and she asked Victoria about the mail. Victoria told her about the reunion invitation and revealed she probably wouldn't attend.

"But you've stayed in touch with several of your close friends from high school all these years, and I'm sure they will be glad to see you. Besides, you really haven't taken a personal trip in... well, I can't remember when. Since you now have your CPA under your belt, don't you think it's time to take some personal time for yourself? You rarely have a social life except getting together with your friend Diana and friends from your firm. I don't think your clients would mind if you take a long weekend away. You deserve it," her mother told Victoria, putting her arm around Victoria's shoulder.

"I don't know, Mom. I really don't like being out there." Just thinking about it gave Victoria the shivers, especially her memories of being bullied in high school.

She felt she always had to keep her guard up. At work, she was strong, confident, and assertive, but in her personal life, not so much. She shied away from social gatherings and relationships and did her best to discourage anyone who showed any kind of interest in pursuing a romantic bond.

"Listen, Honey, the divorce was finalized lickety-split over five years ago. Brandon took a plea deal by naming drug suppliers and other accountants involved in the scheme and is spending his days in a minimum-security prison out of state. You created a new life for yourself, accomplished so much in getting your CPA designation and becoming a partner in the firm by the 'ripe old age' of twenty-eight. You don't date, so to speak, and you've built walls around yourself emotionally when it comes to certain relationships. When anyone has tried to set you up with a blind date, you always come up with some excuse. There's no question you were hurt very badly, but you need to move on. You did it with your career. Now, you need to do it with your personal life. I'm hoping your experience with Brandon didn't sour you on having a loving bond with a man and marriage too. Your father and I had many loving years together. It can be real for you as well. I'm not saying you have to throw a rope around the next guy who crosses your path and hogtie him, but at least get out there, take wing, and see what you can see. Experience life."

Victoria had to chuckle at the "hogtie" phraseology her mother was using, especially after moving to Arizona. Whether it was influence from her friends at the community center or the Vets she worked with at the rehab center, she was becoming more and more a cowgirl.

"Alright, I'll call some of my old high school classmates and get their take on the reunion, then decide," Victoria responded.

Her mother seemed pleased with her response and nodded. "Now, how about some ice cream!"

Marya always seemed to think ice cream solved everything—from a skinned knee to a broken heart.

~

1st Day, Friday - 10-Year Class Reunion

As confident as she appeared, Victoria was "as nervous as a cat in a room full of rocking chairs," as her grandma would say.

She had flown from Phoenix into Chicago and was checking in at the hotel where the reunion events were to be held.

The woman behind the counter told Victoria she already had a message waiting for her. Victoria opened up the message from Robyn, one of her classmates and a very close friend, who had flown in from Seattle a couple of hours earlier.

Robyn was a data scientist in the computer industry and in high school was just as nerdy as Victoria. Both of them were part of the "nerd herd." They always hit it off, telling jokes or making comments no one else seemed to understand. Robyn's note indicated Victoria should call her on her mobile phone to arrange a time to meet in the hotel bar located in the main lobby for a drink before the welcome festivities began for the reunion attendees.

Once in her hotel suite, Victoria dialed Robyn's cell.

"This better be you, Victoria," a cheerful voice answered.

"Yes, it's me... well, I think it's me... wait... I'll check... yep, it's me." The past years disappeared. They still had the routine down to a snap. "I need to unpack and freshen up a bit. Can we meet up in the hotel bar in about an hour?" Victoria asked. "I can't wait to see you!"

"Yes! Me too, Victoria!" Robyn replied.

Victoria had a handful of friends who she stayed in close contact with. Grace, Peggy, and Robyn were all the same demeanor, taking their studies very seriously, always with good grades, and kept out of trouble. Of course, it made for some bullying along the way for some of them. Hopefully, after leaving high school, it remained in the past. Victoria had particularly stayed in touch with the three of them, and they knew what had happened back in Arizona with her ex-husband, Brandon and how deeply she was hurt both mentally and physically.

Promptly an hour later, Victoria nervously exited the elevator in the lobby, and keeping her head down, dodged various groups of people congregating in her path to the bar. For some reason, she envisioned herself walking through a minefield. She had worn her long blonde hair down, gently hugging the sides of her face, softly flowing on her shoulders, which afforded her some concealment. She rarely wore her hair down in public, but this was her personal time away. At the office, it was always pinned up, off her neck, looking every part the professional.

Attired in a forest-green, boat-neck, crepe top which accented the green in her eyes and a knee-length, straight, black skirt with a slight slit on the left side, she entered the hotel bar. The lighting was low, but a familiar female voice from a booth to her right called out her name. Feeling relieved, she headed for the shadowy figure, stepping slowly and carefully in her black stiletto heels.

Robyn, tall and slender with long, ginger hair and big blue eyes, vibrantly dressed in a purple silk pantsuit ensemble, slid out of the booth and greeted Victoria warmly with a hug. As they settled back in the booth, they began to catch up. A barmaid came by, took their order, and went off in the direction of the bartender.

A rather sizeable group of people were off to the other side of the bar, talking and laughing rather loudly. So loudly, in fact, someone from a table nearby asked them to quiet down. A few rude remarks were exchanged, and Victoria and Robyn began to feel a bit uneasy. Someone within the large group intervened and settled everyone down.

Robyn recognized one of the bad-mannered party people as a reunion attendee and made a comment about some people never growing up and being out of control. The comment really hit home with Victoria, and her face must have shown it.

"Sorry, Victoria," Robyn apologized. "That was really insensitive of me. I know Brandon's irresponsibility and ensuing actions weren't of your doing. I better give you fair warning though... the fiasco regarding your ex's accounting firm made the news big time here, along with some of the details of his dealings and his subsequent sentencing. The mismanagement and manipulation of funds affected those clients near and far—some right here in Illinois."

"Not to worry, Robyn. I've moved beyond it. I'm here to have fun and enjoy this long weekend. Now, I just need to find me a rope and a man to hogtie," Victoria added, making light of the conversation.

Robyn looked dumbfounded. "What....?"

"Never mind, I'll explain later," Victoria smiled. Several reunion attendees had walked by, and when they noticed Robyn and Victoria, they were greeted kindly and exchanged pleasantries.

All the while she and Robyn were sitting in the booth talking, Victoria had the uncomfortable feeling she was being watched. Occasionally, she would look around at the various groups gathered throughout the bar, but she never did catch anyone staring. The lighting was extremely dim, and even if there was someone watching her, she couldn't tell who it was for sure. The hairs on the back of her neck gave her the willies, her hand going to her neck, brushing away her long blonde hair trailing down around her shoulders.

~

FRIDAY EVENING – REUNION WELCOME DINNER

IT WAS time for the Welcome Dinner in one of the banquet rooms on the main floor of the hotel. She and Robyn paid their bar bill, gathered their purses, and headed to the hall outside of the banquet room where cocktails were being served. Stopping briefly outside the ladies restroom to the right of the hall, Victoria waited for Robyn as she made a quick pit stop. Victoria leaned against the wall, slightly lifted her foot, and bent to adjust the sling back on her black high heel. Her long hair had fallen over her face and blocked her vision, but she somehow knew someone was watching her. She quickly stood and looked around. A few of the attendees were milling about but nothing indicated they were watching her. She shook it off, reminding herself her uneasiness was due to the fact she really hadn't been out in a social atmosphere for quite some time. Her days of societal hibernation needed to end.

Robyn joined her, and as they entered the banquet hall together, they ran into their friends, Grace Barton and Peggy Hughes with their spouses, greeting each other enthusiastically, deciding to sit together.

Soon the tables were filled, and the meal was being served. The President of their class took a microphone to welcome those who attended and make announcements regarding the class and the reunion events.

Victoria still couldn't shake the feeling she was under surveillance and surreptitiously looked around. *"This is ridiculous,"* she muttered to herself. *"Maybe another glass of wine will settle my nerves."* She was on number two—or was it number three—and was feeling a bit buzzed.

A DJ had been hired and was playing songs from their high school years. Some of the attendees were dancing, some singing along, and some looked like they had already had way too much to drink. Quite a few who had attended the event had either driven quite a distance or flown in for the event, and jetlag seemed to be hitting them.

Grace and Peggy lived in Illinois but had at least an hour or more drive home. They mentioned the next time there was a reunion, they would book a room at the hotel so they and their husbands wouldn't have to do all that driving late at night. Plus, they all wanted to take advantage of the hotel's amenities offered to the guests, especially the spa. Grace and Peggy and their husbands bid Robyn and Victoria a good night, saying they would see them tomorrow at the more formal Reunion Banquet which was being held in the hotel's top floor Grand Ballroom.

The feeling someone was watching her lingered, but Victoria brushed it aside as she and Robyn enjoyed the music. The wine was making her feel more and more relaxed and carefree. She was sure she'd reached her limit several glasses ago.

And then it began...

Alumni's Drew Anderson and Bryan Sullivan came up to their table and introduced themselves as classmates. Robyn had no recollection of either of them, and Victoria only had sparse memories of Drew and Bryan.

Bryan was tall, probably around six-foot-one, shaggy blonde hair, green-eyed, dressed in a dark brown blazer, cream-colored V-necked sweater, and tan slacks. He had been involved in various sports in high school, particularly the swim team but was also into science. People assumed he would become a biology or chemistry teacher someday, possibly do coaching on the side.

Drew, around six-foot with big brown eyes, thick dark lashes, and a head full of the darkest brown hair, reminding Victoria of the color of espresso, was attired in a classic navy sport coat, an open-collared white shirt showing off his deep tan, and fitted navy slacks accentuating his tall and lean physique. Drew had also been involved in multiple sports and was more into hands-on tech science apparatuses.

Victoria could tell both maintained their athletic builds. Because of their "jock status," neither could ever be considered nerds or geeks or even come close to the circle of friends Victoria and Robyn hung out with in high school. Victoria was puzzled why they came by to say hello.

Bryan asked Robyn to dance, and she literally bounced out of her chair, grabbed his hand, dragging him onto the dance floor. Drew held out his hand to Victoria. At first, she was hesitant, but something in those dark eyes, those deep, dark brown, velvet eyes, and his smile made her feel comfortable, so she relinquished, placing her small, delicate hand in his warm, strong one. Sensations sparked through their touching, and she shook it off as a nervous reaction. Drew seemed taken aback as well and with a knitted brow, cast an astonished look at her. His hand grew tighter around hers.

Victoria was mystified; she doubted he even knew who she was. Her wine-fogged brain vaguely remembered they'd had one or two classes together in school but never socialized.

It was a slow dance, and she was consumed with the gentle but profound power of his arms encircling her, almost in a protective embrace. He held her hand on his chest, and she could feel his heartbeat... or was it her heartbeat? It was difficult to tell. She'd never felt more in tune with anyone, and the mere thought caused her to melt in his arms. The feeling was totally foreign to her—never before had she experienced such sensations.

She looked up into his eyes and noticed golden amber flecks in the brown which took her by surprise. He was looking at her as if he was seeing into her soul.

She tried to make small talk while they danced, commenting she liked his cologne and asked what it was—a lame effort to keep her head clear. Well, as clear as she could, considering the amount of wine she had consumed throughout the evening.

She knew her hand trembled against him and desperately hoped he didn't notice. But it was obvious he did when he wrapped his hand around hers.

"Beautiful hands, delicate fingers," he commented. Looking down at her hand, he questioned, "Fuchsia?"

"Yes. It's one of my favorite colors, and I had my nails done for the trip," she replied awkwardly.

She chided herself inwardly for being so inadequate having a conversation with a member of the male species in a social setting.

The idle talk ended, and their heads leaned into one another as they moved to the music. Closing her eyes, she listened to his breathing, inhaling his scent. The music ended, but they continued to move as one on the dance floor.

"Hey, Anderson, you falling asleep out there?" someone called from one of the tables ringing the dance floor. Victoria and Drew abruptly pulled apart. Her cheeks flushed, she walked rapidly off the dance floor to her table, picked up her black clutch purse, then out into the vestibule toward the hallway leading to the ladies room. Her arm was gently but firmly grabbed just before she entered the hallway.

Drew spun her around to face him and caringly pulled her into a telephone alcove. With his hands on her shoulders, he drew her toward him and kissed her with such intensity, she felt her knees weaken and thought she would collapse. It was quite some time before he released her and looked into her glazed hazel-green eyes, his breath ragged. She was breathing heavily, her heart pounding. The kiss... was like none she ever had before. Never. Ever. Before.

"I've been watching you since you walked into the bar before the dinner and wanted to do that all evening, Victoria. And I'm not sorry I did," he said in a rather husky voice with a slight tremble to it. "So, don't ever think I'll apologize for it."

She knew she wouldn't. The kiss was one she would long remember, filled with deep passion but tempered with gentleness. Although it took her breath away, she also felt it breathe life into her. Never had she experienced anything like it—especially not with Brandon. It was an awakening.

It was then she made a move which totally surprised her. She reached up and pulled his head toward hers and kissed him back. Gently at first, then slowly increasing its magnitude until she felt him responding in kind as their mouths gave full access to the other, their tongues probing, entwining, his arms enveloping her, almost lifting her off her feet.

The sound of voices coming down the hallway brought them back to reality. Breaking apart, they made as if they were about to use the phones. Once the hallway was clear, she turned to Drew with glazed eyes, and softly said, "I... I really do need to go to the ladies room."

As she started to walk down the hallway on somewhat shaky legs, he answered back, "I'll be waiting here for you, Victoria. Don't try to escape me now."

As the door of the ladies' room swung closed behind her, she felt her legs giving way and found a dark blue brocade settee to sit on while she gathered her thoughts and strength.

"What am I thinking? I'm recently divorced, and for all I know of Drew, he might be married. He's not wearing a ring, but I know all too well that doesn't mean anything. I'm going to calm down, then walk out and tell him it was all a mistake, an error in judgment, a 'heat of the moment' thing, and we'll go our separate ways. Yes, that's what I'll do."

From where she was sitting, she could look across the room to a mirrored wall above a long ornate dressing table. Her reflection frightened her—a "deer in the headlights" expression. She hadn't seen that look for many, many years... not since... She shook her head to remove the negative vibes.

She rose from the settee, crossed over to the dressing table, and applied fresh lip gloss to her kiss-swollen lips. She was about to brush on some blush but noted her cheeks were flushed and seemed to have a glow all on their own.

Several reunion attendees entered the ladies room, and she knew she couldn't stay there any longer. Snapping her clutch closed, she took a deep breath and walked out into the hallway to face Drew head on. He wasn't there. *Maybe he went into the men's room.*

She waited about a minute—no Drew. She wasn't sure what she felt —relief or disappointment. She was so confused.

Maybe he was the one who escaped. He must have realized what happened shouldn't have.

She thought about going back into the ballroom but opted instead to go up to her hotel room. She'd had enough of socializing for the evening and felt mind-muddled. Little did she know, her decision to return to her room would be a major turning point in her life.

CHAPTER 7

Victoria entered her suite and slipped out of her heels. Walking over to the large windows, she pulled the cord to open the draperies, lost in thought as she gazed out across the skyline and up to the starlit sky.

What just happened? Did I dream it? Must have had way too much wine. She shook her head to clear the cobwebs clouding her mind.

Turning from the window, she picked up the phone and called Robyn's room. No answer. She left a voice message to let her friend know she was in her room and planned to be downstairs in the hotel café for breakfast around eight a.m. if she wanted to join her. Then she called home and spoke with her mom, briefly telling her about the dinner and the old friends she encountered... well, not all of them. The word "encountered" didn't quite describe the time she and Drew had spent together.

What would you call it?

After ending her call, Victoria undressed and entered the bathroom to take a quick shower before going to bed. Standing in the shower, the pulsating streams flowing over her body reminded her of the raw emotions she felt in Drew's arms, and try as she might, those visceral feelings persisted to the point, she turned the water to the coldest setting to send them on their way. It didn't work as planned, so she exited the shower, towel dried her hair and body, then wrapped herself in a white spa robe provided by the hotel. She caught the scent of his cologne still on her body and in her hair. Letting out a deep breath and rolling her eyes, she headed back into the bedroom, flipping on the television to watch some inconsequential program to help her relax and fall asleep.

Just as she was picking up the remote, there was a knock at her suite door. Thinking it might be Robyn, wondering where she had gone, she threw the door open.

"Robyn, I should have called your mobile phone to let..." Her words trailed off as Drew walked through her door, closing it with his foot. His arms scooped her up as he strode across the suite and laid her gently on the bed, devouring her mouth with his undeniably compelling kisses, his hands threading through her damp tresses.

Sitting on the edge of the bed, he pulled back to gaze down at her. Shaking his head, with a ragged voice, he said, "What is it about you, Victoria? I can't think rationally around you. From the time I saw you earlier this evening..."

Was she imagining it, or was his voice shaking and his body trembling as much as hers?

Moments passed, their eyes locked on one another.

"I don't know what's happening, Drew," she whispered, easing into a sitting position next to him. "I can't seem to think logically around you either. There's a feeling... an energy... a force... I can't explain it. I've never felt anything like this... it's frightening," she stumbled for words to describe what she was feeling.

"No, Victoria... please, don't say frightening. I sense it too. It's deep, and yes, it's overpowering," he voiced quietly. "All I know is I have to be with you. I have to hold you... I have to hold on to you. I feel like I'm drowning, and you're the only one who can save me. I know that sounds like a line... it sounds so corny to me, but it's what I'm feeling right now. Actually, it's the feeling I got when I first saw you walk into the bar... I honestly don't know what's happening."

Victoria was listening to each and every word. The sensation she had of someone watching her was now made clear, but she was still desperately trying to reason it out in her own mind, trying to make sense of her own emotions. She felt she was in over her head, and he was her rescuer.

At the same time, past experiences taught her to be wary and not deceived.

She became apprehensive and had to ask, "Drew, are you married?" Her fears were justified.

"Technically, yes, right now I am, Victoria, but it's complicated," he said gruffly. Drew missed her roll her eyes, then dejectedly shaking her head.

Standing, Drew raked his hand through his dark hair. "So complicated in fact, the only reason why I came to the reunion was to get far away from Florida before I lost my mind... and lost everything I worked so hard for over the years."

Victoria was more baffled than ever, and Drew didn't miss the bewildered look on her face.

"I know I'm not making any sense right now," he said desolately. Drew ran his hand agitatedly through his hair and walked over to the windows where Victoria had opened the draperies a short while before. Staring out into the night's abyss, he opened up to her.

"I met my wife, Barbara, in college. She came from a very well-to-do family in Florida. Everyone teased I was dating a Barbie doll. Little did they know how true it was. After graduation, she returned to Florida, and I relocated there as well. Looking back, I think our relationship was one of convenience more than anything else. I wanted to set up a high tech private security and investigations firm which handled high-end, high-profile clients, and Barbara's father was more than willing to fund the seed money for the venture. He knew several prospective clients and was instrumental in getting meetings set up with them. Within a year, my company was thriving, and Barbara was pushing for marriage. I guess I just didn't invest enough time with her to realize it was just a façade. Our wedding was one of the social events of the year in Palm Beach. Looking back, I've made a lot of mistakes in my life, but my marriage to Barbara and being indebted to her father have to be the biggest ones."

Victoria's thoughts ran to the "Brandon" mistake she had made.

Turning to face Victoria, who was still sitting at the edge of the bed, he noticed the understanding in her eyes.

"And what now? Where do you stand with Barbara and your marriage? You know, Drew, no matter the circumstances, I can't—"

Drew abruptly cut her off. "The breaking point was I wanted children. We even talked about it before we married, and she was all for it, but then about six months after the wedding, I approached her about it, and she was adamant she didn't want children, she never wanted children. She said pregnancy would ruin her figure and disrupt her social life. 'Her' social life," he stressed. "The past years have all been smoke and mirrors. We're married on paper only. No intimacy. She's usually off on trips with her friends, traveling the world, going to spas, playing tennis, and playing around with her tennis coaches if you know what I mean. Her father is aware. Barbara is a clone of her mother in all aspects. I feel bad for him, but he raised her to be the spoiled socialite she is. He only has himself to blame. I cringe at the very thought of having a child with her. My God, what kind of mother would she have been?"

Standing up and turning toward Drew, Victoria had to ask, "What about your business?"

Drew turned back to the window, gazing out but not seeing as if he was in a trance, looking deep within himself.

"Ah... yes, the crux of the matter. I've been putting together a new business plan which would buy out the partnership interest held by Barbara's father. Then there is the matter of what Barbara would want in a divorce. I've been walking on eggshells, trying to piece together a settlement. I've already spoken to a divorce attorney, and he's been helpful getting things in order. My gut tells me Barbara may have picked up on what I'm doing, and knowing what a greedy, spoiled brat she is, she will more than likely make my life even more miserable. I can't lose the company I created all these years." Drew turned again to face Victoria, and she could see the stress and strain in his eyes.

"Victoria, I'm so sorry to be dumping this on you. When I saw you earlier this evening, you had this aura about you. I heard you laughing and joking with your friend, Robyn, in the bar, then later at dinner with your friends. You were real. You were genuine. It was obvious your friends adore you and hold you in high esteem. I had heard through the grapevine about your ex-husband and the fiasco you had to go through back in Arizona. When I first heard the story, I couldn't imagine the little blonde girl with freckles in my kindergarten class had grown up and had to face the challenges you had."

Victoria's hand instinctively went up to cover her nose, and her shocked look didn't go unobserved by Drew, a softness coming over his expression.

"You noticed..." Victoria stammered.

"Yes, I remember you, Victoria. The freckles have faded, but yes, I remember. You sat across from me and shared your crayons with me because most of mine were broken. How I remember, I don't know, but somehow, it stuck in my mind. And those years through grammar school, then high school... yes, indeed, I noticed. You hung out with a different group of friends, but I noticed. There were times I saw you being bullied, but your friends stepped in before I could. It was like you had your own pack, and they would circle around to protect you and anyone else in the group."

Victoria, still stunned at his admissions, said, "Drew, I had no idea."

Drew walked over and took her hands in his.

"Victoria, I need to ask you a favor not to say anything about what I told you to anyone. I can't risk this information getting out before I have a chance to get everything in order back in Florida."

Victoria nodded, hoping what Drew had told her was true and wasn't some kind of con. She'd been hurt before and certainly didn't need a replay. Looking deeply into Drew's eyes, she believed him. He pulled her close, and his cologne seeped into her veins. Closing her eyes and taking a deep breath, she knew he was hurting.

"Victoria, I need to ask you one more thing, and depending on your answer... well... do you want me to stay... or do you want me to leave? I can't make any promises to you if I stay, I won't keep away from you."

Victoria sucked in her breath and stepped back, her mind spinning out of control. She walked away from Drew, turning her back to him. The mere sight of him was more than she could bear in order to make a decision. Moments went by. Drew looked down and with a heavy sigh, made for the door. As he brushed passed Victoria, her heart spoke.

"Stay."

It was Drew's turn to be stunned, and he faced her abruptly.

"Victoria... are you sure?" Consternation was evident in his facial expression.

"More sure than anything in my life right now, Drew," she responded, moving into his arms. He buried his face in her hair. They stood there for a long time, each trembling, knowing they were about to cross a line neither had crossed before.

Her heart was beating a resounding tattoo. She could feel her blood coursing through her veins. He raised his hand and slowly grazed her cheek ever so gently, lifting her chin, taking possession of her lips. Gently at first, then with such force, she thought every life source within her was melded with his. The kiss ended, but it was only the beginning.

Ever so slowly, Victoria helped him slip off his sports coat. All the while, their eyes were locked. She started unbuttoning his shirt, her hands creeping inside, savoring the feel of the sprinkling of dark hairs on his chest, then brushing her face gently across his chest, teasing her senses with untold delight. She heard him suck in a breath. Grabbing her wrists, Drew pushed her gently away and with one swift motion, removed his shirt. Backing her up to the edge of the bed, he pushed her, so she fell gently into the softness of the comforter. She went to move her hand to the closure on his slacks, but he brushed her hand away.

"No, Victoria, it can wait," he said huskily. "I need to show you how I feel about you first."

"Do you want to turn off the lights?" she asked quietly.

Drew laughed, a deep throaty laugh which sent tingles through Victoria.

"Hell, no!"

Drew removed the rest of his clothing in a matter of seconds, his cock springing forward, increasing in size, and Victoria felt herself blush. Was it just the heat of the moment? Probably not since her eyes were drawn to parts unknown. She felt the passion building inside her, and when he untied her robe, gently sliding it off, she noticed he too had a bit more rosy color to his complexion, his gaze consuming her and awakening his passion as well.

Drew laid down beside her, then rolled atop her, between her thighs, bracing himself with his arms so as not to crush her, the only sounds their deep and heavy breaths. Drew started kissing her face, working his way around each side and down her neck. Victoria closed her eyes and could hear him saying her name and speaking endearments. He continued his downward journey, trailing soft kisses and gently caressed her collarbone with his lips, descending more into the crevice of her breasts, taking one nipple in his mouth, teasing it with his tongue, then moving to the other nipple and repeating the provocation, her nipples becoming hard pebbles with the arousal. His downward voyage continued to her navel where his playful artistry lingered. Drew moved his body down further and brought his hand around to massage Victoria's sweetness. Victoria was succumbing to his skillful manipulations, letting out low moans of desire, sucking in her breath as his tongue reached her pleasure point, caressing and pulling at her nub. She couldn't take it anymore and reached out for Drew, calling out his name as her mind and body spiraled and soared, then freefalling with aftershocks.

Drew responded, moving up and cradling her face, his look penetrating.

"Open your eyes, Victoria, I want to see your eyes when I make love to you." As she opened her eyes from her mind-blowing freefall, he asked one more question. "Are you sure you want this... want us?"

"Yes, Drew, yes, yes, a thousand times yes."

Again her breath was sucked out of her as he slowly plunged himself into her, gently rocking back and forth until the momentum built within Victoria again, and she screamed out his name, pulsating for the longest time, throbbing while he continued to bore into her with a quicker rhythm until he called out her name as he too was transported to an unsurpassed euphoria—each spent, each relieved, lying in one another's arms, savoring the quietness except the beating of their thundering hearts.

Never before had Victoria felt such completeness and wondered if Drew had felt the same thing. As if reading her mind, Drew spoke aloud.

"That. Was. Amazing. Victoria, you are amazing."

Victoria could still feel tiny reverberations and smiled to herself. *Now I know what it's like.*

They laid together for a long time before Drew turned on his side and propped himself up with an arm.

"You okay, Victoria? I mean—"

Victoria interrupted him, "More than okay, Drew... much, much more."

"Victoria, this isn't a onetime fling for me. I hope you realize it means much more. You mean much more," he said, concerned.

Victoria looked into his sincere dark brown eyes and nodded.

They wrapped their arms around one another tighter, occasionally placing kisses on each other's faces and lips as if they couldn't get enough of each other.

The lights had been turned off, but the moonlight from the window streamed across the bed, providing them with a calming glow to fall into a deep slumber.

Sometime during the wee hours of the morning, Victoria awoke to find Drew clutching her closer to him. It was obvious he was aroused, and Victoria decided to show her witty side.

"Drew, is that you?" she asked coyly.

"What? You little minx..." he whispered as he pulled her so close, she felt they were one—or would soon be.

"It's me alright... let me prove it!" Their lovemaking went on for at least an hour, then totally exhausted, they again fell into a deep sleep.

CHAPTER 8

The ring of the phone on the night table brought them both awake, Victoria scrambling to get the phone, glancing at the clock on the table next to it. Eight-thirty a.m.!

"Hello..." Victoria answered groggily. "Oh, Robyn, so sorry, I've overslept. I had a restless night and must have jet lag."

Drew, now wide awake, sat up and leaned against a pillow, making faces, indicating she was Pinocchio, and her nose was growing for telling lies. She made a face back and stuck out her tongue—all it did was encouraged him. He reached over and tried to grab her, but she avoided his grasp, listening to Robyn on the phone.

"No, not at all, I don't mind. Enjoy your time with your family. I'll see you later this evening at the dinner."

After Victoria hung up, she rose from the bed and swiftly attempted to sidestep the bed to get to the bathroom, but this time, Drew was quicker, pulling her onto his lap.

"You know, when I was growing up if you told a lie, you either got soap in your mouth or a spanking," he stated profoundly.

"You decide, but fair warning, I know what I'd prefer."

Her words were magic to him.

Drew grumbled something under his breath, then spoke aloud.

"Unfortunately, I promised some of my... excuse me... some of our classmates I would meet them downstairs in the café and possibly head over to the old high school for a rally they're holding."

Victoria knew they couldn't be seen together. There was a lot at stake for Drew. She understood how important it was to him to keep their relationship under wraps until he was able to get things resolved in Florida.

"You go ahead and get back to your room to get cleaned up and join your friends. We don't want anyone getting suspicious or any of those suspicions getting back to... Florida," she offered genuinely.

"No, I can't. Victoria, I want to spend every moment I can with you while we're here. I'll get cleaned up, meet up with my friends, and make an excuse why I can't join them for their excursion."

"Drew, I don't want you jeopardizing your business because of me," she responded adamantly.

Drew threw on his clothes and put on his shoes, raking his hand through his dark chocolate hair.

"I'm going back to my room to shower and change clothes. I'll meet up with the group and tell them some business issues popped up, and I have to stay to make some calls and send out some emails for the company."

"Just who is turning into Pinocchio now, Mr. Anderson?" Victoria replied, evoking a smile from Drew. "Seriously, Drew. I'll understand if you spend time with your friends."

Drew took her in his arms and gave her a stern directive.

"You get showered and changed, then head downstairs for brunch. You need to eat after all the exercise last night. I can't imagine how many calories we burned up," he teased. "Somehow, we will connect either in person or by phone. By the way, I need your mobile phone number."

Drew pulled his phone out of his pocket, and Victoria took it, punched in her number, saving it to his contacts. He looked down at it.

"It's not your name?" he asked questionably.

"No, it's not. It's my company's name in Arizona, but the number is my direct office line, and I added my mobile phone number, just in case my name pops up for some reason when you get back to Florida."

"Got it."

Before Drew walked out of her hotel suite, he gave her one last kiss. He didn't like the look of doubt on her face.

"Victoria, I will see you later... you can count on it."

After the door closed, she felt a loss as if a valuable part of her was missing. She shook off the feeling and headed for the bathroom.

After showering, she wrapped the robe around her and proceeded to blow dry her hair, the sound of the dryer almost blocking out the sound of her mobile phone ringing.

"Victoria Hart, here," she answered without glancing at who was calling.

A husky voice replied, "Is Queen Victoria all showered now?"

"Yes," Victoria smiled and laughed out loud. "And is her Knight showered as well?" *Two could play the game.*

"Indeed, My Queen, standing here naked as a jaybird, thinking of you. Can't get you out of my mind."

She envisioned him butt naked with his telltale dark and curly V running its course to...

She caught herself and responded, "Well, Sir Knight, you better get a move on or your men-at-arms will come pounding on your door and find you in your altogether. By the way, your Queen is naked too," she giggled provocatively and hung up before he could respond. *That'll teach him.*

He didn't call back, Victoria guessing he must have finished getting dressed and headed downstairs to meet up with his friends.

Victoria finished drying her hair, opting to leave it hang loose, applying a bit of blush and lip gloss before going back into the bedroom to get dressed. She pulled out a pair of comfortably fitted dark blue jeans and a yellow V-neck cashmere sweater. Tossing on a matching dark blue jeans jacket and a pair of Ann Klein dark blue flats, she grabbed her brown leather tote and headed downstairs to the café for brunch.

While dressing, she'd thought about ordering room service, but the memories of the night before were difficult to keep at bay. She looked around the room and at the bed and chose to dine in the café instead. She hadn't realized how hungry she was until she exited the elevator on the main floor and the aromas from the café assaulted her senses. She was famished.

She was escorted to a small booth in the far corner of the café. The server informed her of the buffet brunch menu, then asked what she would like for a beverage.

Victoria noticed several other reunion guests in the café and nodded hello. She scooted out of the booth and headed for the buffet tables arrayed with various foods. Picking up a platter, she proceeded to "graze" through the buffet tables, and once her platter seemed it couldn't hold one more thing, she headed back to her booth.

As she sat down, she noticed a red rose and an envelope. In the envelope was a note, "A rose for My Queen." She shook her head in wonder and looked around. Drew was nowhere to be seen. She knew he had been there, his cologne lingered. She smiled and set the rose aside, putting the note in her purse.

She enjoyed her time while eating, responding to texts and emails for the company, catching up on social media and the news.

She made another excursion to the buffet tables, this time for something sweet to finish off her meal. Once done, she motioned to the server for the check.

"It's already been taken care of, Ma'am."

Victoria didn't want to make an issue of it but asked her who took care of it. The girl hesitated, then said she didn't remember. Drew had probably sworn the server to secrecy. Victoria left a decent tip for the server, gently tucked the red rose in her tote, and headed into the main lobby.

She noticed there were displays set up for brochures of various places to visit while in the area. She took her time going through them, picking out several brochures she found interesting. Tonight was the big dinner, and tomorrow was open all day for touring. She wouldn't be heading back to Phoenix until Monday afternoon.

Victoria made her way to an atrium in the hotel complex— meandering walkways bordered by trees, flowering plants and multiple varieties of foliage, and small alcoves with fountains and benches. She sat on one of the benches and became lost in thought. So much had transpired over the past ten years—college, her father's passing, marriage, divorce, scandal, her career, and now, the reunion... and Drew. So much, in fact, it was difficult to take it all in.

Her mobile phone ringing startled her. "Hello, Victoria Hart here." Victoria caught her breath... was it Drew?

"Hi, Honey, it's Mom! Just wanted to touch base with you and see how your reunion is going."

"Oh, Mom, sorry. I promised you I would call this morning and with all the activities and events here, I lost track of time." Victoria rolled her eyes, remembering the Pinocchio comments from the morning.

"Not to worry, Honey! I'm just glad you're busy having a good time. Everything here is great. I'm having dinner with some of the other volunteers from the VA this evening. I wasn't sure when you would call and didn't want you to worry if you couldn't reach me."

"Oh, Mom, how wonderful! Glad to hear you're going out with your friends. They truly are a great group of people."

Small talk ensued about the weather both in Illinois and in Arizona. Victoria mentioned more names of the people she ran into at the café during breakfast and her plans for the formal dinner.

After hanging up with her mom, Victoria felt a little guilty for not telling her more. But then again, what more was there to tell? Even Victoria didn't know.

∼

Saturday Afternoon – Reunion Weekend

It was half past noon with no word from Drew, so Victoria started to head back up to her suite to catch a nap before the big dinner at six p.m. She still felt a little sleep deprived and wanted to look her best.

Victoria surmised Drew got caught up with his friends, and they insisted he go to the rally with them. She hadn't seen any of his buddies around the hotel and figured they were gone until the evening's event.

Victoria entered the elevator concourse and pushed the button. After the elevator arrived, she entered and pushed her floor button, followed closely by a couple from the reunion, the Dawson's. She shrank to the back of the elevator, hoping they didn't notice her. They had both graduated with Victoria but clearly ran in a different social circle. Both were bullies in high school and didn't have any compassion for others. Victoria seemed to have a target on her back when Stephanie Baxter was around. Seemed only fitting David Dawson and Stephanie would end up together.

When the elevator door was closing, Victoria put her head down and had the urge to bolt out, but before she could, a hand reached out to stop the doors, and someone else entered. Victoria didn't look up but knew from the scent of cologne who it was. She kept her head down, hoping to be invisible to the Dawson's.

Unfortunately, it was only a matter of seconds when Stephanie noticed her and chided, "You're Victoria Hart, aren't you? The one who married the strung-out embezzler in Arizona?"

Victoria raised a defiant head and was about to respond, but Stephanie continued with her onslaught, "Seems you could have handled your husband better and maybe he wouldn't have turned into the criminal he was."

"And to think about all the clients he ripped off and the companies he destroyed," David Dawson chimed in. "Obviously, since you were his wife, you must have known what he was doing." They both continued their rant, oblivious to who else was in the elevator.

All of a sudden, a hand reached out and pressed a different floor button, a floor the elevator was nearing. Victoria knew who cued the floor, and as the doors opened, she rushed through and made a run for it down the corridor. She turned back to see if anyone had followed her and saw no else in the hallway. She stopped and leaned against a wall for a couple of minutes, catching her breath, her heart pounding, her soul hurt and angry at the words the Dawson's hurled at her.

She spotted another set of elevators further down the hallway and hurried toward them. As the elevator door opened, she was grabbed inside and encased in Drew's strong arms, holding her tightly. He pushed a floor button and a code. Victoria noticed it wasn't her floor.

"The Dawson's suite is on the same floor as yours," Drew explained. "I didn't want you to have to face them and listen to their ugly tirades any longer. We're going up to my suite where you can rest up a bit."

"Are you sure, Drew? What if we're seen?"

"Not to worry, no one will see us."

She wondered about what he said, but in a few short moments, she got her answer. Drew was staying in one of the penthouse suites on a floor only accessible with a code. Once the elevator arrived, Drew ushered her down a private hallway and punched in another code to access the suite.

As they entered, Victoria noticed how much bigger it was than her suite, at least four times larger. It offered a breathtaking view with a separate room off to the side which could either serve as a dining room or a meeting room, a living room with an area for office communications, a kitchenette, and a bar. Double doors led to the master suite and master bath.

As much as she was enjoying the surroundings, she was still visibly shaken. Victoria speculated how many more of their classmates knew about the Brandon debacle in Arizona. She surmised some of the clients and companies affected were in Illinois. The whole situation had made national and international news. She thought back and was glad she never changed her last name to her husband's. Victoria was lost in a haze when Drew put a glass in her hand.

"Drink up, Victoria, it will settle your nerves and relax you a bit." As she moved over to the window, Drew had a worried expression on his face when he looked at Victoria.

"I'll be okay... just need to clear my head. I truly didn't expect... I thought it all was behind me. I thought dealing with the divorce, then Brandon's prosecution would have made me stronger and immune to the verbal onslaughts of people like the Dawson's, people who think I knew what my husband was doing, even the prosecutors and feds who called me in for questioning. Eventually, I made it clear I knew nothing. I'm just surprised there are still some out there who..." Victoria let her words trail off. She swirled the amber liquid around in the glass and took a drink, just about finishing the glass.

Drew reached over and took the glass from her, placing it on the windowsill, pulling her back into his embrace.

"You need to lie down and rest a bit, My Queen," Drew directed.

"Not here, Drew. I'm going to head down to my suite," she responded, then noticed his disappointment. "Truly, I'll be okay. I've weathered tougher verbal assaults. I was just taken by surprise."

"I'll ride down in the elevator with you then."

"No, you stay here, we can't take the chance of being seen together. I'll call you when I get into my suite, okay?"

"Whatever you say, My Queen!" he responded, throwing a bit of light-hearted humor her way with a regal bow.

He walked her to the penthouse elevator, giving her a teasing light kiss on her nose, still displaying a concerned expression.

As the elevator doors were closing, she had to restrain herself from jumping back into his arms and telling him how she felt about him. *How did she feel about him?* He had affected her like none other. His touch left her wanting more... and giving more. With everything that happened in her past, she felt Drew Anderson had somehow gotten to her in a way totally foreign to her—almost magical.

She knew in her heart he stood there at the elevator until the hum of the descending elevator indicated she was on her way back down to her suite.

Exiting the elevator on her floor, she noticed no one else in the hallway and quickly walked to her suite. After entering and sliding the security bolt as the door closed, she turned and noticed the hotel staff had been there, made up the bed, and placed fresh linens in the bathroom.

She dialed Drew's mobile phone, and after only half a ring, he answered.

"Miss you already, Queenie."

"Getting a bit familiar, aren't you, Sir Knight?" she teased. "The Queen is about to rest awhile, then get ready for the evening's festivities. I know you won't be able to join Her Majesty at her table, so I wish you well with your men-at-arms." She heard a deep sigh on the other end of the phone.

"Someday, My Queen, this will all be over, and we will be dining together for all to see—I promise you. Sleep well, Queenie," Drew stated emphatically.

Before she could respond, the call was disconnected. She held the phone close to her breast and closed her eyes. *What is he saying...? What is 'someday'... What is 'together'?*

Victoria lay on the bed and drifted off quickly, still holding the phone close to her.

CHAPTER 9

SATURDAY EVENING – REUNION FORMAL DINNER

It was around four-thirty p.m. when Victoria awoke with a start and sat up in the bed, worried she may have overslept and wouldn't have time to shower and get ready for the dinner. After glancing at the night table clock, she leaned back down, realizing she had plenty of time. The evening's dinner was more formal, and she'd already planned out what she would be wearing. She would be sitting at the table with her friends, Grace and her husband, Peggy and her husband, and Robyn.

Victoria took her time getting ready. She wore her hair up, secured with a crystal comb, leaving a few loose tendrils grazing the back of her neck and shoulders. Her pearl and Swarovski crystal chandelier earrings were the perfect accent, along with matching interlocking bracelets and a pearl cocktail ring on her right hand. She had long ago rid herself of the gauche engagement and wedding band Brandon had given her.

She'd brought her favorite midnight blue, off-the-shoulder cocktail dress with a lace illusion bodice which fitted her lithe body like a glove. She slipped on her glistening pewter-colored stiletto sandals and tossed her lip gloss, mobile phone, and suite access card in her clutch bag. She contemplated throwing in some of her business cards, but this was a personal trip, not a business trip, she reminded herself.

Victoria had delayed leaving her suite as long as possible before heading up to the formal Reunion Dinner in a Grand Ballroom on one of the top floors. She didn't want to run into the Dawson's in the hallway or the elevator and figured they would probably show up early at the dinner in an effort to "make connections."

She opened her suite door and did a fast look up and down the empty hallway, making a dash for the elevator. As a matter of fact, the hallway was unusually quiet. On the way up, other reunion attendees joined her on the elevator, exchanging pleasantries and greeting her warmly.

So far, so good.

Outside the ballroom, tables had been set up to check into the event, and name tags with the attendee's name and graduation picture were handed out. Victoria wasn't sure if she wanted to wear it. Just then, Peggy, Grace, and their spouses arrived, checked in, and made a point of pinning theirs on. Victoria decided there was safety in numbers and put hers on too. Robyn came up behind them, checked in, pinning on her name tag. The ladies were all complimenting each other on their attire, exclaiming how well the spouses cleaned up as well. One of the husbands asked how long he had to keep his tie on—all the ladies said in unison, "All night!" Laughter abounded.

Robyn quietly asked Victoria about the previous evening, implying she knew something was up. Victoria just smiled and gave the impression nothing was going on. The wink and look Robyn gave her suggested she didn't believe her.

The group moved into the Grand Ballroom and found a table to accommodate them. There were six of them, and the table was set for eight. Victoria was quietly hoping whoever joined them wouldn't be anyone like the Dawson's.

As it turned out, another couple, who they knew very well from school, joined them and fit in perfectly.

Victoria couldn't help herself, she covertly scouted the room for Drew. She spotted the Dawson's making their way table to table, broadcasting how successful their business was doing, not asking how anyone else was doing or giving anyone else a chance to talk. Typical. The Dawson's looked over at Victoria's table, whispered between themselves, and avoided their table. Thank heavens! Victoria breathed a sigh of relief.

Just then, "his" cologne surrounded the air around her, and a gentle touch on the shoulder indicated he was standing right behind her. Turning slightly in her chair, Victoria noticed Bryan standing next to Drew.

"Good evening, ladies and gentlemen! We just wanted to stop by and say hello. Bryan here has arranged for the musical entertainment tonight, and if you want to make any special requests, please do," Drew announced. Victoria could feel the warmth of Drew's hand on her shoulder as he was talking, hoping she wasn't giving herself away by blushing. Inwardly, she was hoping someone would turn the a/c on... and make it fast.

Drew asked each classmate around the table their name, commenting how he remembered them from a certain class. Peggy and Grace were amazed he remembered them from Civics and History. Bryan had struck up a side conversation with Robyn, who he had danced with last evening. It seemed like they were really getting along well.

Peggy and Grace introduced their spouses to Drew and Bryan. Drew was quite charming and drew the husbands into the conversations. The couple who were the last to join the table were also enamored with Drew's ability to engage them in the discussion.

Drew still had his hand on Victoria's shoulder and leaned in to take a look at her name tag.

"Victoria, my you have changed! I remember you in several of my classes. I think one was Government, another Social Studies. It's so nice to see you."

Thinking back, it dawned on Victoria he was right. How did he remember?

Robyn was busy talking with Bryan, but hearing Drew's comment to Victoria, she did a fast head turn and sent Victoria an inquiring look. Robyn knew full well Victoria and Drew danced together the night before. Victoria was thankful for Robyn's discretion but knew she would have to get with her privately later.

"Well, we better get back to our table, Bryan. I hope you enjoy the evening, folks. I know I will," Drew stated. Was it a personal innuendo meant for her? He gave Victoria's shoulder a slight squeeze, then slowly and gently removed his hand from Victoria's shoulder—she felt his warmth leave.

Their Class President jumped up on the stage and grabbed a microphone, announcing the meal was about to be served, and during the first part of the dinner, there would be a video montage of photos classmates had sent in for the occasion. He also announced some of the photos would take them all the way back to their earlier days in the school district before high school.

Other than her graduation picture and pictures with her friends in their various "nerd" clubs, Victoria couldn't think of any other photo of her which would be displayed.

The Class President made a few other announcements, including introducing several teachers who were on the high school staff at the time the class was in attendance.

While the meal was being served, Victoria surreptitiously looked around to see where Drew was sitting. She caught sight of him, and he raised his glass in a silent toast. It was obvious he placed himself at a table so he would have a full view of her. A slight smile curved her lips, and her heart warmed.

The video montage began, and soon everyone was nudging and pointing at the screen when someone they knew popped up. Victoria was about to take a sip of wine when Robyn gasped and got Victoria's attention. There on the screen was Victoria in kindergarten with blonde pigtails, sitting at a table next to Drew, holding up their crayons and pictures they made. Victoria was looking at the camera, but Drew was smiling at Victoria.

Peggy was the first to pipe up. "Oh my God, isn't it sweet? Looks like the little guy had a crush on you, Victoria."

Then Grace added, "Wait a minute, isn't it Drew Anderson? The guy who was just here before dinner? Who could miss the dark hair and sweet brown eyes?" All eyes turned to Victoria.

"To be honest, I really don't remember much about back then. All I remember from a kindergarten is I was the scrawniest kid in the class, and someone kept pulling my pigtails."

Peggy interjected, "I'll bet it was Drew."

Victoria was about to jump in and say it couldn't have been Drew because he sat across from her, but then they would know she did remember....

The dinner continued, so did the video montage. There were "oohs" and "ahs" and everything in between as photos popped up on the large screen.

Just as dessert was being served and live music was about to begin, the Class President made another announcement. Awards were about to be given out—the most children, married the longest, and who traveled the greatest distance to attend the reunion. Victoria knew Robyn might stand a chance for the distance traveled, but someone who flew in from Australia got the award.

Victoria casually glanced over her shoulder, but Drew was no longer seated at his table.

The music began, and several attendees gathered on the dance floor. The first song was a slow and sentimental one, the next a fast one. Peggy, Grace, and their husbands had joined the crowd on the dance floor for the first dance and remained for the second. The other couple at the table joined some friends at another table after dinner.

Bryan walked over to the table and asked Robyn to dance. She didn't take but a nano-second to agree before they were maneuvering through the maze of tables to the dance floor.

Victoria sat there, watching the group out on the floor rocking and rolling, shimmying and totally in beat with the music.

Before she even had a chance to take a deep breath and inhale his cologne, Drew was pulling out the chair next to her and sitting down.

"Drew, are you nuts? You can't sit there...." she stuttered quietly.

"Why ever not, Victoria? I'm a classmate catching up with another classmate. That's all. We're talking about a cute picture of the two of us in kindergarten... right? I was as surprised as you when it popped up. I saw the look on your face, it was priceless. Maybe it was an omen back then."

Victoria was speechless. Several times she opened her mouth to say something, but the words just wouldn't come out.

The fast music stopped, and Victoria could see her table mates returning.

Grace spoke first this time, "Drew, wasn't that you in the photo with Victoria in kindergarten? It's such a cute photo. Looks like you had something for her back then."

"Yes, it was me," Drew responded candidly. "Although at age five, I'm not sure what I would have had for her other than a few broken crayons." Smiles were seen around the table.

Damn, he's good, Victoria thought.

Victoria noticed Bryan and Robyn engrossed in conversation, but Robyn looked up at her once and gave her a wink. Did Robyn sense anything? *Of course, she did. Who am I fooling? Robyn knows me too well.*

The band was playing a slow sensual piece, and Drew stood.

"Victoria, my kindergarten buddy, will you dance with me?"

Victoria felt like she had no other choice and took his offered hand.

Entering the dance floor, Victoria said, "Drew, you truly are crazy."

Drew wrapped his right arm around her waist as she put her left hand on his shoulder. He pulled her close, taking her right hand and placing it on his heart. She tried to put some wriggle room between them, but he just held her tighter.

She felt warm and was sure the three—or was it four—glasses of wine were taking effect. Or maybe it was something else.

"Yes, Victoria, I am crazy. Crazy for you. I thought I could keep my distance tonight, but it was killing me sitting across the room from you, watching you eat, watching you interact with your friends. I wanted to share the time with you. Have I mentioned you look absolutely lovely this evening? You took my breath away when you walked through the door. And I know I wasn't the only one who noticed. I was standing at the bar, and quite a few of the gentlemen voiced their appreciation when they noticed you. I wanted to clobber them and tell them hands-off." He ended his last statement between gritted teeth.

Victoria didn't know what to say. They finished the dance in silence, each in their own thoughts, sensing what the other was feeling.

The song ended, and an upbeat, fast one began. Instead of leaving the dancefloor, Drew twirled her around, and they kept beat with the music, Victoria moving seductively to the rhythm, their eyes locked on one another. The music ended, and they were breathless. Victoria now knew what the term "Dancefloor Foreplay" meant.

Returning to the table, Victoria noticed Robyn and Bryan with their heads together again in deep discussion, but not about anything romantic—algorithms and bytecodes. Victoria smiled. Robyn had finally met her match. Drew must have picked up on it too and gave Victoria a wink as he nodded his head in their direction.

When Victoria took the chance to excuse herself to go to the ladies room, Robyn jumped up.

"Me too! Drew, entertain Bryan for me while I'm gone. Don't let him wander off." Bryan smiled and told her he wasn't going anywhere. Once out in the hallway leading to the restrooms, Robyn opened up.

"I can't believe I went through four years of high school and never noticed Bryan. He's so intelligent and has the most beautiful green eyes. And he's so witty. He totally gets my weird sense of humor and understands my quirky lingo when it comes to tech things."

Victoria looked at Robyn and smiled.

"What?"

"Robyn, you're smitten. I've never seen you like this. It's wonderful to see you glow like this."

"Me? Glow? You should talk, lady! Don't think, for one minute. I haven't noticed what's going on between you and Drew."

"What are you talking about?" Victoria stammered. "Nothing's going on."

"Well, if you say so, Victoria," Robyn sniffed, then winked at Victoria. "Not to worry, your secret is safe with me."

Victoria didn't know what to say, so she just kept quiet as they walked on to the ladies room. There were so many other attendees in there, it would have been impossible for them to continue their conversation.

On their way back to the banquet hall, Robyn mentioned Bryan was planning a trip to Seattle and wanted to see her while he was there. He had made the excuse he wanted to scout out prospects for his tech business. Robyn intimated she and Victoria might not see one another the next day, giving Victoria an enigmatic smile. Victoria totally got the message.

As Victoria and Robyn approached their table, she noticed Drew was missing. *I swear he's a regular Houdini sometimes.* She surmised Drew quite possibly didn't want to be so obvious staying around her and made a getaway to dispel any rumors which might have been created.

She looked up and saw Bryan taking Robyn by the hand, leading her back out to the dance floor. Something told her this was only the beginning for them.

Other classmates stopped by the table to catch up, and Victoria listened to the various discussions around the table, but if someone asked her to repeat what was said, she doubted she could—her mind was indeed elsewhere.

The Class President again approached the microphone and thanked everyone in attendance, announced the band would be playing for at least another hour, and for everyone who drove to the event to have a safe trip home.

Victoria gazed around the room and wistfully noted the various couples. Bryan and Robyn had returned to the table and had their heads together again. She wished she and Drew could be out in the open but knew it would definitely create havoc in his life.

Just then, a server came to the table, asked if she was Victoria Hart, and when she nodded yes, handed her an envelope. Victoria discreetly opened it to find a suite access card and a code written on the back of a business card. She turned the card over and noticed it was Drew's.

Victoria looked around the table to see if anyone had noticed. Robyn was the only one who seemed to take notice and with a raised eyebrow and a smile, gave Victoria an "I told you so" look.

Victoria got up and walked around the table, bidding her friends goodbye, promising to stay in touch, saying she was looking forward to the next reunion. She should be traveling back to Illinois before then for business and would make it a point of getting together with them. There were lots of hugs and some tears.

Robyn mentioned she wouldn't be flying back to Seattle until Sunday afternoon and hoped maybe they would be able to get together again before she left, but if not, they would talk during the week either on the phone or by Skype. Victoria knew exactly what Robyn was saying.

Victoria gathered her clutch with the envelope from Drew in it and headed to the hallway.

The Dawson's were lingering near the entrance to the banquet hall. Victoria was sure they were trying to snare more clients for their brokerage agency. As they saw her exiting the hall, David and Stephanie stepped in front of her, blocking her from leaving. Before they could say anything, Robyn and Bryan barreled through between them.

"Oh, so sorry," Robyn apologized. "We didn't notice you there. Hope we didn't step on your toes. Lord knows, nobody likes to get their toes stepped on."

The obvious positioning of Bryan and Robyn gave Victoria a clear pathway to avoid any altercation the Dawson's had planned. Instead of heading to the closest set of elevators, she proceeded to a different set further down the hallway, hoping the Dawson's weren't on her tail.

Victoria pushed the elevator button, and when the doors opened, she hurried in and inserted the penthouse floor access card and code.

CHAPTER 10

A s the elevator rushed up two floors, Victoria knew Drew had figured out the Dawson's might try to corner her again and didn't want her to take the chance of a replay of running into them in the elevator or in the hallway near her suite.

The elevator doors opened, and the first thing she noticed were rose petals scattered on the floor in the private hallway leading to Drew's suite. She inserted the access card, and no sooner had she heard the click of the door unlocking, the door swung open, and she was pulled into Drew's arms.

"Waiting for you has been torture. I was worried the Dawson's might ambush you. I overheard them making comments about you to each other, so I gave Bryan the heads up about them," Drew told her, all the while holding her tightly in his arms.

"They tried, but Bryan and Robyn ran interference. Now I know how they picked up on it."

The worried look on Drew's face disappeared and was replaced with a totally different look.

"You're safe now, My Queen. And... we're alone. Is it alright for me to kiss you now?"

There was no need to ask. Victoria reached up, holding the back of his head, and brought his lips to hers. Victoria wasn't sure how long the kiss lasted, all she knew was both of them were gasping for breath when it ended—a tsunami of massive proportions, sending wave after wave of emotions and senses, twisting and turning Victoria, body and soul. A need so great, she felt the relevance to her core.

She stared glassy-eyed into his espresso-colored eyes, taking a step back and a deep breath.

Victoria noticed the scent of roses and glanced down to find yet another trail of rose petals, deducing they led to the master bedroom.

"I do believe you ought to speak to the housekeeping staff. It seems they need to do a better job of cleaning up," she whispered huskily, nodding to the floor.

"If you think that's something, wait until you see what else is awaiting you," he said cryptically. Taking her hand, they followed the petal trail into the master bedroom.

Victoria gasped—the bed was strewn with petals.

"Fit for My Queen?" he questioned as his hand waved in the direction of the bed.

Victoria was speechless. Drew motioned for her to sit in an armchair, took her clutch and laid it on the side table, then knelt down and removed her stiletto heels.

"I can't for the life of me understand how you ladies are able to dance, let alone walk in these things... but they are pretty."

Then he asked her to stand. Victoria knew all too well where this was heading. Turning her around, he slowly, very slowly unzipped her dress. He was doing it on purpose, and she couldn't help but smile. Nor could she help the beginnings of a pleasant, sensual ache from her nether regions.

Finally, her dress floated down, and he gently took her hand as she stepped away from the dress pooled around her feet. Without missing a beat or taking his eyes off her, he swept up the dress and laid it on the chair.

Victoria stood there in her dark navy-blue, strapless demi-bra and matching bikini panties. She noticed his breathing had changed pace as much as hers. She pursed her lips and moved toward him, closing the gap between them. Enveloping her against him, the bulge between them indicated just how aroused he was.

Pulling back, he led her barefoot into the master bath. As they continued through a trail of petals, she spotted the oversized Jacuzzi spa tub on a raised marble surround. Steam was rising from the full tub which clearly was scented with rose oil. Drew reached down and pressed a control button, and the water swirled gently.

Turning to face Victoria again, Drew reached behind her and within seconds, had unsecured her bra. *Wow… he's pretty adept at this.* Refocusing on what Drew was doing, she felt his hands sliding down her sides to the top to her panties, his eyes watching her facial expressions. She couldn't biting her lower lip. That particular little act emitted an expletive from Drew.

"Damn, Victoria, I'm trying hard to go slow and make this as pleasurable as possible for you… but the hell with it!" Drew removed her panties and scooped her up in his arms, setting her on the edge of the spa, and guided her lithe body into the effervescent waters.

Drew made haste removing his own clothing and entered the spa, facing her. Victoria observed his arousal had reached unimaginable heights. Drew's eyes were boring into hers as he clenched his jaw. The telltale pulsing of his jawline indicated the tension was building. Drew pulled her to him, having her straddle his lap. The steaming water churning around them, droplets forming on their faces as they stared into each other's eyes. Words weren't necessary to convey what they were feeling.

Drew took the natural sponge from the side of the spa, soaking it in the rose-scented water, and started stroking Victoria's arms and shoulders, eventually pulling her close, so her head was burrowed in the crook of his neck as he caressed her back with the sponge, her arms wrapped around him.

She felt so relaxed, yet the sensual ache increased to the point, she thought she would shatter at any second.

Drew must have sensed it. Positioning her atop his manhood, he gently eased into her, causing Victoria to let out a small moan. Throwing her head back, she exposed her neck to the onslaught of Drew's lips, kissing his way around her neck, then onto her lips, his tongue exploring even deeper, entwining with hers.

The water splashed to the pace of their undulating bodies locked in a primal coupling. Victoria had never experienced such pure ecstasy and spasms of release, transporting her mind and soul to a domain unknown before.

While she was still in the downward spiral of the euphoric state of mind, Drew pulled her tight as his moment of release overcame him, calling out her name, over and over again.

The water roiled around their spent, interlocked bodies, Victoria nestling in Drew's arms as his head lay back along the edge of the spa.

A few minutes passed when Drew placed kisses on the top of Victoria's head, taking his hand and gently touching and lifting a damp tendril of Victoria's hair which had come undone. He cupped the side of her face, then stroked her cheek. Victoria was able to see their reflection in the mirrored wall and noticed the expression on Drew's face. He seemed lost in his thoughts.

A short while later, he said, "Victoria, what I'm feeling right now is something new to me. I'm at a crossroads in my life and need to make some pretty serious decisions. I'm asking you be patient with me while I sort this all out. I'll totally understand if you want to erase this time we shared from your memory."

Victoria angled her head to look up at him.

"Removing what we have had between us is impossible. I don't think I could if I tried, and I definitely don't want to try." She paused long enough to gather her thoughts. "Neither of us knows what the future has in store for us. We're all subject to outside influences. I learned that the hard way. We just need to forge ahead and make the best possible decisions, not only for ourselves but for those people we care about. I totally get what is at risk here for you. I can't make any promises and neither should you. Not here. Not now."

Drew lifted her chin, looking deeply into her eyes.

"You're an amazing woman, Victoria. I don't know how anyone in their right mind could have let you go, but I'm thankful they did. I wish we would have connected years ago, long before I made the mistakes I've made. I know things would have been different... much different and much better." Leaning in, placing a gentle kiss on her lips, he whispered, "Much different."

"Yes," she whispered, framing his face with her hands, then raking her fingers through his damp hair.

He gently guided her off his lap and rising from the spa, helped her out of the spa and grabbed a fluffy towel to wrap around her, gently patting her dry, then grabbing another towel and wrapping it around himself.

Taking her by the hand, he led her to the bed adorned with rose petals, lifted her up, and laid her on it. He came around the other side of the bed and laid down beside her.

"It's late, and you need your rest. We'll talk more tomorrow," he said as he placed a kiss on her forehead, nose, and lips. "Sweet dreams, My Queen."

Victoria did feel exhausted in a warm and cozy way. She soon drifted off into a deep slumber with Drew breathing softly beside her, adoring her with his eyes, her left hand interlaced with his right.

CHAPTER 11

Her eyes fluttered open, and the aromatic scent of coffee pervaded her senses. Sometime during the night, she was placed between the sheets, and the down comforter had been pulled up around her. She rolled to her side and saw Drew was gone, but the scent of his cologne was on the pillow. She drew the pillow to her, hugging it, burrowing her face, and inhaling his scent. She pushed back the bed linens and sat up, noticing the towel she had wrapped around her when she went to sleep was now lying on the floor beside the bed.

Victoria walked over to the master bathroom and took a spa robe from a hook and eased her body into it, stopping once to undo her hair, brushing it and letting it cascade onto her shoulders. Padding quietly on bare feet, she moved through the bedroom out into the suite's living room.

Drew was sitting at a desk, reading through documents, a distressed look on his face. When he felt her presence, he looked up. The troubled look disappeared, replaced by a broad smile, his big brown eyes turning from worried to gentle. It was obvious he had already showered, evidenced by his damp, dark chocolate locks and clean-shaven appearance.

"Good morning, Your Majesty," he said, rising from his chair. Wrapping his arms around her, she again caught the scent of his cologne. "I wasn't sure what you would like for breakfast, so I ordered room service." Drew ushered Victoria to an alcove with large windows offering an expansive view of the area. A table was set, and several covered platters lay in the center with a large carafe of coffee.

"I wasn't sure if you took tea instead, so I asked them to bring both." Drew seated Victoria, uncovering the hot plate dishes.

Victoria looked astonished at all the food. "Drew, you ordered enough for an army! I doubt we could even put a dent in all of this."

"I didn't know what you normally have for breakfast and wanted to make sure I covered all the bases," he responded with a quirky smile.

"Covered the bases? I think you hit a home run!" responded Victoria, still trying to take it all in. There was Eggs Benedict, bacon, toast, potatoes, smoked salmon, cream cheese, bagels, yogurt, fresh fruit, and an assortment of jams and preserves. An additional glass carafe containing juice sat to the side.

Drew intervened when Victoria was reaching for the carafe of coffee. "This is my pleasure, Victoria. How do you take your coffee, Your Majesty?"

"Cream and sugar, please, two sugars. I have an incurable sweet tooth," she said innocently.

Drew was quick to respond, "Me, too," waggling his brows and promptly placed a kiss on her lips, lingering ever so slightly—just enough to cause breathlessness for both of them.

Pulling away, he finished dispensing her coffee, adding cream and sugar, then sat in the chair beside her. Drew served food from the platters with a flourish, intimating he was her servant, bestowing his best smile upon her whenever she looked at him.

"You're spoiling me, Drew. I could really get used to this."

At first, she noticed slight consternation cross his face, but it immediately disappeared.

"Victoria, if it was up to me, you would be served like this each and every day," he said seriously. "Let me enjoy being at your beck and call today. Tomorrow will come soon enough," he said cryptically.

Victoria shrugged off the feeling of disquiet in his words, and the two of them enjoyed the rest of the meal in mutual ease. Drew told her he had a rental car and mentioned going for a drive, away from the prying eyes at the hotel.

After they both were sated, Drew leaned back in his chair and suggested she shower in his suite, then they head down to her room for her to get a change of clothes. Victoria was concerned they might run into someone from the reunion, suggesting they go separately. Drew wasn't happy about it but understood. He agreed to wait a half an hour before he joined her in her suite.

Drew pulled the chair out for Victoria, and she rose to find herself drawn into his arms again. This time his kiss lasted longer, and Victoria responded in kind. When they finally broke and came up for air, each was winded.

"My Queen is an enchantress, and if she doesn't get a move on..." Drew whispered in her ear. Victoria slightly pulled away with an impish grin. This time, Drew sent her on her way to the master bath with a light smack on her buttocks.

While Victoria made haste showering, lightly blow drying her long hair, and getting dressed, she heard Drew talking on the phone. She knew the strained look he wore earlier had to do with his business and fought hard not to inquire and bring up any negativity. She wanted this day to be special since they were going their separate ways tomorrow. What happened afterward was anyone's guess. Victoria knew deep down what she wished would happen, but it was a big wish, and a lot of issues had to be resolved before she could even contemplate any "what ifs."

Victoria walked out of the master bedroom, dressed in her navy-blue dress from the night before but left her hair down.

"Victoria, you always seem to take my breath away," Drew declared, rising from the desk chair. He walked her out into the private hallway to the penthouse elevator, holding her hand in his, kissing her knuckles as she entered the elevator.

"Thirty minutes is all I'm giving you. Watch out for..."

"I know, Drew. I'll be as stealthy as possible, avoiding any and all ill-mannered curmudgeons," she said with a nod and a wink as the elevator doors closed. Even though he worried about her and what she could possibly run into on the way to her suite, he had to chuckle at the way she handled it—a bit of wit and humor to cover her anxiety.

Victoria arrived at her floor, exiting the penthouse elevator, and walked to the adjacent hallway which would eventually lead to her suite. After a cursory look down the hallway, noting no one was about, she hurriedly got to her suite door and slid her access card. One inside, Victoria breathed a sigh of relief.

Kicking off her heels and taking her mobile phone out of her clutch, she looked to see if she had any texts or messages from the night before. There weren't any, so she phoned her mom to touch base.

"Hi, Mom! How's it going?" she said lightheartedly.

"Fine, Honey. How was the big dinner and did you get to do any dancing?"

"Dinner was great. Loved being with my friends. Dancing?" Victoria asked.

"Well, Victoria, normally they have dancing after those dinners. Did you get to dance?"

Victoria quietly mused her mother was psychic.

"Yes, Mom, I danced a couple of times," Victoria responded, knowing full well the next thing her mother would ask would be with who. Victoria beat her to punch. "It was a classmate I've known since kindergarten. So, how was your evening out with your friends, Mom?" Victoria asked, attempting to change the subject.

"Oh, it was lovely, truly lovely spending time with... with the group," her mother responded, almost reflectively. Victoria knew she needed to discuss her mother's evening out in more detail when she returned to Arizona.

"What's on your agenda today?" It was her mother's turn to switch subjects.

"I picked up a few tourist brochures in the lobby, and there are a couple of things which look interesting. I thought I might see if Robyn or anyone else in the group would like to join me. Several of the sights are a short ride from the hotel, and Robyn has a rental car, so do several others. I'm enjoying playing it by ear." Victoria hated not being upfront with her mom but felt she had good reason.

"Good for you, Honey. It means you're relaxing and enjoying yourself. You so deserved this time away."

"Thanks, Mom. I'll give you a call either tonight or tomorrow morning. My flight home isn't until tomorrow afternoon, and checkout is noon. I may decide to spend time here at the hotel for a couple of hours before heading to the airport or hang out there."

Victoria and her mom exchanged their goodbyes, and Victoria raced to gather casual clothes. She struggled with the zipper on her dress, remembering how Drew was so sensual when he unzipped it. She finally had her dress and underwear off, heading to the bathroom to freshen up. Her hair was still slightly damp from taking a shower in Drew's suite, so she gave her hair a quick once over with the blow dryer. A little of gloss, a pinch of the cheeks, a tad of mascara, and she was off like a jackrabbit, putting on fresh underwear, a cream-colored knit turtleneck, a pair of rust-colored jeans, and her dark blue jeans jacket. The weather had turned cool. She wasn't exactly sure what Drew had in mind for an outing and thought it best to dress in layers.

She emptied her clutch on the bed, putting away her chandelier earrings she wore the night before, putting pearl studs in her ears. Taking her ID wallet, a mini-comb, her mobile phone, and lip gloss, she dropped the items into a rust-colored, leather purse. After adding a light mist of her favorite perfume with essences of balsa, bamboo, lotus flower, and nashi and zipping her purse closed, there was a quiet knock at her door. Looking out the peephole, she saw it was Drew and threw the door open.

"You're ready!" His look of surprise was quite noticeable. "Damn, Woman, you are one in a million!"

Not a second later, Drew had her in his arms, bestowing her with a kiss, lifting her off her feet! HER FEET!

"Oh my God, sorry to disillusion you, Drew, but I'm not quite ready. I think I'd better put some shoes on!" Victoria walked over to the closet and took out a comfortable pair of rust-colored Ann Klein flats.

"I expected you to pull out a pair of cowgirl boots," he joked.

"Nah, Buckaroo, I left those back at the ranch. These here are my city shoes," she said with a twang and a wink, slipping on the shoes.

Drew sat down on the side of the bed, staring at her and shaking his head. "You continue to amaze me, Victoria."

"So what's our agenda today, Drew? You alluded to a couple of things. You have my curiosity in overdrive."

Drew gave her a sideways glance. "Overdrive? Lady, you've had me in overdrive the past two days if not longer.

"I have a rental car parked in the hotel's underground parking. We'll head out in a westerly direction, making our way to the Rockford area. There's something special I want to show you, something I think you'll like."

"Okay, I'm game. Head 'em up and move 'em out as they say out west," she teased. Drew just shook his head and smiled.

Victoria checked to make sure she had her room access card in her purse and took two small water bottles from the mini-refrigerator for the ride, slipping them into her purse. Drew opened the suite door and glanced down the hallway—the coast was clear. Closing the door behind them, Drew held her hand as they meandered the hallways until they reached the penthouse elevators. Victoria gave Drew a quizzical look.

"The penthouse suite guests have their own private parking areas, only accessed by this elevator." Entering the elevator, Drew pressed the button for the parking garage and entered a code. The doors closed, silently moving to the underground level, and a few moments later the doors opened, and they walked around the corner to where his rental car was parked.

The lights of a silver Audi A6 lit up, and its doors unlocked as Drew pressed the button on a key fob. Opening the front passenger door, he helped Victoria into the car, making a point of helping her secure her seat belt, leaning in and placing a kiss on the tip of her nose. After closing her door, he rushed around to the other side. Victoria took the water bottles out of her purse and placed them in the cup holders. Getting settled in, Drew asked Victoria if she was comfortable and what kind of music she liked. Once she told him, he programmed the satellite radio to her choices. Victoria's taste in music was very eclectic, ranging from country to the classics, rock to pop, classical to new age. She didn't care for frenetic music. Victoria told him she liked lyrics she could understand and weren't offensive. Growing up, Victoria's parents took her to as many musical theater productions as possible. Drew appeared definitely pleased with her choices.

As they traversed the tollway and roads to Rockford, Drew's right hand held her left. It was mid-day on a Sunday, and traffic wasn't heavy. The music was background for their talk—exchanging stories of growing up, college days, describing friends and cohorts.

Drew was an only child, and his father had passed away when he was very young. Drew then lost his mother while he was in college. Both his parents died of natural causes. Victoria sensed he felt a deep loss over losing both his parents at such young ages. No wonder he wanted a family. Hearing Victoria speak of the circumstances of her father's passing, he squeezed her hand.

They only touched lightly on the subject of her marriage to Brandon, his incarceration, and their divorce. Drew was careful not to dwell on those years of upheaval in her life. He could sense the heartache, the pain, and the shaming she had to endure, brought down on her by someone she had loved and trusted.

Drew vigilantly watched the GPS navigation screen, and an hour and forty minutes later, they pulled into Anderson Japanese Gardens.

Before Victoria could ask, Drew stated, "No... no relation. Just happen to share the same last name."

Drew parked the car and ran around to help Victoria out of the car. She noticed as they walked to the main entrance, the fall foliage was in full splendor and was eagerly looking forward to seeing what lay behind the gates. After paying the admission fee, Drew suggested they have a light bite to eat at the onsite café before roaming the grounds.

Entering the garden café was like walking into an atrium, certainly surpassing the atrium in the hotel complex. Drew and Victoria were seated and given menus boasting "Farm to Table" cuisine. Still somewhat full from breakfast, Victoria opted for a simple Apple Chicken Walnut salad, and Drew chose a corn chowder, both electing to have iced tea. Service was excellent and quick.

Victoria learned from the brochure given them at the entrance, the gardens were usually open from late April through October, and guided tours were available. They decided to forego a guided tour and allow themselves to experience the gardens on their own, following a map of the grounds contained in the brochure.

After leaving the café, they entered the main pathway and found themselves entranced by the vibrant autumn beauty laid out before them. Wandering from different points of interest was putting Victoria into sensory overdrive. There were streams, ponds, unique waterfalls, a teahouse, bridges, pavilions, and every so often, they found wooden benches and chairs in small meditation areas to accommodate those seeking refuge from the chaotic, noisy outside world.

Victoria and Drew stopped several times at these little hideaways and gave peaceful recollection a time of its own within themselves. At the last stop along the way, they sat quietly, listening to the sounds of the birds, gazing out over a fairly large pond surrounded by lush foliage displaying a riot of fall color. Victoria looked over at Drew. He looked as if in a trance. She was so happy to see he seemed at peace. She knew he would have a lot to deal with when he returned to Florida and prayed this little respite would give him fond memories to fall back on when times got tough.

Drew turned to her. She knew he was struggling to say something, but she placed her index finger against his lips and shook her head. He took her hand and kissed it. She swore in this tranquil and quiet place, she could hear the beating of their hearts, beating as one. No words had to be said.

Their tour of the gardens had come to an end, and they silently walked back to the car, their hands entwined. A few minutes later, they were back on the road, heading to the hotel.

Finally, Drew spoke, "I didn't think it would be this overwhelming, nor did I figure at this point in time, it would be so difficult knowing tomorrow we'll go our separate ways. I don't want this to end."

"I know, Drew. I feel the same way. But we both need to take it one day at a time. Neither of us knows what the future will hold. It would be unfair for either of us to make promises we don't know we would be able to keep. Days from now, weeks... months from now, this could be only a distant memory of a wonderful interlude we shared. Time we could look back on with a smile. No regrets," Victoria answered, knowing full well part of what she was saying she didn't believe herself.

The rest of the drive to the hotel was in silence, only the muted sounds of the music playing. Drew pulled into the underground parking, and after they were in the elevator to his penthouse suite, he asked if she would stay with him that night.

Victoria reached over and pressed the button for her suite floor. He looked at her with hurt in his eyes.

"I'm just stopping at my suite to pick up a change of clothes, check for messages, then come up to your suite," she said calmly, squeezing his hand. He relaxed, smiled, and nodded.

CHAPTER 12

SUNDAY EVENING – REUNION WEEKEND

The elevator doors opened, and she headed down the winding hallway to her suite, catching Drew's voice from the elevator saying, "I'll be waiting with open arms," as the doors closed and started to ascend to his penthouse floor. Victoria didn't look back but kept walking to her suite.

Immediately after entering her suite, Victoria went through her suitcase and the closet, picked out clothing, placing the items in a large canvas tote along with a small bag containing her toiletries, and put her phone charger in her purse.

She sent a text to Robyn's mobile phone, presuming she was either inflight back to Seattle or had already arrived.

Looking around her suite to see if there was anything else she needed to take with her, she turned and left her suite, but not before checking if the Dawson's were in the hallway. She wasn't sure when they were checking out, but guessed it would have been by noon. Fortunately, the coast was clear, and she stepped lightly down the hallways to the private penthouse elevator and upon entering the elevator, slid the access card. She was gripped by an anxiousness filled with both calm and excitement.

No sooner had she arrived at the Penthouse floor, the doors opened, and Drew was standing there with a single red rose he held out to her. She wondered how the heck he got one so quick. Drew took her canvas tote and escorted her to his suite door which he had left open.

"What? No petals this time?" she joked.

"Sorry, My Queen, but the hotel florist was all out of petals. It seems somebody wiped out their supply last evening, but hopefully, this single rose will do," he countered.

"Yes, it will do nicely, Sir Knight," Victoria responded, holding the stem and gently brushing the side of his face with the rose.

It was too much for Drew to take. Dropping the tote on the nearby chair, he pulled her to him, and gave her a toe-tingling kiss... and there was a whole lot more tingling than her toes. A warmth was spreading from her core. His tongue invaded her mouth, and she responded. The two of them locked in a swirling primal embrace, carrying them into the master bedroom, falling onto the bed, cushioned by the down comforter. Clothes were removed posthaste. In moments, Drew was looking down at her, admiring what he saw—her toned body with its full, perky breasts, their aroused nipples and her slim waist.

"Every time is like the first time with you, Victoria."

Victoria used her body as leverage to throw Drew off to the side, intentionally ending up on top of him, straddling his lean, muscular body. It was her turn to look at him, leaning down to nuzzle and kiss the soft tuft of chest hairs. With a look similar to the cat that swallowed the canary, she positioned her body above his aroused member and eased her body down around it with her wet heat.

"Damn, Victoria... you're tearing my heart and soul apart."

No other words were needed. The ritualistic cadence began, building momentum until each reached a crescendo at the same time, calling out each other's name in unison.

It took a while to regain clarity and calm the lingering shock waves. Every time Victoria would experience one, it was felt by Drew and a smile formed on his face.

"You are one very passionate woman, Victoria. I wish..." His voice trailed off, leaving Victoria to wonder what he wanted to say.

They laid there for a while, enjoying the moments of closeness, knowing full well their time together was growing short.

Victoria rested her head on his chest, listening to his heartbeat. She made a motion to move to the side but Drew held her tight to his body, laying a kiss on top of her head. It was her turn to smile.

They must have fallen asleep as the sound of a mobile phone ringing startled them awake. Drew looked over and noticed it was his phone, looked at the caller ID, and ignored it. Victoria wondered who it was but declined to ask. Drew rolled Victoria to the side and placed a kiss on the tip of her nose.

"I'm hungry... clarification... I'm hungry for food," he teased. "How about I order up room service? Is there anything special you would like?" After he asked, he realized it was a loaded question when Victoria gave him a mischievous smile and waggled her brows.

As if on cue, both of their stomachs made noises, indicating it was definitely time to eat something, laughing together until both had tears in their eyes. Drew read the room service menu to her, then called down with the order and was given a time frame of thirty minutes.

"I guess we better throw some clothes on before they arrive." Victoria scurried over to the side of the bed and walked into the master bath to wash up. She glanced over to the spa tub and smiled, reliving memories from the previous night. Drew entered behind her, and Victoria again noticed his tanned, lean, muscular physique. She felt no inhibition with both of them there butt naked—a feeling previously foreign to her. She felt as if she had been awakened from a deep intimacy sleep. Or maybe, just maybe, she had never ever been awakened before, and this experience was indeed a first. Glancing over at Drew, she sensed a normality of them together, a comfort level she had never encountered before now.

Once washed up, she put on one of the spa robes. Drew, wrapped in another robe with his tousled dark hair, came up behind her and wrapped his arms around her. Victoria looked into the mirror in front of them and loved what she saw. Obviously, Drew did too.

"Victoria, what do you see?" Before she could answer, he spoke again, "I see two people who care deeply for one another. Two people who have the same principles and understand the needs of others. Two people who belong—" Drew didn't get a chance to finish what he was saying due to the knock at the suite door. He hung his head down and shook it.

While Drew went to open the door for room service, Victoria

pondered his words and took a deep breath, tightened the belt on the robe, and ran a brush through her long hair, pushing it back. She heard Drew talking to the staff, then the door closing.

Drew was standing near the table, set and laden with the menu items they had chosen.

"They'll be back shortly, they forgot something."

Victoria looked at the platters on the table and couldn't imagine what they would have forgotten. It seemed everything was there.

Drew walked over to the bar, pulled a bottle of wine from the chilled wine cabinet, and snatched two wine glasses from a shelf.

Standing at the bar, he deftly opened the bottle, poured some into one of the glasses and tasted it, declaring it to be a good wine, then filled both glasses and brought them over to the table.

By the time he had seated Victoria, there was another knock at the door. Room service rolled a service cart into the room. Victoria's back was to the door and couldn't make out what Drew was saying to the staff. Then she heard the door close.

"What's on the cart?" Victoria asked, noticing whatever was there was covered.

Drew responded, "It's a surprise... for dessert." This time it was his turn to look playful. Victoria made a pouty face. "No, Victoria, I'm not going to tell you until you finish your dinner," Drew reprimanded with an admonishing pointed finger. Victoria responded by sticking her tongue out.

"Be care, Victoria, your tongue could get you in a lot of trouble," Drew teased back.

Drew sat down and started uncovering the various platters on the table. Victoria had ordered a salad and seafood pasta while Drew opted for a salad and lamb shank with roasted vegetables. Drew caught her eyeing the dessert cart on several occasions and gave her an authoritarian look. She just sniffed and continued with her meal.

She intentionally broke off a piece from a warm loaf of bread, dipped it into the remaining sauce on her plate, allowing the sauce to drip down onto her fingers and hand. Seductively, she licked the sauce from her hand, then each finger, staring at Drew.

"You know what they say about payback, don't you, Drew?" she asked coyly.

He had been watching her intently, and she could see his Adam's apple rising and lowering as he swallowed. Pushing his plate aside, laying his napkin down, he turned toward her in his chair.

"You know, Victoria, for someone who wants dessert, you aren't behaving very well. Maybe I should send this cart back—"

Victoria interrupted, "You do that, Sir, and you will get your just desserts."

"Promises, promises," he replied with a smile.

Drew reached over to the cart and pulled off the covers. There was an assortment of fruit—berries, cherries, bananas, and side dishes— chocolate syrup, chopped nuts, chocolate chips, and a cooled container of fresh whipped cream. Victoria's curiosity was obvious. The Drew raised another cover—a large chilled container holding a massive amount of ice cream. Victoria's eyed the cart's contents in amazement.

"I remembered you telling me about how you love ice cream, and your mother thought ice cream could solve any problem and make things better."

Victoria was deeply moved. Some would think it was silly, but she actually was touched by Drew's thoughtfulness and the fact he had remembered such a little, insignificant piece of information.

"Trust me, Victoria, I do have a hidden agenda regarding this little surprise," he said ambiguously.

Victoria raised her left eyebrow to indicate she understood all too well what he had in mind.

"Would you like to create your own, or would you like me to do it for you?" Drew gathered two large bowls from a shelf under the cart.

"Oh, you do it, Sir Knight. I'd like to see how creative you can get," she challenged.

Drew sat down next to her and started by placing a heaping amount of ice cream in a bowl, adding sliced strawberries, bananas, blueberries, and chopped nuts. Then he added the whipped cream, sprinkled chocolate chips, drizzled the syrup, and placed a cherry on top. All the while Victoria was watching intently and wide-eyed.

"Ta-Da! For My Queen," he said with a flourish.

"Well, done, Sir Knight!" Victoria applauded. "Now do yours!"

Drew went to work on his, and a short while later, he was finished. Another round of applause from Victoria. "Bravo!" she exclaimed.

"I guess working in an ice cream shop while going to school helped. Who knows, if all else fails, I could work in one of those shops again. After all, I am experienced. I think I'll add it to my resume," he said jokingly.

"Come on, grab your bowl, and let's get comfortable," Drew told Victoria, leading her over to a leather sofa in the living room. He lowered the lights, then pressed a button on a remote, and the gas fireplace lit up. He tapped another button, and they were surrounded by music. They sat together on the sofa, watching the flames flicker while indulging in their special dessert.

Drew, noticing Victoria had a smidge of chocolate syrup at the corner of her lip, leaned over to lick it off, and proceeded to conquer her lips with his tongue, ending with a sweet kiss.

Leaning back on the sofa, he commented facetiously, "Didn't want to waste the chocolate." He wriggled his eyebrows, causing her to laugh.

Victoria deliberately saved the cherry from her bowl, and picking it up by the stem, she dangled it in front of Drew. "I know it's too late, but at least you can tell yourself you—"

Drew didn't let her finish, snatching the cherry off the stem with his teeth, smiling as he chewed it. Victoria bust out laughing again.

"You're grinning like a Cheshire cat, Drew."

Two can play this game, Drew thought. Reaching over, he pulled a dollop of whipped cream out of the bowl with two of his fingers and put his fingers to her lips. Victoria took the cue, licked the whipped cream from one finger, then the next. All the while Drew was watching her, Victoria could see his jaw clenching.

Drew slowly undid the belt on Victoria's robe and let it fall open. He was about to embrace her, but she pushed him back, untied the belt on his robe, and opened it, leaving him naked to the eye and obviously, quite stimulated.

She gathered more whipped cream from the bowl, and just when he thought she would be placing it on his lips, she gently deposited the whipped cream on his aroused member.

"Victoria..." he gasped as the chilled cream worked its way downward.

Before he could finish his sentence, she was on her knees in front of him, her mouth causing him to close his eyes and lean his head back against the sofa. She worked her magic, and soon, he was hoisting her on his lap, lowering her gently onto his now engorged cock. His eyes opened slightly and glazed over as she straddled him, arching her back and weaving her fingers through his hair. He leaned forward and took one of her breasts in his mouth, slowly circling the nipple with his tongue, then ever so slightly, gently used his teeth to tug. He moved to her other breast and repeated his assault on her senses.

The steady rotation of her hips soon brought both of them to a level of pleasure, consuming them both. Her thighs quivered from clenching aftershocks.

Drew held her tightly, so tight, in fact, she found it difficult to breathe. Drew released her a little, and she slid off to his side. Recovering from their passion, the music played on, and the fire burned, including the one within them.

"That was some dessert."

Victoria responded with a quiet, "Yes, it was... some dessert."

Drew suggested they shower since they seemed to have more dessert on their bodies than in the bowls. Victoria got up and headed in the direction of the bathroom while Drew gathered the bowls and put them on the cart. He looked around the room, and a bit of melancholy came over him. He wondered how many times he would replay the weekend in his mind.

The sound of the shower brought him back to reality. It was late, and tomorrow they would part. He wished he could extend his trip, but there were things that needed to be taken care of back in Florida. Things which would either make or break him and his company.

He also knew Victoria had to get back to Arizona and her company. From everything he heard about her company, it was quite successful, and most of it was due to her skills and tenacity.

Drew walked into the master bath and watched her showering for a few seconds before he walked over to the glass enclosure and joined her. She was facing the other way, but Victoria felt the cool air when he opened the glass door, wrapping his arms around her under the pulsating spray. The embrace was sensual instead of sexual. They were both laying out their feelings without saying a word.

Drew gently took a soapy cloth and stroked her limbs and torso, almost with reverence. Victoria felt tears prickle the backs of her eyes.

Not wanting Drew to see what she was feeling, she bowed her head under the shower spray. He kissed her neck and hugged her tightly. She wondered if he was feeling the same thing.

Coming out of the shower, Drew took a big, thick spa towel and wrapped it around Victoria, not saying a word, just looking at her, then grabbed a towel for himself.

Victoria walked over to the counter, ran a comb through her hair, and turned on the blow dryer to dry her hair while Drew busied himself at the counter. They locked eyes several times, but no words were spoken— none were needed.

They walked into the bedroom together and settled onto the bed, spooning with Drew's arms wrapped around her. He kissed her head, and she kissed the hand she was holding, sleep coming quickly.

CHAPTER 13

Monday morning came too soon and too abruptly. The jarring sound of a mobile phone woke Victoria and Drew.

It was Drew's phone, and the caller ID indicated it was his office. It was eight a.m. in Florida, and he wondered who would be calling. He answered the call, swinging his legs to the side of the bed, and standing up.

Victoria could tell by the look on his face, and the clenching of his jaw, the call wasn't a good one.

He walked into the master bath and closed the door. Victoria could hear him, and he clearly was mad. She caught some of his conversation.

"Dammit, I don't care what she says. She CAN'T have it, and under no circumstances are you to release it to her. I'm flying back today and will deal with her when I get there. Make sure her father knows what she's trying to pull."

Then silence.

It was well over ten minutes before Drew opened the master bath door and came out, wearing a spa robe. He glanced over to Victoria, who had gotten out of bed, dressed, and was gathering her things to put in her canvas tote. He stopped and stared at her.

Following a deep sigh, Drew said, "Victoria, you're the only bright spot in my life right now."

Victoria didn't know what to say. She felt his pain and wished she could help, but it was up to Drew and Drew alone.

"My flight is scheduled to leave at one p.m., but I may try to take an earlier one if it's available. I wish—"

"Drew, it's okay..." she responded before he could finish.

"No, dammit, it's not okay," he answered angrily. "This isn't how I wanted it to be today... not when... one way or another, you've got to know, I'll be back in touch with you... this isn't over between us, Victoria, I promise you with everything within me."

She walked up to him, framing his face with her hands.

"Drew, we knew this day would come, regardless of any phone calls. We knew we each had things which needed to be done. The things affecting you and your company are far more important than anything I would have to face. We need to say goodbye here and now. Whatever the future holds... I have no idea, and neither do you. We know in our hearts what we would like to happen, but as I said before, time will tell. If it's meant to be, it will happen. I'm leaving now. If I stay, it will only prolong the agony of leaving you. You know where to find me and how to get in touch with me."

Victoria reached up and gave him a tender kiss. His response was a deeper one. She pressed her fingers against his lips as he was about to say something and shook her head. She picked up her purse and tote and walked to the door.

Turning around she said with a forced smile, "The Queen only wants the best for her Knight." She opened the door and walked to the elevator, not looking back.

As the elevator descended to her floor, she couldn't help but feel she was falling too... the realization hit full force...

Victoria took her time packing, gazing through the window in her suite with teary eyes, looking out over the communities ringing the hotel. So much had changed over the past years. So much had changed over the past few days. She had changed.

The teenaged girl in high school, the naïve young woman in college, the battered wife—she learned lessons hopefully no one ever does. Those who do can only survive if they put the past behind them and rise above it all, striving for success in both their private and professional lives.

Taking a deep breath, she noticed his telltale scent on her clothes and skin. She'd never felt such deep longing for a man. This man was indeed her own personal catalyst, throwing her into the depths of passion and the complexities of caring so much, of loving too much.

In the distance, Victoria took sight of a passenger jet lifting off from O'Hare Airport, and her heart clutched, an ache causing her to gasp. With tears falling from her eyes, she stepped away from the window and went about finishing her packing.

Victoria wasn't sure what airline Drew was flying on and decided to stay at the hotel after she checked out at noon. She didn't want to take the risk of running into him at the airport, It would just draw out their parting. She checked out and had her luggage held at the bell station. The Bell Captain advised her when she was ready to leave for the airport to let them know.

She was walking through the Atrium in the hotel complex when her mobile phone rang. Answering it immediately, thinking it was Drew, she said, "Hello, Victoria Hart, here."

It was her office. One of her junior accountants called to tell her their receptionist, Heather, who was over seven months pregnant with her first child, was hospitalized. Heather had already told Victoria she was going to take maternity leave soon. Heather and the baby were fine, but her doctor told her she needed to quit work for the remaining weeks of her pregnancy. Victoria was more concerned about Heather and her baby than the receptionist position. Heather had worked for her for a long time and was quite adept at the position, even taking on some accounting tasks. George, the junior accountant, handled the payroll and benefits for the firm's employees and informed Victoria they had called a temp agency to provide someone on a temporary basis to cover the position. Victoria had wanted to interview anyone who might be a prospect during Heather's maternity leave but was okay with the temp for now. George relayed some additional client information, and within a few minutes, Victoria hung up.

Leaving the Atrium, Victoria walked into the café and had a bite to eat. She hadn't had breakfast, and her last meal was with Drew in his suite the night before. Nothing seemed to taste good now. Memories of the past weekend were coming at her from all directions.

A short while later, Victoria notified the Bell Captain she was ready, and he called for the hotel shuttle to take her to the airport. Fifteen minutes later, she was on her way to O'Hare Airport to catch her flight home to Arizona.

Victoria, early for her flight, checked her bag and went through security quickly with her TSA preapproval and found a secluded corner near her gate, trying in vain to relax, wondering how Drew was doing.

As time went by, more and more passengers were gathering in the gate area, and Victoria passed the time "people watching," a game she always amused herself with when traveling. Trying to figure out why people were traveling, what they did for a living... anything to make the time go by and not think about Drew.

She checked her phone for emails, voice messages, and texts... and ended up playing a game of Sudoku.

Finally, an announcement came over the speakers, informing passengers her flight was boarding. Victoria had priority boarding, so she grabbed her carryon and purse, handing her ticket to the attendant to scan. Walking down the ramp to the plane, an overall ache formed in the pit of her stomach. She couldn't help thinking about Drew. He was no doubt already back in Florida and facing heaven knows what.

Finding her assigned seat next to a window, she placed her carryon in the bin above her and burrowed in. She looked out at the tarmac with planes coming into gates and others lining up for takeoff, people coming and going in all different directions. *What direction was she headed?* Her mind was in turmoil, except one thing... her undeniable feelings for Drew. *Were they truly reciprocal? Only time would tell.*

The ball was in his court, she would wait to hear from him. As much as she wanted to talk to him, she didn't want to add to his burden and knew he had business to take care of. He certainly didn't need the pressure of her contacting him.

Normally, she engaged in congenial conversation with fellow passengers. This trip, she just wanted to be alone in her thoughts. Fortunately, so did those in the row with her.

CHAPTER 14

After the plane landed at Sky Harbor Airport in Phoenix, she thought about taking the shuttle to her office but opted instead to go straight home. Everything was being covered at the firm, and it would behoove her to go home and get rested up for work the next day.

Her mom was delighted to see her and was full of questions about the reunion and her trip. After noticing Victoria's rather tired and somewhat disquieted look, her mom stopped the questions and suggested she have something to eat and head for bed. Victoria was more than ready to call it a day.

Although Victoria tried to make light of the events of the past weekend, her mom sensed there was more—a lot more—but respected Victoria's privacy and refrained from prying. She figured if and when Victoria was ready to talk and needed an ear, she would be there for her as she promised.

VICTORIA ARRIVED at her office bright and early on Tuesday. She wanted to meet the temp and make sure she was a good fit for the office. The position of receptionist set the tone for the firm, their clients' first impression of what lay behind the big doors. It was vitally important the receptionist be knowledgeable about the company and the staff, present themselves with confidence, dress and speak appropriately, and above all, respect confidentiality.

As a partner in the firm, Victoria was adamant about those qualities in all the staff.

She had hoped the temp agency George contacted would send someone with those attributes. They had used a particular agency for many years and they always seemed to send the right people for the positions needed. If they worked out, the possibility of a temp-to-perm position might be viable if they had an accounting background and one of the accountants needed an assistant.

There was no way of knowing when Heather would be returning after the maternity leave or if she would decide to be a stay-at-home mom. She knew Heather and her husband didn't need to depend on both their salaries. Whatever she decided, she knew Heather would make the best choice for herself, her husband, and their baby. Although Victoria secretly hoped she would return even if on a part-time basis.

Victoria unlocked the main entry door to the firm and turned off the security alarm. It was still at least thirty minutes before anyone else would arrive. Walking past the reception desk and down the hallway to her corner office, she again thought about Drew and wondered how he was doing. She missed hearing his voice and the scent of his cologne. And missed a lot more... the way he held her... the way he looked at her... the way he...

"Oh, for God's sake! Come on, Victoria, get it together," she muttered to herself.

Entering her office, she noticed messages stacked near her phone and her phone set blinking, indicating she had voice messages. She rushed around the corner of her desk, almost knocking over her cherished bronzed statue of a Phoenix rising from the ashes. She had noticed it one day in a 5th Avenue gallery in Scottsdale and bought it on impulse. To her, it represented her personal rising above the tumultuous events of her past. Her rebirth... her new beginning.

She sat down in her desk chair, swiveled to toss her purse in the drawer of the credenza behind her desk, swung back around, and went through the written messages. Then she pressed a button on her phone and went through the voice messages. After listening to the last message, she sat back in her chair with a heavy sigh, disappointment quite apparent from the look on her face. *What was she expecting? He's probably got his hands full right now.*

Staff was arriving, and several stopped by her office door and greeted her.

Victoria rose and walked up to the reception area. It was past the starting time, and no one was there. Fortunately, the phone system allowed callers to go through a directory to be connected to one of the staff, but Victoria preferred the personal touch and having a live person answer the phone call on the main line. She walked down to George's office. He already knew why she was there.

"I know, I know. I'll call the temp agency and see what happened to the gal," he said. "I'll let you know what I find out."

Victoria walked to the office break room, poured herself a cup of coffee, added her usual cream and heavy dose of sugar, and headed back to her office. She spent the better part of an hour going through client files and responding to emails. Off to the side of her office was a conference table and chairs and a small sofa on the other side with a coffee table. She turned behind her and opened a mini-fridge built-in to the credenza and took out a bottled water. Grabbing a file from her desk, she stood and walked over to the sofa, sat down, and started reading through the file, making notes.

George knocked and entered. He looked frazzled.

"What's up, George?" Victoria asked.

"The gal they had lined up canceled on the temp agency, but they're sending over a temp-temp until they can find one who fits the bill for us," he responded.

How odd, the agency never dropped the ball before.

"A temp-temp? What's... never mind... I don't want to know," Victoria stated. "Just send her or him in to see me before they start."

George nodded and left her office.

An hour later, George was at her door again, this time with a young lady he introduced as "Tiffany the temp." After introductions were made, George sheepishly left, and a wide-eyed Victoria asked "Tiffany" to sit, motioning to the armchair next to the sofa.

Victoria had to control herself. Never before had the agency sent over anyone like this. There was Tiffany, gum snapping and wearing an outfit which was totally inappropriate for the office. Torn leotard tights, a low-cut top leaving little to the imagination and a skirt... well, it looked more like a large belt than a skirt. On her feet she wore what only could be described as army boots—stacked army boots, making her look an additional four inches taller, looking as if they weighed twenty pounds each.

Victoria took a deep breath. "Tiffany, I understand you're a 'temp-temp' until the agency finds someone to be a temp for our firm. Correct?" Victoria asked.

"Yeah, I guess. All's I know is they gave me this address and told me to ask for George," she mumbled, making it difficult for Victoria to understand her.

"Do you have your resume with you?" Victoria asked, taking a calming breath.

"Sorta," she replied, snapping her gum and handing Victoria a sheet of paper with only half of the required information filled out.

Victoria looked it over and asked, "Do you have phone experience, answering phones, transferring calls, taking messages? And what is your experience in handling the public, such as when a customer or client calls in person?" Victoria was inwardly cringing at what her response would be.

"Well, I use the phone a lot. And worked in my uncle's takeout pizza place for a while. Does it count?"

That's when Victoria noticed a slight speech defect, it was difficult to understand what Tiffany was saying. Victoria then saw the glint of something in her mouth—she had her tongue pierced, and the sound of the bead clicking against her teeth was in competition with the gum snapping.

Victoria couldn't help but think this was some sort of prank being played on her.

"First of all, Tiffany, we have a dress code here. Office attire is to be appropriate. No torn clothing. Clothing fitting correctly and covering..." Victoria hesitated and calmly asked, "Do you know what I mean?"

Tiffany just shrugged. Victoria grimaced inwardly.

Victoria arose from the sofa, asked Tiffany to wait in the lobby, and walked down to George's office.

"You're kidding me, right? This is a joke?" Victoria said, waiting for his reply. George just sat there looking like a schoolboy who just got reprimanded.

Finally, George spoke, "I used a different agency than what we usually use for staffing. They were cheaper, and they were recommended by a friend of a friend."

Victoria mentally counted to ten—maybe even twenty—before responding.

"George, cheaper doesn't cut it. We have a good rapport with the agency we've always used, and they have always sent us qualified people, not... well, you know. You need to explain to Tiffany her services are not needed, contact our usual agency, and get someone in here—the sooner, the better. And when a candidate gets here, I'll do the interview. George, I know you meant well, but you can't cut corners on staffing. Understood?"

George nodded, and Victoria left his office and went back to her office, closing her door to give herself some time to think. She hated being tough on George, but his actions were not in the best interest of the firm. "You get what you pay for," she muttered to herself, a statement she had heard over and over from her Dad.

Victoria walked over to her desk and sat down. The mere thought about her Dad brought tears to her eyes. Oh, how she missed him. She was sure her mom missed him too. She wished she could talk to him one more time.

Victoria felt herself getting overly emotional.

"What's wrong with me," she thought aloud. "Get it together, Victoria. You have a business to run, no time for emotions right now."

She glanced down at her mobile phone and noticed there was a text message. It was from Drew. Her heart leapt, and she clicked on the message. *"Taking care of business,"* was all it said, nothing else. Disappointment was felt from her head to her toes.

The rest of the day went a lot smoother. George had contacted the correct temp agency and gave them the requirements for the position. They promised to have someone there as a temp first thing in the morning. George was avoiding Victoria, sending her a message with the information.

It took over a week to find a temp who would work out, going through at least five different temp interviews and three prospective candidates before hitting the jackpot.

Abby showed up on time and was impeccably dressed in office attire. What a difference! Victoria interviewed her and brought her back out to the reception area to show her where she would be working. She gave her a brief rundown, then handed her a packet containing information on the firm, the staff roster, policy and procedures, etc. She asked Abby to take it home and look it over, and if she had any questions, either Victoria or one of the staff could help her.

Victoria realized it might take a while for Abby to fill Heather's shoes but had high hopes for her. She was bright, cheery, full of energy, and dressed conservatively. Victoria had one of the assistants sit with Abby at the reception desk for two days and explain the phone and messaging systems.

During those days, Victoria took note on how well Abby handled the phones and the clients who came to the office. She was a quick study, and it seemed all the assistants in the office had taken Abby under their wing.

It had been ten days since she and Drew parted. Except for the one terse text, there hadn't been any word from him—no call, no other texts, no voice message.

On a whim while out shopping, she stopped and purchased his cologne. Why she did, she didn't know. Later in the evening at home, just before going to bed, she dabbed a little bit of the cologne on her neck and the pulse points on her wrist, the small act bringing vivid memories back. Hugging her pillow, now with the scent of his cologne, she felt tears running down her cheeks.

"What's wrong with me?"

Soon, more weeks had passed, then a month, and Victoria still hadn't heard from Drew. She Googled his company and was relieved to find it was still in operation. The company bio contained photos and information on the officers of the company. Drew's photo jumped out at her. She took her index finger and touched it.

Oh, Drew, what's going on? Victoria was finding herself doubting Drew's sincerity more and more as each day passed.

Abby was indeed working out fine as the receptionist. She was attending the community college in the evenings, taking accounting courses, so she was familiar with the lingo in the office.

Heather's husband had called into the office and announced he and Heather were proud parents of a baby boy. Heather and her husband would be taking family leave for several weeks, and Heather hadn't yet decided what her career plans were going to be.

Victoria didn't mind and left the option open for Heather to work part-time if it would appeal to her once her family leave was over. If she did choose to be part-time, it would work out beautifully with Abby. One of the accountants needed an assistant, and Abby would be able to fill the position as a temp-to-perm. Both Abby and Heather could work out a flextime schedule.

Things were running smoothly at the firm. The client base was growing. As a matter of fact, a company with a suite of offices next to the firm was moving out soon, and Victoria and the other partners had discussed expanding into the vacated suite of offices. It would mean they would be able to take on additional accountants, support staff, and more clients.

Victoria thought back to where she was four or five years ago in the business world, and a feeling of accomplishment overwhelmed her. Her mom was so supportive and very proud of her. Her dad would have been so proud too.

Victoria wished she could share her excitement of her firm's success with someone else. Someone who obviously had erased her from his memory. Tears were blurring her sight, emotions getting the better of her again, and she shook it off.

Just prior to Thanksgiving, Victoria's mom was talking about the upcoming holiday at breakfast. She looked over at Victoria.

"Honey, you look tired... I mean really tired. Are you sure you want to go into work today?"

"Yes, Mom. I have several appointments coming in this morning, and I have an appointment out of the office this afternoon. I'll be okay. It's Friday, so I'll have the weekend to rest up. We have so much going on now since we're taking over the offices next to us. More accountants and staff are being interviewed. Heather decided after January 1st, she would like to come back to work part-time in the afternoon, three days a week. Then depending on how it works out, maybe more. She really enjoyed working at the firm, and her husband is able to work from home and care for the baby on the days she's working."

"I'll bet their handsome baby boy is already breaking hearts. It brings back fond memories of when you were an infant, holding you in my arms, and your father beaming. Nothing like a baby to make you feel all is right with the world."

Victoria didn't respond to her mother's remarks—she couldn't.

"I've got to get going now, or I'll be late. See you later, Mom. Love you!" Victoria said as she bent down to give her mom a hug and kiss on the cheek.

Her mom watched Victoria closely as she grabbed her purse from the kitchen counter and left. Marya wanted to say more but held back.

It was well past seven in the evening when Victoria came home. Her mom was in the kitchen and looked up as Victoria entered. Intuitive, Marya read the look on Victoria's face and knew. Mother's intuition. Marya embraced Victoria, holding her daughter tightly, whispering to her, "It's going to be alright. Everything will work out, you'll see."

Marya paused and pulled back a little, trying to make light of the moment. "Would you like some ice cream?"

Victoria gave a weak smile and responded, "Always with the ice cream, Mom.... always with the ice cream."

CHAPTER 15

THE "NOW TIMES"
THE 15-YEAR CLASS REUNION

Only a few minutes had passed after the wheels of the jet touched down at O'Hare Airport, and the plane was taxiing along the tarmac to its assigned gate.

Victoria took a deep breath and shook off the uneasiness she felt as she gazed out the window. She came all this way because of a promise she made to some of her dear friends. She would attend the Fifteen-Year Class Reunion, beginning with a Welcome Dinner on Friday evening and an optional tour on Saturday of the old high school which had been totally renovated with new additions. The more formal Reunion Banquet would be held on Saturday evening. Most reunions were only held every ten years, but it was someone's bright idea to now do them every five years so everyone could stay in touch. Classmates were spread out over the globe on seven continents, and it became evident ten years was way too long to maintain contact even with social media. However, she did keep in touch on a regular basis with Robyn, Peggy, and Grace. They were the mental touchstones in her life, giving her balance, loyalty, and encouragement.

She still had misgivings about the trip but decided to live up to her promise to her friends. Not everyone lives up to their promises—a lesson learned multiple times before, especially at the last reunion.

Her mom had been relentless in convincing her she should attend, claiming it would be a great getaway for her to be with her longtime friends. Her social life in Arizona was basically non-existent, except for a handful of friends who basically gave up on trying to arrange blind dates or fix her up with someone's brother's friend.

Arriving at the gate, the senior flight attendant announced their arrival information and welcomed them to Chicago's O'Hare Airport where the temperature was seventy-five with sunny skies and the current time was two forty-five pm.

Victoria knew the late-September weather in Chicagoland could be "iffy" and made sure she packed to adjust to any changes in the weather, and more than likely, she had over packed as usual. At least in Phoenix, there was never much of an extreme temperature deviation.

There always seemed to be a mad rush when the chime sounded indicating passengers were now able to unbuckle and disembark from the plane. Seated by a window, Victoria took her time gathering her purse and the carryon she had stowed in the bin above the row of seats. Was she subconsciously delaying her arrival?

She waited until most of the passengers had made their way to the exit and followed the pack, exiting the gate area and heading to baggage claim. She stood back from the baggage carousel to avoid getting jostled but stepped forward when she saw her checked bag that matched her Hartmann Tweed carryon coming down the conveyor onto the carousel. As she was reaching for her bag, an older man smiled at her, grabbed her bag, and set it down next to her. *Wow! A gentleman still exists!*

She thanked the man and walked over to the bank of phones which connected directly to the various airport hotels and shuttle services. She picked up a phone, pressed the appropriate keys for the hotel, and gave her name and reservation number to the clerk who answered. He informed her what terminal door the hotel shuttle would be picking her up and advised her it would be there in fifteen minutes.

She interlocked her carryon with her larger bag and headed out to meet up with the shuttle. The shuttle was on time, and because of the proximity of the hotel, the ride only took thirty minutes. Considering the high volume of passenger traffic at O'Hare, it was pretty good.

Inwardly, she kept questioning her reasons for attending the reunion, then after chiding herself for being too critical of her decision, she became more determined than ever to enjoy the time spent with her friends. Her classmates, Grace, Peggy, and Robyn, were thrilled she decided to attend. They were an integral part of her high school years, and she felt fortunate she was able to maintain close contact with them, especially over the past five years. Their loyalty, love, and support got Victoria through some pretty rough spots. Without them and her mom, she wasn't sure she could have survived mentally and emotionally.

Her friend Robyn had made a name for herself in the tech industry and was still based in the Pacific Northwest but constantly traveling. Robyn made a point of flying to Phoenix at least once a year in June to spend time with Victoria. They connected often through email and Skype, and the last time they talked, Robyn told her she would be at the reunion but not sure when she would arrive, and she had something important to share with her.

It was the same hotel that hosted the Ten-Year Reunion weekend five years ago. Some of the time she spent there then seemed like a blur for more than one reason.

The hotel was one of the few in the area which boasted elegantly appointed rooms with views, fabulous food, and stylish ambiance, catering to conventions, reunions, wedding receptions, and similar events for a number of years. The hotel had been recently refurbished and updated, and Victoria looked forward to seeing the new look. The Grand Ballroom on the top floor of the hotel was renovated as well as the smaller event venues on the main lobby floor.

After checking in, she followed the bellman up the elevator to her suite, noting how fresh and wonderful the hotel looked. It seemed every nook and cranny had been redone. After the bellman left, Victoria kicked off her shoes, familiarized herself with the room and its amenities, and unpacked her clothes. Then she called home and to her office to let them know she arrived safely and to call her on her mobile phone if needed. She had taken an early non-stop flight, so she had a couple of hours until the reunion welcome dinner being held in one of the hotel ballrooms at the top of the hotel.

She decided to take a brief nap, leaving herself enough time to shower and dress for the dinner. Rest didn't come easy though. Her thoughts rambled around in her head, reliving the past and jumping to the "now." All the "what ifs" came into play... and no matter how hard she tried, she couldn't erase the past or a fear she had to be careful—a lot was at stake. Butterflies were waking in the pit of her stomach.

It was a little after six as she stepped into the elevator and pushed the button for the Starlight Ball Room. The last time she was near the top of the hotel, memories were made, memories never to be forgotten.

As Victoria stepped out of the elevator, she caught a glimpse of herself in a hallway mirror and straightened her "little black dress," smoothing down the sides with her hands. She brushed her long blonde hair back from her shoulder. Then her right hand went to her midriff, hoping to calm down the butterflies... those pesky butterflies were back!

Other than the sounds of her black stiletto heels on the travertine floors, she heard a myriad of voices coming from the opposite end of the large foyer. She took a deep breath, straightened her shoulders, held her head high, walked across to the reception hall doorway, and peered into the room. The lighting was more muted than in the hallway, and it took a little time for her eyes to adjust.

She let her gaze scan the room, skimming over the countless heads turned in every direction. All at once, her head snapped back and returned to one facing in the opposite direction. Her breath caught. Her hope he wouldn't be there was a lost cause. She'd recognize the wonderful shock of dark, thick hair and broad shoulders anywhere. How many times had she run her fingers through his hair, nibbled and kissed those shoulders? Her body began to tremble, and as if those tremors reverberated across the room, he sensed her presence and slowly turned toward the doorway, his profile igniting her hidden deep-felt passion to her core.

Their eyes met, her eyes apprehensive, wondering and inquisitive, his eyes penetrating, then a smile slowly forming as his gaze consumed her head to toe.

She noticed a clenching of his jaw. He raised the glass in his hand as a toast, raking her up and down with his eyes and nodded his admiration. She was spellbound, holding her breath as if time stood still. He still had a way of reaching her mentally.

Suddenly, a hand touched her arm, startling her from her mesmerized state, and she heard an indistinct voice call her name.

"Victoria, you made it! We were beginning to think you changed your mind and weren't going to come to the reunion."

She turned to find several former classmates sidling up to her and giving her hugs, including her friends Grace and Peggy and their husbands. It was so difficult to not glance over her shoulder to see if he was still looking in her direction. But she dared not turn back for fear she would freeze up... or worse yet, collapse into a puddle of emotions. She was never very good at hiding her feelings. A catch twenty-two of sorts—an asset and a liability.

She made small talk with her friends but felt as if she didn't hear a thing being said. Was it her imagination, or did she sense him watching her every move? She excused herself from the group to get something to drink and decided to make her way through the crowd in the opposite direction. At this time, distance was her friend. Somewhere along the way, a waiter offered her one of the drinks on his tray, which she snatched and downed quickly in an effort to calm herself. After putting the empty wine glass back on the tray, she picked up another from the tray, giving a rather sheepish smile to the waiter who looked rather shocked, then she walked away, delicately sipping the wine.

She was starting to doubt herself for ever coming to the event. Eighteen hundred miles and five years didn't seem far enough or long enough now to quell the apprehension she felt. She started to feel a little lightheaded. *Was it the crowded room, the hastily drunk wine?* The air was stifling. She noticed a set of open French doors leading out onto a terraced balcony. She darted through them, heading to an unlit corner overlooking the city lights.

She inwardly reproached herself. *How could someone so successful and with a calm, cool demeanor in business be such a wimp when it came to her personal life?* Here she was with her stomach all tied up in knots, butterflies doing a fast Texas two-step, and her brains scrambled just knowing he was in the next room.

She stood before the elaborately carved stone balcony balustrade, silently berating herself for feeling so foolish, deciding to enjoy the evening with her old friends. She chose to wait and relax a bit, then go back inside to mix and mingle with her friends while maintaining a safe distance from him.

She took a deep cleansing breath. The air was permeated with the scents from the potted flowering plants scattered around the balcony. The reception hall outside the Grand Ballroom was situated near the top of the hotel complex with only two other floors above it, which were reserved for the guests of several penthouse suites—one suite in particular which she was well acquainted with. Only the muted sounds of traffic below could be heard where she stood. The night was crisp and clear, and because of the faintly lit area, a sky full of stars sparkled like crystals on blue velvet.

She was lost in gazing up at those stars when something aroused her senses—his scent

Damn! He's close by. He hasn't changed his cologne after all these years.

She quivered at the thought of the last time she inhaled the scent here at the hotel. How she had buried her face in the pillow he had laid on. How she wrapped her arms around a pillow at home and pretended he was there. And how, when loneliness would creep into her life, she would still hug her pillow and relive those special moments.

She felt his presence behind her. His hand gently brushed the silken blonde tendrils from her shoulder, exposing her vulnerable bare skin. Her pulse quickened. Time stood still.

He leaned close and whispered her name, "Victoria."

Her breath caught in her throat. She closed her eyes. His hands gently touched her shoulders, and she could feel his breath in her hair as he pressed his face into it. A long-dormant feeling started to rise from the pit of her stomach as he slowly turned her to face him.

She opened her eyes and mouthed his name, "Drew."

She looked into his eyes and tried to read what was in them.

Regret? Passion? It was difficult to say, and she dared not to think it was anything more.

He removed his hand from her shoulder, took her chin, and rubbed his thumb along the side of it.

"It's been a long time, Victoria... you still take my breath away. You're more beautiful than ever," he said in a slow, hoarse whisper.

Was it her imagination, or was he affected as much as she was?

She wanted so much to tell him the time apart had been heart-wrenching, and her thoughts of him were endless. But most of all, she wanted to tell him how much he hurt her.

She was about to respond when the noise of a shoe scraping on the terrazzo tile startled them both, and they froze for an instant.

Drew looked over his shoulder to see a couple standing at the opposite corner of the balcony, engrossed in a very animated conversation. He recognized them as the Dawson's, the same couple who had gone all through school together, married, and the very same couple who had created havoc for Victoria at the ten-year reunion. All through school and beyond, they had based their relationships on power and money. From the gist of the conversation, the raised voices, name calling, and body language, their marriage was in trouble. He knew all too well, a successful marriage had to have respect as one of its foundations, and theirs was definitely faltering.

He looked at Victoria and pulled her closer to him as if shielding her from the scene.

Was he protecting her or hiding her? She recognized the couple as well from the sound of their voices. They were vocal about anything and everything and always appeared to gloat at the misfortunes of others. Victoria cringed at the memory of her encounter with them at the previous reunion. How they chided her for marrying someone without any ambition to be more than an accountant, particularly an unethical one, and how she only had herself to blame for the divorce for not inspiring her spouse to be more than what he was, which was a drug addict and criminal. As if it was as simple. They didn't have all the facts, and she certainly wouldn't share those with the likes of them. Although she had to give them credit for being one of the catalysts leading to a very special time in her life. One which ultimately impacted her to realize what love truly was.

It became obvious the Dawson's noticed they weren't alone on the terrace but weren't able to recognize Victoria and Drew in the darkness of the corner. They quickly moved back into the reception hall.

After the Dawson's left, Drew relaxed his hold on Victoria and pushed back ever so slightly, looking down at her face. Her hands still clenched her wine glass between them, holding onto it as if it was a lifeline. His hand took the glass from her and set it on the bench seat at his side.

"You know how you get with wine, Victoria. One relaxes you, two makes you giddy, and three, as I know so well... makes you one very passionate woman. So what number is it," he asked with a slight curve on his lips and a twinkle in his eyes.

His question surprised her. *Why was he asking how much wine she drank?* She cocked her head to the side and gave him a somewhat discerning look.

"Two... almost," she responded. Before she could think, she surprised even herself, and raising an eyebrow and displaying a minx-like smile, she snidely asked him, "Were you hoping for three? Because it's not going to happen, Drew."

She knew she had to display an air of detachment and not show how much he was affecting her. *No emotions, Victoria... show no emotions,* she said over and over in her mind. *Play it cool, play it like he doesn't matter... like he never mattered... oh, heaven help me!*

He tilted his head back and let out a hearty laugh.

"You still have your quick wit. It's one of the things I adored about you. Our conversations were always like friendly duels, and for days on end, I would remember them and laugh to myself."

Her sassy demeanor abruptly changed. She remembered them all too often—among other things. She felt a warm blush arising in her cheeks. *Did he notice?*

She held her hands together tightly to stop the trembling which seemed to be surfacing. Indeed, it was noticed, and he took her hands in his, bringing them slowly to his lips, lightly kissing her palms and fingertips, all the while looking into her eyes, then smiling.

Another quirky smile of his. Now what?

"Another thing I adored about you... your deceptively delicate hands, long sensual fingers, and fuchsia-colored nails... ah... you changed the color... sort of coral, maybe? Haven't had a decent massage or back scratching for years."

She pulled her hands out of his, and with her right hand, gave him a light punch on the shoulder.

"Serves you right, Drew! You never had it so good. At least I know there was something you missed about me."

Her tone had fallen somewhere between joking and sarcastic, using humor and mockery to hide her hurt feelings. She turned her back to him and faced out over the balustrade. His eyes squinted, and he actually looked hurt.

Her mind raced, thinking about their last time together, and since then, only one text message on her mobile phone, informing her he was "taking care of business," the tone of the text bordering on cool and distant, belying what had transpired between them and leaving her with the impression either it was all a dream, or he felt what happened between them didn't matter. Then... nothing. No calls or emails. How many times had she checked her messages, knowing full well if he wanted to contact her, she always had her mobile phone, and he had her phone number? Days turned into weeks, then months, and finally, years. Time was supposed to heal, but this hurt would never go away. It couldn't. He'd left her with a reminder never to trust again, lies and broken promises, a time filled with nothing but deception.

She knew he had commitments. What did she expect? Did she truly believe he would come riding back into her life on a white charger and carry her off to begin a "happily ever after" life?

He had been taken aback by her response. She missed seeing the clenching jaw and the furrowing of his brow. He sighed deeply and nodded.

"Yes, of course, there were things I missed about you, Victoria. And you know very well I had responsibilities to take care of when I returned home to Florida."

She thought she would feel a deep satisfaction hearing he missed her, but they seemed to be said in such a melancholy manner, she felt a sadness overcome her.

A microphone voice was heard out on the terrace, announcing the "Welcome Dinner" was about to begin and requesting everyone move into the adjacent ballroom and be seated.

She knew they shouldn't and couldn't sit together in such an open forum. It would be challenging if they did, and she wasn't sure if she could actually be so close to him and manage not to have the rebellious butterflies in her stomach.

Turning back to Drew, she tried to hide her anxiety, saying in an almost too perky manner, "I guess we better head in and get to our places. Have a nice—"

He cut her off saying, "Shall we, Victoria," more as a statement than a question. He brusquely took her elbow and escorted her through the

French doors and across the room to the large double doors leading into the Ballroom.

"Victoria! We saved a place for you at our table," Peggy called out.

Victoria was about to accept when Drew firmly stated, "She's sitting with me, but thank you just the same."

Peggy looked surprised and gave Victoria a concerned look. Victoria looked back over her shoulder and quietly said, "*Thank you*" to her as Drew whisked her away, pulling her through the maze of tables to one situated almost dead center in the room.

Oh my God! What was he thinking? Didn't he know how chancy this was going to be? How precarious?

CHAPTER 16

He pulled out her chair for her, and as she sat down, she looked around the table to see her dining companions were comprised of his close friends from school who he had stayed in contact with all these years. Some had brought their spouses and "significant others" with them.

How was he going to explain this? How was he going to explain her?

Victoria's circle of friends in school was small and were known as the "nerd herd," most belonging to the same afterschool clubs. Victoria Hart was very much the wallflower. Traversing the hallways in school, the petite, overly shy girl would always keep her head down and had her arms loaded with books, trying to be as inconspicuous as possible. Unfortunately, this also made her the perfect target for those who took great enjoyment in bullying.

It wasn't until just before graduation, the butterfly finally started to open up, and she couldn't escape the school days fast enough. Graduation was like a reprieve to her. Once away from the taunts and ridicule, she blossomed even more.

Drew Anderson, on the other hand, had a bounty of friends in school, male and female. He was witty, intelligent, personable, involved in sports, and attractive. A real jock. What's not to like? He was extremely popular and was invited to just about every party ever thrown during their high school years. Victoria had questioned his veracity when he had told her at the last reunion five years ago, he remembered her in school

Now, seated at this table with his friends, she felt totally out of her element. Introductions were made around the table, former classmates raising a few eyebrows when they heard her name. Two had no recollection of her at all.

During the course of the dinner, it was becoming more and more obvious his friends were curious about her, asking questions which seemed to delve further and further into her past and her private life. She had to be careful, giving minimal responses. It felt like she was being interrogated, and she was stressing inside. Drew must have sensed her discomfort and deflected some of the questions with his humor, turning the tables on them.

Again, she wondered who he was protecting. Drew's intervention seemed to make them even more determined to find out more about her. The ladies at the table appeared to be a little unnerved by the attention she was getting from their male counterparts. Fortunately, dinner went by rather quickly with all the verbal sparring.

Victoria reached for the beaded shoulder strap of her purse which had been placed on the floor between her and Drew. He noticed her intention and attempted to pick it up for her, bumping heads as they both leaned over. A nervous giggle arose from her throat, and he smiled warmly at her. She felt the heat rise in her cheeks, and she started to push out her chair.

"Just where do you think you're going?" he asked with the all-knowing smirk of his.

"The ladies' room, and this time, I don't need an escort," she responded, knowing full well this was déjà vu as another memory from the past was triggered.

Drew's eyes narrowed, and there was the clenching of his jaw again.

She thought her comment about not needing an escort to the ladies room would remove the smirk on his face with memories of the last reunion, but it didn't. Instead, he stood up, helped to pull out her chair, and handed her purse to her. Then taking her by the hand, he led her back through the labyrinth of tables and chairs, avoiding the servers who were busy clearing the tables for coffee and dessert.

Another hallway, another time. He accompanied her to the entrance of the ladies room, not making any gestures or moves along the way. She did notice he had an unusual twinkle in his eyes. *Oh, those eyes.* How she could fall deeply into those dark pools of melted chocolate, almost as if she could see into his soul. Her thoughts drifted to another time, and she caught herself.

Stop it, Victoria... it's all in the past, never to happen again.

Without wanting to drag the encounter out any longer and without hesitation, she walked into the ladies lounge without looking back. She knew full well she was treading on thin ice and needed time to compose herself and think things out. After stalling for a good ten minutes, she took a deep breath and walked back out into the main foyer, hoping he did another Houdini and disappeared like he did five years ago—no such luck. There he was, and he had his hand behind his back as if hiding something. As she got closer, he brought his hand forward, holding a beautiful red rose. She looked at him quizzically.

"A rose for my Queen," he answered huskily.

"Drew, why? Why are you playing games with me? Don't you realize how much you hurt me five years ago?"

He looked aghast. He realized they were standing out in the middle of the foyer. Only a handful of people were nearby, but not close enough to hear their conversation.

"We need to talk but not here," he replied rather brusquely, grabbing her arm and steering her down a long hallway toward an elevator.

She was about to object, but the elevator door opened as soon as he hit the call button. He gently pushed her inside and quickly pressed the button to close the doors, then pressed the Penthouse Suites button. The suite was two floors above, and they arrived at the floor in seconds. Just as before, the elevator doors opened into a hallway with entrances to penthouse suites. Still holding onto Victoria's arm as if he was afraid she would escape, he headed to a door at the end of the private hall and inserted his access card. All the while, Victoria kept trying to talk to him, but he was having none of it.

"Drew, please, not this. Not again," she snapped as he was dragging her by the arm.

He turned to her as they entered the suite and shut the door. She couldn't tell whether his look was one of anger, frustration, or both.

He started to speak, then exasperated, he countered, "Oh hell!"

He crushed her to him and ground his lips into hers, taking her off guard and taking her breath as well. He finally released her, both of them gasping for breath.

"What... what's this all about?" she asked, catching her breath and bringing her hand up to touch her sore lips.

Backing up and putting some distance between them, her body still reeling from the kiss, she said, as calmly as she could, "Drew, I can't do this again. I can't allow myself to get hurt again. Five years ago was foolishness. It was poor judgment on my part. You told me you were separated and in the midst of a divorce and would finalize everything when you returned to Florida after the reunion. I returned to Phoenix, thinking you and I had something special going between us. I was a fool to think it was real. You played me. You were nothing but a predator. I was a very naïve and easy target back then. I'm not naive and gullible now."

Her words stung him, especially the word "predator" and hit him as if someone poured ice water on him and sucker-punched him. He ran his hand over his head through his espresso-colored hair with an agitated motion.

"You don't understand, Victoria. I had my business and my marriage interlinked, and a divorce needed to be handled carefully in order for the business to survive," Drew tried to explain.

"One text message, Drew. Really, only one text message? 'Taking care of business?'" she asked incredulously, doing air quotes with her hands.

"I realized how important your security investigations business was to you but not contacting me...? Did I mean so little to you, a phone call was too much to ask from you? What was I to believe?" She took a deep breath.

"Enough, Drew!" she snapped, waving off his movement toward her. She walked determinedly to the suite door, opened it, and turning to Drew, she said, "If you have any feelings for me at all, no matter how little, you'll respect my wishes and keep the hell away from me. Goodbye, Drew."

She pulled the door shut, quickly walked to the elevator, and pushed the elevator call button. Trembling, she opened her purse and pulled out the access card to her hotel room. As she stepped into the elevator, she feared Drew would come running to stop her. She hurriedly jabbed at her floor button and drew another deep breath. As the doors closed, she breathed a sigh of relief, yet a wave of disappointment came over her. *What was she disappointed about?*

SHE ENTERED her hotel room and immediately double-latched the door. She thought about turning on the lights, but the floor illuminators were all she needed to move about the suite. If "someone" came to her door, she wouldn't answer, and it would appear as if she wasn't there. She quickly and quietly took off her heels and her dress, noticing his cologne's scent left a trace on her dress. She even noted his fragrance had clung to her skin. Peeling off her underclothes, she headed into the bathroom and stood in the shower, turning the dial and letting the hot water stream down from head to toe, hoping to erase those vestiges of him.

"Dammit, Victoria, you have to get hold of yourself. You can't let him get to you. You have a lot at stake. You have to protect yourself... and those you love."

A few minutes later, she was toweling off, and there was a knock at the hotel room door. She froze. She had purposely closed the bathroom door in her suite so no one would hear the shower running if they were outside her suite door in the hallway. Another knock. She stood still for several minutes. She was about to walk back into her bedroom area when the hotel phone rang. After several rings, it went to voice mail. It couldn't have been home or her office calling. They would only use her mobile phone number. It had to be one of her classmates... or possibly Drew?

She stood there with the towel wrapped around her for another minute and decided to just call it a night and get to bed. It had been a long day, and although flight travel didn't bother her, she felt drained.

It wasn't even nine p.m. in Illinois and only eight p.m. in Arizona, but she knew she needed her rest. Her anxiety and worry had taken a toll on her mentally, emotionally, and physically. Tomorrow was another day, and she hoped the "Drew" issue was finally over. She didn't like to be deceptive but had to be.

She checked the room phone voice messages. There was only one call, but the caller hung up and didn't leave a message. Deep down, she knew who it was.

She got under the covers, picked up her mobile phone, and made a call home. The voice on the other end made her smile, and her spirits rose. After ending the call, she reached over and connected the charger to her phone, nestled deep into the sheets, and fell asleep with a smile on her face.

CHAPTER 17

Victoria was awakened by the hotel phone ringing beside her on the nightstand. She was still groggy, and without thinking, she picked up the phone to answer it. Then realizing what she'd done, she held her breath.

"Hello... Victoria, are you there?" a female voice asked. "Are you okay?" It was her classmate Peggy.

"Oh, Peggy, yes, I'm fine. Just a bit of jet lag."

"Oh, good, we were worried when we didn't see you after the dinner and thought maybe something happened." Peggy was one of her closest friends and a strong ally and confidante.

"I saw Drew walking you out after dinner. Then a little over an hour later, he returned without you, proceeded to hang out with his old buddies, then they moved down to the lobby bar. From what I heard, they closed the bar around two in the morning. Are you sure you're alright?" The innuendo was there.

"Yes, really. I'm okay. Just tired from the trip... and from a bit of anxiety."

"I understand, Victoria, I really do," Peggy responded. "Hey, we're going to tour the old high school later and see what changes they made. Would you like to ride along with us? It might be good for you to get out and about."

Victoria pondered and replied, "I don't know, Peggy. Not sure if I want to relive some of those memories if you know what I mean, plus I'm wondering who else will be on the tour."

"Victoria, we did have some good memories too. It's where we first met, and our group had some good times together. I don't know who else is going, but you just stay with us. We watched out for one another in high school, and you know we'll watch out for you now, just like back then."

"Okay. Against my better judgment, but okay."

"Have you eaten breakfast yet? It's just after eight a.m. I hear they have an awesome breakfast buffet downstairs, and I'm ravenous. We could meet you downstairs in an hour," Peggy asked.

Victoria agreed to meet her friends downstairs at the buffet in an hour. Enough time to call home and check on things, take a quick shower, do her hair, a bit of makeup, and throw on her teal warmup suit and sneakers. The phone call home was brief but bolstered her emotions. She went about getting ready with a smile on her face.

Timing is everything, and she ran into Peggy and Grace with their respective spouses in the hallway. Hugs all around. In the elevator, descending to the lobby, Peggy eyed Victoria carefully and asked if she had called home, and Victoria responded with a wink, a grin lighting up her eyes.

Soon, they all were seated in the restaurant, ordering beverages from the waiter. Victoria cautiously and discreetly glanced around the room. *No sign of Drew. Thank goodness.*

The waiter brought their beverages, and Peggy suggested the husbands head to the buffet and scope it out for them, then the ladies would go. Victoria knew full well it was Peggy's way of having private time for some girl talk.

With the guys gone to the buffet tables and more than likely heaping all kinds of things on their plates, Peggy dove in, "Well, what happened last night after dinner? We were truly worried about you but figured you could handle it." Grace leaned into the conversation.

"Nothing much, really," Victoria responded. She hoped her cheeks weren't turning red. "We talked very little." Oh, that much was true. "It got a bit intense, and I told him it was a no-go, it was over and done with. I was in bed before nine."

"Alone?" Grace interjected. Victoria choked on the coffee she had just sipped.

"Yes, definitely alone," Victoria replied, gasping. She looked at Peggy and Grace and smiled. "Absolutely alone. I'm not falling into the Drew pit again."

The husbands had returned, and just as expected, each was trying to do a balancing act with their abundantly full plates.

"You know this is a buffet, and you can go back as many times as you want," Grace laughed. The guys looked at each other, rolled their eyes, and responded they knew but wanted to make sure they didn't run out of food before they got back there again. This time, Grace and Peggy rolled their eyes and shook their heads.

The ladies rose and headed to the buffet tables. It was quite a spread —fresh fruit and freshly baked rolls, breads, and muffins. Another table was laid out with smoked salmon with sides of capers, lemons, chopped onion, cream cheese, and bagels. There were potatoes prepared several ways. Yogurt, cereals, and smoothies were spread out for those guests looking for something healthy. Another table station had a chef preparing made-to-order omelets and another for crepes and pancakes. Additional buffet tables wrapped around until you could start over at the beginning. No wonder the guys had their plates full.

Of course, Victoria and her sweet tooth noticed the dessert station which took up three tables and included a chocolate fountain. "Oh, dear," she thought aloud. "I'm in trouble."

As if reading her mind, both Peggy and Grace chimed in with the same sentiment as they spotted the fountain with cascading chocolate.

Victoria announced she would head to the fresh fruit, then on to the omelet station to request a made-to-order omelet. Peggy and Grace headed to the smoked salmon and breakfast meat tables.

After choosing strawberries, grapes, and melon, Victoria waited behind a woman in the omelet line while the woman gave her order to the chef. She was deciding what she would tell the chef she wanted in her omelet when the scent of "his" cologne reached her. She knew he was behind her and really didn't have anywhere to run. She hoped to place her order quickly and get back to the table with her friends.

"Good Morning, Victoria," he said softly in her ear. "I hope you slept well last night. I certainly didn't."

Before she could reply, the chef said, "Excuse me, Miss, what would you like in your omelet?" Victoria felt frozen but managed to give the chef her order without stumbling over her words.

Turning ever so slightly toward Drew, whose shadowed eyes and unshaven face looked like he had a bad night, Victoria responded.

"I slept very well, thank you. A little bird told me you were out with your friends until the wee hours. Hope you had a good time."

"Checking up on me, Victoria?"

"Not hardly. Don't be so full of yourself, Drew. It was mentioned to me in passing by another classmate. That's all. There was no inquiry on my part. I couldn't care less what you do or who you're with," she answered matter-of-factly. She noticed he was clenching his jaw again. She turned her back to him and faced the chef.

The chef had her omelet ready, reaching out to hand the plate to her. She slid away from the buffet station, away from Drew, and walked in the direction of her table.

Peggy met her halfway. "We saw your encounter with Drew, so I was headed over to cause a diversion in some way. Sorry I didn't get to you sooner."

"No, worries, Peggy. It was brief, very brief. And hopefully, he got the message loud and clear."

By then, Peggy and Victoria had gotten back to their table, and the remainder of the main meal was enjoyable. Victoria noticed Peggy and Grace looking around occasionally, appearing as if they were guarding her with Grace seated on one side of Victoria and Peggy on the other. Victoria smiled inwardly—she had her own secret service detail protecting her.

Victoria's mobile phone rang. Reaching into her purse, she recognized the number. "Robyn, where the heck are you girl?" Victoria asked.

"I'm at the airport, ready to board my flight to O'Hare. As soon as we... er, I get checked in at the hotel, I'll call you. Gotta run, we're boarding now. Love and hugs!" Robyn responded.

"See you later!" Victoria answered. "Wait... who's with you?" Too late, the call disconnected.

Grace and Peggy were thrilled Robyn was going to make it to the reunion and catch up with them. Victoria had a feeling there would be a lot of "catching up" when Robyn arrived.

Grace suggested the three ladies head for the dessert table together. *Safety in numbers.* The gentlemen had already made a run to the desserts and returned again with their plates full of sugary and high carb treats. Grace commented she got a sugar rush just looking at their plates.

The ladies left the gentlemen to their sweet dreams, and the three agreed to head to the chocolate fountain. Each was picking pieces of fruit and pastry and holding them under the flowing chocolate. Victoria accidentally slipped, holding a strawberry on a skewer and ended up with melted chocolate on her thumb. As she was putting her thumb in her mouth to lick it off, she looked up and found Drew was on the other side of the fountain, staring at her intently, looking at her mouth. She quickly grabbed a napkin from the table and wiped her thumb. Drew cocked his head to one side and smiled.

Oh, hell, another memory from the past. She felt her face heating up and decided she had enough of the chocolate fountain and went back to the table, Peggy and Grace close behind.

"You okay, Hon?" Grace asked after catching some of the interaction between Victoria and Drew.

"Yes, at least he didn't try to engage me in conversation this time," Victoria responded quietly.

Peggy said softly, so only Victoria and Grace could hear, "But if eyes could talk, he said a whole lot. Even I felt the vibrations!"

The rest of the meal conversation revolved around their upcoming tour of the old high school and what time they would meet in the lobby. With arrangements made, they all headed up to their suites to change clothes. Victoria whispered to herself, "Safety in numbers."

VICTORIA FRESHENED UP, putting her long blonde hair up in a ponytail, and picked out a turquoise V-necked sweater and dark blue denim jeans with a matching denim jacket. As she was sliding on her comfy, navy-blue sneakers, there was a knock on her door. She sucked in her breath. She wasn't sure if anyone outside the door had heard her moving around in the room and stopped in her tracks.

Another knock. She didn't dare move. Then a large envelope was slipped under the door, and she heard footsteps moving down the hallway. Waiting a few seconds, she quietly walked over to the door and scooped up the envelope.

It had the high school name and logo on it. Inside was the information and dinner ticket for the formal dinner in the evening. It also contained a questionnaire should anyone like to fill it out and a comment card, asking for suggestions, comments, etc. regarding the reunion. There also was a booklet listing the contact information for her class members. Victoria remembered receiving a notice in her email months earlier, asking for contact information to be put in a booklet to be shared with her classmates.

Victoria had to be very careful. The information requested was personal, regarding spouses, family, career, etc. Victoria only responded with her accounting firm's name, noting she was a senior partner and the address, phone number, and email at the company. Nothing more.

She looked through the booklet and found Drew's name. His information was just as vague. No family information, just the name of his company and its address, phone number, and his email info.

"Just because he didn't supply personal information, doesn't mean he's not married to Barbara anymore," Victoria murmured to herself, an ache in her throat. *But why?*

Victoria glanced down at the time on her mobile phone, and seeing she needed to get a move on, put on a pair of southwestern turquoise earrings and a thin matching bracelet. Gathering a bottle of water out of the mini-fridge and her purse, she headed down to the lobby to meet up with her friends.

The elevator arrived on her floor, and she entered as soon as the doors opened, instantly inhaling a waft of a familiar cologne and realizing too late Drew was there, right behind her. He quickly hit the button to close the doors, and the elevator descended.

He turned to face her, looking as if it was difficult for him to talk, but quietly and slowly as if he was having a difficult time controlling himself said, "We're not done talking, Victoria, not by a long shot. And *we* are not done." His last words ground out with a clenched jaw. She wondered what he meant.

Victoria was trembling from within. Just then, the elevator doors opened to the main lobby, and she rushed passed him. She felt him reach out to grab her arm but averted his grasp and quickly headed to the center of the main lobby, knowing full well Drew wouldn't want to make a scene there.

Peggy and her husband were already in the lobby, off to the side, and Peggy noticed Victoria coming out the elevator with Drew fast on her heels. Peggy nudged her husband, and with her husband close behind her, they made a beeline for Victoria, arriving at Victoria's side before Drew caught up.

"Victoria, you look like all you need now is a Western hat to complete your ensemble," Peggy said emphatically, gathering Victoria in an embrace. Whispering, Peggy said, "Not to worry, we got your back."

Victoria gave a silent nod.

Drew stopped short, veered away from them, and stood off to the side about fifteen feet away with both his fists and jaw clenched.

Good thing because around the corner came Grace and her husband who had just come down in an elevator. Peggy gave a look to Grace, and Grace nodded.

"Wow, Victoria, you look fabulous. Love those turquoise and silver earrings. So 'Southwesty'... is that a word?" Grace commented lightheartedly.

"Thanks, Grace. I picked them up on a short business trip to Santa Fe a couple of months ago. Amazingly, they're lightweight. I don't knock myself out when I turn my head," she smiled as she swiveled her head side to side.

Grace and Peggy replied with laughs. She knew they all were making light conversation, but it didn't matter.

Drew had his own agenda though and purposely walked up to the group, standing behind Victoria. Peggy and Grace's eyes didn't have to tell her to turn around, his cologne was already there.

Resting his left hand on Victoria's shoulder, sending electric pulses through her and giving the butterflies a jolt, he reached around her to shake the hands of Peggy, Grace, and their respective husbands.

"Hello, Ladies and Gentlemen, hope you're having a pleasant time."

It was Victoria's turn for jaw clenching.

Drew then slid his arm around Victoria's shoulders, and looking down at Victoria, said, "And what do we have here... a cowgirl from

Arizona, right? Hello, Victoria... or should I call you Miss Vicky? I'm sure there are plenty of cowboys out there who would love for you to rope and brand them or maybe vice versa!"

Victoria could feel herself grinding her teeth.

Everyone feeling a bit uneasy, Grace was the one who came to the rescue.

"Drew, it's been really nice to see you again. We were all just on our way out, but maybe we can catch up later this evening at the dinner."

Drew got the message loud and clear. As he removed his arm from her shoulder, his hand traveled down her arm to her hand, and grasping it, he gave it a gentle squeeze and released it. Victoria felt his hand tremble, and an ache consumed her from inside, her heart drumming an erratic beat.

As Drew bid everyone goodbye, his piercing eyes lingered on Victoria. When he was well beyond earshot, there was a collective sigh of relief even from the husbands.

Victoria looked around at her friends. "Well played, my friends, well played."

CHAPTER 18

The next hour was spent in Peggy's car, her husband driving and Grace's husband riding shotgun. The three girls were in the back with Victoria between Grace and Peggy, sharing stories about school days, looking at family pictures on their mobile phones, and sometimes laughing so hard, they had tears in their eyes.

At one point, Peggy and Grace stopped talking and looked at each other and took one of Victoria's hands. *This is what unconditional friendship was all about.*

For a Saturday, it was pretty busy at the old high school. Victoria, Peggy, and Grace were amazed at how it had expanded. The main building had been added onto several times. Although Peggy and Grace still lived in Illinois, neither had made any recent road trips in the vicinity of the high school, so this was new to them as well.

There was a "Welcome Alumni" banner hanging near the front entrance. After they parked the car, they walked through the entrance and stood in awe.

"Wow," Peggy exclaimed, "They've done a lot in fifteen years!"

Students were manning tables in the main entrance hall, handing out information sheets and a guide showing the new layout of the school. There were also tables set up in the cafeteria for alumni to sit and have light refreshments. The girls teased their husbands about being hungry again so soon after having such a big brunch.

They all opted to tour the classrooms with the additions, then head out to the sports fields. There was a rally going on early in the afternoon, and everyone was enthused about seeing it.

After visiting the new sections of the school, they walked out to the stadium area. It had been a while since any of them had to climb stadium bleachers, and they laughed that even at age thirty-three they were winded. One of the husbands joked, as he climbed to the top section of the bleachers, it was because of the altitude, which caused a round of laughter. It was breezy up there, but the temperature was comfortable. Victoria's ponytail was whipping around slightly in the wind, causing some of her hair to come loose and block her vision.

The entire stadium was filled with either current students or alumni. Victoria had the recurring sense someone was watching her. She looked around but didn't notice anyone, and her loose strands of hair didn't help matters. Peggy had brought along mini-binoculars and handed them to Victoria when she asked for them. Victoria scanned the field and laughed along with her friends at the antics of the mascot and the cheerleaders.

Aiming her sight across the field, she skimmed the stands on the other side. No way! There was Drew, sitting with a couple of his friends with a pair of binoculars—looking at her. Putting down his binoculars, he raised his fingers to his lips and gave her a salute.

Victoria felt herself turning red and handed the binoculars back to Peggy.

She picked up on it and said, "It's Drew, isn't it?" Victoria nodded.

Grace overheard, and replied, "He's certainly not making it easy for you, is he?"

"Afraid not. But he's just going to have to accept the fact what we had —or what I thought we had—wasn't real. I'm not falling for it again. I have more important things in my life to think about," Victoria replied, "Much more important."

Peggy and Grace both nodded knowingly.

The rest of the rally was entertaining, but Victoria was uncomfortable, knowing Drew was watching her every move from across the field. At one point, she took down her hair from the ponytail, allowing her hair to fly with the wind about her face in an effort to shield her face from his view. Although she couldn't help herself from stealing a look across the field once in a while.

During the ride back to the hotel, the ladies talked about what they would be wearing at the formal dinner that evening. Peggy opted for a black, cold-shoulder, knit sheath with silver embellishments, and Grace chose a royal blue dress with a beaded and sequined top and chiffon skirt.

Victoria brought a chain-collared, chiffon-layered shift dress in vibrant poppy, measuring a few inches above her knees. She remembered when she tried it on at the store how the layers of chiffon fluttered around her as she walked. It was a "fun" dress. And it had been a long time since she had fun! Victoria was determined to have as much fun as possible on this trip.

It was half-past three in the afternoon when they got back to the hotel. They all headed to their suites, agreeing to meet upstairs later in the reception area of the hotel's banquet hall.

Victoria was grateful her friends were staying in suites on the same floor, just down the hallway from her suite. She was more determined than ever to put as much space between herself and Drew and to avoid him as much as possible. With her friends nearby, she knew they would run interference for her.

As Victoria entered her suite, she saw the telltale flashing on the room phone, indicating she had messages. She hit the speaker button and voice message button to retrieve any messages. The first was from her friend Robyn, telling her she had arrived and would meet her outside the reception area before the dinner.

The next one was a "hang up." Victoria could only guess who it was.

No other messages. Victoria checked her mobile phone. There was only one call from a Realtor friend who was doing some scouting for her. Victoria had finally made the decision to start house hunting. She was financially secure with money in the bank and wanted to find something with a nice back yard. Being under her mother's roof for the past years had been a godsend, but she really wanted to get her own place.

Her mom had been spreading her own wings, as she said she would, and Victoria got the feeling one of her mom's volunteer friends from the V.A. was getting to be more than a friend, and she didn't want to stifle her mom's activities. Victoria knew moving out on her own would be a good thing for both of them.

She decided to call home before getting ready for the dinner. No answer. Odd, she thought, Mom didn't mention going out anywhere. Victoria left a message for her mom to call her, and if she couldn't reach her on her mobile phone, to leave a message either on her room phone or at the hotel desk. Victoria knew she shouldn't be concerned but wanted to make sure everything was okay back home.

Victoria laid back on the bed and closed her eyes, trying desperately to relax. It seemed the activity so far today was taking a toll on her. She needed to focus on enjoying her time with her friends and removing the anxiety over Drew.

Victoria spent extra time and care getting ready for the evening's event. After applying her makeup, which included a poppy lipstick, her fingers nimbly put her hair in an upswept hairdo with tiny Swarovski crystal pins scattered in her hair to keep it from falling. She had let her hair grow much longer over the past years. Her friend Tonia at TM Hair Studio made sure when she trimmed Victoria's hair, the longer style would be easier to manage, particularly for her exercise and fitness activities.

She had joined a cycling club close to the house, and three times a week, a little after dawn, they would meet at a designated location sent by text and cycle around the vicinity, riding anywhere from five to ten miles. Victoria was feeling the best she had ever felt. Her mom always made sure there were fresh fruits and vegetables in the house for her to make blended healthy drinks. Marya had even become an expert at whipping up smoothies. A gentleman who also volunteered at the V.A. had schooled Marya on the drinks and was instrumental in making them available to the "wounded warriors" they worked with.

Victoria went to the closet and pulled out her poppy-colored dress. Smiling, she laid it on the bed and went about opening a small zippered bag in her luggage, taking out a pair of crystal chandelier earrings and matching bracelet.

Before she'd left Phoenix, she went to see her dear friend, Jeanine, who owned a spa and had a manicure and pedicure done in a matching poppy. Sliding on a pearl and diamond ring in a gold setting, she held up her right hand to admire the luster of the pearl in the light—simple and elegant.

Victoria slid the dress over her head, over her poppy strapless demi-bra and matching bikini panties. From being outdoors, her skin had a golden tan on her toned body, exhibiting good health and fitness. She was glad she would have the cycling exercise to fall back on after all the crazy eating she was doing this weekend.

Reaching behind her neck, she hooked the clasp of the chain collar ring. The shift dress floated down around her, brushing her thighs about two inches above her knees. As she turned, the swirling, orange-infused red chiffon resembled a transparent cloud. The muscles of her tanned and toned calves gave proof of her deep regard for physical activity and exercise.

She looked at herself in a full-length mirror on the bathroom door and swirled again. Yes, she was so happy she brought this dress. Walking over to the closet, she reached into her bag and pulled out the peekaboo poppy stiletto sandals. Stepping into them, she slid the back strap up her ankle and wiggled her toes with nails the same color.

She went over to the dresser and filled her beige, beaded evening bag with her mobile phone, lipstick, a blush compact, her room access card, and some tissues.

One last gander in the mirror, her thoughts drifted to Drew. *Would he notice her? Would he like what he saw? Why should it matter? Dammit, Victoria! Stop it! Forget it! Forget him!*

Taking a deep breath, she looked around the room and checked if she forgot anything. *Was she stalling?* Victoria shook her head. She looked at her watch and headed to her suite door. Before opening it, she heard someone in the hallway. She peeked through the peephole and saw it was Peggy and her husband. *Whew!*

Peggy looked stunning in her black dress. A look of admiration was on her husband's face as he looked at his wife. Both noticed Victoria and together gave out wolf whistles.

"Victoria, you are going to drive all the guys wild the way you're looking... particularly one guy," Peggy commented.

Just then Grace and her husband came out of their suite and joined them in the hallway, Grace looking absolutely gorgeous in her blue ensemble, her husband also enamored with his wife.

"Holy Smokes, Victoria... the color is so good on you and so appropriate. You're going to set hearts on fire," Grace remarked.

Victoria thanked her friends for the compliments, then commented on how lovely they looked and how handsome and debonair their husbands appeared.

They entered the elevator together to go up to the Grand Ballroom floor with the elevator stopping at the floor just above their floor. As the door opened, Robyn appeared... then Bryan!

"Hi, all!" Robyn exclaimed, giving hugs all around. "So glad we were able to make it, and we can all be together again."

Victoria raised an eyebrow at Robyn. So Bryan is what Robyn had hinted at when she said she had something to tell her. Robyn winked back at her. Victoria had had her suspicions and felt complete joy for Robyn. They were two peas in a pod.

They exited the elevator and walked across the travertine floor to the reception hall, decorated in their school colors of black and gold. Quite a few of the male attendees had gathered around a bar to the side of the entry, and when Victoria walked through the doorway, conversation at the bar came to an abrupt halt except for some side comments and several wolf whistles.

Robyn gave Victoria a nudge and whispered, "Eat your hearts out, boys, her heart belongs to only one guy right now." Victoria knew exactly what Robyn meant and smiled at her as Robyn put her arm around Victoria's shoulder, giving her a hug.

Peggy and Grace had heard Robyn's comment. Peggy responded, "Oh so right, Robyn!"

Before Victoria could quietly ask Robyn how much Bryan knew, Robyn took the moment to say, "Not to worry. He's sworn to secrecy and loyalty, or his mainframe will get trashed... if you know what I mean." Victoria couldn't help laughing at her comment—Robyn sure had a way with words.

Bryan and the husbands went to get drinks while the ladies waited off to the side, noticing classmates and commenting on who was who. Some hadn't changed one bit and others quite a lot. Peggy's husband brought a glass of wine for Victoria, and she thanked him.

"I was getting the third degree by the guys up at the bar, wanting to know who you were and if you were with anyone. I'd better tell you,

Drew was up there, and he was almost apoplectic. He shut a couple of the guys down with a few comments of his own."

Victoria kept her back to the bar area and shook her head. *What right did Drew have making any comments?* Victoria ended up chugging her glass of wine.

Grace noticed, nudging her husband, and told him, "Go get her another one. I think she's going to need it tonight." A few minutes later, Grace's husband came back with another glass of wine for Victoria.

Victoria felt a tap on her shoulder and apprehensively turning and upwardly angling her head, noticed it was Travis McCollum. She vaguely remembered him from school, but again, they hung out in different social circles since his playing on the basketball team gave him "jock" status.

After exchanging introductions with the group, Travis asked, "Would it be possible for me to steal you away from your friends for a while, Victoria?"

Victoria looked around at her friends. It was Robyn who piped up, "Sure, Victoria, go on. We'll see you later at the dinner. We're saving a place for you." The last comment was made looking straight at Travis.

"Oh... okay. I'll see you in there then," Victoria responded.

Travis had dark auburn hair and amber eyes, was very tall, probably over six-three, and appeared to be someone who worked out regularly. He took her by the arm, leading her through the maze of people and out to the veranda—the same place Victoria had been with Drew the night before.

Victoria caught a glimpse of Drew still standing off to one side of the bar. Even at such a distance, she could see the scowl on his face and the clenching of his jaw while he watched as Travis led Victoria out onto the balcony.

Travis motioned for Victoria to have a seat on a bench surrounded on three sides with flowering pots and sat beside her. He seemed nervous, and Victoria broke the ice.

"Travis, tell me what you've been up to these past years." Victoria saw an ease come over his face.

"I'm an attorney, working primarily in corporate law."

"And family?" Victoria asked.

"Nope, never have. By the time I went through law school, passed the

Illinois State Bar exam, and joined a firm, I found my practice had taken a lot of my free time. Plus, I did a stint in the military in the National Guard, doing two tours in the Middle East. I still offer my services to my fellow Guardsmen pro bono. Not much time for searching for the 'right one.' I've just recently decided to open my own practice but not sure where yet. What about you, Victoria?"

"The condensed version... got my accounting degree, got engaged, worked at my future father-in-law's accounting firm, married briefly, actually very briefly, divorced, joined a new accounting firm, acquired my CPA, became a partner in the firm... currently living and working in Arizona. That's it in a nutshell."

"I have to be totally honest with you, I only have a scattered memory of you in high school. I'm sorry now I didn't make an effort back then to get to know you better," he confessed.

Victoria laughed, the sound of her laughter echoing around the balcony and placed her hand on top of his.

"Travis, trust me, back then you wouldn't have gotten to know me. I was a scrawny geekette who always had her head in a book, braces on my teeth, and was a target for the bullies. Our social circles would never have overlapped."

Travis looked intently at her and placed his on top of hers. "Definitely my loss, Victoria Hart. I wish I could turn back time."

Victoria was truly moved by his words and shyly looked down. She didn't know what to say. Travis was like a breath of fresh air.

"Victoria, when you walked through the door, the whole room lit up. I had to make a point of talking with you, and I'm so glad I did. I know you plan to dine with your friends, but would you mind if I joined you... if there's space?" Travis asked.

As if on cue, an announcement was made for the alumni to go into the ballroom and be seated for the dinner.

Victoria didn't want to lead Travis on. She wasn't totally forthcoming with him about her life and hesitated to answer.

Travis prompted, "It's only a dinner, Victoria... and maybe some dancing," presenting a sincere smile.

Victoria nodded. They rose up from the bench and taking their drink glasses with them, entered the ballroom and found the table where her friends were seated.

"Victoria and I were wondering if there was a seat available for me to join you?" Travis inquired.

The ladies all looked at one another, then at Victoria who nodded, and each spoke at the same time, "Of course... definitely... sure thing."

Travis pulled a chair out for Victoria, and once she was seated, he pulled out the one next to her for himself. Victoria had her right hand on the table, and after seated, Travis placed his left hand on it.

Victoria glanced over at Robyn who bestowed her with a smile.

The Class President announced from the podium a video presentation would be shown and asked for a few moments of silence as it contained names and photos of those alumni from the class who had passed, several who had perished in the Middle East conflicts serving in the military.

Victoria had noticed a tremor in Travis' hand when this was mentioned, his eyes introspective. Victoria could tell Travis was very moved and took her left hand, placing it atop his and gave a little squeeze. Travis looked over at her and smiled.

After the solemn presentation, the wait staff came out and began serving the tables.

Halfway through the meal, Victoria caught the scent—Drew. He had brushed past her chair and stopped around the other side of the table, standing just behind Bryan, purposely causing Victoria to look straight across at him.

Déjà vu!

"Good evening. Did you all have a good time this afternoon up at the old high school? I know, I did," he said with a smirk.

Victoria's friends all concurred, but Victoria kept quiet.

"Travis, did you attend as well?" Drew asked.

"No, I didn't, but I wouldn't have minded spending a little extra time with Victoria," he responded, glancing at her and giving her a gentle look.

Victoria smiled at Travis, then caught Drew with his exasperating jaw clenching. Victoria knew she had to be careful and not get involved with Travis, but realized his enamored looks would be a deterrent to Drew making any more advances.

Victoria was catching a late flight out on Sunday and didn't want anything to complicate her life back in Arizona.

Drew bent down and whispered something in Bryan's ear, wished everyone well, and returned to his table. Once Drew was gone, Bryan leaned into Robyn and told her something. Robyn just shrugged. Whatever it was Bryan passed on to Robyn didn't faze her, which was a good thing.

CHAPTER 19

The main course was over with, and by then, Victoria was on her third... or maybe it was her fourth glass of wine. She lost count. She was having a wonderful time with her friends. Drew was no longer in sight, and Travis was entertaining, conversing with friends around the table, totally relaxed among them.

During dinner, they had piped in music, but now a DJ was almost done setting up and made an announcement for requests. Travis excused himself and went up to the DJ while the ladies decided to make a trip to the restroom before the dancing started. Of course, one of the husbands commented about how women always go together to the restrooms.

Victoria felt like she was surrounded by bodyguards and inwardly chuckled to herself.

She asked Robyn about the conversation with Bryan and Drew, and Robyn told her Drew asked Bryan to meet with him later to talk, but Bryan told Robyn he was going to avoid any discussion with Drew involving Victoria. It was obvious Bryan and Robyn were a couple and didn't want anything to interfere with their relationship. Robyn trusted Bryan to be discreet in any dialog he had with Drew.

As the ladies walked out of the restroom, Drew was spotted nearby, but he didn't approach them. He appeared to be resigned to the fact

Victoria didn't want contact with him. He reached up and raked his fingers through his hair in an agitated motion, staring at Victoria.

After returning to the dinner table, the music began and the strains of a sultry rendition of "One Fine Day" could be heard.

Travis looked over at Victoria and said, "Please?" reaching out his hand.

Smiling, she took his offered hand and rose, walking toward the dance floor. Travis took her in his arms, and as they swayed to the music, they laughed quietly as they caught themselves singing the lyrics. Travis twirled her around, and the cloud of chiffon drifted around her legs. Between the wine, the music, and her chivalrous dance partner, she was enjoying herself immensely.

The music ended, and Victoria figured the next dance would be a fast one, but instead the song "The First Time Ever I Saw Your Face" began.

Travis remained holding Victoria tightly but was tapped on the shoulder. It was Drew.

"Would you mind if I had this one dance, Travis? Just this one?" Drew asked pointedly.

Travis looked at Drew, then Victoria. His instinct took hold, and being the gentleman he was, he backed away and allowed Drew to move in.

Victoria didn't know whether to be furious with Drew for intruding or disappointed with Travis for allowing Drew to take over. She kept her cool, not wanting to create a scene.

Drew pulled Victoria tightly to him. "Listen to the words, Victoria, just listen," he whispered in her ear. Drew held her hand over his heart.

She closed her eyes, and the lyrics drifted around her. And there it was again—the beating of their hearts as one.

As the song ended, Drew stepped away from her.

"The dance may be over, Victoria, but we're not. Goodnight, My Queen." Taking her hand, he kissed it, then leaned in, kissed her forehead, and walked away.

Travis was watching the interaction between Victoria and Drew from the table and came to her side. "Are you okay, Victoria?" he asked.

"Yes, I'm fine. Couldn't be better, but it is a bit stifling in here," she responded, knowing full well she wasn't okay. *Was it the wine... something else... or someone else?*

Travis suggested they go out onto the balcony for some air. Once they were out on the balcony standing at a balustrade, he turned to her.

"Is there... or was there something between you and Drew? I know asking such a thing may be crossing the line about your privacy, but I... I would like to know for my own personal reasons."

Victoria pondered how she could answer... how she should answer. Everything that happened five years ago came rushing back—her time with Drew, the dreams they shared, his promises, then later, the crushing blow and realization she had been naïve, and more than likely, used by Drew. And now, he was attempting to do it all over again.

Victoria finally responded, "Travis, yes, Drew and I had a brief... extremely brief encounter years ago. But it's over and has been for quite some time. It's all behind me now. No attachment."

"It didn't seem like it's over for Drew."

"If there is one thing I learned about Drew Anderson, it's he doesn't like to be rebuffed. And he'll go to any lengths, including using and hurting people, to get his way. He makes promises he doesn't keep."

Travis looked deeply into Victoria's eyes and seemed satisfied with her answer. Tilting her chin up with his fingers, he said, "Then I guess it's okay if I do this." He brought his lips to hers, a soft, gentle kiss at first but increased with intensity. Victoria found herself responding. Flashes of Drew's face, then Travis' face entered her mind, competing for her sanity.

Victoria had wrapped her arms around Travis and pulled herself tighter to him, trying to erase the intruding thoughts of Drew. Victoria felt those invasive memories fading to oblivion, and Travis' kisses rekindled a fire within she had thought was extinguished long ago.

The sound of a glass breaking on the darkened far side of the balcony startled them, and they broke apart. Catching their breaths, they smiled at one another.

Travis spoke first, "I guess our kiss answered my questions. How about we head back inside for another dance, Victoria?"

"Yes, Travis, I'm ready if you are," she responded with delight.

As they entered the dancefloor, the song "Someone Like You" began.

"How apropos," Travis whispered in her ear as he brought her close.

Victoria looked up at him and smiled, causing him to draw her even closer.

After the song was over, they headed back to their table, weaving in and out of the maze of tables with Travis leading the way, holding on to her hand, running interference against the hustling wait staff.

As they came to their table, the ladies all looked at Victoria. It was obvious Victoria was having a grand time by the glow about her. And Travis was holding onto Victoria's hand as if for dear life, looking at her every chance he got.

Victoria reminded herself she needed to tread lightly. She was enjoying her time with Travis, but at all costs, she couldn't become romantically or physically involved and more importantly, didn't want to mislead him or hurt him—like Drew did to her.

Everyone at the table had included Travis into their conversations. At times, funny stories were shared, and exuberant laughter from their table echoed around the ballroom. Victoria was laughing so hard, at one point, she took a napkin to dab the tears in her eyes.

Peggy, Grace, and Robyn looked at each other and smiled, happy for their dear friend, hoping the happiness and carefree attitude would finally be lasting for Victoria.

The DJ was playing more upbeat and fast dance music. Everyone at the table got up to dance, including Travis and Victoria after Victoria told Travis, "I'm game if you are."

"You got it!" he responded.

The DJ had played three in a row of the faster dance songs, and Victoria was rocking it out on the dance floor, her poppy chiffon swirling around her thighs like the eddying of the tide.

Travis spun her around, and she softly crashed into his arms. They stood still, looking into each other's eyes, and Travis placed a brief kiss on her lips.

"How anyone can make out on the dance floor to this music is truly a feat worthy of praise," Grace commented as she and her husband were gyrating next to them. They all laughed and continued their cavorting on the dance floor.

Grabbing Victoria's hand, Travis whirled her around. As she turned, she caught a glimpse of Drew standing near the balcony doors with a distressed look, the ever-clenching jaw, noticing he had a napkin wrapped around his right hand.

Exhausted from several fast dances, Victoria motioned in the direction of their table. Collapsing in her chair, she reached down to massage her ankle.

Travis took note, and said, "I'd be happy to help you, but maybe here isn't the right place."

Victoria, in her bent position, looked up at him, and responded, "No, I think you're right, but I appreciate the gesture. Stiletto heels aren't really conducive to marathon dancing," she laughed lightly as she straightened herself.

The crowd was thinning, and one couple at time excused themselves from their table for the evening, reminding everyone about meeting up for brunch in the morning. Bryan and Robyn were the only ones left at the table with Victoria and Travis.

"Do you want us to stay and walk you to your suite?" Robyn whispered to Victoria.

"No, you go ahead. I'll be alright."

After they left, Victoria finished off her glass of wine—she'd lost count how many she had. All she knew was she felt totally relaxed for the first time since arriving at the reunion. Things were going smoothly... well, as smoothly as possible. Her encounter with Travis had put off Drew and relieved Victoria of any further conversations with him.

Victoria told Travis it was time for her to retire as well.

"May I escort you to your suite?" he asked. Victoria looked up at Travis as he pulled out her chair.

"Yes, that would be nice," she responded, taking his offered arm.

As they rode up in the elevator, they talked about his law practice. Victoria found it fascinating, particularly about his serving the needs of veterans on a pro bono basis. Victoria told him about her mother volunteering at the V.A. hospitals and clinics in the Phoenix area, and Travis praised her mom for her work.

Exiting the elevator and walking down the hallway, Travis mentioned he would be checking out of the hotel Sunday afternoon and returning to his condo along Lakeshore Drive. Since he knew she would be brunching with her friends in the morning, he wondered if she wouldn't mind if he joined them.

"Travis, it would be wonderful if you could join us. We're supposed to meet in the café around nine o'clock. Hopefully, my feet will recover by then," she retorted.

"Sweet Dreams, Victoria. I've had the most incredible time this evening, and I owe it all to you," he said tenderly as they came to the door of her suite

Victoria inserted her access card, the door unlocked, and she pushed it slightly open. Travis held the door for her, then took her in his arms, kissed her gently at first, then imprinting his face in her mind with a kiss, rocking her to her core. A noise down the hallway interrupted their sweet interlude, and they breathlessly broke apart.

"Thank you again, Victoria, for a most memorable evening," he whispered, holding her tightly to him.

Victoria snuggled into him, noticing his cologne, different from someone else's but very memorable. They stood there for a while, embracing. Travis pulled away slightly, cocking his head to the side.

"Good night, Victoria. I'll see you in the morning. I can swing by before nine and take you down to the brunch if it's okay with you?"

Victoria nodded and went the rest of the way through the doorway. Travis took her hand, kissed her palm, turned, and left. Victoria closed the door and set the security bolt. Walking over to the bed, she kicked off her heels, sitting down to rub her feet.

"Maybe I should have taken Travis up on his offer... no, it might have led to something more... can't ever let it happen again... besides Travis is really a nice guy, and soon, we'll have over a thousand miles between us," she mumbled to herself.

Victoria glanced over at the clock and noticed it was late but not too late in Arizona and called home. Her mom answered on the first ring.

"Hi, Honey! How's it going there?"

"Great, Mom. It's really been so much fun, especially spending time with old friends." There was a bit of silence on the other end of the phone. Victoria knew why and added, "Peggy and Grace were there with their husbands, and Robyn came with Bryan. They are definitely a couple now. Plus, I ran into Travis McCollum, and he joined us for the evening. He's an attorney here in the Chicago area. We're all meeting up for brunch in the morning, then I'll pack it up and check out for the flight back to Arizona." Victoria knew she was rambling, totally avoiding any mention of anyone else.

"So, did you go out this evening?" Victoria asked. "I tried to reach you."

"Oh yes, we went out to a new restaurant in the area. We had to get there for the 'Early Bird' specials. We'll have to go there sometime after you get back," her mom replied.

Victoria wondered about the "we" her mother mentioned and how many were in the party of "we." Victoria bid goodnight to her mom, undressed, then went into the bathroom to wash up for bed.

Thoughts of five years ago invaded her mind. A lot of time had passed between then and now—a lot had happened.

Victoria's head hit the pillow a short while later, and she was sound asleep within seconds.

CHAPTER 20

Victoria's wake-up call roused her from a deep sleep. Only half awake, she stumbled into the bathroom. She thought about throwing on her workout clothes and using the fitness facilities of the hotel, but instead decided to do some pre-packing before she headed down to brunch.

She combed through her long hair, brushed her teeth, threw off her nightgown, and headed into the shower. The pulsating streams of hot water massaged her muscles as she soaped her body. She dialed the spray all the way up, and the strong jets of the water felt so good. After washing her hair, she turned the water control to a refreshing temperature. More memories popped up, and in an effort to dispel them, she quickly turned off the water, grabbing a spa towel while exiting the shower.

The steaming water from the shower had left her body glowing, including her face. She gently smoothed on some moisturizer. She finished getting ready, blow drying her long hair, leaving it down. She added the lightest of makeup touches, a bit of mascara, and a layer of lip gloss. Removing clothes from the closet and the drawers, she picked out a pair of black, boot-cut jeans, a matching jacket, and a dark berry cashmere, V-necked sweater.

While dressing, she had opened her suitcase and started folding and adding items. She caressed her poppy dress from last evening and thought about the wonderful time she had. And what a surprising time she had too. After carefully placing the dress in the suitcase, she sat down and slipped into a pair of black ankle boots with a short heel. *Lots more comfortable than stilettos.*

By the time she was all but finished packing, it was almost time to leave for the brunch. A knock at the door indicated Travis was there. Peeking out of the peephole to make sure, Victoria opened the door.

Travis, all six-foot-three of him, stood there, looking absolutely... well, suffice it to say, Victoria's delighted expression didn't go unnoticed. Travis was looking pretty pleased with himself, noting the smile on her face. He was wearing dark blue jeans, a cream open-collared shirt, a camel sports jacket, and dark brown slip-ons.

Victoria could only think back to comments recently made and heard about roping, hogtying, and branding.

His dark auburn hair was still a little damp, a stray lock falling forward. When Victoria reached up to brush it to the side, Travis took her hand and drew her into his arms. His lips came down to hers, and she found herself answering his probing tongue with her own. They stood in the doorway, oblivious to everything... and everyone within sight. A door opening and closing down the hallway stirred them from their sensual ventures.

Victoria ushered Travis into her suite, commenting she just needed to grab her purse. She turned, picked the strap of her purse up, and turned back to Travis.

"One more before we go down to breakfast?" he whispered. Without replying, Victoria stepped back into his arms. This time the kiss was gentle, caring, and short.

They exited her suite, Travis' arm around her protectively. Anyone who saw them would have thought they were a couple and been happy for them—anyone except for the one who watched the scene play out from down the hallway.

Victoria and Travis joined her friends at a large table in the café. Her friends noticed Victoria discreetly touched up her lips with gloss right after sitting down. Secret smiles traveled around the table. Victoria told Travis about the brunch offerings and warned him when it was over, he wouldn't be able to move.

This time, instead of the ladies going up together, Travis and Victoria went together. Victoria pointed out the various buffet tables, displayed with fruits, salads, seafood, etc. She expressly mentioned the dessert table.

They were moving from one table to another, having fun picking out each other's food. They came to the seafood table, and Victoria was attempting to snap up an Oysters Rockefeller. Travis put his platter down, reaching around from behind Victoria, and grabbed it with a pair of tongs. Putting it on her plate, he gave her a light kiss on her cheek.

"Thank you, kind sir!"

"My pleasure... totally, Victoria," Travis smiled.

Victoria turned back to the table to pick out some shrimp and was surprised to see Drew standing on the other side, helping himself. She didn't catch him looking at her but noticed the telltale jaw clenching, and the tongs in his hand were brutalizing the shrimp he was choosing. She doubted the shrimp could be more crushed if he had stomped them with his foot.

"Well, I'm finished here. Ready to head back to our table?"

Travis nodded, and by the time they got back to their table, everyone had already returned with their platters full.

"So did you give Travis the rundown on the buffet tables?" Peggy asked,

"Oh, yes, she did! I understand there's going to be a quiz later to find out if anyone missed anything."

The table erupted in laughter. Victoria glanced across the dining area and saw Drew sitting with his friends, the scowl on his face speaking volumes.

"I really hate the fact we only get to see one another at reunions," Grace said. "Even those classmates who live in Illinois don't really get together as much."

"I agree," piped up Peggy.

Robyn chimed in, "Well, I... or should I say 'we' are planning a trip to Arizona in a couple of months, preferably in January or February to escape the winter. Or quite possibly maybe even sooner."

Victoria excitedly turned toward Robyn, "Really, you are?"

"Yes, we are, Victoria, and hopefully, by then you'll be in your new house and be able to show us around town."

"Oh, that would be great. Actually, my Realtor left me a message he's researching several possibilities." Looking around the table, she added, "And, of course, you all are welcome to come visit. I would love it!"

Soon, everyone's plates were emptied, and Peggy's and Grace's husbands excused themselves, announcing they were heading for the dessert table. Bryan jumped up to join them.

Peggy, Grace, and Robyn decided to hold off a bit before attacking the desserts, ordering coffee from the server.

"Victoria, are you ready to forage through the sweets?" Travis asked.

"Sure. Let's go do some damage!" she giggled.

"A girl after my own heart. Or is it a Hart after my own heart? Who could ask for anything more!" he responded. The butterflies in Victoria's stomach started doing a cha-cha.

Pulling out her chair as she rose, Travis placed his hand on the small of her back and walked with her to the dessert table. The chocolate fountain beckoned to her. Travis picked up berries, cake, and sliced kiwi and banana. With wooden skewers, he pierced the fruit and held them under the velvet chocolate cascading down the fountain's multi-levels. Taking a banana slice he had just dipped, he held it up to Victoria's lips. She took the hint and closed her mouth around the banana slice, her lips pulling it from the skewer.

"Who knew a chocolate fountain and a piece of fruit could be so erotic?" Travis said, rolling his eyes.

Victoria almost choked on the slice she was chewing. More memories flashed, and she pushed them aside.

Victoria felt a drip of chocolate at the corner of her mouth, and when she went to wipe it with her finger, Travis leaned over and licked it before giving her a gentle kiss.

"Don't want to waste any of the chocolate," Travis said tenderly, looking into her eyes. The butterflies amped it up a bit and were now doing a full-on rave.

Victoria caught the scent of Drew's cologne. He was standing not more than four feet away. She caught his look, and it wasn't nice. She vowed to herself before she left Chicago, she would have to straighten him out.

The rest of the brunch went smoothly. Peggy and Grace and their husbands were checking out shortly and bid Victoria and Robyn fond goodbyes, promising to Skype in the next day or two.

Robyn and Bryan got up to leave, but Victoria interceded and suggested she and Robyn go to the ladies room first. Robyn took the hint and agreed. Once they entered the restroom, Victoria whispered to Robyn, "Did Drew get with Bryan?"

"No, as a matter of fact, after last night, he hasn't even approached Bryan. We're hoping he's just accepted the fact there's nothing between you and him and moves on," Robyn quietly answered.

Victoria shook her head. "My gut tells me he hasn't accepted it, and it worries me. I've got to stop him in his tracks, but I don't like putting Travis in the foray. I really like Travis, and I don't want him to get hurt."

"Victoria... have you opened up to Travis... I mean really opened up to him about things? If not, if you're really getting to like him, you need to be upfront with him... about everything. It's only fair to the both of you," Robyn consoled.

Victoria agreed but wondered how much she should tell him. After all, they had only reconnected in the past twenty-four hours, and soon, they would be going their separate ways.

Robyn gave her friend a hug. "Call me tomorrow. Promise?"

Nodding, Victoria gave Robyn a hug, then they exited the restroom.

Bryan and Travis were waiting patiently in the hallway. They rode the elevator back up to their respective suites, and as Victoria and Travis exited the elevator on her floor, Bryan and Robyn said their goodbyes. Victoria and Travis walked to her suite, and arriving at her suite door, she turned to Travis.

"Travis, could you come in?" she asked, stumbling on her words. "I need to talk to you about... something."

"Sure, Victoria. You have me worried with your expression though. Did I do or say something upsetting to you?"

"Oh no, Travis, definitely not!" she replied emphatically. She unlocked the suite, and they walked in together. She asked him to sit down, then sat next to him on the sofa.

"Travis, I honestly don't know where to begin other than to say, the time spent with you this weekend has been absolutely wonderful. You made it wonderful. And to think I even hesitated about coming to the reunion."

Travis made as if he was about to say something, but she gently pressed her fingers to his lips.

"Please, let me go on. I have to get this out," she nervously said.

"Please know I've grown truly fond of you although it's only been a short while since we've gotten to know one another again. And I realize what I'm about to tell you... well, you may never want to..."

It was almost an hour later when Travis and Victoria walked to her suite door. She watched him as he digested what she had told him.

"I'll totally understand if you don't want to make any further contact wi—" Her words were cut off as he kissed her.

"That's not the person I am, Victoria. I do my best not to judge people until I've walked in their shoes. And even then, I judge people by what's in their heart. You're an amazing woman, Victoria, and I consider myself lucky having you as a friend. My perception of you will never change. I don't know if our paths will ever cross again, but I certainly hope they do. Please know my feelings are genuine."

Travis kissed her once more, deeply and with enormous feeling. He turned and walked down the hallway to the elevator. Victoria stood in the doorway, hearing the whoosh of the elevator doors opening and closing.

Victoria felt a chill, wrapped her arms around herself, and went back into her suite, closing the door behind her. Tears prickled the back of her eyes. She had no regrets telling Travis what she did. She truly cared for him, and the last thing she wanted was for him to get hurt. Without even asking, he promised her he'd never tell anyone what she'd told him. He truly was a gentleman, an honorable one.

A knock on the door startled Victoria from her reverie. Thinking it was Travis returning, and opening the door, she said, "Travis, wha...?"

It was Drew.

"Travis left... I saw him leave," he ground out as he walked through the doorway, closing it securely behind him.

"Victoria, we need to talk and talk right now. I'm not leaving this room until we do."

Victoria grit her teeth. "Yes, Drew, we do need to talk. But first, I get to do the talking, not you, you arrogant Neanderthal. You came into my life five years ago, making all kinds of innuendos and promises. You made a fool of me in more ways than one. You gave me some sob story about your wife and the business. Well, it seems everything you told me was bogus. Your business is thriving, according to the latest reports on the internet... yes, I checked on you. I have the feeling you didn't once check on me. I waited for a phone call or a message from you. Only one off-handed text message after what we shared together and nothing after. For the life of me, I don't understand how you could act so wounded the past couple of days, interjecting yourself with my friends and into my affairs. You have no right at all—none, zip, zero. You don't own me and never did. I'm sorry I ever let you into my life. If it wasn't for... never mind. Go back to Florida, back to your precious Barbie Doll, and your business and stay out of mine. Who I see and who I spend time with is none of your damned concern. Understood? Five fucking years, Drew, and you expect me to fall into your arms all over again. You're delusional and despicable."

Victoria was beet red and breathless by the time she finished her tirade. She was never one to lose her cool or use vulgar language. It had been building up all these years she had felt deceived and used. It was time for her to set herself free and rise above it.

During her tirade Drew had fallen down into a chair, looking totally shell-shocked.

Victoria didn't expect Drew to say what he did.

"Victoria, you may not believe me, God knows you have every right not to, but I truly care about you, and I care about us. I did call you the week after the reunion, and the receptionist told me you were in a meeting and took the message. You didn't respond, and I figured... I don't know what I figured. All I know is you didn't call me back. I needed to know when you returned to Arizona your feelings for us were the same, and you didn't regret the time we spent together, you weren't sorry for what we shared. But you didn't return my call. I picked up the phone and dialed your number so many times but hung up before the call went through. I believed you had gotten my message and would have called me back if you felt the same.

"I lost hope after months had passed and focused on my business. I found an investor to help buyout my father-in-law... correction, my ex-father-in-law."

Victoria's head snapped up.

"Yes, Victoria, the divorce went through although pretty costly, considering the ties to the business. But the business survived with the influx of funds from my investor and continues to be successful to the point of imminent expansion. But there is something missing in my life. No matter how successful my business is, it can't fulfill it. This time, I came to the reunion in the hopes of running into you and finding out why you never contacted me. My gut told me to stay away from you, but my heart wouldn't listen. I see now you've moved on with your life, and I'm truly happy for you. I only wish I could have been part of it."

As Drew was talking, he had risen from the chair and was pacing slowly back and forth, looking at Victoria for some sign of acceptance and understanding. There was none.

She was numb. Victoria was trying to assimilate everything he was saying. She wasn't sure she should believe him about the call. She remembered how hectic and disorderly things got at her office when they were trying to hire and train a new receptionist. *Could the chaos explain it?* She just wasn't sure... she wasn't sure of anything right now.

Then she noticed the bandage on his right hand and remembered the sound of breaking glass when she and Travis were out on the balcony. She knew then it had to have been Drew out there, hidden in the shadows.

Drew walked over to the door and opened it, looking back to face Victoria.

"You left me with some wonderful memories, Victoria, I only hope I left you with some as well," he quietly said. He left her sitting on the edge of the sofa, her hands folded in her lap. The click of the door closing broke her thoughts.

"Yes, Drew, you left something with me," she said quietly to herself.

CHAPTER 21

ARIZONA

The late afternoon flight home to Phoenix had taken its toll. Victoria tried to sleep on the plane, but the activity around her was incessant. She kept going over again and again what Drew had said. She really needed some quiet time to get her head together.

Thinking back, she was grateful Drew didn't pry into her life in Arizona.

A shuttle picked her up at Sky Harbor Airport and brought her home to her mother's house just as the Arizona sun was setting. Her mom greeted her at the door, and as soon as she saw Victoria, she knew something had happened in Chicago. Although the house was quiet, the tension emanating from Victoria was resounding.

"Do you want to talk about it now, or would you rather rest up and talk about it later?"

"Later, Mom. I need to freshen up first."

A short while later, Victoria joined her mom out on the back patio, carrying two bowls of ice cream on a tray.

Marya raised an eyebrow. "So, it's an ice cream kind of talk, I guess."

Victoria nodded and set the tray down on the coffee table and sat next to her mom on the settee. Reaching for the bowls, she handed one to her mom and took the other one for herself.

Victoria relayed the happenings, day by day. About running into Drew, meeting and spending time with Travis, the reunion events, the dining and dancing, and last but not least, the discussion she had with Travis and later, the confrontation with Drew.

"Honey, what are you going to do?"

"Honestly, Mom, I don't know. Trust is a valuable thing in any relationship, and I don't know if Drew told me the truth. I want to believe him. And if it is the truth, what do I do about it? I'm fearful he could..."

A small voice came from around the corner out to the patio. "Mommy, you're home... I missed you. Did you miss me?"

Victoria scooped the pajama-clad little guy with tousled dark chocolate hair and big dark brown eyes up onto her lap. "I sure did, Tyler. I sure did," Victoria said tenderly as she kissed the top of his head.

Tyler was holding a small snow globe. It had a miniature of Chicago's well-known Water Tower inside. Tyler shook it and giggled as he watched the sparkling crystals float down.

Victoria took a deep breath. As long as she could have her son in her arms that was all that mattered.

WHILE DRIVING Tyler to preschool in the morning, he was all excited about a project they were doing in class for Thanksgiving, which was still about two months away. It had something to do with the seeds they were planting. Victoria was grateful the preschool was nearby, and her mom, who volunteered in the mornings at the V.A., was able to pick Tyler up at mid-day dismissal.

After dropping off Tyler, Victoria arrived at her office early, determined to find out if Drew was telling the truth. Because of the character of the business, phone records were maintained for at least seven years.

She called one of the assistants into her office and asked her to locate the phone and message records from September through October from five years ago. She knew those records were in storage, and it would take at least a week or more to retrieve. They hadn't started digitalizing phone records data until three years ago. There were two avenues of research--one, check the carbonless copies of handwritten messages and the other, the incoming call records printouts. She would just have to be patient.

Victoria worked through the day like a demon, trying to put as much energy into her work to dispel the memories and thoughts plaguing her mind.

Marya texted Victoria when they arrived home, and Tyler always asked "Gramma" to attach one of his "goofy faces" as he called them. It always put a smile on Victoria's face to receive the text.

Shortly after three in the afternoon, the receptionist buzzed Victoria in her office, advising her there was a personal delivery for her.

Victoria wasn't expecting anything and walked to the reception area. On the divider ledge of the reception desk was a vase filled with several dozen long-stemmed yellow roses with a single red rose in the center. Victoria had a sense of what it signified but wondered who sent them. She could only guess one of two people, and she was pretty sure it wasn't Drew.

Victoria withdrew the small envelope from the bouquet and removed the enclosed card, silently reading the card.

"It only took 24 hours to find a genuine 'heart' touching me like none before. Thank you for all that you are and for all the trust you put in me this past weekend. To beginnings... with deep affection, Travis."

Victoria smiled to herself, put the card back inside the envelope, and took the vase of flowers back to her office. After placing the vase on her desk, she sat back in her chair. Taking the envelope and card out again, she reread it several times.

"So, it didn't matter to Travis about what she told him," she said to herself. What an amazing man.

Deep down, she had secretly hoped somehow they would stay friends and stay in touch. She had doubted their paths would ever cross again unless there was another reunion.

She was shaken from her reverie by the ringing of her mobile phone.

"Hello, Victoria Hart, speaking," she answered.

A familiar voice asked, "Are you sure?"

"Wait, let me check. Yes, it's me! Hi, Robyn!" Victoria responded happily. "So good to hear your voice."

"Victoria Ann Hart... spill the beans!" Robyn said emphatically.

Victoria laughed. Robyn only used a middle name when she was serious... very serious.

Victoria told Robyn about the time spent with Travis and her sharing information with him, then told her about the confrontation with Drew and what she had said to him and his response. Robyn listened without responding.

"And this afternoon, I received a beautiful bouquet of yellow roses with a red rose in the center."

"Okay, and I'm guessing they're from one of two people... and I think it was Travis. Am I right?" Robyn asked.

"Yes... may I ask why you picked Travis?"

"Because if it was Drew, he wouldn't send the roses, he would be at your door with them. Of course, Drew doesn't know everything, does he? As a matter of fact, right now, Travis knows more than Drew does," Robyn reasoned.

"You're right, Robyn," Victoria said somewhat dejectedly. "I worried while at the reunion I would let something slip. If Drew found out, there's no telling what he might do. He might try to force me to share custody or try to take Tyler to Florida. My trust level where Drew is concerned is not good. When he told me he did try to reach me after the ten-year reunion, I found it difficult to believe. I'm having the phone records for the office pulled for that particular period of time. They're in storage, so it may take some time to get them. Drew said since I didn't call him back, he figured I didn't want anything to do with him or the relationship. It bothers me he didn't try again to reach me. I know we were only together for a little over three days—three incredible day— but somehow, I thought he knew how I felt and what we shared wasn't a flash in the pan," Victoria spoke dolefully.

"Victoria Ann Hart, now listen to me. You have to get it together. You've always been the solid one. Even if he did call, would he have just given up after one call if he really cared? I doubt that. I would think he would want to hear it directly from you whether you wanted to have a continued relationship or if you wanted to completely forget what happened. Anyway, that's my way of thinking."

A heavy sigh came from Victoria.

"You're right, Robyn. You make it sound so logical."

"Okay, so let's change the subject now. How would you and your mom like to have some company for Thanksgiving dinner? I really would love to see my little godson!"

"Oh, Robyn, it would be great. Will you be bringing anyone with you... anyone special?" Victoria hinted.

"Why, yes, I will. Bryan actually has a meeting in Scottsdale the Wednesday before Turkey Day, and the company is putting us up at the JW Marriott Resort and Hotel through Saturday, so we'd be checking out and leaving around noon on Sunday. Isn't the Marriott close to where you live?"

"Yes!" Victoria exclaimed. "Very close. What about a car?"

"We're getting a rental at the airport. It just makes it simpler. This way, Bryan can drop me at the hotel, go to his meeting, and I can nest at the hotel until he's done."

"Actually, my office is closing at noon on Wednesday, the day you arrive, and I can come get you at the hotel if you like. Bryan can meet up with us at our house after the meeting," Victoria suggested.

"It might work. We can play it by ear since there's no telling how long his meeting will last. I'll email you the flight and hotel information. I'll make sure to text you when we land and call you from the hotel. Oh, Victoria, I can't wait to see you! Time for some 'girl' time." If Victoria didn't know any better, she would have bet Robyn was dancing around like a loon.

They said their goodbyes with promises to Skype in a couple of days. No sooner had Victoria hung up, her office phone rang again. It was her Realtor, telling her he found some good prospects and was emailing her the MLS listings. Victoria swung around in her chair, her gaze falling on the bouquet. Travis' roses must be a good omen.

When Victoria arrived home that the evening, Tyler came running at her. She picked him up and spun him around, both of them giggling all the way. Marya came out of the kitchen; she loved how her daughter was beaming.

"Mom, so much happened today. All good. First, I get a beautiful bouquet of flowers delivered, then Robyn called and asked if she and Bryan could join us for dinner on Thanksgiving, then my Realtor called and said he has some listings he thought I might be interested in seeing!"

Marya looked at Victoria and said, "First of all, who are the flowers from... second, it's wonderful Robyn and Bryan are coming. Hopefully, you said it was okay. And thirdly, well, I know you have been house hunting, and I know you'll find something, but I sure am going to miss you both being here. Although Tyler will always have his Gramma to watch him."

Victoria told her mom the flowers were from Travis and how thoughtful it was of him. Her mother agreed. Then she told her about Robyn and Bryan's itinerary and what plans they made so far. Lastly, Victoria told her the listings were located close to her mom's house, just a little further north and east. It was Marya's turn to be ecstatic. It was pretty obvious Marya had been concerned about the location and distance, but all the prospective listings were nearby.

THE NEXT COUPLE of weeks sped by. Victoria met up with her Realtor several times in the afternoon. On one such afternoon, as soon as she walked through the entrance of one home, she felt something special.

The home had been custom built, but just prior to the escrow closing, the owner was transferred out of state, and the home had to be put on the market. As luck would have it, it had the single-story floorplan and the amenities Victoria wanted—a secure, large stuccoed block-walled backyard for Tyler, a pool and hot tub with safety features, and a large master suite with access to a den she could use as her home office. The master suite was large and inviting with telescoping sliding doors opening to the back patio. A large walk-in closet and the master bath with spa tub and over-sized glass shower with beautiful deco tile took her breath away. There were two other bedrooms, one of which would be for Tyler, and the other she would use as a guest room. Each of the other bedrooms had its own walk-in closet and bathroom, and there was a powder room off of the kitchen.

A large great room with a fireplace, high vaulted ceilings, and a perfect view of the backyard opened to the light and bright kitchen. The horizontal glass tile backsplash caught her eye immediately. The u-shaped kitchen had two islands in a separated "T" configuration. One for food prep with an additional deep sink and the other contained a surplus of lower cabinet storage with barstools on the opposite side. There was a butler's pantry in one corner, and the kitchen opened on the other side to a separate and more formal dining room. The space could easily accommodate seating for twelve hungry eaters if need be.

Just outside of the dining alcove, a large patio offered additional outdoor dining. The landscaping was xeriscape with little or no maintenance. The side yard had plenty of room and the right amount of sunlight for her to put in a garden for vegetables and herbs if she wished. She always wanted to have a raised garden, and the area was perfect for it.

The house was located on a cul-de-sac which offered privacy and security. The front courtyard had a half-wall with a gate. As she had pulled up to the house, she noticed several children playing outside adjacent houses. This put a smile on her face, knowing Tyler would have some playmates. It was truly a deal maker.

Since there was a "quick sale" order on the house, Victoria and her Realtor came up with a realistic offer, and within twenty-four hours, there was an acceptance. There was no financing contingency in the contract, and Victoria was pleased to learn the escrow would be closing the end of October. She would have several weeks to "customize" the house for her needs. Her plan was to move in right after Thanksgiving weekend if everything was finished. She and Tyler would be celebrating Christmas in their new home.

Marya was so happy when she heard the news, and had gone over to see the house. Victoria looked at her mom and saw tears in her eyes.

"Mom, are you okay?"

"Oh, yes, Honey. I've just got mixed emotions right now. I'll definitely miss seeing you and Tyler walking through my house, but I couldn't be happier you found your dream home. The fact it's only ten minutes away is a big plus." Victoria put her arms around Marya and gave her a big hug.

"Maybe then, Mom, you can do some personal entertaining if you know what I mean," Victoria commented wryly.

Marya was speechless at first. "Victoria..." she stammered.

"Mom, I'm not naïve, nor am I completely oblivious to your social life. I have a hunch someone has piqued your interest. Am I right?"

Marya made several attempts to say something and finally blurted out, "Well, maybe... time will tell."

"Don't forget to get the rope and hogtie him, Mom," Victoria laughed. Marya just rolled her eyes, but Victoria could tell she hit the nail on the head.

"And let me know when you want to share the particulars... I'm dying of curiosity. He must be really something special to make you blush," Victoria teased.

Marya put her hands up to her face, and sure enough, she could feel the warmth in her cheeks. "Brock said I blush all the time," Marya said softly and abruptly stopped from saying any more.

"Oh, I heard that, Mom. So, his name is Brock?"

Marya waved her hands, dismissing further discussion. "After we pick up your little man at preschool, let's go out for a celebratory dinner tonight," she said, changing the subject.

VICTORIA and the firm were incredibly busy due to the addition of new clients, most of whom had come from referrals through current clients. Personally, she had a full plate as well.

She began the process of customizing and moving into her own home, including contacting the various utility companies to put the accounts in her name effective the day of the closing, acquiring moving boxes, and arranging for a moving company. Every wall in her new home was off white, and she knew she wanted to change the look even if it was only to add color for an accent wall. Tyler had put in a few requests of his own.

Fortunately, she was able to gain access to the home several times prior to closing to take measurements for window treatments and furniture placement, which brought up a whole other personal cause.

Victoria and her mom took Tyler shopping for his bedroom furniture. Of course, Tyler was overwhelmed with all the choices, but Victoria and Marya were able to tamp down his rambunctious frolicking by narrowing down the choices.

Tyler was outgrowing his "toddler" furniture in the room originally set up as an office at Marya's house and was thrilled to have a "big boy" bedroom set which was geared for him to use for many years.

Victoria decided to either sell or donate Tyler's old furniture, and

Marya had picked out a white wrought iron daybed to put in Tyler's old room, figuring he could use it when he has a sleepover at Gramma's.

The bedroom set Victoria was using at her mother's house was hers while growing up and was going to stay at her mom's house in the guest suite. Victoria was now shopping for her own new bedroom suite. Her new master bedroom was massive in comparison, and she really wanted to get a king size bed with matching dresser, armoire, and nightstands. There was also a sitting area perfect for a lamp table, coffee table, and chairs. She opted for a double chaise lounge, envisioning herself snuggled up with Tyler while she read him one of his storybooks.

When she got married, Marya had surprised Victoria, gifting her a refurbished cedar-lined steamer trunk handed down in the family for years and a beautifully carved cedar hope chest that had belonged to Marya's mother. Victoria was so moved, and as tears trickled down her cheeks, Marya gently brushed them away.

"Victoria, these pieces of furniture are heirlooms, and I want you to have them. I can't think of a better place for them to end up than with you and Tyler."

Victoria already pictured in her mind where she would place them in her new home—the hope chest would go at the foot of her new bed, and the steamer trunk in the guest bedroom to hold additional linens.

Victoria arranged for professional painters for the high walls running up to the vaulted ceiling in the family room on both sides of the fireplace wall and the accent walls in the guest bedroom and its bath. She opted to do the painting in Tyler's room and bath herself.

Landscaping was minimal since it was a new build, so Victoria hired a landscaper and worked on a design. Fortunately, the landscaper was also able to lend his services in designing an outdoor kitchen in the patio area with a gas grill center. She loved eating out on her mom's patio and looked forward to many meals with Tyler on their patio.

Victoria arranged for a high-end security system to be installed which she could monitor away from home.

Everything was coming together, and Victoria felt it was a new adventure for her and Tyler.

CHAPTER 22

Thanksgiving was just around the corner, and Victoria was finalizing the plans for the house. She was in her office when the receptionist buzzed her, saying there was a delivery at the front desk and asked if it should be brought back to her office. Without hesitation, Victoria said she would come up to the lobby.

As she rounded the corner, she noticed a huge planter basket of fall flowers. She took the envelope and removed the card.

"Victoria, wishing you and your family a wonderful Thanksgiving. Expecting to make a trip to Arizona soon and hoping we could get together. With deep affection, Travis."

A smile formed on Victoria's lips, thinking how thoughtful of Travis and how she would like to see him again when he came. She picked up the basket and brought it back to her office, placing it on the coffee table.

It didn't take but a few seconds, then Victoria picked up her mobile phone and called Travis on his mobile phone.

The phone rang only once and Travis, noticing the name on the caller ID, picked it up and said, "Hello, Victoria!"

"Oh, Travis, the flower arrangement is beautiful! Thank you so very much. It was very thoughtful of you, and I plan on using it as my table centerpiece for our Thanksgiving dinner."

"I'm so glad you like it. I hope I'm not being forward in suggesting we get together when I come to Phoenix. It's just you have been on my mind so often... actually, quite often. And this opportunity to come to Phoenix on business presented itself, and I had to say yes. I'm truly hoping we could spend some time together, and if agreeable with you, meet your family."

For some reason, Victoria didn't hesitate, answering, "Travis, that would be very nice. Do you have the trip date scheduled?"

"Actually, I do. It's for the week after Thanksgiving. I'm working with some clients and committees over at the VA. I'm staying a hotel in north central Phoenix."

"Travis, I'm essentially only working Monday of that week since the rest of the week I'll be moving into my new home. I'm sure we'll be able to squeeze in some time," Victoria answered sincerely.

"Victoria, you just made my day... heck, you just made my whole month! I'll email you my itinerary, and if you can work me in, that would be great. And if I can be of help with the move while I'm there, please let me know. I'm so looking forward to seeing you again, Victoria."

"Travis, the feeling is mutual. See you soon."

A few moments after hanging up, Victoria closed her eyes and leaned back in her chair, thinking to herself Travis was indeed a special guy. She did have feelings for him, but there was physical distance between them, and her life was here in Arizona. She knew she needed to take it a day at a time and not get ahead of herself. But thoughts of Travis' kisses invaded her mind... then another face appeared... Drew's face and his kisses. She abruptly opened her eyes and sat up straight.

"Drew Anderson, why are you messing with my mind?" she whispered agitatedly.

Victoria left her office and charged down the hallway, approaching the desk of the assistant who was researching the phone and message records for her.

"Did you locate all those files yet and get me the printouts?"

"Not completely, Miss Hart. There was a delay. We found some of the storage boxes were mislabeled during the office expansion, but they were found, and the storage company will be delivering the boxes here tomorrow, and I can go through them. I'm terribly sorry it's taken so long, but we've been deluged with the new client files, and the research was put on the back burner."

"I understand. The new clients and their files should come before the research. I truly appreciate your help in this matter. Please let me know when you're able to zero in on the timeline I gave you."

Victoria walked back to her office somewhat dejectedly. Drew's comments the last time they were together weighed heavily on her. She needed to find out the truth.

The assistant somehow knew the research was very important to Victoria and made a point of putting extra effort into getting the data to her as soon as possible.

THE WEDNESDAY BEFORE THANKSGIVING, Victoria was finishing up paperwork when the assistant knocked on her door. Victoria motioned for her to come in. The assistant walked over to Victoria's desk and told her the four thick pocket folders she was carrying contained the data she was asked to research. Victoria thanked her and told her how much she appreciated her taking the time to put the data together and wished her a Happy Thanksgiving.

It was just after noon, and the office was closed for the long Thanksgiving holiday. Robyn and Bryan would have already arrived with Bryan having a meeting downtown and Robyn getting settled in at their hotel. Victoria gathered the research folders and put them in her briefcase. As much as she wanted to dive into them immediately, she had last minute grocery shopping to do and pre-dinner prep. The data would be there later, and she would go through it when she had time over the holiday.

As Victoria walked down to the underground parking garage, she had an eerie feeling someone was watching her. She looked around quickly but saw no one. The feeling lingered. Most of the firms in the building had closed early, and there were few vehicles remaining in the garage.

She quickened her step, and as she neared her car, she clicked the remote to unlock her car, grabbed the door handle, and basically, threw herself and her briefcase into her car, quickly hitting the lock button.

She put on her seat belt and started the car, backing out of her parking space. As she maneuvered to exit the garage, she put the car in drive and moved forward. Glancing in the rearview mirror, she was startled as she caught the shadow of someone behind her and gunned her car, hurriedly exiting the parking garage. Was it just her imagination?

Shadows playing tricks on me? Goosebumps formed on her arms, and she made an effort to shake off her uneasiness.

Victoria stopped at the grocery near her mother's home and picked up the few items she needed. She no longer felt someone was watching her and relaxed her hands on the steering wheel. As she entered her mother's kitchen, carrying the grocery bags and her briefcase, she was assaulted from behind by a thirty-eight-inch tall dynamo. Maybe because of what happened in the parking garage, Victoria's nerves were on edge, and she screamed, taking Tyler by surprise, causing him to scream.

Tyler's normally happy face was replaced with one of panic. Marya came running in from the dining room to see what the commotion was all about. Victoria set the bags and briefcase down and leaned on the counter for a couple of seconds, then knelt down to Tyler giving him a hug.

"Oh, Tyler, I'm so sorry I screamed. I was just so surprised."

Tyler's scared expression changed immediately to one of an imp. "I scared you, Mommy? Really... I scared you?"

"Yes, you little monster... you really scared Mommy. Next time make some noise before you scare Mommy... like stomp your feet or growl like a tiger or something," Victoria said jokingly.

Marya looked at Victoria and knew something was amiss, noticing the tension so apparent in Victoria's face.

Victoria sent Tyler off to build something special for her with his Legos while she worked in the kitchen.

Marya touched Victoria's arm. "Honey, are you okay? You seem tense... and jumpy."

"It's the oddest thing, Mom. When I left the office and got to the parking garage, I noticed almost all the cars were already gone for the holiday. But I had the eeriest feeling someone was following me. I looked around but didn't see anyone. Then when I backed out of my space and was going to exit the garage, I caught a glimpse in my rearview mirror of someone behind my car. Of course, I hightailed it out of there. Probably just my imagination," Victoria explained with an air of brushing it off with a shrug.

Marya's concerned looked was obvious. "You can't be too careful, Victoria. You always need to be aware of your surroundings and listen to your intuition."

What Marya didn't tell her was she had an odd incident recently as well. She opted not to say anything to Victoria, preferring to push it aside for now and enjoy the holiday.

VICTORIA'S MOBILE PHONE RANG, and she noticed it was Robyn. "Hey, Robyn! Welcome to Arizona!"

"Thanks, Victoria! Bryan's meeting didn't last long, and he was able to get back to the hotel a little bit ago and is getting cleaned up. When would be a good time for us to pop over?"

"Anytime... the sooner, the better. I can't wait to see you both!"

"Great! Us too... can't wait to see you and Tyler and your mom. I'll text you when we leave the hotel. Looks like it will take less than ten minutes from here to your mom's."

"Okay, see you soon!"

After hanging up, Victoria told her mom about Robyn and Bryan's arrival plans, and they busied themselves putting together salsa, chips, and dip. Marya had already planned to serve her special chicken and rice dinner. Victoria prepped a salad to have with the dinner later and placed it in the refrigerator to chill.

"Victoria, is this going to be a margarita, sangria, or wine evening?"

"Let's shoot for the sangria tonight, Mom. Tomorrow we can do wine with the turkey. Probably do margaritas later in the week. How does that sound?"

"Sounds like a plan to me," Marya exclaimed, pulling out fruit and a cutting board. Victoria reached in the wine cooler and took out a bottle of Spanish red wine and a large pitcher.

By the time Robyn had texted Victoria they were on their way, everything was prepared and ready to be served.

Soon after the doorbell rang, Tyler was the first one at the door, yelling his Auntie Robyn was there, impatiently waiting for Victoria to open the door.

Immediately after the door was opened, Tyler rushed at Robyn, almost knocking her backward into Bryan.

"Hey, Tyler! My goodness, you have grown since I last saw you," Robyn said as she picked Tyler up into her arms. Tyler wrapped his arms around Robyn and was rocking excitedly against her.

"Hey, Mama told me you have something to show me... something to do with some a visit from the tooth fairy, maybe?" Robyn asked.

Tyler's eyes lit up, then opened his mouth and pointed to a gap where one of his baby teeth had fallen out.

"Oh my, Tyler! And I suppose the tooth fairy took your baby tooth and left you something?" Robyn hinted.

"Yes. One whole dollar!" Tyler squealed.

"Tyler, this is my... friend, Bryan. Bryan, this is my godson, Tyler," Robyn said, introducing them.

Bryan extended his hand to shake, and Tyler reached over and shook it with erratic little jerks.

"Nice to meet you, Tyler. I've heard so many nice things about you and even saw some of the pictures you drew and sent to your Auntie Robyn," Bryan responded. "You are quite an artist."

Tyler gave a shy smile, not quite sure yet how he felt about Bryan.

Victoria suggested Tyler go get washed up for some snacks, the magic word being "snacks." Tyler slithered to the ground out of Robyn's arms and took off, running to the bathroom to wash his hands.

Victoria was now able to embrace her dear friend and Bryan and have them move from the foyer into the great room. Marya came out of the kitchen area and gave Robyn a hug and as she was introduced to Bryan, gave him a hug as well.

"Get used to it, Bryan, we're all huggers here," Marya told him.

"No problem, Mrs. Hart."

"Please, call me Marya. Mrs. Hart sounds a bit old fogeyish," Marya responded. Bryan nodded.

Victoria was quick to notice a ring on Robyn's finger and lifted her friend's left hand. "Robyn... is this what I think it is?" Victoria asked slyly.

Giving Victoria a sly smile, Robyn enthusiastically replied, "Why, yes, it is, Victoria! We're engaged. Bryan proposed to me a couple of weeks ago. I wanted to phone you right away and tell you, but Bryan thought it would be better to tell you in person. No date set yet, but we've been talking about next spring." Robyn was talking so fast, she hadn't taken a breath and finally took one, inhaling deeply and looking wide-eyed between Victoria and Bryan.

"Oh, Robyn!" Victoria said, engulfing Robyn in a tight hug. "I'm so happy for both of you," she said tearfully.

Marya clapped her hands together and excitedly. "Well, this is cause for a celebration. Let's break out the bubbly to toast the occasion!"

Marya ran off to the kitchen as Victoria brought Robyn and Bryan through the great room onto the back patio area. Appetizers had been set out, and it wasn't long until they were enjoying the late fall breeze and raising their glasses. Tyler brought out some of his prized Legos to show Robyn and Bryan.

Talk revolved around Bryan's business connections in the Phoenix area and what Robyn had been up to in Washington. Victoria quickly learned Robyn had now been promoted twice within her company and had more opportunities to travel, which she had dreamed of for many years. Bryan was relocating to Washington State after the first of the year.

Their conversation was shattered by a loud bang coming from the direction of a neighbor's house where a gazebo was being constructed. Victoria jumped out of her chair so fast, she almost knocked over the side table. She ran to Tyler who was oblivious to the commotion while he was playing with his Legos.

Robyn and Bryan looked at one another, then at Marya and noticed a look of concern on her face. Victoria picked up Tyler and brought him over to the sofa next to Marya.

"Hey, Tyler, I'll bet Bryan would love to see your room and all the other Legos you have," Robyn piped up and nudged Bryan.

"Yeah, Tyler, I played with Legos when I was your age and would love to see your collection. How about it?"

Tyler looked over to Victoria, she nodded, and within seconds, Tyler was pulling Bryan's hand, leading him down the hallway to his room.

Robyn waited until Tyler and Bryan were out of earshot.

"Okay, so what's going on. Victoria, you're so tense, I can feel it."

Victoria knew it was no use trying to keep things from Robyn, so she went into detail about the garage incident, but tried to blow it off as probably something foolish.

While Victoria was telling Robyn about it, Robyn noticed Marya's eyes looking down, and she was biting her lip. Robyn nodded her head to Marya.

"Marya... is there something on your mind?"

Marya sheepishly looked up and confessed she too had a similar experience earlier in the week. She felt someone watching her, following her when she was volunteering at the VA. Fortunately, she was meeting a friend in the parking lot, and they walked to her car together. Being cautious, she purposely drove in a roundabout way, making erratic turns on the way home.

Victoria was shocked. "Mom, why didn't to say something earlier?"

"Honey, it was just one time. I had such a weird feeling, so my friend Brock said he would walk me out to my car from now on."

Victoria breathed a sigh of relief.

Trying to make light of the conversation and raising an eyebrow, Victoria asked, "So is this the same Brock you've had some one-on-ones with for lunch or dinner and movies lately?"

Marya blushed and didn't answer, but instead said she needed to tend to the dinner in the kitchen and scurried back into the house.

Robyn spoke first, "Victoria, you have always had a good intuition about things..."

"Except with men," Victoria chimed in.

"Okay, except with men. But don't discount your intuition now. Please be careful. And make sure you and your mom don't take any chances. If things feel amiss, they usually are. Listen to your gut," Robyn warned.

Robyn then asked if Victoria had ever gotten to the bottom of Drew's phone call. Victoria told her about the records research and how she now had copies of the records but needed to go through them.

"Victoria, if you need help, let me know."

"I appreciate your offer, but it's something I have to do. I just need to find some time to sit down and go through them, but now is not the time.

Whatever is in the records can wait. It's certainly not going to change anything right now," Victoria responded somewhat soulfully.

"Do I dare ask...Victoria, have you heard anything from Drew?"

"Nothing, nada... pretty sure our past is a done deal. Probably for the best as far as I'm concerned."

"And Travis?"

Smiling, Victoria sat back, totally relaxed and gave an upbeat reply.

"Ah... yes, Travis. As a matter of fact, he'll be here next week. He has some business in Phoenix, and we promised to get together."

"Are you going to bring him by to meet your mom and Tyler?"

"Not sure yet. I think I'll play it by ear. It's still early in our relationship if there is one. I wouldn't want Tyler growing attached to anyone unless it looks like it would go deeper," Victoria stated. "Besides, we do have a geographical logistic issue."

"I totally get it. Tyler is one smart little cookie, and he probably could steal anyone's heart really easy. Besides, he's my godson, and I think he's perfect!"

Robyn and Victoria helped Marya get the dinner on the table. The dinner conversation included what subjects Tyler liked and where he would like to travel. Of course, Disneyworld was first on his list. Talk then revolved around Victoria's new house, its layout, what décor she had picked out, and the landscaping.

"So, maybe next time, we'll get to see you in your new digs when we come in?" Bryan asked.

"What do you mean 'see'? Hopefully, you'll stay with us," Victoria answered. "We'll have plenty of room. The escrow has already closed, and our move is next week. Since you're in town, I would love to show you the house, and Bryan, maybe you can give me some pointers on tech things. I'm having a high-end security system installed."

Bryan didn't miss the looks passed between Robyn, Victoria, and Marya.

"Good idea, Victoria, very good idea," Bryan agreed.

AFTER DESSERT WAS SERVED, Victoria announced it was time for Tyler to wash up and get ready for bed. Of course, Tyler tried to negotiate some extra time and gained only about five more minutes. Marya offered to get Tyler ready for bed and let Victoria know when to come for his prayers. Robyn asked if she could come then too. Tyler's smile was beaming when he heard Auntie Robyn's comment.

Victoria and Robyn cleared the dishes and table with Bryan helping load the dishwasher while Marya saw to Tyler. A short while later, it was time for bedtime prayers, and Tyler's normal prayer was decidedly much longer than usual, blessing everyone in the house, all his stuffed animals, and the lizard he saw out on the patio earlier that day.

With Tyler tucked in for the night, the adults went back out on the patio.

"Hard to believe it's the end of November with this gorgeous weather," Robyn stated.

"I know. Sometimes, I feel so spoiled with our weather, remembering the snow, cold, and ice back in the Midwest. How many Halloween costumes had to be oversized so we could wear our winter jackets under them," Victoria chimed in. "Although July and August are pretty warm here. But there's always air-conditioned cars, stores, offices, houses, etc. I'd rather have two to three months of hot and over nine months of great weather anytime!"

"Yeah, I remember thinking winter was never going to end. Always seemed like it lasted six months at least," Robyn added.

"And what about the snow shoveling and icy roads? At least up in the Washington area, it's not as bad as the Midwest. I remember all too well the term 'lake effect snow.' Heavy and wet and within twenty-four hours, dirty," Bryan stated.

Robyn turned to Bryan. "Well, Honey, I think it's time for us to head back to the hotel. We had an early start today and want to be well rested to come back tomorrow for Thanksgiving. We really want to help with the prep, so what time would you like us to return to the 'Hart Hearth?'" Robyn asked.

Victoria deferred to her mom.

"Dinner is at three in the afternoon, but if you came about noon, it would be fine. The turkey will already be dressed and in the oven, but you could help with the pies, and I need a strong man to mash some potatoes," Marya hinted.

"You got it," Robyn and Bryan said in unison.

A round of hugs ensued at the front door, and Robyn and Bryan were off to their hotel.

Victoria threw her arms around her mom and walked with her back to the kitchen. She knew they all had so much to be thankful for, and what better way to celebrate than to be with those you love. All was good in the Hart household.

CHAPTER 23

The morning of Thanksgiving Day, Tyler sat on a barstool at the kitchen island, totally mesmerized by the turkey sitting in the roasting pan, watching his mom and grandma cramming stuffing into the huge bird.

"Mom, this turkey is huge. Are we going to feed an army... did you invite the 6th Battalion?" Victoria asked.

"Nope. It was on special and figured there would be leftovers and more to freeze and make soup. Winter's coming you know," Marya said with a wry smile.

"Oh yeah... right... winter... here in Phoenix with freezing temperatures and blizzards... snow drifts... I forgot," Victoria laughed.

Tyler's ears perked up. "Snow... really?"

"No, Tyler, we're just kidding. No snow. But I promise you, come January and February, we'll take a drive up to northern Arizona where years ago Mommy would ski, and we can go sledding if you want."

Tyler's eyes were all bug-eyed. "Yay! We're going sledding!"

He took off toward his bedroom.

Leaning close to Victoria, Marya commented, "I'll bet he's trying to figure out how to make a sled out of Legos."

Victoria nodded and continued stuffing the turkey... remembering how she felt when she was a little girl and her dad took her out sledding. It was at times like this, the memory of her father brought tears to her eyes, and she brushed them away, but not before her mother noticed and reached over and gave Victoria a hug.

Promptly at noon, the doorbell rang, and Robyn and Bryan arrived with their arms loaded.

Victoria asked, "What's all this?"

"Well, we stopped on the way and picked up a few things. Like a couple of bottles of vino, which I know are your favorites, a fresh bouquet of flowers for Marya, the Hostess with the Mostest, and... a little something for the 'man' of the house," Robyn said.

By this time Tyler had come into the foyer to greet them.

Bryan knelt down in front of Tyler and asked, "Tyler, are you the man of the house?"

Tyler looked quizzically from Bryan to Victoria.

"Yes, you are, Tyler, indeed you are the man of the house," Victoria answered.

Bryan reached inside a bag and pulled out a Lego set Tyler hadn't seen before.

Tyler's eyes grew large, his mouth dropped open, and he squealed.

As Bryan handed it to him, Tyler looked at Bryan and said, "Thank you. I love Legos. Is it okay if I go put it together now, Mommy?"

Victoria nodded, a lump in her throat. What a sweet gesture it was to give Tyler one of his favorite things. Words were beyond her right then. She motioned everyone into the kitchen. Tyler took off like a cannon with his Lego gift, heading for his room.

"Okay, troops, let's get this show on the road! We have a turkey roasting, potatoes to peel, and veggies to prepare," Victoria exclaimed as they entered the kitchen.

The food prep was filled with laughter and remembering old times, some of which led to teasing between them all, which then led to rounds of laughter, bringing on teary eyes. Victoria looked around the room at her mom and friends and felt a warmth in her heart, realizing how wonderful it was they were able to share the holiday together.

Tyler made a careful entrance into the kitchen, carrying a small tray holding his Lego creation. "Mommy, I did it!"

"Wow, Tyler, it's amazing," Victoria exclaimed.

"Hey, Tyler! How awesome! You did it really fast," Bryan piped in as he knelt down beside Tyler to get a good look at the project.

SEVERAL HOURS LATER, Bryan carried in the platter of turkey, and Marya, Robin, and Victoria placed the side dishes on the table in the dining room.

With the aroma of the roasting turkey still lingering and the floral centerpiece arrangement from Travis in the center, all were settled around the dining table. Marya took Victoria's hand, and they all joined hands around the table. Marya said grace, adding a special blessing for all at the table and asked Tyler if he wanted to add anything to the prayer to express his thanks.

"Grandma, I'm just glad we are all here to eat turkey... it smells so good... oh... and thank you for the Legos."

Bryan proposed a toast to Marya and Victoria for hosting the dinner, and once the glasses were raised and the toast completed, almost total silence overcame the room as the dinner was consumed, the only sounds being those emitting appreciation for good food.

The pies made earlier in the afternoon had already come out of the oven and were cooling for dessert.

Robin turned to Marya and enthusiastically said, "Thank you so much for the pie baking lesson. I'd never made a pie before. I always felt so intimidated baking one. You made it seem so easy, especially the lattice-top."

Victoria passed around dessert plates with the apple pie slices topped with ice cream.

Bryan took a bite and looking at Robin, exclaimed, "Wow, this is delicious! So, now you know how to bake an apple pie, does this mean you'll be baking them for me?"

"Only if you behave yourself, Bryan. Otherwise, it may be a mud pie," Robin teased. "And what's in it for me if I do?" she asked, waggling her eyebrows.

Victoria watched with a little jealousy at the interaction between

Robin and Bryan. She was so happy for her friend Robin and the fact she'd found a "good guy."

After dishes were done and food put away, they sat out on the patio.

"I feel like the turkey... stuffed," said Robin.

"Yes, me too," Victoria added.

Over the next hour, they made plans for the following day. Victoria wanted to take them over to see her new house with the ulterior motive of checking to see if all was ready for the move. She also wanted to show them points of interest she thought they might like to see and experience while in the area.

Tyler had sleepily walked down the hallway to his bedroom, singing a little song Robyn had taught him earlier.

After calling it an evening, Robyn and Bryan headed to the hotel.

Marya went about turning off the lights throughout the great room, kitchen, and patio.

"Mom, thanks for everything you do and for this wonderful Thanksgiving."

"Oh, Honey, we're family, no need to thank me. Everything we do for each other is out of love. And it will always be that way. Now, let's get some sleep. Tomorrow is going to be busy, and the move over the next days is going to be twice as busy."

As it was planned on Friday, Robyn and Bryan drove to Marya's home, and after arriving around ten in the morning, they got into Victoria's SUV and headed over to her new home.

It was Marya's wish to spend time with Tyler, and they left earlier to visit a petting zoo about twenty minutes from the house. Victoria knew her mom was giving her space and time to spend with her friends.

As Victoria pulled into the driveway of her new home, Robyn exclaimed, "Oh my God, Victoria! It's wonderful!"

No sooner did Victoria put the car in park and turn the engine off, Robyn was out the door and exploring the outside of the house.

"Victoria, this is so you! Love the landscaping, and the cul-de-sac with the center landscaping feature is so awesome. Now, let's see the inside," she yelled over her shoulder, basically running up the walk to the front entry. Victoria and Bryan looked at one another, laughed, and ran to catch up. Her exuberance was catching.

Before Victoria unlocked the deadbolt on one of the double front entry doors, she pressed a button on a remote, heard a beeping sound turning off the alarm.

"Whew, I was concerned they hadn't activated the security system yet. Nice to know it's been done."

Victoria explained most of the furniture she recently purchased wouldn't be delivered until the day she moved in. They went room to room with Victoria telling them what furniture would go where and what the pieces looked like.

In the great room, Robyn stood in awe at the fireplace with colored accent walls on each side and built-in cabinetry. Some rooms had quarried stone floors, some had tongue-and-groove plank flooring.

For someone who didn't cook, Robyn fell in love with the kitchen, commenting as she ran her fingers on the granite countertops, "I would definitely make an effort to learn to cook if I had a kitchen like this."

Bryan laughed. "It's okay, Honey. I'll do the cooking... your talents lie... elsewhere," he teased, waggling his brows.

Robyn's mouth opened to say something, nothing came out, but she gave Bryan a friendly clip on the shoulder, along with a wink.

Entering the master suite, Robyn stopped dead in her tracks, turning around to face Victoria.

"You have got to be kidding me. Your own fireplace in your bedroom. How romantic... how sexy! Bryan, I hope you're taking notes!" Noticing the built-in hot tub outside with access through the master suite, Robyn turned to Victoria... "I guess someone has some 'tub time' planned."

Victoria just rolled her eyes. "Purely therapeutic," she responded.

"Yeah, right," Robyn smirked.

Once Robyn saw the master bath, she was speechless, which was saying a lot. Robyn walked back through the wide, mirrored hallway between the master bedroom and the master bath.

"Okay, don't tell me," she said as she slid one of the mirrored sections to reveal a walk-in closet. Walking to the other side of the hallway, she repeated her actions and found another walk-in closet.

"One question, Victoria... when can I... er... we move in?"

Robyn insisted on going through each room again, including the laundry room, and when they got to the guest room, Robyn made a point of reminding Victoria what her favorite colors were.

Bryan asked to see the garage. "It's a man thing," Robyn said over her shoulder at Victoria. This time it was Bryan's turn to be awestruck.

"Oh man! Look at those built-in cabinets and the seal-coated floor. This could be turned into the most awesome man cave. A sound system could be hooked up, and a sixty-five-inch flat-screen TV over there can be cased, then opened up for viewing, and..."

He detected it was noticeably quiet and turned around to face Robyn and Victoria. They stood there with their hands over their mouths, quietly shaking with laughter.

"What? I'm just saying there's a lot of potential here!"

Robyn walked over to him and threw her arms around him. "Sweetheart, when we get our own home, you can do whatever you like with the garage."

Bryan looked lovingly at her. "Thanks, Honey... I think." Looking somewhat bewildered at their conversation, he just shrugged.

Victoria turned and walked back into the house with the lovebirds following her.

"How about a trip out to the backyard? I want to make sure the BBQ and outdoor kitchen island are hooked up, and everything is ready for the delivery of the patio furniture next week." Victoria opened the telescoping slider to the backyard.

"Oh, Victoria... it's beautiful. You've got your own piece of heaven out here."

The landscaping was all in, and Victoria noticed the telltale drip lines were still wet from an early morning sprinkling. She went over to a control panel inside an enclosed case on the wall and flipped one of the switches, and the waterfall feature above the pool started flowing.

"Wow... I'd be spending all my free time out here," Robyn said dreamily, taking off her sandals and sitting down on the stone patio, dangling her feet in the water and wiggling her toes. Victoria and Bryan joined her

"Victoria, truly this is all so amazing. I... we're so happy for you. You so deserve this," Robyn said, putting her arm around Victoria.

"Thanks so much. I look back, and I have to pinch myself sometimes. Can this be real?"

"Of course, it's real. You worked so hard in school, making your folks proud. Getting a great job and now a partner in the firm. Plus, you have one very handsome little man in your life, and I'm sure he'll be a heartbreaker when he grows up. You've come a long way, baby."

It was Bryan's turn to say something he had been holding in.

"Victoria, I know you have seen the best of men with your father and the worst of men with your ex-husband, then quite possibly Drew. I hope you don't let the latter color your world, and you'll give someone good a chance to bring light and love into your life. You've been through a lot in your short time here on planet Earth. More than most people experience in a lifetime." Waving his arms around at the beautiful house and yard, he continued, "You do deserve this, all the happiness you can garner, and so much more."

The silence was deafening.

Victoria and Robyn were sitting there, their mouths agape.

Robyn was the first to speak, "Who are you, and what have you done with my Bryan? I have never heard anything more beautiful than what you just said to Victoria."

Robyn leaned into Bryan and gave him a kiss.

Over the past months, indeed there were times Victoria had been questioning herself to the point she was beginning to doubt her decision-making capabilities. She wanted to create a perfect house, a perfect world for Tyler.

Most of her life, it had been difficult for Victoria to accept compliments. The bullying she experienced in school left a deep mental scar, and after the fiasco of her marriage to Brandon, her self-confidence shattered very easily.

A quiet contemplation had come over the three of them, each one in their own thoughts. Minutes passed, and Robyn pulled her feet out of the water.

"Oh, now look what you made me do. I've got wrinkled toes," she laughed, breaking the silence. Victoria and Bryan laughed as well and lifted their feet out of the water, and all three scrambled getting up and gathered their shoes. Victoria turned off the water feature and opened the door leading into the kitchen. As they walked back into the house, Victoria took the hand of each.

"I don't know how anyone could get so lucky having friends like you."

After walking through the rooms once more to make sure lights were turned off, they walked to the front entry. Victoria set the alarm and locked the deadbolt to her home... HER HOME!

CHAPTER 24

The rest of the day was spent traveling around the area. First, they went to the Boulders up in Carefree and had lunch at El Pedregal, then checked out the shops. It was, after all, the Friday after Thanksgiving and everything was on sale.

Robyn admired a pair of earrings, and Bryan swooped in and bought them for her. They both fell in love with a bowl they found made of turned wood with copper and turquoise inlays crafted by a local artisan. Each wanted to buy it for the other and finally settled on Robyn paying for it, saying she wanted to use it in their home when they got married.

"Consider it part of my dowry, Bryan," she teased.

"Your dowry? You have a dowry? How come this is the first I'm hearing about this?" he joked back at her.

Victoria spied a beautiful painting in a gallery. It was just the size she needed to fit in a niche in the entry hall of her new home. It was an original oil by Lorna Sanders, another local artist whose name was well known to her and many art collectors in the area. After purchasing the painting, she made arrangements for it to be carefully wrapped and delivered to her mother's house to be stored until the move.

Neither Robyn nor Bryan had any desire to tour downtown Phoenix or Scottsdale, especially due to the hordes of Black Friday shoppers, but they did express an interest in going to WestWorld of Scottsdale. They had heard the venue was where events—horse shows, rodeos, music festivals, and colossal celebrity style car auctions—were held.

As luck would have it, there were two events happening— a miniature horse show in the Equidome and a massive hall adjacent to the Equidome was showcasing a canine agility competition. Bryan and Robyn were eager to see both.

After spending several hours there and consuming a couple of churros, Bryan admitted he really wanted a dog after they were married, in particular, a border collie. Robyn was leaning toward an Australian shepherd. Victoria was rooting for a German shorthair pointer, and a debate ensued as to which each would be better suited.

Robyn said she changed her mind and decided on a miniature pony which had all three of them in hysterics.

"And just who will be cleaning up after your 'pretty little pony,' Robyn? Don't look at me," Bryan kidded.

After they left WestWorld, they headed back to Marya's.

Tyler ran to greet them at the door, insisting he show everyone the pictures on Gramma's camera of him with the various animals at the petting zoo. Tyler exclaimed how thick the wool was on the sheep and the fact his hand disappeared into the wool when he petted it. He shared stories of each of the animals and soon yawning took over his dialogue. Marya had already given him an early supper and suggested it was probably time to call it a day for him.

Victoria excused herself, picked up the sleepy Tyler, and carried him to his room.

A half hour later, Victoria joined Robyn, Bryan, and Marya out on the patio.

"He's down for the count. Mom, I don't know how you did it raising me and now caring for Tyler. You must be Superwoman!"

"Hey, it wasn't just me raising you. Your father was a big help, so were your grandparents. Everyone pitched in, especially when I had night shifts at the hospital in the trauma ward. It's what family does, and as I've said before, it's what love is," Marya spoke sincerely as she squeezed Victoria's hand.

Marya rose from her chair and bid everyone good night, saying she was calling it an early night and wished she had someone to tuck her in.

"Mom!"

All they heard was gentle laughter as her mother headed into the house.

She really needed to sit down with her mom and discuss this "Brock" guy soon. But then again, her mom seemed to be more "with it" than Victoria, and probably could give Victoria a run for her money in dealing with relationships.

The plan for the evening was to head over to Handlebar J's for a genuine western dinner and dancing. Victoria was familiar with the band and knew Bryan and Robyn would enjoy the music. This time, Bryan insisted on driving to dinner with Victoria giving him directions. All three ordered the slab of BBQ ribs, and by the time the meal ended, they felt like they needed to be hosed down.

Robyn had a bit of BBQ sauce on her cheek, and Bryan leaned over and gently licked it off. She squealed and feigned disapproval, but then laughed and gave Bryan a big BBQ sauce kiss.

The playful teasing between them brought back memories to Victoria of a weekend just over five years ago, and she felt a pang of jealousy wrap around the ache in her heart.

The dance floor was crowded, but the three of them did manage to join in on a line dance. Then when the music changed, Victoria headed back to their table to watch Bryan and Robyn try to do the Texas two-step. They gave up just in time for the music to change to a slow romantic song. The lovebirds wrapped their arms around each other and moved in a gentle, swaying rhythm.

More memories came flooding back to Victoria, and she had to look away for fear the tears forming in her eyes would give her away.

Would she ever find her special someone? Maybe she had... but... who?

Hours later, Victoria was dropped off at home, and Bryan and Robyn headed back to the hotel. They had arranged to meet up again around ten in the morning and drive out to the Salt River to see if they could spot any of the wild horse bands residing along the river. Victoria knew Tyler would get a kick out of seeing the horses.

Morning came, and Tyler went charging into Victoria's bedroom, jumping up on her bed, bestowing "wake up" kisses on her face. The room was filled with giggles between both of them.

"Okay, Ty! Let's go get breakfast, then Mommy has a surprise for you."

"What is it, Mommy?"

"Like I said, it's a surprise, but I know you'll like it. Auntie Robyn and Bryan are going to be here soon, and they're going to go with us."

"Where are we going?" Tyler asked coyly.

"Oh no... you're not getting any more information out of me... race you to the kitchen!" Victoria said, changing the subject and jumping out of bed.

The patter of feet running down the hallway to the kitchen was heard by Marya who was already up and had the coffee brewing.

"Well, look at you two all energized. What are your plans today?" Marya asked.

"Oh, just a little surprise for Tyler."

Tyler was listening closely to see if Victoria was going to spill the beans—no such luck.

Once she had him settled down at the breakfast table with his fruit and cereal, Victoria motioned for her mom to step around the corner into the hallway with her and told her about the trip out to see the wild horses at the Salt River.

"Oh, Honey, he's going to love it," she whispered.

"Mom, please come with us. It'll be so much fun," Victoria asked.

"Victoria, if you don't mind I'll take a pass. I've got some errands to run... and I thought I might meet up with a friend for lunch," she said hesitantly.

"A friend? Hmmm... I don't suppose your friend's name would be Brock, would it?

Victoria was surprised to see a blush come over her mother's face.

Their discussion was interrupted by a snicker coming from around the corner of the hallway.

"Tyler Benjamin Hart! Are you spying on us?" Victoria teased.

His giggles gave him away, and he rushed back into the kitchen, sat down in his chair, and pretended to be eating his cereal.

∼

AT A FEW MINUTES AFTER TEN, Bryan and Robyn arrived, and it was decided Victoria would drive her SUV since she knew the area where they would be going, and it would give her friends the chance to admire the scenery while she drove.

Robyn called out "Shotgun" as they got to Victoria's car in the garage. Victoria had already loaded the back of her SUV with a cooler, picnic basket, and a blanket.

Victoria had given them the heads-up the ride was a surprise for Tyler who was buckled in his car seat in the backseat next to Bryan. Of course, Tyler tried his best to get one of them to let the cat out of the bag —but again, no such luck.

The total drive time would take just over an hour and a half, and Tyler asked about every fifteen minutes if they were there yet. Victoria pulled into a gas station close to where they were heading and said she had to pick something up. After getting back into the car, she hung a placard on the rear-view mirror.

"Mommy, what's it for?"

"It's a permit, Ty."

"What's a permit?"

"Well, we need permission to go where we're going, and this allows us to go there," Victoria explained, watching she didn't say too much.

Tyler scrunched up his face, thinking hard about what she said.

Soon, they were traversing a winding and hilly road. Victoria knew it was vitally important for drivers to go slowly through the area—no telling what might suddenly cross the road in front of you. She finally spotted the turnoff she needed to take. As they came around a bend in the road, there was the Salt River. Victoria found a parking spot and turned off the ignition.

Tyler, strapped in his seat, pulled himself up as far as he could and was so excited to see the river with its greenery on its sides.

"Ty, look over there at the beach area."

"Mommy! Mommy! Horses!" he exclaimed.

"Okay, Tyler. We're going to get out of the car now. They are wild horses. You can't get too close to them, or they'll get scared, particularly some of the little ones. So, we have to keep our distance. I brought my camera to take photos and videos, and I've got a pair of binoculars for you. Will you remember what I said, Tyler?"

"Yes, Mommy. We can't go close to the horses. Can we feed them? Gramma packed some picnic food for us."

"Nope, sorry, Tyler, the horses have their own food growing around here, and when they eat something different, it upsets their tummy, and they get sick."

Bryan and Robyn were taking this all in and commented how Victoria was such a great "Mommy."

"Best job in the world," Victoria replied.

They exited the SUV and grabbed the blanket, picnic basket, and cooler out of the back. Once they got to a section of the beach, a safe distance from the horses, they laid everything out. Tyler asked if he could take his shoes off and walk in the water. Victoria told him it was okay, but he had to stay close to shore and never more than knee deep in the water. Robyn and Bryan were busy with their cameras, taking pictures of the river and the horses.

"Oh, Victoria, this place is awesome. I never had any idea it would be like this. Those horses are beautiful and so healthy looking. What do they eat?" asked Robyn.

"Scrub, mesquite pods, but they love the eelgrass that grows in the river. They go out in the river and 'snorkel,' pulling up the eelgrass to eat. It's full of nutrients, and the horses thrive on it. The mares teach their offspring how to put their whole head in the water and pull it up. I was out here in the spring with some friends and watching the mares with their foals was such a beautiful sight. There are several bands. Each band has a stallion and several mares with one mare being a lead mare, sort of the matriarch of the band. I knew I had to bring Tyler here to see this," she explained, smiling.

Victoria grabbed her camera and took some videos of Tyler playing in the water with the horses in the distance. Then she snapped pictures of Tyler splashing with his feet.

With her special zoom lens, she took photos of the horses and made a mental note to make sure she printed them up and framed them for Tyler's room.

They later picnicked on the blanket, eating the turkey sandwiches Marya had made for their excursion, then rested, listening to the sounds of the river flowing, birds calling, and the whinnying horses. They could tell from a whinny if it was from one of the younger ones.

Tyler fell asleep in the car on the way back home. Victoria glanced up in the rearview mirror and noticed Bryan had dozed off as well.

"Victoria, thanks ever so much for this. I'll never forget it. As soon as we get home, I'll download the pictures and videos and email you a link to them," Robyn said.

"I'm so glad you enjoyed it. There's so much to do and see here, but I wanted it to be fun and relaxing for you. I know you and Bryan have busy work schedules and some 'kick back' time was needed."

"No kidding! Now with our wedding coming up in the spring, we're going to adjust our schedules to accommodate the planning. I sure hope you will be there... after all... you're the maid of honor," Robyn said hopefully.

"Oh, Robyn! Of course, I'll be there. And thanks so much for asking me to be your maid of honor, I'm honored."

"Which brings up another point. Do you think Tyler would be our ring bearer?"

"Wow! I'm pretty sure he would, but I'll make sure he gets lots of practice time before the wedding. How sweet."

CHAPTER 25

As they pulled into the driveway at her mother's house, they found her mother standing very close to a gentleman near a car on the other side of the driveway. He was around six foot tall, fiftyish with silver-streaked dark hair.

"Aha," Victoria exclaimed. "I'll bet he's mom's mysterious friend and co-worker, Brock." Victoria had filled Robyn in earlier on her mom and "her friend."

"So, do we give him the third degree now or wait," Robyn teased.

"No, I'm pretty sure mom feels he's okay, or she wouldn't have him at the house."

Tyler and Bryan awoke, and Victoria and Robyn grinned, noticing "the boys" were rubbing the sleep from their eyes in unison. As they all exited the car, Victoria noticed Marya was blushing but not at all flustered.

"Good sign," mused Victoria aloud.

"Hi, Mom."

Victoria waited for her mom to make introductions.

"This is my... friend, Brock Collier," Marya said, stepping forward and putting her hand on Brock's shoulder. "Brock is a captain with the Phoenix Fire Department and also volunteers at the V.A.

"Brock, this is my daughter, Victoria, and her friends Bryan and Robyn who are visiting from Washington State."

Handshakes ensued, then Tyler went running to Brock. Brock knelt down and gave Tyler a "high five."

"Hey, Ty. How ya' doin,' Buddy?"

It was obvious Tyler had met Brock before.

Yes, about those dinners Mom went to when I was out of town.

"We saw horses... real horses... and there was a big river... and..." Tyler was beside himself with joy being able to tell Brock all about the horses, the beach, and the river.

Victoria loved the way Brock related to Tyler. Her heart warmed at the thought. Victoria stood with her mom and listened to the verbal exchanges between Brock and Tyler.

Bryan and Robyn unloaded the back of the car and brought everything inside the house.

"Okay, Tyler, it's time for you to get washed up. I think you have sand in every nook and cranny of your body."

"Can Brock stay?" Tyler asked.

Marya piped up, "No, Honey, Brock is on special duty tonight at the fire station because of the holiday, but you'll see him again soon. I promise."

"Tyler, how about you and your mommy and gramma come down to the fire station sometime? If it's okay with them?" Brock said inquiringly.

"Oh, can we, Mommy, please?" Tyler pleaded.

Victoria looked over at Marya and saw her smiling.

"Of course, Tyler, we'll plan on it," Victoria answered.

"Brock, it was a pleasure FINALLY meeting you and thank you so much... for everything," Victoria said, giving him a hug.

Tyler turned to Brock and whispered loudly, "Thanks, Brock." Brock bent down, and they exchanged hugs.

"C'mon, Tyler, time to get you cleaned up," Victoria said, taking Tyler by the hand, heading into the house.

Marya called to her, "I'll be in shortly."

"Don't hurry, Mom."

Robyn and Bryan had unpacked the cooler and picnic basket and put everything away, and Robyn told Victoria she set the sandy beach blanket in the laundry room. Victoria sent Tyler down the hallway to his room to get ready to shower the sand off. A few minutes had passed, and Robyn looked over to Victoria.

"Your mom hasn't come back in yet. Should we check to see if she's okay?"

They both looked at each other and started laughing hysterically. Calming down and wiping the tears from her eyes, Victoria excused herself, saying she needed to get Tyler showered. Fifteen minutes later, Victoria entered the kitchen and walked out to the patio to find Robyn, Bryan, and her mom enjoying sangria with chips and salsa.

"You all seemed to have a nice day out at the Salt River with the horses," Marya commented.

"Yes, Mom, we did. And I guess we don't have to ask how your day went. Near as I can tell, you had an enjoyable day too," Victoria kidded.

"I'll have you know, I had one of the finest days of my life actually," Marya replied. Quickly changing the subject, Marya asked where Tyler was. The sudden switch in conversation took Victoria off guard, and she stumbled with her words.

"Ah... he's... back in his room, attempting to create a river and horses with Legos."

That evening, they all enjoyed homemade pizza, one of Tyler's favorites.

After dinner, Tyler made sure Auntie Robyn and Bryan went to his room where he had used his Legos to create a scene reminiscent of the time they had at the Salt River with the horses. Bryan knelt down to get a better look at what Tyler constructed and reached in his pocket for his digital camera.

"Tyler, is it okay if I snap a picture of it?" Bryan asked.

"Sure," he responded. Tyler was thrilled someone would think enough of his creation to take a photo of it. He beamed. Tyler's bedtime ritual lasted a bit longer than usual. He knew Auntie Robyn and Bryan were going back home the next day and gave them hugs, then more hugs.

Once he was tucked in, they gathered back out on the patio where the atmosphere turned melancholy. Victoria didn't like thinking about them leaving tomorrow morning, and Robyn felt the same way. Robyn was the first to speak after a long spell of silence.

"Victoria and Marya, I know I speak for both Bryan and me, we so appreciate all you've done for us while we visited. We've had a lovely time here." Tears were forming in Robyn's eyes, and when she looked up at Victoria, tears were trickling down Victoria's cheeks. They were sitting together on the settee and wrapped their arms around one another.

"It's been great having you here," Victoria said, sniffling. "And remember, you're always welcome, and next time, you get to stay at my house. Forget about making hotel arrangements, or I'll be mad at you."

Robyn nodded. "Who knows... the Christmas and New Year's holidays are coming... maybe we can break away for a bit." Looking over at Bryan with inquiring eyes, he nodded and smiled.

They said their goodbyes and walked out to Bryan's car, Robyn promising to call Victoria before they left for the airport on Sunday morning. As their car pulled away, Marya put her arm around Victoria.

"You have some wonderful friends, Honey."

Victoria cocked her head and nudged her mom. "So do you, it seems, Mom," Victoria winked.

All was right in the Hart household.

CHAPTER 26

The Monday after the Thanksgiving holiday was a busy day at the office, and Victoria was eager to get home. She hadn't as yet gone through the folders containing the phone records she had requested and wondered if she was delaying for a reason. She promised herself she would start reviewing the reports in the evenings after Tyler went to bed.

This evening, she planned to have a light supper with her mom and Tyler, then meet up with Travis. Travis had arrived in Phoenix earlier in the day and would be in town for several days, during which time she would decide whether or not to bring Travis into her life and those of her little family.

As she pulled out of her parking spot, she noticed her SUV didn't feel right. She hoped the mechanic near her mom's house would still be open and could take a quick look to see if there was an issue. It was just after five in the afternoon, and normally, "Doc" was open until six in the evening, sometimes later.

Victoria turned onto the access road to Route 51 and entered the stream of traffic on the highway. It was rush hour, and Victoria thought to herself it was an oxymoron since it was moving so slow and way under the speed limit. *No "rush" about it.*

She noticed the steering was difficult. Looking down at her dashboard gauges to check the system, she noted her tire alert had a red light—all four tires! She put on her emergency flashers and attempted to pull off to the side onto the shoulder, but the steering became worse, and she felt panic as she tried desperately to control her vehicle.

Other vehicles were passing her, honking their horns, waving furiously, pointing to her wheels. She was able to maneuver to the side of the road, but skidded perilously close to a cement barrier, sending up gravel around as her vehicle pivoted to a stop.

She put the transmission into "Park" and sat shaking in her seat. Two vehicles pulled over and stopped on the side of the road, one in front of her, one behind her, and put their emergency flashers on. Victoria was oblivious to their arrival. Shaken from her state of duress, she was startled when someone knocked on her driver's window.

"Miss, are you alright?

Victoria lowered her window. "

I think so. I don't know what happened... all of a sudden, I couldn't control the car."

"Well, it's no wonder... your wheels are just about off your car."

Just then the driver of the other car approached. "Wow, you sure are lucky you were able to pull off when you did. If you had been going the speed limit and those wheels came off, you could have been killed!"

Realization sank in, and Victoria rested her forehead on her steering wheel, tremors going through her body.

Someone had obviously called 911, and two Phoenix police cruisers arrived. One stayed behind the car behind Victoria with lights flashing, and the other pulled in front of Victoria between her car and the other vehicle. One of the officers went to speak to the other drivers, and the other officer came to Victoria's window.

"Ma'am, are you okay? Do you need any medical assistance?"

Stammering, she replied, "I think I'm fine... just shaken up. My car just..." Victoria's voice trembled and tears were forming in her eyes.

Flashes of what happened and thoughts of her mom and Tyler hit full force. Her face was a ghostly white.

The other officer walked over to Victoria's car and was inspecting the wheels and with a concerned looked, motioned for the other officer to join him.

"Excuse me, Ma'am... I'll be right back, but if you could, please have your license, registration, and insurance card ready for me when I return... for our incident report." It was obvious the officer was trying to be compassionate and allay any stress—it was more than apparent Victoria was somewhat in a state of shock.

While the officer joined the other officer, Victoria complied with the officer's request and with shaky hands dug out the documents requested. A short while later, both of the officers returned to Victoria and seemed very troubled.

"Ma'am, it appears quite a few of the lug nuts and bolts have been removed from your wheels." The officer noted Victoria was digesting what he was saying and watched her pallor turn gray.

Victoria looked up at the officer. "I don't understand... but how... what would cause it to happen?" she slowly asked.

"We couldn't say for sure... but is it possible someone may have tampered with your vehicle? Someone may have been attempting to steal your tires... or... is your car secured in a safe area when you aren't using it?"

"At home, it's in our garage, but it was fine this morning. I just left work where it's parked in the building's parking garage. I'm not sure if there are any surveillance cameras there.

"Here's my driver's license, registration, and insurance card," she added as she handed them to the officer.

"Well, your vehicle is impossible for you to drive, so a tow truck will have to come and load it, and we'll need a statement from you while we wait for it. Do you have a towing company you use?"

"Yes, I'm a member of Triple-A and can contact them to tow it to my mechanic."

After arranging the tow, Victoria knew she would have to get someone to pick her up, but she didn't want it to be her mom. She also realized Marya would already be wondering where she was since she called her as she left the office and knew it would now be some time before she got home. She called home, dreading telling her mom what happened and causing her to worry.

Marya answered on the first ring. "Victoria, are you okay? You called from your office saying you were on your way..." Marya hesitated. "Victoria... what's wrong?" Marya's mother's intuition kicked in.

"I had some car trouble... a tire issue... but I'm okay. My car is being towed shortly to our mechanic, Doc, and I'm going to be home soon. Not to worry... really, I'm okay." Her mom didn't seem assuaged by her answers but didn't want to press Victoria. She knew she would get all the answers when Victoria got home.

"Wait. How are you getting home? Do you want me to come get you?"

"No, Mom. I don't want you to have to load Tyler in the car and drive all the way down here. It's just easier for me to call Lyft... or even a friend close by."

"Oh, alright then... be safe and see you soon," Marya replied hesitantly. She sensed there was more to the story than what Victoria was letting on.

After disconnecting the call with her mom, Victoria took a deep breath and dialed Travis' mobile phone number. The sound of his voice as he answered gave her some relief from the stress she was feeling.

"Travis, it's Victoria, and I hate to ask you this, but I had some car issues and need a ride home, and I thought maybe since you and I were meeting up later anyway, you wouldn't mind..." she spoke tentatively. Victoria wondered if she was making any sense. Her hands were still trembling slightly.

"Victoria, are you kidding? I'd be delighted. Just tell me where you are, and I'll be on my way," Travis answered enthusiastically.

Victoria gave him her location and told him she was waiting in the tow truck.

"Oh, thank you so much, Travis. I hated to ask my mom to come get me. She would have to wrangle Tyler and get him strapped in and—"

Travis cut her off saying, "Victoria, don't even think about it. Besides, it means more time spent with you, and I get a chance to meet your family. You sound quite a bit shaken up, actually. You mentioned car issues. Is there something you aren't telling me?"

"I'll tell you about it when I see you. Just know I'm fine... and I'm looking forward to seeing you."

The other drivers had left after giving their statements to the police, and the officers were finishing up with Victoria's statement when the tow truck driver arrived and started assessing how to hook up and transport her vehicle. It was tricky, but they managed to switch some of the remaining lug nuts to the back wheels and temporarily straighten them while hoisting the entire vehicle onto the flatbed of the tow truck, then chaining the vehicle in place.

Travis arrived, driving an SUV similar to Victoria's, as they were locking down the chains securing her vehicle. He pulled over to the side of the road, put on his emergency flashers, and got out of his car. His look said it all as he observed the vehicle. He knew this wasn't a fluke. He approached Victoria as she was thanking the officers for their help.

"Victoria, this was no accident," he exclaimed, noting as he said it, neither of the officers seemed surprised by his statement.

"Ma'am, if you think of anything else we need to put into the report, please contact us at the number on the report copy we gave you." Victoria nodded.

Victoria was glad her mechanic, "Doc," answered the phone and told him a tow truck carrying her SUV was on its way to him shortly. Doc was more than a little concerned about Victoria when she relayed what happened and asked if she had a ride. Victoria confirmed she did, and that she had given the key fob to the tow truck driver.

The officers guided the tow truck out into the mainstream of highway traffic, then after both Travis and Victoria got into Travis' vehicle, assisted Travis in merging into the traffic flow as well.

Victoria gave Travis directions where to merge onto Highway 101 and where to exit on Tatum Boulevard. The only acknowledgment was a nod from Travis.

Minutes passed, and finally, Travis couldn't hold back any longer.

"What exactly happened, Victoria... and don't sugarcoat it. I know what I saw, and the stress I see in your face tells me there is more at play here than 'just an issue' with your car."

Victoria closed her eyes, took a deep breath, and launched into what occurred, relating the officers had their suspicions as well. By the time she finished, they were approaching the highway exit, and Victoria gave additional directions to her mother's home.

Travis was uncomfortably quiet, but Victoria could tell he was concerned and was holding himself in check. As they pulled into the driveway at Marya's, he turned to Victoria and took her hand.

"We won't discuss it now, especially in front of your little boy, but we will discuss it soon. This isn't something to be taken lightly. You could have been hurt or worse yet, killed. We both know this was no accident." He raised her hand to his lips and placed a gentle kiss on it.

As they exited Travis' car, Marya came out of the house.

"Oh, Victoria, you had me worried. I told Tyler you had to work a little later so he wouldn't fret."

"I'm fine, Mom. Fortunately, I was able to hitch a ride with Travis," she said, motioning to him.

Looking up at Travis, Marya threw a hug around him. "Travis, so nice to finally meet you. I've heard so many wonderful things about you." Marya caught a glimpse of Victoria rolling her eyes.

So much for keeping this relationship neutral for a while.

"Mrs. Hart, the feeling is mutual. I'm just glad I was able to come to Victoria's rescue," he teased.

"Oh, please, call me Marya. Mrs. Hart sounds so old and formal, not at all like me. Well, at least not the formal part," giggled Marya.

Victoria was at a loss for words. She hadn't heard her mother giggle in a long time... or maybe she just wasn't around to hear it.

As they entered the house, Tyler came barreling down the hallway and around the corner, running smack into Travis' solid long legs.

"Whoa!" Tyler exclaimed looking up... and up. "You're like a tree!" he said, wonder in his eyes. All three adults bust out laughing.

"Tyler, I would like you to meet Travis, a friend of mine from when we were in school together," Victoria explained while introducing them.

Tyler reached out his small hand to Travis, and Travis knelt down, took it gently, and shook it.

"Nice to meet you, Tyler. Your Mommy and I have known each for a very long time. We went to school together. I'm so glad to finally meet you."

Tyler was cocking his head side to side, examining Travis.

"What is it, Tyler? Marya asked.

"Do I call him Mr. Travis or Tree or Travis the Tree?"

"How's about you just call me Travis?"

Tyler seemed very pleased with his answer and asked if Travis was going to eat dinner with them. As Travis rose to stand up, Victoria glanced over to Travis.

"I hope you haven't eaten dinner yet. I know we were going to meet up later this evening, but I know for a fact, my mom usually cooks enough for an army, and we would love for you to eat with us."

"Oh, please do, Travis. I just need to set an extra plate. Nothing fancy tonight. Just my homemade turkey and vegetable soup with a salad," Marya interjected.

"Your expertise in the kitchen is well known, Marya. I'd be delighted to join you."

Tyler shouted, "Yay!" and promptly grabbed Travis' hand to lead him into the kitchen.

"Well, it sure smells good in here... and if it tastes as good as it smells, I'm in for a real treat. I hardly ever get a home cooked meal."

The talk was easy between them all during dinner, but there were undertones of stress lurking, especially in Victoria's face. Her eyes were troubled, and neither Marya nor Travis broached the subject of the car incident in front of Tyler, knowing full well it would just add to any pressure Victoria was feeling.

After a dessert of ice cream and berries, Victoria suggested Tyler get washed up and ready for bed. Marya offered to get him prepared and would let Victoria know when he was tucked in and ready for his prayers.

"Can Travis come hear my prayers too... please?" he pleaded.

"If it's okay with your mom, it's okay with me," Travis said, glancing at Victoria. She nodded, and Tyler was off down the hallway to his room, Marya trailing him.

Travis quietly helped Victoria clear the dishes and load the dishwasher, all the while watching her face and noting the stress lines.

After tucking in Tyler and hearing him say his prayers, Travis and Victoria joined Marya out on the patio. Marya had already put out some stemware and opened a bottle of wine.

"I wasn't sure what your plans were for the rest of the evening, but I thought the three of us could enjoy a glass of wine together," Marya said quietly.

Victoria knew a setup when she saw one... and it had nothing to do with her and Travis.

Travis took the cue, pouring three glasses and passed them around.

Raising his glass, he toasted, "Here's to smart and intuitive mothers!" After they all had taken a sip and put their glasses down, Victoria folded her hands in her lap. It was so quiet, you could hear a pin drop. Victoria sat up and voiced what had been brewing in her mind.

"No... it definitely wasn't an accident. It was intentional. And I fully intend on getting to the bottom of it, no matter where it leads," she firmly stated. It was obvious she was trying desperately to hold herself together.

Wringing her hands, Victoria conveyed the series of events regarding the "accident." As she was talking about the car spinning out of control when it hit the gravel on the shoulder and she saw her car was heading to the cement embankment, her whole body shuddered, and she closed her eyes, tears falling down her cheeks.

Marya, sitting beside her, put her arm around her. Travis, sitting across from Victoria, jumped up and knelt in front of her, taking her trembling hands in his. She held it in a long as she could. Wracking sobs came from Victoria. Travis took a handkerchief from his pocket and handed it to her.

"All I could think about was my son and my mother, and I wouldn't be able to say goodbye."

"But you survived... and I must say, Victoria, you really handled your car well. The police officers were amazed," Travis commented.

Marya sat quietly, absorbing all the information Victoria had imparted.

It was then Victoria noticed her mother had reached over to take Victoria's wrist and was looking at her watch—forever the nurse. Her mother was checking Victoria's pulse.

Knowing she was caught, Marya said, "Victoria, you experienced an event that was a shock to your system. I hate to put a damper on the evening, but may I suggest instead of going out, you two just enjoy yourselves out here on the patio for now and plan on getting together tomorrow. Tomorrow Doc will be able to tell you more about your car."

"Sounds like a great plan to me, Marya," Travis said.

"I'm going to turn in for the night. You both stay out here and enjoy the quiet." Marya gave both Victoria and Travis a goodnight hug and went inside. Travis moved to sit next to Victoria.

Only a few seconds later the house lights were dimmed and "someone" turned on the sound system to light contemporary music which was barely audible. Only the landscaping lights and those in the LED candles on the patio tables were lit.

A soft breeze blew long strands of Victoria's hair across her face.

Travis reached over, brushing them out of her eyes, and curled them behind her ear.

His touch was so gentle. Maybe it was the events surrounding the car accident or the fact she hadn't been with a man in such a long time, or maybe... just maybe because Travis seemed to be hitting all the right buttons.

Victoria looked into Travis' eyes and asked, "Can I kiss you?"

There wasn't any need to ask. Travis, holding her face in his hands, softly possessed her lips and lingered, erasing the stress and strain engulfing Victoria for the past hours.

It was with deep reluctance he pulled away, but not before what they shared in that one kiss made a lasting impression on both of them. The quiet between them spoke volumes. Travis took her chin with his fingers and placed a gentle kiss on her forehead.

"You've had a rather eventful and somewhat disquieting day, and I'm sure you are mentally and emotionally exhausted. I'm going to head back to my hotel now, and I want you to call it a night and get some rest. Call me in the morning, and we'll make our plans."

She acknowledged what he said with a nod and reached out. "Thank you, Travis... for everything... I..."

Travis put his index finger to her lips to stop her from saying anything further.

"No 'thanks' is necessary. I'm just glad I was here to help... and please, never hesitate to ask for my help."

She walked Travis to the front door and touched his arm.

"Call me when you get to your hotel?" she asked hesitantly.

"Are you sure... what if you're already asleep?"

"Somehow, I don't think I'll be falling asleep all that quickly. So much going on inside my head."

Travis nodded and put his arms around her. "One more for the road?"

Her smile said it all. He leaned in and pressed his lips to hers, tightening his arms around her. She responded in kind. The kiss was slow and gentle at first but soon deepened to much more.

He pulled away gradually, and said a bit remorsefully, "If we don't stop now, I'll never leave... ever."

Victoria, breathless from the kiss, could only smile and nod.

"Good night, Victoria... and yes, I will call you when I get to my hotel room. Make sure the house is locked up tight before you go to bed."

Travis strode down the walkway to his car and went on his way but not before lowering his window and waving to Victoria as she stood in the doorway.

Victoria shut and bolted the door, leaning her back against it. She could still hear the sounds of the music coming from the speaker system and closed her eyes. Travis' face, his touch, his kisses were like magic to her senses. With all she'd experienced, his magic seemed to dispel most of the anxiety plaguing her.

She walked through the house, making sure the lights were turned off as well as the sound system and the doors were locked, then headed for her bedroom. She washed up for bed and went to check on Tyler who she found sleeping away with a smile on his face, "Arfer," his favorite stuffed dog, next to him. She gently laid a kiss on his forehead and closed the door to his room.

Back in her bedroom, she fluffed up her pillow and looked around. If all goes as planned, this would be one of her last night's sleeping in her old bed. She had taken the rest of the week off to move into her new home with Tyler. New beginnings—she hoped nothing would interfere.

She plugged her mobile phone into the charger on her nightstand and lowered the ringtone. Sliding between the sheets, she relished the comfort she felt. A gentle tone came from her phone, and as she reached over to grab it, she noticed Travis' name on the caller ID.

Leaning back into the softness of her pillow, she answered, "Hello, Travis."

"Hi, Victoria. Made it safe and sound to my hotel room... as much as it is a beautiful hotel and the room is full of amenities, I regret not overstaying my welcome at your place... at least for another bowl of ice cream."

Victoria laughed out loud.

"I love your laughter! It means you're relaxed. Am I right?"

"Yes. I'm snuggled in and trying not to think about the gazillion things I have to get done this week for the move."

"Wait a minute... is gazillion really an accounting term?" he jokingly asked.

Victoria laughed again.

"I highly doubt it, but it does work in this case. I really would like to take you over to the new house tomorrow if you can make it."

"I have an eight o'clock meeting which will probably last about an hour to an hour and a half, then I'm free. I can call you when I get out of the meeting and head up your way then if it's alright with you."

"Oh, Travis, it would work out beautifully. I'm looking forward to showing the house to you and getting your opinion on some things."

"Sounds like a plan to me. Sweet dreams, Victoria."

"Sweet dreams, Travis."

After disconnecting the call, Victoria rolled over on her side and gazed out the window at the moonlight streaming from the sky. Mental and emotional exhaustion took hold. Sweet dreams were on their way.

CHAPTER 27

Victoria was awakened by the telltale "ding" on her mobile phone sitting in the charger on the bedside table. She knew it was the text blast going out every morning from her cyclist group, specifying where and when to meet up.

She rolled over, looked at the clock, and debated whether or not to join them. It was still dark outside, but by the time she was ready, it would be light enough to ride safely. She would have plenty of time for a ride, come home, shower, eat breakfast, and call Doc about her car, all before Travis arrived around ten o'clock.

She knew a ride would be beneficial. Feeling uptight about the car incident had taken its toll on her, both mentally and physically.

Tyler and her mom were still sound asleep as she arose from bed and headed into the bathroom. Within thirty minutes, Victoria was dressed out in her gear, including her helmet and exiting the garage on her bike, clicking the remote she had in her pocket to close the overhead garage door.

She loved this time of day just before dawn. The air was clean and crisp, and she could just make out the beginning of the chittering of the awakening feathered denizens in the area. There wasn't any traffic right then, but she knew, it would soon change and was thankful for the reflectors on her bike and reflective strips on her clothing.

The meet-up point was only a half mile from the house. She checked the gears to make sure they were working properly.

Riding in the designated bike lane, she was blinded momentarily by a bright flash of lights in the mini rearview mirror attached to her helmet. A vehicle seemed to come out of nowhere behind her and startled her. She maintained her speed and position in the bike lane, noticing the vehicle was keeping pace with her.

Why weren't they passing me? An uneasy feeling went through her.

Keeping in the bike lane, she sped up, only to realize the vehicle did the same. It was impossible for her to determine what kind of vehicle it was or who was driving because the driver had his high beams on, and the lights continued to obstruct her vision.

The driver then swerved the vehicle into the bike lane and closely followed her. Within seconds, the vehicle was less than ten feet behind her and closing in. She was now in a new development area under construction, and there really wasn't anywhere to turn into. She thought about pulling off the road onto the shoulder but thought whoever was in the vehicle would have her cornered, and heaven knows what their intention was with such blatant aggressive behavior.

As she was coming to the next intersection, the vehicle revved up and bumped the back of Victoria's bike, then suddenly veered away, kicking up dust, and racing down the street, passing her as she was struggling to stay upright. It was then she noticed several members of her cycling group approaching the same intersection from the street to her right. She steered toward them, dragging her foot to regain balance. The cyclists came to a sudden stop.

"What the hell, Victoria, who was that idiot?" one of the cyclists shouted.

"I don't know," she replied, visibly shaken. "What I do know is it was deliberate. Whoever it was had every chance to pass me along the road, but instead entered the bike lane and rammed my bike, trying to either shove me off the road or run me down."

"We could see it happening when we came down our street," another rider called out.

"Listen, I think you need to get back home." Two other cyclists chimed in to say they would go with her. Besides, her bike might have been damaged, and they didn't want her stranded with some moron out there driving around.

Normally Victoria would have brushed it off, but after the ordeal with her car, she decided to accept their offer.

There was definitely an issue with her bike but nothing major. It was Victoria's sense of security that needed to be restored. After her friends saw her home and she thanked them, she stowed her bike and helmet in the garage and entered the house.

Marya was up and already getting the coffee brewing. She looked up and saw Victoria's face.

"What happened?"

Victoria considered not telling her mom but knew if someone was out to get her or—worse yet—her family, they needed to be warned.

Her mother looked aghast as Victoria detailed what happened.

"Victoria, you need to go to the police and report this. This and the other incidents. These are not coincidences. These are premeditated attacks."

Marya was usually the calm, cool, and collected one in the house, but now she was a mother tiger, her voice raising enough to make a point but not enough to awaken Tyler who was still asleep.

BY THE TIME Travis called to say he was on his way, Victoria had showered, dressed, eaten breakfast, and called Doc to get his take on what happened to her car.

She called her office to check messages and spoke with Abby at the front desk.

"How's the move going, Victoria?" Abby asked.

"Well, almost everything is packed and ready to move. Friday is the big day for both the move and furniture delivery. A good friend of mine from high school is in town on business and offered to help while he's here. He's going to help me move some of the smaller boxes over to the house before then."

"A good friend, huh?'

"Okay, Abby... yes, a good friend."

Changing the subject, Victoria asked if there was anything needing her immediate attention. Abby informed her all was quiet and wished her well with the move. Victoria didn't want to say anything to Abby about the car or bicycle incidents yet.

Marya had taken care of Tyler, getting him fed and dressed and had already left to drop him off at preschool on her way to the V.A. Rehab Center. She had offered to forego her time volunteering, but Victoria insisted she would be fine, and Travis would be at the house shortly.

Marya conceded but told Victoria she would pick up Tyler when preschool was dismissed so Victoria wouldn't need to break up her day. Marya knew Victoria had a lot of things to take care of between the move, her car, and making a police report.

Travis knew as soon as Victoria greeted him at the door something was amiss. The strain on her face and the fact she was favoring her left foot was evident.

Furrowing his brow, he asked, "Victoria, what happened?"

Victoria waved him in, and he followed her into the kitchen.

"Coffee?" she asked as he was lowering his long torso onto the counter barstool. Nodding and looking even more concerned, he started to ask again, but as she was pouring his coffee, she began her account of what happened earlier. By the time she was finished, she noticed he was clenching his hands around the coffee mug.

"I spoke with my mechanic, Doc and got a report from him." Within a heartbeat, she launched into what Doc had told her. On close inspection, there was no way the lug nuts came off by themselves. It appeared only one or two were intentionally left on each of the four wheels but were probably loosened.

"You know you have to go to the police now, don't you?"

Victoria nodded and said she had made another call earlier to the precinct and spoke with a detective, setting a time to meet and file a report around noon.

Before she could even ask, Travis informed her he was going with her... besides, her car was in the shop for repairs, and her mom was using her own car. He wasn't going to take "no" for an answer. Victoria wasn't going to argue about it. In fact, she was relieved.

Travis reached over and took her hand. "Victoria, we're going to get to the bottom of this."

Looking somewhat at a loss, "I just hope nothing else happens in the meantime."

Travis leaned back in his seat and hesitated before he asked, "Victoria, do you have any way to defend yourself?"

"I took a self-defense class a while ago... soon after I had filed for divorce... so it would have been about nine years ago. Why?"

"I'm talking about a weapon... mace, a taser, or a gun."

"I've got my Dad's old handgun. Mom brought it with her when she moved to Arizona. A couple of years ago, I took the CCW class at the nearby gun club, passed the written exam, the range exam, received the FBI clearance, and my concealed weapons permit. The last time the gun was used was at the range during the exam."

Realization set in why he was asking. Travis recognized the look of shock in her face.

"Victoria, listen to me. You need to take control of the situation. You need to be prepared to do whatever it takes to protect yourself and those you love. A gun is the last resort. Mace is temporary, and most of the time, the spray can even debilitate the one using it. A taser is safer, but it doesn't work well on some attackers. It depends on their build, if they're under the influence, and you have to be within a certain distance to them. I'm more than willing and able to take you to the gun club to get some practice in to make you feel more secure handling the gun."

Victoria was taking in everything Travis was saying. She trusted his knowledge and experience and knew he was right. Victoria jumped at the sound of her mobile phone ringing and moved to answer it.

"Hello..."

"Hey, how's the move going?"

When Victoria hesitated to respond, Robyn sensed there was something wrong. Travis motioned to Victoria to tell Robyn what was happening, and Victoria relayed the events of the past couple of days.

Robyn was speechless at first. "Oh my God, Victoria! I'm glad you're getting the police involved and hopefully, get it taken care of quickly."

Victoria mentioned Travis' help and also how she was going to take him up on his offer about a trip to the gun club. Robyn was all for it. After hearing that, Travis reached over, placed a kiss on Victoria's forehead, got up, and poured himself another cup of coffee, then sat back down on the barstool at the counter.

Robyn made a point of telling Victoria if she needed anything to give her call, and she would be contacting her again in a day or two to get an update.

After she hung up, Victoria sat quietly for a minute and raised her eyes to Travis, then got up and faced Travis

"Thank you, Travis. I usually have my act together, but all this has thrown me for a loop. I so appreciate you being here."

He took her hands and pulled her between his long legs.

"You know what I would appreciate right now?"

"No."

"This."

His lips found hers and what started as gentle coaxing turned to heated passion. When they finally pulled away, they were both breathless. Somewhere in the vicinity, seismic activity was registering on the Richter scale and setting off alarms.

"I don't know about you, but I sure needed that," he stated, somewhat winded.

Victoria smiled and nodded, enjoying the warmth of his touch and the security of his arms around her as he tightened his embrace.

THE FIRST STOP Victoria and Travis made was to see her mechanic and pick up a report from him regarding her car, addressing what he'd found. Doc had been her mechanic since she moved to the Phoenix area after college and thought of her more as a niece than a normal customer. His concern was written on his face, and as Victoria was getting back into Travis' car, Doc looked at Travis.

"You take care of her now. She means a lot to me and a lot of other people."

Travis had noticed the military tattoo on Doc's arm, and replied, "Roger that."

The next stop was the police precinct. After introductions, Detective Casey told Victoria and Travis the records of the vehicle incident were pulled, and he reviewed the reports with them.

Victoria had given the detective the report from Doc which only confirmed what the officers had written in their reports. Victoria's vehicle had certainly been tampered with, and there was a clear intention to bring harm to the driver and any passengers in the vehicle.

Victoria then relayed what had happened that morning. After writing down her account of the incident and the names of several cyclists who offered to be witnesses, the detective leaned back in his chair.

"Miss Hart... or can I call you Victoria?"

"Please do."

"Victoria, were there any other incidents prior to this? Anything causing you concern?"

Victoria hesitated, but then told the detective what happened in the parking garage a week prior when she had left work.

"Victoria, do you know of anyone who would have a grudge against you or someone who thinks you may have wronged them?"

Victoria took less than a New York minute to reply.

"Only one comes to mind... but he's incarcerated in prison out of state." She then went on to tell the detective about her ex-husband, Brandon, the domestic violence, the embezzlement, and his subsequent imprisonment.

Hearing what Victoria was saying caused Travis to clench his fists, thinking she should never have experienced the terror her ex-husband had subjected her to. Travis reached over and placed his hand on hers.

"I'm going to place into the record all you've told me, including the previous police report regarding your vehicle and the report from your mechanic. I'll be delving into the records and talking with the witnesses pertaining to both your vehicle and cycling incidents should they have any further information, such as the make and model of the vehicle trying to run you down. I promise you, I'll do my very best to find whoever wants to cause you harm. In the meantime, I want you to take as many precautionary actions as possible. Make sure you aren't in a position of vulnerability. Advise your mother of the same. Be aware of your surroundings. And if something doesn't feel right, get to a safe place as soon as possible. I'll keep you updated on what I'm able to find out. By the way, I've asked the patrols covering your area to add an extra drive-by or two." Handing Victoria a business card, the detective told both Victoria and Travis to call with any concerns, questions, or if any questionable occurrences arose.

Back in Travis' car, he reached over and took her hand.

"I know you're shaken up about all this. The detective seems confident they'll get to the bottom of it soon. Just promise me you'll heed his advice and make sure you don't put yourself in a precarious position. Have someone walk with you to your car and check it all around and underneath before you get in, and for now, please, no more cycling until this gets resolved."

Victoria nodded. She wouldn't be getting her car back from the mechanic until the next day, and Travis made himself available, telling her he had only one other appointment mid-morning on Wednesday he needed to attend, and all the time before and after, he would be at her beck and call.

Victoria welcomed the fact he was there to help.

CHAPTER 28

Friday was her big move day, but she had wanted to move as many of the small boxes over to the new house before then. Not having her car back until sometime the next day set her back a bit.

Travis lessened some of her anxiety.

"Hey, one of the reasons I rented this SUV was so I could help transport items for you. The middle seat section folds down, and we can really pack a lot of stuff back there, including Legos! It'll get done, Victoria."

Travis asked if she was hungry, and she told him her nerves were getting the best of her, wreaking havoc on her appetite. He didn't want to push it, so he pulled into an ice cream and smoothie shop.

"Your mom told me ice cream is always the best thing when things go haywire."

Victoria laughed out loud.

The rest of the afternoon was spent moving boxes and small items from Marya's house to Victoria's. While they were loading, unloading, and on the road, Victoria noticed Travis was on high alert, watching for vehicles trailing them or anyone in or out of a vehicle who seemed to be watching them.

Upon arriving at the new house, Victoria would unlock the door and disarm the security alarm, but Travis would enter first. When they left,

Travis would make sure everything was locked up, and Victoria would turn on the security. Every time the security was either turned on or turned off, Victoria would receive a notification on her mobile phone, and she had cameras installed, sending live videos directly to her phone, her laptop, and her office computer as well.

Marya had picked up Tyler at preschool earlier in the afternoon and had Tyler helping with the move, asking him to put colorful stickers on the boxes with his name written on them. He was so excited to be helping, and every time Travis and Victoria returned for another load, he was waiting by the front door.

When dinner time rolled around, they took a break. Marya had made a large turkey pot pie for them. Travis smiled when he noticed Victoria's appetite had just about returned to normal by the big helping she put on her plate.

After dinner, Victoria asked Travis if he was up for to move one more, and on his way to the door, he replied, "Head 'em up! Move 'em out!" After unloading the last load for the day at her new house, Victoria sat down on the raised hearth surrounding the fireplace in the great room.

"Penny for your thoughts," Travis said, sitting down next to her.

"Oh, just thinking about all the changes in my life the past dozen or so years and hoping nothing would happen to take away the good things, the happy things."

Travis understood what she meant. He leaned forward with his elbows on top of his knees and rested his chin on his hands.

"What life teaches us is we need to be resilient. We need to be patient. We don't always get what we want. And sometimes when we do, it's taken from us. That's where faith comes in, believing there's a reason for it to happen. It's pre-ordained. Events shaking up our lives can either make us or break us. You have strength of character, Victoria. You've already overcome challenges most people never survive. You didn't allow it to destroy you. You rose above it all."

Cocking her head toward him, Victoria whispered, "Like a Phoenix rising from the ashes." Now she understood.

Lifting his head and turning toward her, he uttered, "Exactly... and knowing what I know of you, you'll continue to rise above it all. You're an amazing woman, Victoria Hart." His hand stroked her cheek, and she pressed it to her with her hand and closed her eyes. Lifting her chin, he placed a tender kiss on her lips and pulled away, only to return with a kiss that rocketed her to her very core.

Houston, we have liftoff!

Wrapping his arms around her, he pulled her down onto the thick carpet in front of the raised hearth. Raising up on his elbows, he blazed a trail of kisses from her mouth to her neck, murmuring words of endearment. She could feel the strength of his long brawny body as he leaned over her, his hands caressing her almost reverently. She heard soft moans and realized they were emanating from within her.

While his left hand cradled her head, his right hand moved provocatively down her side, his fingers kneading the backside of her hip.

Taking his head in her hands and taking control of his lips, she bestowed him with kisses above and beyond, probing his mouth with her tongue and feeling an exhilaration when he reciprocated.

The jarring sound of a mobile phone brought them crashing back to earth, gasping for breath. Darkness had fallen, and only the lights in a hallway illuminated the room.

They both scrambled to get to their mobile phones with Victoria working her way to the kitchen counter where she laid her phone, and Travis picking up his jacket off a doorknob in the hallway to retrieve his from a pocket.

By the time Victoria got to her phone, it stopped ringing, but the caller ID was still lit. It was her friend Diana. She attempted to call her back, but her phone went directly to voice mail. A few moments later a notification popped up, telling her she had a text message from Diana.

All the message said was "Call Me. Urgent."

Travis looked at Victoria and inquired if something was wrong.

"No... I don't know... it was from my friend, Diana. I spoke to her last week, and she had hoped to come over on Saturday to help unpack. Maybe something came up, and she can't make it now. I'll try to reach her later."

Travis threw his arms around Victoria.

"It's late, and we've had a busy day. Time to drop you off at your mother's house and for me to head to the hotel. Although I would like nothing better than to spend tonight with you... all night. Tomorrow, I have a meeting in the morning, then I'll head over to take you to pick up your car. Hopefully, the repairs will be done and your car is ready for you. Then we can load up both cars and make more runs."

"Travis, are you sure? You've done so much already."

"Yes, I'm sure. I promised I would help. Besides, as I said before, the more time I get to spend with you, the better."

After locking up and setting the security system, Travis walked out to his car, scoping out the area, including the street, checking around and under the car, then waving Victoria to get into the car.

Victoria had a hunch his actions were drilled into him while in the military and on the tours of duty he had in the Middle East. While driving, he was constantly checking the rearview and side mirrors, making sure he left plenty of room between the vehicle in front of him and his car. He never took the same route either coming or going.

"Why do you check under the car?"

He hesitated before answering, "I'm not checking for a boogeyman if that's what you're thinking. Sometimes you can detect if a vehicle has been tinkered with... such as a brake line cut, leaving a puddle of fluid, or some kind of device attached such as a tracker... or... an explosive device."

Victoria's head jerked. "Oh..."

"Better safe than sorry. I don't want you getting all paranoid. From the looks of it, whoever is behind these attacks appears to be an amateur. Just promise me you'll be careful, be alert, and don't take any chances. Victoria, you're very special to me. Always remember that."

Although he remained vigilant while he was driving, he reached over and took her hand and gave it a light squeeze. When she gave him a squeeze back, he smiled, never taking his eyes off the road.

Arriving back at her mother's house, he walked her to the door, then followed her inside and was greeted by Marya.

"Well, you two have to be exhausted. Can I get you anything... ice cream maybe...?

Victoria and Travis both broke out in laughter.

"No, thank you. I would love it, but I really need to get on the road and to the hotel. I've got a meeting in the morning and need to prepare for it, plus get some beauty sleep. But I'll be by after the meeting to take Victoria to pick up her car and make more runs between the houses."

Marya wished him a good night with a hug and scurried down the hallway.

"Good night, Victoria. Please rest up. Things will get resolved. Promise me you'll have sweet dreams tonight."

"I will. How could I not... especially after... well, nothing like knocking my socks off and getting interrupted by a ringing phone, just when things were getting... interesting."

"Tell me about it," Travis teased.

"One more for the road," he said as he bent to capture her lips with full-on intensity. Pulling away and leaving Victoria breathless, he said, "Had to make it so it would last me until I see you tomorrow." Kissing her forehead, he turned and went out the door, walking with a decidedly buoyant step.

Victoria closed and locked the door, watching from the side window as he pulled away. As she turned off the light in the hallway, she leaned her back against the front door, took a deep breath and murmured, "Be still my heart."

CHAPTER 29

Victoria was lying on her left side, her head half buried in her pillow when she felt something probing her right eyelid. She gradually opened her right eye, coming eyeball to eyeball with Tyler who let out a snicker as he pulled back his finger from her face.

Tyler greeted Victoria in a loud whisper, "Good Morning, Mommy! It's time to get up."

"Mornin', Tyler."

"Gramma told me to be very quiet and see if you were awake."

"I am now," she said, pushing herself up to look at the clock on the nightstand.

"Wow, seven o'clock already. Guess Mommy was super tired. Head on back into the kitchen and tell Gramma I'll be right there, okay, Sweetie?"

"Okie-dokie!" he said, zooming out of the bedroom.

Victoria kicked off the covers and stretched, feeling muscles she didn't know she had. *Wow! I'm truly out of shape. With all the boxes and things I lifted and moved yesterday, I didn't think I'd feel this sore.*

Then she remembered the muscle strain was more likely a delayed reaction to her trying to control her bike and putting her leg out to slow down when she almost got run down. *Hopefully, a hot shower after breakfast will ease the soreness.*

Marya had everything well in hand in the kitchen, especially Tyler who was busy eating his scrambled eggs and bacon.

"How d'you sleep, Honey?"

"As well as can be expected. At first, I had a difficult time falling asleep, but then I must have really zonked out. Sure can feel some aches and pains today. I'll take a hot shower after breakfast to get the kinks out."

"Instead of a shower, why don't you soak in the tub with some bath salts? That's what we recommend for our patients after an intense physical therapy session."

"Hey, sounds pretty good, Mom. Thanks."

Tyler had finished eating, and Marya scooted him off to his bedroom to get cleaned up and dressed for preschool, reminding him his clothes were already laid out on the chair in his room.

Victoria threw a smoothie together with protein powder, fruit, honey, oats, and almond milk. "This should get me through to lunch."

An hour later, Marya took off with Tyler to drop him at his preschool, then head to the rehab center in the V.A. complex.

Victoria called her office and checked in with Abby again, then checked her phone for messages, hoping to hear from the detective. There was only one text message from Doc, saying her car would be ready after nine-thirty.

She tried Diana's number again, and again it went straight to voice mail, so Victoria left her a message. She didn't want to call Diana at work since she still was employed at Victoria's ex-father-in-law's accounting firm. Except for Diana and a handful of other employees who worked with Victoria while she was there, she had cut all ties with anyone else at the "Barkley" firm.

Over the years, Diana and Victoria had gotten together socially, and Diana told her Ross Barkley still worked at the firm but lost his officer position, most of his staff, and was moved to an office on a lower floor. His salary had been cut substantially, and his standing in the company and community was, for all intents and purposes, no longer viable, including their membership at the country club.

According to Diana, the Barkleys were in bankruptcy court, and their home, which was rumored to now be owned by the bank, was currently on the market. Claudine Barkley was nowhere to be seen. No more extravagant parties or luncheons, binge shopping at luxury shops, limousines, private jets, or day spas. Oh, how the mighty had fallen.

Victoria tried to summon up some sympathy for the Barkley's, but after what she went through, it just wasn't going to happen.

Victoria took her mother's advice and relaxed in the jetted tub with scented bath salts, the rippling and churning water bringing memories back to a time just over five years ago. Leaning back in the tub, she could almost feel his touch again. Her hand touched her face and stroked her neck, running over her shoulder and down her arm.

Oh my God, what am I doing thinking about Drew?

She suddenly sat upright, causing the water to nearly splash over the edge of the tub. She hit the button to turn off the jets and turned the lever to drain the tub, stepping out carefully onto the bath mat. Grabbing a towel, she briskly dried herself, trying to erase the vestiges of a phantom caress.

She tossed on her robe, walked over to the counter, and wiped the fogged mirror, taking note of the face looking back at her—a face sometimes she didn't recognize.

Am I the same girl who once laughed with glee as she skied the slopes in northern Arizona? Am I the same girl who walked down the aisle to a man I thought was going to be my "forever?" Am I the same girl who had been made promises only to be disappointed? Am I the same girl who trusted, then was betrayed twice?

Sometimes, she felt like a fraud. No matter how many steps she had taken forward or how many successes she found in her life, there were times when the past hurts, the past disappointments, and the past mistakes always seemed to pull her back into a dark place filled with self-doubt and self-recrimination. And now, intense fear was trying to get a foothold in her life.

She raised her eyes to look again into the mirror.

Realizing where this demonic void was coming from, she shouted, "NO! Not now. Not ever again will I be a victim."

All those counseling sessions during and after the divorce—trying to put herself together again, restoring her self-esteem and self-confidence, realizing her self-worth—weren't in vain.

She was knocked down before, and she got up. These recent attacks were playing with her mind. Yes, she was afraid, but fear can be a good thing too. It can keep you alert, keep you aware, and in turn, keep you safe.

She wasn't going to hide, but at the same time, she wasn't going to take chances either. She would do anything to protect herself and those she loved—at all costs. She would be prepared.

By the time Travis arrived, Victoria was dressed and ready to go. He immediately noticed something different about her—her look of determination, of strength, and something more, but he couldn't put his finger on it.

"Travis, after we pick up my car, I have a favor to ask you."

"Sure, Victoria, anything."

IT WAS WELL after one o'clock in the afternoon when they made their first trip over to the new house with both of their cars fully loaded with things from her mother's house.

After organizing some of the boxes so they wouldn't be in the way when the movers and the furniture store deliverymen got there on Friday, they sat on the floor in the great room. Travis and Victoria both started to talk at the same time and stopped.

"You first, Victoria."

"No, you first, Travis," she laughed.

"Okay. I saw your mom this morning."

"You did? Where?"

"At the V.A. It's where I had the appointment. I'm working with a couple of vets undergoing treatment there, and I happened to meet with him in one of the physical therapy centers. Boy, do they love her there. And you can tell she really enjoys being with them. She introduced me to her friend, Brock who volunteers on his days off as a captain with the Phoenix Fire Department."

"Funny, you should mention him. As a matter of fact, mom told me Brock and a couple of his firefighter buddies are going to help on Friday. I'm renting a small U-Haul to move the pieces of furniture going from mom's house to mine, along with some other things, and Brock offered his services for both loading, unloading, and driving the truck. He's even going to pick it up for me Friday morning."

"I think your Mom picked a winner there... and vice versa."

"So, you got the same feeling I got. There's something more there than what meets the eye?"

"Oh, yeah. Definitely."

"Then it's probably a good idea I'm moving into my own house and giving my mom some space."

"I'm sure your mom will miss having you and Tyler around, but you're still going to be close by and more than likely, will still be seeing one another often."

"We've already talked about me dropping Tyler off at school in the mornings and her picking him up in the afternoons. She'll either take him to her house where I would get him after work, or she bring him to my house and wait there for me to get home. I want her to have her free time to spend... with whoever. Next year, Tyler will be going to all-day kindergarten, so it will be a bit easier."

"I'm sure everything will work out."

"So, you're working with the vets on legal matters. You mentioned a while ago you did pro bono work for them."

"Yep. It's my way of giving back. My trip here was actually three-fold. I needed to meet up with them and work out legal matters, and, of course, I wanted to come see you."

"And the third reason?"

"Well, it's not cast in concrete yet, but I've been offered an opportunity to join an affiliated law firm here. They're expanding the one they already have in Arizona. I would need to pass the Arizona State Bar exam and update my knowledge on Arizona statutes. While I'd be going through that process, I would have legal reciprocity to assist the vets. But like I said, it's not a done deal yet."

Victoria was mentally grasping what he was saying, and it certainly shed new light on things between them.

Victoria and Travis spent the remainder of the afternoon making additional trips back and forth between the houses.

She still hadn't heard back from Diana and was becoming more and more concerned. It wasn't like her at all. She normally would make contact within a short time after Victoria left a message.

Victoria checked her phone again, but nothing from Diana. She noticed she missed a call from Detective Casey and hurriedly hit the call button. Another detective answered and told Victoria the detective working her case was out on an investigation. Victoria left her number and asked to have the detective call her back.

Victoria and Travis had returned to Marya's house with their cars empty, discussing whether they should load up again or take a break when Marya pulled in with Tyler. Tyler immediately got out of the car and ran to give his mom a hug, then went over to Travis and held out his little hand. Travis knelt on one knee, took Tyler's hand, and gave it a gentle shake.

"How was school today, Tyler?" Travis asked.

"We had Show-and-Tell, and I brought photos of the horses we saw at the river."

"What did everyone say when they saw the pictures?"

"They thought it was pretty cool, and they all want to go there. But I told them if they go, they have to obey the rules."

"What are the rules, Tyler?"

"Well, you can't get too close, or you'll scare them, especially the baby horses. And you can't feed them. They have their own food to eat, and some of it's in the river. We saw them eating it, and it looks like big green vines. If you give the horses something else to eat, it would probably make them sick."

"Wow! I'm impressed, Tyler. You learned a lot from going to see the horses at the river."

"Yep! Mommy knew all about it!"

Travis looked over at Victoria. "You have a very smart mommy, Tyler."

Marya motioned Tyler into the house, commenting about rustling something up to eat.

CHAPTER 30

A little while later, they were in the kitchen when Victoria's mobile phone rang—Diana.

"Diana, thank heavens, I thought you fell off the face of the earth."

Victoria could hear the alarm in her voice and listened to her as the doorbell rang. Marya walked over, opened the door, saw a police car out in front of the house and a police officer and another person standing there. After they introduced themselves, Marya escorted them into the kitchen, noticing Victoria's face was terror-stricken.

Victoria and Travis immediately recognized Detective Casey who was investigating her case. Something was up by the look on the detective's troubled face.

"Diana, hold on a second."

"Tyler, would you do Mommy a favor and go back to your room and surprise me by making something special with your Legos?"

She didn't have to ask twice, he raced to his bedroom.

"Diana, the police are here, and I'm going to put you on speaker phone."

From the look on the detective's face, he knew it would be another piece to his investigation. The puzzle pieces were coming together.

Clicking the speaker button, she told Diana, "Okay, you're on speaker now. Tell me again what you told me."

"At work the other day, some of the staff were talking about seeing Brandon. I told them it was impossible because he's in prison out of state and his sentence wasn't completed. They insisted he was in the offices, and in particular, his father's office, and they were having a heated argument. That's when I tried to reach you.

"When I left work, I was walking to my car in the parking garage, and out of the blue, I got mugged. I was knocked down and hit my head on the pavement. I still had my shoulder strap of my purse around me and felt someone try to roll me over and try to rip my bag from me. I was dazed but managed to reach up and hold tight to the strap. Then I got slugged. The next thing I knew, I woke up in a haze and paramedics were around me. And my purse was gone.

"Victoria, I'm sure it was Brandon even though whoever it was wore a large, dark hoodie. Brandon knew how close we were when we worked together and that I picked you up at the hospital when he hurt you and helped you get an attorney."

"Oh, Diana, I'm so sorry. Where are you now?"

"I'm safe. I couldn't go back to my condo because my keys were in my purse, along with all my personal information, including my address book. I'm staying with a friend until I can get the locks changed and get all my IDs reissued. I had the mobile phone company cancel and block my old mobile phone and got a new phone. Oh... and by the way, the very next day I was let go from the firm, stating my position was being eliminated."

"What? You oversaw all the paralegals and legal admins in the legal department. How could they? Well, I guess Ross Barkley still has some influence there."

"Not to worry. They did give me severance, more than likely to cover their butts. I have feelers out, and I actually had been looking to move away from that environment."

"Diana, I'm going to let you go, but I'll make sure the detective has your contact information. Please stay in touch with me."

"Will do. Please take care of yourself, Victoria. We know how dangerous Brandon can be. No telling what he might try to do."

Victoria had wanted to tell Diana more about the incidents she experienced but wanted to talk to the detective first. After she hung up with Diana, she looked over at the detective who was busy writing in a notebook.

Looking up at Victoria, the detective said, "That's why we're here. I found out Brandon Barkley is out of prison on early release. You were to be notified, but someone dropped the ball. How it happened, we don't know yet. His early release certainly wasn't for good behavior. He got into trouble while in prison and was moved from minimum to maximum security but then back again to minimum security. Although we don't have direct proof it was Brandon who tampered with your car or tried to run you down while cycling, it's my opinion he had his hand in it somehow."

"And the person I saw in my office parking garage?"

"Very possible. But the security camera footage we were able to obtain is grainy, and the lighting was poor, so it's difficult to make out the facial characteristics. At least we know someone was definitely there. We also found it interesting your office property management service told us they had just replaced all the lights in the parking garage the week prior, and on the day you said someone was there, some of the new lights had their wires cut, and the property management had to reconnect them a day or two later."

Travis and Marya were listening intently, along with Victoria.

"So, now what happens?" Victoria anxiously asked. "I can't go into hiding or live in a bubble and neither can my family."

Travis went to Victoria's side and laid his hand on her shoulder.

"First off, with your permission, we'll process a restraining order. As far as we can tell, he definitely returned here to Arizona, and we're trying to pinpoint the exact date he arrived here. He's supposedly living with his parents at their home. After I spoke with his parole officer, he's checking on him almost daily, especially when I shared with him what has been happening to you. I need to check to see what it would take to get an order to have an ankle monitor put on him. I'll have the squad beef up the patrols around here too."

With a concerned look, Victoria said, "I'm moving into my new home on Friday."

"Where is it?" the detective asked.

After Victoria gave him the address, he excused himself and went into the other room to make a phone call. He came back shortly and advised Victoria there would be additional patrols at her new house as well. If it was proven Brandon was the instigator, there would be a twenty-four-hour police presence at both homes until he was incarcerated. The detective was positive after the review of circumstances, there would be no bail, and additional time would be added to the original sentence with no provision for parole with additional charges being made.

The detective told Victoria he was concerned about her security when she was at work.

Victoria advised him she really needed to continue her work and would take as many safety measures as possible to protect herself. Knowing glances passed between Travis and Victoria.

As the detective and the officer were leaving, the detective said he would be in touch often to update her, and she was to call with any questions or if something seemed amiss.

Marya had swiftly disappeared into her bedroom, and Victoria could hear her talking to someone on the phone. She returned to the kitchen just as Tyler came down the hallway, saying his surprise was ready.

Victoria walked back to his room and saw he had built yet another masterpiece and praised him, taking him in her arms and holding him tight. He was her everything, and she vowed no matter what, she'd never let any harm come to him.

A PALL SETTLED over the Hart household. The adults tried to keep things light-hearted. Travis asked if it would be alright if he stayed the night, sleeping on the sofa. Victoria mentally debated whether or not he should, but after the urging of her mother and Travis... then Tyler, she caved in.

His excuse was they could get an early start on unpacking at the new house, emptying as many boxes as possible, and recycling them to make room for Friday's big move. Victoria knew darn well Travis really wanted to stay as an extra line of protection. Well, primarily it seemed like it was his reason.

Later in the evening, they were all enjoying bowls of ice cream in the kitchen when Tyler innocently asked, "Mommy, if Travis is going to stay over, why doesn't he sleep with you in your big bed instead of the sofa?"

A unified gasp was heard. Victoria had just taken a big spoonful of ice cream and had to slap her hand across her mouth to prevent the cold confection from flying out.

Travis cleared his throat, and Marya snickered.

Tyler looked around the table at the adults and just shrugged.

Travis saved the day. "Tyler, I snore like a grizzly bear and... I'm sure I would keep your mommy up all night."

He added the last part with a grin, looking over at Victoria.

Tyler seemed satisfied with Travis' answer and went about finishing his ice cream.

"Okay, Ty, it's your bedtime. Head to the bathroom, get washed up, and brush your teeth," Victoria said, adding, "Mommy will be there shortly."

Marya had kept her head down, but Victoria could tell she was laughing inside from the shaking of her shoulder and the sassy smile on her face when she looked up.

Travis' look wasn't much better.

"You two are no help at all. I'm not sure who the adults are here."

Then to Victoria's utter amazement, they both broke out into laughter and gave each other a high five.

"Oh great! I'm surrounded by children this evening."

Travis sat back in his chair and challenged her, "I wouldn't count on it, Victoria." Then he presented her with a wink and a waggle of his eyebrows.

Victoria felt herself turning red and fanned herself with her napkin. Rising from her chair, she said, "I'll go get Tyler tucked in. You two can... clear the dishes." Peals of laughter echoed from the kitchen as she walked down the hallway to Tyler's room.

Once Tyler was settled in and his prayers finished, Victoria gave him a loving kiss on his forehead. As she closed his door, she quietly said a prayer.

The good-natured kidding changed the atmosphere, and everyone seemed more at ease but nonetheless guarded.

Marya peeked out the front window and reported there was indeed a patrol car parked outside. Travis didn't want to sound any alarms, but he voiced if Brandon saw the police presence at the house, he might change his tactics and try to do something elsewhere.

He had to get back to Chicago on Sunday and expressed his concerns about Victoria going back to work at her office the following Monday.

After Marya had gone to bed, Victoria went into the linen closet and pulled out sheets, a blanket, and a pillow. Travis watched as she pulled the back pillows off the sofa and laid the sheets down on the wide seats, tossing the blanket on top. She fluffed the pillow and put it at one end of the sofa.

"Do you really snore, Travis?" she asked innocently.

"I have no idea. I never stayed awake to listen," he answered with a smirk. "Why do you ask?"

As she was smoothing the blanket, she replied, "Well, I never slept with a grizzly bear and just wondered."

Her smart-ass smile didn't get past Travis, and he jumped up from his chair at the table and gently threw her down on what now was a neatly made bed on the sofa.

"I guess there's only one way to stop your smart mouth."

Travis ambushed her lips and did a full-on plundering of their soft flesh. Victoria felt herself falling off the edge of the world and clung to his kisses, reciprocating with a need and desire to draw him into her. Again Drew's face came into her mind.

A roller coaster of emotions was beginning to overwhelm Victoria. The incidents with her car and the cycling and realizing Brandon might be out for revenge were overwhelming to her—add the stress of the move, mentally and emotionally acknowledging Travis was becoming more to her, and Drew's claims, Victoria's heart was thundering, and her body was tensing up.

Travis could feel her becoming taut and pulled away, looking down at her with a concerned look.

"Victoria, what is it? What's wrong?"

"Travis, I'm so..." Taking a deep breath, she continued, "If we have something... you and I... I want it to be real, not because of everything happening now. I don't want you to be caught in the crosshairs of all this drama. I've become very fond of you, Travis. I'm grateful you're here, but there's so much going on right now. I've made so many mistakes in the past, I don't want to make another one, based on outside influences. I know I'm not making much sense. It's so difficult to…"

"Victoria, you're under a lot of strain right now. Actually, that's an understatement. I don't know how you've managed to keep it together. I certainly don't want you to ever think I would take advantage of you in such a vulnerable state. I care about you… a lot. More than you realize. As much as I would want to take our relationship to another level, let's just take it a step at a time. Take it slow. But I promise you if the opportunity presents itself and you're okay with it, I want to show you just how much I do care."

Victoria had tears in her eyes, thinking how lucky she was to have such an extraordinary friend and maybe someday more than that. She was in the arms of someone who put her well-being first instead of his own. Someone who hadn't broken a promise. Someone she could trust.

As her tears flowed down her cheeks, Travis rose, lifted her in his arms, and carried her to her bedroom where he laid her on her bed. Giving her a gentle kiss on her lips, then her forehead, he covered her with the bed comforter.

"Sweet Dreams, Victoria… no harm will come to you or your family if I can help it," Travis said softly as he quietly closed her bedroom door.

CHAPTER 31

T he next morning, Victoria woke to the aroma of brewing coffee and the sounds of conversation coming from the kitchen. How she managed to sleep through the night was a wonder to her. She still wore her clothes from the day before and went into the bathroom to remove them and take a quick shower.

After throwing on underwear, a pair of sweatpants, and a sweatshirt, blow drying her hair and putting it up in a ponytail, she entered the kitchen to find Tyler and Travis sitting at the kitchen table, in deep discussion about wild horses. Marya was busy at the stove, whipping up breakfast.

"Morning, Mommy!" Tyler jumped down from his chair and threw his arms around Victoria.

"Good Morning, Tyler. That's quite a morning welcome."

Taking Victoria's hand, he led her over to the table, maneuvering her to sit beside Travis who was displaying an affectionate grin.

"Good morning, Victoria. I hope you were able to get some decent sleep," Travis commented as his appreciative eyes traveled over her.

"I think I did. I felt so mentally and emotionally exhausted, my body must have just gone into numb mode and shut down. I remember closing my eyes, then the next thing I remember is waking up a short time ago."

Marya came over to the table, and after placing the platters heaping with breakfast sausages and scrambled eggs in the middle for everyone to help themselves, she gave Victoria a loving hug.

Before Victoria could get up to pour herself some coffee, her mom placed a cup of the hot brew in her hand. Victoria looked up at her mom and received a warm smile and a kiss on the cheek.

"Victoria, I think it best if I stayed home today. I'm really feeling a bit under the weather, and I think I'd like some company as well. I thought maybe Tyler would like to stay home as well to help me finish up on packing... especially all those Legos," Marya added, along with a wink to Victoria.

Tyler's ears perked up, and he looked pleadingly at Victoria.

"Is that okay with you, Tyler?"

Giving Victoria two thumbs up, Tyler responded, "You betcha!"

Victoria had purchased rolls of drawer and shelf liner for the new house and had planned to get it taken care of before the move. She knew enlisting the help of her mom, it would all get done in time.

"You know, Mom, I think it's a great idea. And later, if you're up to it, you can come with us to the new house and help me line some drawers and shelving."

Victoria and Travis both knew what Marya was up to—keeping the family together, keeping them safe.

"Oh, and by the way, Brock is going to come by as well, possibly with a couple of friends to size up the move tomorrow," Marya said, raising an eyebrow, so only Victoria and Travis noticed.

"Tyler, Honey, I'll call the preschool and let them know you won't be there today and probably not tomorrow as well because it's our big move day."

"Yay! It means I get to spend more time with Travis!"

Travis and Victoria exchanged looks and smiled.

After finishing her meal, Victoria told her mom she would clean up the kitchen since Marya had made them all a wonderful breakfast.

Travis chimed in, "I'll help, four hands are better than two."

WITH THE DISHES done and the kitchen put back in order, Victoria wandered over to the side windows near the front door and looked out. Travis came up behind her.

"Are they out there?"

"Yep. Still there. It feels so strange having the police guarding us, watching us. I don't want Tyler getting alarmed. I want him to feel safe. I don't know what to tell him if and when he asks why the police are out front. He's very aware of things, and I know he's going to ask, eventually."

Laying his hand on her shoulder, he whispered, "Hopefully the detective will get some answers soon and resolve this, then there won't be a need for the protection or an explanation."

"We can only hope," Victoria stated with a degree of trepidation.

Travis gave her shoulder a gentle squeeze, and she looked up into his eyes and found understanding.

Only a few moments passed before the silence was broken by Tyler pushing a box down the hallway from his room. In big bold marker the words "TYLER'S LEGOS – BOX #1" was emblazoned on the sides and the top.

"I guess we know what's in that box. I wonder how many more there are," Victoria commented.

The rest of the morning was spent packing, sealing and labeling boxes, then staging them near the front door and the door leading to the garage to be loaded into the cars.

Travis could bring in the smaller boxes, and Tyler could help by directing where the boxes would go. Yet another reason why the labeling was done in large bold lettering.

By noon, the loaded cars had arrived at the new house with Travis, Victoria, and Marya noticing a police presence at the entrance to the cul-de-sac. Moments later, a crew cab pickup and an SUV pulled into the cul-de-sac. Brock got out of the SUV and waved at the officers in the patrol car while two well-built gentlemen exited the pickup. Victoria noticed both vehicles had firefighter decals in the windows.

Marya exclaimed, "The cavalry is here! And, my oh my, aren't they a sight for these eyes?"

Brock greeted Marya with a very affectionate hug, then looked a bit sheepishly at Victoria.

Victoria put her arms out, motioning for him to come toward her, and she gave him a hug, bringing on a beaming smile.

Brock reached out his hand to Travis.

"Travis, it's good to see you here, and thanks for all you're doing," Brock said with a nod of understanding. Brock went on to introduce the two men who had arrived with him as his buddies Riley and Jamie, who also were firefighters.

Tyler stood in awe as he was dwarfed by the muscle-bound men, including Travis.

"Wow! All you guys are so big!" he exclaimed, causing the men to laugh.

Travis reached down and picked Tyler up, putting him up on his shoulders. "Someday, Tyler, you're going to be just as big as us."

As Victoria unlocked the door and turned off the security alarm, she and Marya, Brock, and Travis, with Tyler holding on tight atop Travis' shoulders, entered the house.

Riley and Jamie went back to their pickup and grabbed a large cooler out of the truck bed, along with several large, flat boxes and a grocery bag.

Brock explained since it was around noon, everyone was probably a bit hungry. Brock, Riley, and Jamie unloaded the cooler filled with cold bottled water. Marya and Victoria emptied the grocery bag containing paper plates, napkins, and plastic ware. The flat boxes were opened to reveal a variety of pizzas. Since there was more than enough to go around, Brock and Travis carried out a couple of full plates and bottles of cold water to the patrol car out on the street, for which they received hearty thanks.

The guys gathered and discussed the move the next day as if it was a military operation. They planned when the moving van would be picked up and by who, how many hand trucks and furniture dollies would be needed, and how many mover's blankets were required to protect the furniture while being transported.

Victoria and her mother had made a list of the pieces of furniture to be moved from Marya's house to Victoria's house, where they were currently located in Marya's house, and where they would be placed in the new house.

The guys walked through the new house to familiarize themselves with the layout. Victoria watched as Travis fit right in with these guys. She had found out they were all ex-military and worked seamlessly as a team while plotting out the move. They even joked about naming the move "Operation Tyler" which, of course, just made Tyler's day.

Sometime during the afternoon, she noticed she hadn't seen Travis for a while. When she asked where he was, Brock was quick to answer that Travis needed to pick something up and would be back shortly. About an hour later, Travis returned.

Victoria received calls from the various delivery companies servicing the furniture stores, confirming arrival times the next day and advised the guys so they would be aware. Brock pulled a notepad out of his pocket and jotted something down.

Wow... this really is like a military operation!

Victoria and her mom finished up the shelf and drawer lining and decided to unpack a couple of the smaller boxes containing towels and linens for the bathrooms, thinking they would probably be using them soon.

Next, they opened the boxes containing kitchen utensils and began placing them in the organizers in the kitchen drawers. There were so many more of the smaller boxes to open, but they elected to push the pause button and take a break.

It was almost five-thirty, and they knew "Operation Tyler" would be an early and very busy day and didn't want to get burned out. Besides, it was time to eat, then for Tyler to get ready for bed. Victoria doubted Tyler would get to bed on time since he was so wound up about the move.

Riley and Jamie called it a day and told Victoria they would give Brock a lift to the truck rental center to pick up the moving truck early the next morning and follow him to Marya's house. After they left, Brock pulled Marya aside, wrapped his arms around her, and gave her a gentle kiss.

"See you in the morning, Honey," he whispered and walked to his SUV. Victoria watched as her mother raised her fingers to her lips and smiled. Yes, there was a lot more between Marya and Brock, and it made Victoria smile.

A short while later, Victoria set the security system, locked up her house, and left with Tyler, Marya, and Travis. As they pulled into her mother's driveway, they couldn't help but notice the patrol car parked up the street. Victoria made a mental note to thank the detective for all he was doing to ensure their safety.

Tyler had nearly fallen asleep in the car, so Travis walked over to Victoria's car, picked him up, carrying him into the house.

"I have a hunch between all the scurrying around he did and his six pieces of pizza at lunch, plus the one he had before we left the new house, it has totally crashed him," Travis said.

"I think you're right. Let's just put him in bed. Tomorrow's going to be a busier day for him. His new bedroom furniture is going to be delivered, and it's all he's been talking about. Some of the pieces may need to be assembled, and I'm sure he's going to supervise as much as possible," Victoria said quietly so as not to rouse Tyler.

Travis carried Tyler into his bedroom and laid him on his bed, drawing the covers up around him. Victoria watched with admiration and something else she couldn't comprehend. She felt the prickle of tears in her eyes and quickly bent her head, wiping them away.

She walked over to Tyler's sleeping form and laid a kiss on his forehead, then she and Travis left the room, closing the door quietly behind them.

Marya was in the kitchen, throwing together something to eat for the three of them.

"Victoria, Travis is staying the night... or maybe more. It was my idea... and Brock's. We discussed it earlier, and I know I would feel better if he was here, and besides, then he wouldn't have to drive back and forth to a hotel."

It wasn't just a comment from Marya, it was a directive. Victoria knew better when her mother issued an assertion like that, there was nothing to do but acquiesce.

"Your mom is quite convincing. I ran over to the hotel and picked up my things this afternoon. If it's not okay, I understand."

Before Victoria could answer, her mother piped up.

"And Travis is going to sleep in my bed, and I'm bunking with you, Victoria. The sofa is no place for a big guy like Travis to sleep."

"I... No... It's fine, Mom." Victoria added jokingly, "And besides, now you'll have a man sleeping in your bed!"

Travis waggled his brows toward Marya.

Victoria thought she was being funny but noticed her mom was turning several shades of red and overheard her mom whispering under her breath.

"It hasn't been that long."

It didn't get missed by Travis either, and he and Victoria exchanged glances. Yes, it definitely was time for Victoria to get a place of her own and none too soon.

After pasta and a salad, they worked together and got the kitchen cleaned up.

"Any room for ice cream?" Marya asked.

Victoria and Travis looked at another and bust out laughing.

"Of course," Travis said. "Who would possibly turn down ice cream?"

Even though there was still an undercurrent of tension about the events surrounding the car and cycling incidents and her friend Diana, Victoria looked around the table as they sat, dipping into their bowls of ice cream and felt a tranquility come over her. She knew how fleeting the calm could be and sent up a silent prayer this peace would be lasting.

Marya rose from the table and placed her empty bowl and spoon into the sink.

"Mom, I'll take care of the dishes. You head to bed. We have a long day tomorrow, and we all need to get our sleep. And you want to look your best for Brock, don't you?" Victoria sassed.

Marya shook her head, admonished her with a wagging index finger, and walked down to her bedroom to gather her nightclothes. As Travis and Victoria cleaned up the dessert dishes, they heard Marya exiting her bedroom and going into Victoria's.

Victoria was wiping down the counter when Travis came up behind her, wrapping his arms around her. No words passed between them as she leaned back and snuggled into him. Her exposed neck was a target for his lips as he bent his head.

"I don't suppose you sleepwalk during the night, do you?" Travis murmured in her ear.

Victoria had to chuckle, "No, but I'm kind of wishing I did."

Turning her to face him, he bent and gave her brief gentle kiss.

"Just in case you do, make a left turn at the end of the hallway... but if not, I'll see you in the morning. Sweet Dreams, Victoria." Travis released her, turned and left the kitchen, picking up his suitcase near the hallway and walking to Marya's bedroom.

Victoria knew she was getting in deep with Travis. She also realized she had so much going on with the move and the incidents, now wasn't the right time. She needed time. Time to resolve things. Time to clear the slate. Time to make sure what she was feeling was real. She knew she cared for Travis... a lot.

But was it enough? Was it out of gratitude? Yes, he made me feel things. Things making her feel warm, secure, and loved. But—yes, there was a "but," and she just couldn't put her finger on it—there was a missing piece that would complete her jigsaw puzzle life.

She thought she had it before—twice before, as a matter of fact. The first time it was pretense, the second time it a deception... until proven differently. The emotional and physical haven she felt now... would it be enough? She had her doubts.

She wanted a certain something, a certain thrill, the longing she felt only once before. As a tear fell, she realized only one person made her feel that way. Made her feel totally open, entirely uninhibited, completely safe, and perfectly loved—and perfectly whole. But until confirmed otherwise, it too was just a fantasy.

She still had those moments, especially at night, where memories flashed, and her heart beat double time, and Drew's face and touch were there. No matter how hard she tried, she couldn't shake those recollections nor the ache spreading through her core.

Victoria checked the locks on the doors and turned off the lights. Just before entering her bedroom, she looked down the hallway to where Travis was sleeping. Breathing a deep sigh, she turned the knob on her bedroom door and entered. Something told her sleep would not come easily tonight.

CHAPTER 32

"Operation Tyler" began bright and early on Friday. It was a clear, bright day with temperatures in the seventies.

Travis had already showered, dressed, and was in the kitchen, starting up the coffee maker with Tyler sitting at the island counter, drawing a picture.

Marya had awakened and was already back in her own bedroom, changing clothes.

As expected, sleep was fitful for Victoria. She took a quick shower, gathered her long hair into a ponytail, and threw on her underwear, a pair of jeans, and an old NAU sweatshirt.

Walking through the house, she stopped near the front window and saw the squad car just up the street. As she entered the kitchen, Travis put a cup of coffee in her hand and gave her a kiss on the forehead. His look said it all. He didn't have a good night's sleep either, and Victoria was sure he noted the dark circles under her eyes.

Sounds out on the driveway indicated a rather large vehicle had arrived. Sure enough, it was Brock and his guys. Marya must have heard them as well and came into the kitchen.

Marya had removed a quiche from the freezer the night before and put it in the refrigerator to thaw, and now, it was going into the microwave to heat up. She pulled out a couple of plates from the cabinets and stacked them on the counter with utensils. Fresh fruit was laid out, along with a container of yogurt. She insisted everyone have something to eat before they started. And there was absolutely no arguing with her about it.

Riley and Jamie had brought two huge coolers filled with water bottles and ice. They planned on leaving one at Marya's house and taking the other to Victoria's.

After everyone had a bite to eat, Brock went over to Tyler and picked him up.

"Okay, Tyler, we're ready. All you have to do is give us the order to begin 'Operation Tyler.' Are you ready?" Brock asked.

"Yes, Sir!" Tyler saluted Brock. "Let's do it."

Victoria couldn't help smiling and had to stifle a giggle.

The move was going like clockwork. The guys loaded the rental truck, being very careful with the treasured heirloom furniture pieces being loaded first. Then larger boxes and other pieces of furniture were loaded. Only a few other things were left to be moved, and they would go on the second and last load.

Victoria noted her bike would be going on the last load and looked forlornly at the rear damage. She knew she would have to make time to get it over to the bike shop in the next week or two. Travis noticed her reaction as she looked at the bike and went to her, throwing his arms around her. He knew she was thinking about the incident when he saw her biting her lip.

"Hey, about tomorrow, if we get a break in the action from the move, we can haul the bike over to the bike shop and have them fix it."

Victoria nodded. There he was again. Travis to the rescue.

Surprisingly, the deliveries from the furniture stores all came on time, and the pieces of furniture were in place.

Tyler was beside himself with joy with his new bedroom furniture and invited each and every one of them to go into his bedroom to see it after it was assembled and put in place.

By four o'clock in the afternoon, everything needing to be moved had been moved, and everything to be delivered was in place in Victoria's house.

Unpacking the remaining boxes, putting up curtains, draperies, and blinds, hanging artwork and pictures was next on the agenda, all of which could be done at a leisurely pace.

Riley and Jamie followed Brock over to the truck rental center to return the truck, then they all returned to the house, carrying takeout containers filled with hot dogs, Italian beef sandwiches, and fries.

Victoria cornered Brock and tried to give him money for the food, but he refused. When Victoria first called in the order for the truck rental a week prior, she had given them her credit card number, but when the receipt came up on her mobile phone, it had a different number. When she asked Brock about it, he told her it was already taken care of and for her to consider it a house warming gift. She was so moved, she threw her arms around Brock and gave him a big kiss on his cheek.

Marya stood off to the side with a smile on her face. Victoria looked at her and winked.

With the patio furniture delivered and set up out on the patio around the pool, everyone opted to sit outside and enjoy their meal.

Tyler ran around, pointing out different areas of the back yard. He knew his mom wanted to put in a raised vegetable and herb garden and explained in detail what would be planted. The landscaper had done a wonderful job prepping those areas.

The outdoor kitchen setup was ready to go and connected for gas, water, and electricity. The outdoor security system and lighting had already been activated. Victoria had several other cameras installed as well. She hated the thought of having to make these security measures part of her life, but the world was changing, and she would do anything to protect those she loved.

She knew she needed to spend time with Tyler talking about security. He already knew about "stranger danger" and how to dial 911, but she wanted to go over things about the house security and the "what ifs."

Victoria caught a bit of conversation between Tyler, Travis, and Brock. Something about a dog. She had talked with Tyler about getting a dog but wanted to hold off a bit and get settled. Then she would need to decide about access for the pooch to get in and out of the house. She had heard stories about doggie doors not being as safe and secure and wanted to check out other options. Travis noticed she was listening and waved her over.

"Brock mentioned an electronic doggie door which is triggered by the dog's collar when the dog gets near the opening, allowing it to go in and out. We can check into it if you like."

Tyler was all enthused, and Victoria made sure he understood things needed to get settled around the house first and made a point of telling Tyler it would more than likely be a rescue pet who needed a home.

Riley and Jamie asked if they could help put window treatments up, especially for the privacy factor. Some of the windows already had large white wooden shutters, but others were totally bare. Victoria had purchased a six-foot ladder and an electric drill, and with her direction, the guys went to work, installing brackets and rods where needed.

By nine o'clock, Victoria told everyone to call it quits. Marya told them all to come into the kitchen for dessert. She had laid out a spread of ice cream with all the fixings. Victoria had another flashback to a time and place over five years ago.

"Holy Cow, Marya," Brock exclaimed as he patted his flat stomach. "You're going to put the pounds on me!"

Marya looked at him and said sassily, "I'm sure you'll find some way to work it off," and realizing what she spoke out loud, ducked her head.

Silence followed, then a snicker came out of Victoria who quickly disappeared around the corner.

By the time they finished, it was way past Tyler's bedtime, and Victoria walked him down to his bedroom. Marya had made sure the linens were already on the bed and ready for him. Tyler washed up, and Victoria helped him into his superhero pajamas. Marya came into the room, and Tyler said his prayers, yawning in between each phrase. He was tuckered out from Operation Tyler.

Since this was all new to him, Victoria left a night light on near the door and quietly exited the room with Marya.

Riley and Jamie bid goodnight and said they would be available the next day if anything needed to be done. Victoria told them she couldn't think of anything but would let them know if there was and thanked them for all their help. Walking them out the door and to their pickup truck, Victoria noticed the police presence at the entrance to the cul-de-sac and gave them a wave, receiving an acknowledging gesture.

Brock and Marya were sitting out on the patio, enjoying the evening when Victoria walked out to join them. They all could hear the faint sounds of music coming through the speaker system.

Victoria turned abruptly when she heard footsteps behind her. "How....?"

Travis said, "Riley and Jamie hooked it up this afternoon, exactly where you mentioned you wanted it. So, if you need it moved, they offered to move it and reconnect it."

"Wow... I thought it would be a couple of days before everything got hooked up."

"Nope. While you were unloading the kitchen boxes and putting things away, they hooked up your televisions. I took care of your computer set up, along with the internet connections. So, you're good to go."

Marya mentioned Brock was going to take her home, and she would be over in the morning to help unpack more boxes. Victoria gave her mom a big hug.

"Mom, you've been a trooper helping me with this move. Thank you so much for being here."

"Honey, I told you before... I'll always be here to help. I love you, Victoria," Marya said as she gave her daughter a loving kiss on her cheek. Marya reached over and pulled Travis into a hug.

"Now, you see to it she gets to bed and gets some rest. I expect you to stay the night and look after things... understood?"

"Roger that!"

Victoria reached around to Brock and gave him a hug. "And you make sure my mother gets her rest as well!"

"Yes, Ma'am! Boy, these Hart women can be so bossy."

Victoria and Travis waved goodbye as Brock and Marya pulled out of the driveway.

"Brock is lucky to have found your mom."

"Mom is lucky she found Brock... and I'm guessing they're both going to get lucky tonight." Victoria and Travis both started to say something at the same time, causing them both to laugh.

"Okay... you first," Travis said.

"I was just going to say it really is no use for you to be driving back to the hotel when there's a guest room all made up here for you."

"Well, I was counting on that... since I already checked out of the hotel, and I am under strict orders from your mother. I figured if you wouldn't let me stay here tonight, I would just camp out at your mother's in your old bedroom. Of course, it might be a little awkward with Brock being there."

"You knew I wouldn't let you stay at my mom's tonight. By the way, when did you check out of the hotel?"

"Yesterday, when your mom ordered me to. It was Mother Edict! It's when I disappeared for a bit in the afternoon. I packed up everything at the hotel and checked out."

It all added up, Victoria thought to herself.

"Time to turn in, young lady. Tomorrow we have a lot of unpacking to do. I thought, if time permits, we might drop your bike off for repairs."

"Okay. Hard to believe I'll be sleeping in my very own house tonight. Overwhelming, in fact, with everything that's happened."

Travis went around and checked all the doors to make sure they were locked, the security system activated, and turned off the lights.

"Remember, the system is on, so if you have to open a door to go outside, you have to punch the code either on the wall panel, with the remote clicker, or on your mobile phone."

"Got it," Victoria nodded.

Travis picked up the bag he had stowed near the front hall closet, and as he walked Victoria to her bedroom door, he set it down.

"Can I have a goodnight kiss for some sweet dreams?"

"Oh, yes," she said breathlessly.

Victoria wasn't sure if she moved first or if Travis did, but they locked lips and held tight. She could feel her heart pounding and Travis' warm breath as his kisses traveled to her cheek, then her earlobe, then back to the soft flesh of her lips. Their tongues danced around each other, and she felt her legs give way. He must have sensed it and picked her up, maneuvering to open the bedroom door, carrying her to her bed.

Laying her carefully down without breaking their lip-locked connection, he leaned over her. Victoria's head was swimming, and all she knew was she wanted him to stay. She needed to find that missing piece... the missing "something," and if there was a chance they truly had it, there was only one way to discover it. They needed to go deeper into their relationship.

She felt Travis' apprehension as if he was fearful of moving too fast. She knew he wanted her to take the lead, so she started to pull up his tee shirt from his waist. He sat up and looked into her eyes, then pulled his shirt off over his head. She had watched him lifting and moving furniture during the move and couldn't miss the rippling of his muscles under his shirt or the bulge of his biceps. Every time they came in contact with one another, she could sense his strength, but now she could see it. She trailed her fingers down his shoulder and across his chest with a sprinkling of burnished hairs.

A vision came to her, causing her to stare glassy-eyed with her hand trembling against him—an image from the past. Travis must have sensed it.

He stopped her hand—no words. He rose from the bed, gathered his shirt in his hand, bending to brush a gentle kiss on her lips, and whispered, "Good Night, Victoria. Sweet Dreams." Ever so quietly, he left her room, closing her door behind him.

An empty feeling she experienced so many times before hit her full force. She still had ghosts entering her mind, stopping her in her tracks from moving forward. She knew she had to break free of them. If she didn't, she would stay in this limbo and never feel the "something" again. The tears fell into the night.

CHAPTER 33

Saturday morning came too soon. Victoria awoke to the echoing sound of someone tapping the code into one of the security panels located in the house. Her mobile phone on her nightstand registered the security was turned off. Only Travis, Marya, and Victoria knew the code.

She jumped out of bed and ran out of her room. Looking out the kitchen window, she found Travis already out on the patio, checking the pool skimmers. He had on a pair of swim trunks and a t-shirt. He turned as Victoria open the patio door.

He couldn't possibly be thinking about swimming right now.

It was still a bit brisk out, and she was sure the water would be chilly. Cocking his head toward her and smiling, he slowly backed his way to the edge of the pool. She was just going to yell to stop before he fell in when he laughed, threw his arms out, and landed in the water.

"Travis, it's freezing. Are you crazy? I haven't had the pool heaters turned on yet."

"No kidding! Hey, why don't you join me? It's really quite refreshing."

"Ah, no thank you. Now, come on out, and I'll get some coffee brewing to warm you up."

"Alright then. Give me a hand," he said as he swam to the side of the pool.

As Victoria reached down, he grabbed her wrist and pulled her in.

As she surfaced, her face expressing shock, she sputtered, "You honestly didn't do that on purpose, did you?"

"As a matter of fact..." he trailed off, hitching a brow and cocking his head.

Victoria made her way to the steps and got out of the pool with Travis right behind her. As she got to the top step, she turned and gave Travis a shove with her foot, so he fell back in. They were both laughing so hard, it was difficult to tell if they had tears in their eyes or it was water dripping from their hair.

Victoria was about to run into the house to get some towels, but Travis called to her that there were towels already on one of the chairs on the patio.

As she walked over to get a towel, she admonished, "You planned this, you stinker."

"No. Really? Would I do that?"

Travis was out of the pool and picked up the other towel, drying himself off. Victoria was hard pressed not to notice how he looked standing there. Her breath caught in her throat.

As she was drying herself off, she totally missed Travis' eyes devouring her, head to toe. She had fallen asleep in her t-shirt and a pair of boy shorts, and their wetness left little to the imagination. Looking up, she caught his gaze and realized what he was looking at, turning a vibrant shade of red. But then she noticed he was having some personal issues himself from eyeing her.

Looking down, he exclaimed, "Hey, what do you expect, Victoria. You're a beautiful woman, and I'm a red-blooded man. It happens."

"Yes, you are, Travis, indeed you are and a very handsome man to boot," Victoria countered as she turned to walk back into the house.

Travis sighed heavily and spun his towel and gave her a slap on her butt. "Let's get some coffee before I do something to ruin a good thing."

$\sim$

AS MUCH FUN as they had that morning, there was an undertone of tension. Both Travis and Victoria knew answers were needed and hoped the detective would be able to get resolution for the incidents and confirm whether Brandon was indeed behind them. Waiting for answers was stressing everyone out.

After breakfast, Brock and Marya arrived, ready to help unpack boxes and put things away. Victoria had to smile when she saw her mother had a certain glow about her, and Brock made sure he was constantly by Marya's side.

Victoria had purchased two large bookcases matching Tyler's bedroom furniture, and he was more than content putting away his storybooks, then using some of the shelves to display his latest Lego creations.

Travis and Victoria put more window treatments up. She couldn't get enough of watching Travis as he scaled a ladder. He was wearing cutoffs, and his calf muscles flexed as he moved on the ladder, and his t-shirt rose up, exposing his six-pack while reaching up to make adjustments to a bracket. Her heart was doing flip flops, and several times, she had to look away quickly, so he didn't catch her ogling him.

The property was surrounded by a stuccoed block wall over six feet high, but it didn't obscure the view of the not too distant mountains. Victoria still wanted to maintain indoor privacy, particularly in the bedrooms and baths. Quite a few of the windows had between-the-glass blinds operated by remote control. These afforded Victoria privacy and security, but other windows required some form of window treatment, and Travis was delighted when she asked for his opinion.

Around noon, the doorbell rang, and after looking out the sidelight window, Victoria saw it was her friend Diana. After she opened the door, the two of them rushed together with hugs.

"Oh, Diana, I'm so glad you came. I thought maybe you wouldn't after what happened."

"Nope. Nada. I'm here to help. Besides, I really need to get focused on other things." Diana quickly noticed Travis close behind Victoria and the protector stance he exhibited.

Victoria noticed Diana looking over her shoulder and turned to introduce Travis.

"Oh, Diana, this is my... friend, Travis. We reconnected at the reunion. He's in town on business but has been helping with the move... and other things."

Travis reached out his hand, and Diana took it, followed by a light but warm shake.

Marya came around the corner and gave Diana a hug. Brock was fast on her heels, and Marya introduced him. Tyler came running out of his bedroom to see who arrived and threw his arms around Diana's thighs.

"Aunt Diana, I'm so glad to see you. You have to come see my bedroom!"

"Hi, Ty! I'm glad to see you too. I hear Mommy got you all new furniture, and I can't wait to see it, but first I need to talk to Mommy for a couple of minutes. Okay?" Diana asked sweetly.

"Okay... but come after?"

"Yep, I sure will. I promise," Diana said, ruffling Tyler's head of dark hair.

He joyfully bounded down the hallway toward his room.

Marya and Brock disappeared into the kitchen while Diana walked with Victoria and Travis through the house as Victoria explained what she had planned for each room once everything was unpacked. When they had been through all the rooms, including Tyler's, they went into the kitchen.

Marya offered freshly made lemonade, and after everyone was served, Diana asked Victoria what she could do to help.

"Well, there are still linens to be put away and, of course, wardrobes to unload into the closets and drawers. But I know you still must be hurting from the attack, so please don't do anything that might make it worse."

The scrapes and bruising were still visible on the side of Diana's face. Travis cringed at the thought someone, more than likely Brandon, had done it.

"No, I'm fine really." After making sure Tyler was out of earshot, she asked, "Any new reports from the detective? He's been keeping me posted, but I haven't heard anything for two days."

"Same here. Travis believes since we have a police presence here, Brandon might have backed off but try something elsewhere."

"Yeah, I noticed the patrol car just outside of the cul-de-sac when I pulled in. How long will they be able to do that?"

"Not sure. The detective said they were going to pull Brandon in for questioning and quite possibly, anyone who he's been associating with. His parents too."

"Oh, that's going to go over like a lead balloon. I'm sure the Barkley firm is in an uproar. I'm so glad I'm out of there. I was able to get all my locks changed and updated my security system on my condo. Hate to say it, but I now carry pepper spray with me and a few other things. I should have done it a long time ago. I'm still volunteering with the women's crisis center hotline, and there are times I need to go pick up someone in distress. You never know, nowadays."

"What about the job prospects?"

"I've got feelers out. I updated my resume a while ago and had been making contacts in the legal community. I just want it to be the right fit. You know me. Being an advocate for spousal protection from domestic violence, I want to work for a firm and with people who have the same ideals, not for some company only worshiping the almighty dollar and might be swayed by influential people."

Travis was listening closely to Diana with deep admiration and found himself suggesting Diana email him her resume.

A short while later, Travis asked Brock to help him in the garage, putting together a tool bench and cabinets delivered the day before but not fully assembled. A pegboard needed to be hung as well. Before Brock extricated himself from Marya, he gave her a hug and kiss. Victoria hid a chuckle, but it didn't go unnoticed by Travis.

While Marya enjoyed herself putting things away in the kitchen and pantry, Victoria asked Diana to help her unload the wardrobe containers and put things away in the master bedroom walk-in closets. Diana had teased Victoria about having two walk-in closets, a "his" and a "hers."

"What gives with you and Travis?"

Taking a deep breath, Victoria said, "It's complicated."

"Really, is that all you're going to give me... it's complicated? I may have gotten my head injured, but I'm not blind. He's definitely a little more than a friend."

"Like I said earlier, we reconnected at the reunion. We had a great time together, and when he found out he was coming to Phoenix on business, he made a point of offering his services... for the move."

"This business trip here... was it purely for business?"

Victoria hesitated, "No... I don't think so. I think he extended his trip to help me. He's an attorney back in Chicago and has a condo along Lake Shore Drive. He served a couple of tours in the Middle East and does pro bono work with injured veterans. His business here was to get together with some of those vets needing legal assistance. He's also been offered a position here with his firm's affiliate branch offices. He's really a good guy, Diana. He's actually the one who helped me out after the car incident, then again after the cycling incident and made sure I contacted the police."

"Wait a minute, hold on. Tell me more about these so-called incidents," Diana gently insisted.

As they were unpacking and putting things away, Victoria launched into the details of what happened. By the time she was through, Diana had to sit down on the floor in the closet, her mouth agape.

"Holy Cow! Victoria, you know Brandon has to be behind all of this. He is definitely out of control and off his rocker. He's more than that... he's demented! I knew from some of the questions the detective asked me there was more going on. I had no idea," she said, shaking her head slowly as if it was difficult to believe.

"I know. And I would have called you, but everything happened in a very short time span."

"Hey, we've gotten off the topic. So, tell me more about that handsome guy out there in the garage. You know, the one who looks at you with puppy dog eyes."

That made Victoria smile. "We're just friends. Good friends. Nothing more. Right now. I can't help holding back, especially with all this other stuff going on. There's nothing I would like more than to have someone in my life like Travis."

"Is there something... or someone else holding you back, besides all this crap you're having to deal with?"

"At the reunion... I ran into Drew."

Diana's head snapped up.

"Yes, I ran into Drew. THE Drew. He tried to tell me how much he cared and how much he wanted us to be together and all that, but I responded by confronting him about not following through and the fact he only sent me one message. Of course, he denied it, saying he did try to contact me at the office. I actually had my staff pull the phone and message records from storage to see if he did."

"Well, what did the records show?"

"I don't know. By the time the records got pulled and I finally got them in my hands, I had the car accident, then the cycling episode. I've been so preoccupied with those events and the move, I haven't had the energy to sit down and go through the reports."

"Victoria, as your friend, I know you have a lot on your plate right now with the Brandon issue, but until and unless you substantiate what Drew said, you're going to have this barrier between you and anyone else. What are your plans the next couple of days?"

"Working through the move here today. Tomorrow Travis goes back to Chicago although I know he would rather stay here. Then Monday, I plan on going back into my office. I'm not sure if I will put in a full day or not. I had planned on taking time getting settled in the house, then going full steam ahead the following week. I've got a great staff who've really covered everything for me during my move."

"I'll tell you what... I'm coming back here tomorrow, and we can do more unpacking and putting things away, then we're going to sit down and go through those records. You need to do this, Victoria, for your own peace of mind. Once you have the answers, you can move forward with a clear understanding and not be pulled back by a ghost from the past."

Victoria knew Diana was right. For all of her thirty-one years on the planet, Diana was wise beyond her years. Victoria attributed her intelligence and understanding to her victim's advocate work and her own personal experience.

CHAPTER 34

Marya put out platters of sandwiches she had made and had a pot of chili simmering on the stove. Whenever anyone felt like grabbing a bite, they helped themselves.

Small kitchen appliances had been either stowed or placed on the counters. Victoria's grandmother's crystal and china were carefully placed into the lighted china hutch in the dining room. Victoria noted her mother had been very busy. But that was her mom—she moved like the wind, humming softly to herself. Victoria stood in the doorway to the dining room and envisioned her traditional Christmas Eve dinner.

Christmas! Oh, wow, it's right around the corner.

Victoria looked around and found the perfect place to put the tree.

Travis had come in from the garage, noticed the smile on her face and the far off look in her eyes.

"What's making you happy right now, Victoria?"

"Believe it or not, Travis, I'm thinking about Christmas and where I'm going to put the tree! And how Tyler and I are going to be spending the holidays here in our very own home."

His warm smile told her everything.

They walked into the kitchen together, joining Brock, Marya, and Diana, chowing down on the sandwiches and chili. Marya had made

Tyler a chili dog, and he was happily sitting at the end of the counter, explaining the interlocking mechanisms of Legos to Brock.

"No doubt about it. Tyler's going to be an engineer when he grows up," Brock exclaimed.

"No, Brock! I want to be a fireman like you. And then maybe a 'turney' like Travis."

Travis leaned into him. "Tyler, you can be whatever you want to be. What we all want for you is to be happy and enjoy whatever you do."

Tyler looked up and around at everyone and beamed, "Okay! Then I want to be a cowboy!"

Victoria watched the interaction between Tyler, Brock, and Travis. Tyler related so well to the guys, and it hit home a male influence was needed in his life even if it was just as a friend and not as a parent. Victoria walked over to Tyler and ruffled his dark hair.

"Tyler, let's get you cleaned up and wash that chili off your face, then we'll have dessert."

The magic word "dessert" had him hopping off the stool and rushing to the bathroom.

"We'll be right back," Victoria said, following Tyler down the hallway.

Diana reached over and touched Travis' arm.

"Is she going to be okay? I mean, safe?" I know you're leaving tomorrow, and I worry about—"

Travis interrupted her, "I know. I'm concerned too. We all are. But until the police can actually prove Brandon has been behind the attacks, all they can do is keep up the patrols. I know they planned on questioning him and confirming his whereabouts since he's been in Arizona. I'm sure the detective is also checking on Brandon's appearance at the Barkley office and the timing of your own attack. I wish I could stay longer, but I need to get back to Chicago and wrap things up there. I've just accepted the position here in Phoenix. I haven't told Victoria yet."

Victoria overhead his last comment as she walked back into the kitchen with Tyler, and asked, "What haven't you told me yet?"

"I'm now a partner in the firm here and am relocating as soon as I can get everything wrapped up in Chicago."

Victoria's heart did a somersault.

"Wow, Travis, that's wonderful!"

"The firm really needed me here to work with the veterans, and since I've already worked on several of the cases, it was a good fit. Plus, there are side benefits... like the weather and getting out of the Midwest winters. I'm not blind to the fact the summers are hot here, but I'll take a/c over shoveling snow and driving on icy roads any day."

"Hey, if you want to see snow in the winter, northern Arizona has plenty of it, and it's only a two- or three-hour drive up north," Brock interjected.

Tyler's ears perked up. "Yeah, and Mommy told me we're going sledding up there. And we're going to build a snowman and throw snowballs!"

Marya chimed in, "Speaking of snow... how about some ice cream?"

"Now, that was a smooth transition, Mom," Victoria joked.

After indulging in servings of ice cream with all the toppings, Victoria spooned the last bit out of her bowl and reached up to the back of her neck. Travis could tell she was tired and achy from all the activity the past couple of days. He went behind her and placed his hands on her shoulders, massaging her neck and shoulder muscles with his fingers and palms.

"Oh, that feels sooooo good. If all else fails, I think you have a career in massage therapy, Travis."

"Hmmm... I'll have to give it some thought. Of course, I'll have to fine tune my technique a bit, so I'll need a volunteer to practice on," he teased.

Diana was listening to the verbal intercourse between Victoria and Travis and noted the physical contact.

"Hey, it's late, and I'm really bushed, so if you don't mind, I'm going to head home. I'll call you in the morning, Victoria, and we can figure out the best time for me to come over to help you with things."

Victoria knew what "things" Diana was referring to and nodded.

Diana said her goodbyes and gave her hugs to everyone, holding onto Tyler and telling him how much she enjoyed seeing his new bedroom.

"Thanks for all your help today. Please be careful on the way home, Diana. And make sure you lock your doors," Victoria whispered as she walked her friend to the door.

"I will. And as I said before, I'm prepared. See you tomorrow."

As Victoria walked back into the kitchen, she noticed Brock and her mother had gone out to the patio and were standing out in the far corner, deep in quiet conversation.

Tyler had his own deep conversation going on with Travis, discussing the type of sled he wanted for Christmas, one he could use up north in the snow.

"Hey, Ty... it's way past your bedtime. Let's head back to your room and get you ready for bed. Travis can come back and hear your prayers in a bit."

After Tyler was tucked in for the night, Travis helped Victoria clear the table and the counters, drying the dishes as she washed.

Brock and Marya walked back into the house and told Victoria they were heading home as well, but would be back on Sunday to do more.

"Mom, you and Brock have already done so much. Why don't you just do something fun tomorrow, just the two of you?"

"Victoria, your mother and I enjoy helping you," Brock firmly said. "We'd rather be here with you, getting you and Tyler settled in. Tomorrow, we can break down all those empty moving boxes and bring them to the center to be recycled by someone else who might need them for moving."

"Wish I could take them with me. I'm sure going to need them for my move although most of what I'm moving are books, fifty percent of which are law books. I have a few personal things and photo albums and such. Most of my furniture wouldn't fit the lifestyle here, so I'll be getting new furniture after I find a place. I'll more than likely get a condo or patio home. The firm put me in touch with a Realtor, and I was advised it wouldn't take very long for me to find something. The condos in my building on Lake Shore Drive are in high demand, so I'm sure selling won't be an issue."

After Brock and Marya headed home, Victoria and Travis sat on the sofa on the patio. It was crisp and clear, and Victoria gasped as she looked up at the star-blanketed sky. The area where her home was located had a "Dark Sky Ordinance," designed to control the use of outdoor artificial illumination devices emitting rays into the night sky.

"Wow, Travis, have you ever seen anything more beautiful?"

"Never," he responded, looking directly at her instead of the sky.

Victoria knew she blushed from the heat she felt rising up from her neck.

She started to say something, but Travis placed his fingers on her lips and turned to face her.

"Victoria, don't say anything. I know you have a lot going on right now. I'm really torn about leaving tomorrow. I wish this Brandon issue was already resolved. I would know you and your family needn't be in a position where you had to have protection. You all mean a lot to me, and if anything happened, it would devastate me. I've seen so much on the battlefield, but nothing compares to the fear and anxiety I'm feeling right now."

Victoria tried to say something, but he stopped her.

"It's been pretty obvious you're holding back from me, both physically and emotionally. That's a whole other matter needing to be worked out, but only you can do it. I just hope when you do, there will be a place for me in your life and in your heart. Our relationship did play a part in my decision to move to Arizona, but it's not the only reason. My work with the vets here is very important to me. No matter what's down the road for us, my being an advocate for them is truly significant to me.

"You've brought a light into my life. I feel like I was just existing before, and now I truly understand what living is. Things happened while I was in the service, things that caused me to shut down. No matter how hard I drove myself, I couldn't find the spark to reignite myself. You've been the spark without even knowing it. Just sharing a quiet moment like this, hanging pictures, moving furniture, or sharing ice cream... it made me appreciate those simple things we all take for granted.

"I don't know if I'm making any sense, but I just wanted you to know how much you mean to me, and you always will... no matter what the future brings."

Victoria couldn't help the tears flowing down her cheeks.

With a catch in her voice, she responded, "I do understand what you're saying. And you must know by now, I have strong feelings for you. Very strong feelings. I have things I need to get settled before I can take a step in any direction. I've made mistakes in the past and have regretted them. I don't want to go down that path again. Depending on what happens, hopefully, in the not too distant future, I'll be able to make a solid decision. Travis, there's nothing I would like more right now than to be able to close the door on the past and begin a future... with you, but I can't."

Travis listened quietly and patiently, then he took her hands in his and vowed, "Victoria, whatever happens, whatever your decision, I will always be there for you whether as your friend or as more."

"Travis, I'm so very blessed to have you in my life and in Tyler's life." She pulled her hands from his and wrapped her arms around him, holding him tightly, placing her cheek next to his. "So very blessed."

Travis embraced her and whispered, "I'm the one who's blessed." Then pulling away he stood and reached for her hand.

"It's really late. We both need our sleep."

After walking back into the house, locking the doors, and setting the security system, they walked back to her bedroom door where he gave her a brief sweet kiss and walked down the hallway to his room.

A while later, Victoria laid in bed, remembering the words he had spoken. She needed him to know just how much she cared, but at the same time not giving him false hope.

She threw the covers back, left her room, and walked down the hallway to his bedroom. She raised her hand to knock on his door several times but stopped. Just as she was going to follow through, Travis opened the door, startling both of them. No words passed between them as he led her to his bed, then he lifted her and laid her down.

It was then he finally whispered, "Only to hold you," as he moved to lie beside her and snuggled them into a spooning position.

He knows, Victoria thought to herself. *He knows.*

CHAPTER 35

The days were getting shorter and the nights longer, but Sunday morning still came too soon... again.

Victoria's eyelids fluttered open to find Travis staring at her.

He teased, "You snore."

"I do not!"

"How do you know? You're asleep!"

"Oh! Do I really snore?" she asked with a grimace.

"No. Just kidding. Besides, if you did, it wouldn't matter to me."

Victoria grabbed the small pillow next to her and bonked him on the head as she got up and stood on top of the bed.

Travis decided two could play that game and grabbed his pillow and smacked her in the butt with it.

A pillow fight ensued, and with all the commotion, Travis and Victoria didn't notice Tyler coming through the door.

"Wow, Mommy and Travis! A pillow fight! YAY," he exclaimed as Travis and Victoria looked like they just got caught with their fingers in a cookie jar.

Tyler ran and jumped on the bed and started tossing pillows.

Victoria shrugged and slammed another pillow into Travis. Travis grabbed her and held her face down while he told Tyler to grab her feet and tickled her toes.

"No!" Victoria screamed.

"Mommy's really ticklish, Travis."

"Oh, really? Let's just see how much."

Travis started tickling her ribs, and Victoria was trying to hold in her laughter. The tickling got the better of her, and she gasped for breath.

"Okay, I give! I call 'uncle'! I can't take anymore," Victoria squealed.

The three of them collapsed on the bed.

"That was fun, Mommy! Can we do it again sometime?"

"Sure, but not now. We need to get up and get breakfast, and soon Gramma and Brock will be here, and you need to finish putting things away in your room. Then maybe, you can help flatten all those empty boxes out there in the garage."

Tyler went down the hallway to the kitchen, and Victoria did a feline stretch on the bed to get the kinks out. Travis watched and waggled his brows at her.

"Don't be getting any crazy ideas, Travis," she teased.

"Ideas? Yes! Crazy? No!" he kidded her right back.

He reached out his hand and pulled her up off the bed, bringing her to an abrupt stop against his bare chest. His amber eyes zeroing in on her lips, he kissed her with a controlled intensity. When she was just about to respond in kind, he pulled away and ran his hand down the side of her cheek, brushing a long golden tendril from her shoulder.

Breathing a deep sigh, he walked over to his cutoffs lying on a chair and slipped them on over his jockey briefs that left little to the imagination. Victoria slyly watched him with squinted, hungry eyes, biting her lip, but her gaze didn't go unnoticed by Travis.

"You like what you see?"

Victoria turned red and sped out of the room.

"I'll be right out in the kitchen in a minute."

She heard his chuckles as she walked to her own bedroom.

A little while later, Victoria stood in the entrance to the kitchen. Tyler was eating the cereal Travis had obviously prepared for him, and Travis was pouring himself a cup of coffee. He noticed her standing there with a smile on his face and raised the cup of coffee to his lips, peering over the rim at her.

She stood there, watching Travis and Tyler as if it was a scene out of a commercial about a family—a father and son having breakfast. Her smile changed to a look of wistfulness as an ache settled in her chest, and she was reminded again.

What do I tell Tyler about his own father?

Travis must have sensed her deep thoughts, and quickly said, "How about a cup of java to kick start your day?" His question brought her out of her reverie, and she walked over to Travis as he poured her a cup.

As they sat and enjoyed a breakfast of scrambled eggs and sausages Victoria prepared, Travis broached the subject of Diana.

"Exactly what did Diana do at the firm? Her duties and responsibilities?"

"She has a paralegal background and oversaw the administrative staff in the legal department. I know she did some law clerking as well. Why do you ask?"

"Just wondering. I imagine she got along pretty well with the staff, co-workers... well, except maybe the Barkley's after she helped you."

"Oh, definitely. Except for the Barkley's, she was well-liked by everyone, and I can well imagine quite a few people were unhappy when they let her go. You didn't really answer my question."

"Well, I hate to see someone of her caliber and work ethic being treated the way they did. As I asked, she did email me her resume, and I'd like to hand it off to someone in human resources at my firm here in Phoenix. Do you think she would be okay with that?"

"Oh, Travis, I know she would. From what you told me about your offices here, they are pretty much in the same general location, not far from her condo. It would be great if they found an opening for her. I won't say anything until and unless you tell me to go ahead."

"You can tell her. I'll be putting in a good word for her too. I noticed she had you listed as a reference, so you would be getting a call."

"It's really nice of you to do that. I know she'd be so appreciative."

"I like being appreciated as well as the next guy," he said as he reached over and took her hand, kissing her knuckles. Victoria could only smile... a big smile.

"I'm going to finish up some unpacking with you this morning and see if Brock will need help when he and Marya get here. I guess they must have slept in a bit this morning," he teased, hitching his brows at her.

Victoria cocked her head to the side and winked.

"My flight leaves at four this afternoon. I'll head to the airport around two so I can return the rental car and get through security on time."

Victoria felt an ache in her heart, but this time it was for Travis and her.

Tyler piped up, "Travis, are you going to come back soon? I hope you are."

"Yes, I am, little buddy. And soon I'll be living here, and if it's okay with your Mommy, we'll see one another often and have fun. Besides, you need to take me to see those horses out at the river... right?"

"Oh, yeah!" Tyler squealed.

The doorbell rang shortly after; Marya and Brock had arrived.

Tyler ran to greet them.

"Mommy slept in Travis' room last night, and this morning we had a big pillow fight! And then we tickled Mommy, and she screamed so loud, and we all laughed so hard!"

Victoria froze, turning the darkest shade of red. Travis put his head down and compressed his lips, but shudders of laughter could be seen in his quaking shoulders. Marya and Brock looked at Victoria, then at Travis, then at each other, and bust out laughing.

Tyler looked at all four of them and started laughing.

As promised, everyone hopped right to it, getting things done. Diana called, and when Victoria told her Travis would be leaving around two o'clock, Diana insisted on coming by to say goodbye, then staying to help.

At one in the afternoon, Travis went into his bedroom to shower and pack. A melancholy settled around Victoria. It was noticed by Marya and Brock, and they tried to engage her in spirited conversation, teasing her about the morning and who won the pillow fight. At a little before two, Diana arrived, and she could feel the cloud hanging over Victoria.

Travis came out of the bedroom, placing his suitcase and briefcase near the front door. He looked so handsome standing there—his burnished hair still damp from the shower, his long legs encased in dark denim jeans, a crisp fitted white shirt open to display a few golden tufts of chest hairs, and a camel sports jacket. Although he had wanted to buy a pair of custom boots while in Arizona, he didn't have the time, so he wore his oxblood loafers. He took Victoria's breath away.

Victoria's mouth had turned to chalk, her heartbeat pounding in her ears. She wanted so much to ask him to stay, but she knew she didn't have the right... at least not yet... maybe. A big maybe.

Diana walked up to him and thanked him for everything he did to help Victoria.

Travis told her he had already taken steps to get her resume to his HR department, and she was ecstatic.

Marya gave Travis a hug and thanked him, making him promise to come back soon and to call if he could. Brock shook his hand and wished him Godspeed.

Tyler ran to Travis and hugged him around his knees. Travis knelt down in front of Tyler and gave him a high five, told him to take care of his mommy, and make sure he remembered to say his prayers at night, then gave him a big hug.

"I'll be back soon, Ty. I promise." Travis was rewarded with a slobbering kiss only a little kid to give.

Rising up to his full height, Travis looked at Victoria who tried in vain to blink away her tears. Diana, Marya, and Brock herded Tyler into the back of the house, leaving Victoria and Travis alone.

"This is harder than I expected," she said quietly.

"Tell me about it. I packed and unpacked three times back in the bedroom. We both know I need to go and take care of things back in Chicago. The sooner I get that accomplished, the sooner I can get back here."

Travis wrapped his arms around Victoria and pressed her tightly against him. With his head against the top of her head, he inhaled the scent of her shampoo... apples and vanilla. He knew when he got back to Chicago, he had to pick up a bottle if only to remind him of her.

"You've really left your mark on me, Victoria. It's never going to go away. I never knew I could feel this way... so quickly and so deeply."

Victoria pulled away slightly, looked up into his amber eyes, and noticed the glaze of tears. Her own green eyes reflected the same unshed but very real tears. His hand caressed the back of her head and pulled it toward him.

"Oh, Victoria, I'm so torn right now."

Victoria's tears unleashed and fell upon the exposed skin at the opening of his shirt. She knew he could feel their moisture, along with the shudders of her weeping.

He pulled away and raised his hand to her face, wiping her tears. His head bent, and his lips seized hers, dominating her soul. She pulled him tighter as if they would merge into one and she could feel the blood streaming through his veins.

Breaking free to gasp for breath, they backed away from each other. Travis reached down, picked up his bags, and walked to the door. He strode down the walkway to his car as Victoria softly bit at her lower lip, holding on to the front door frame for support. He got into his vehicle, turned, and smiled. As he drove away, she felt an extreme loss—as if a part of her died—and she shivered.

Diana had come up behind her. "Are you okay, Victoria?"

"I don't know, Diana. What I do know is I have things to sort out when it comes to Travis and me. I can't put it off any longer. And this concern with Brandon needs to get resolved. There's no way I can move forward until these things get worked out."

"Well, then, let's get started on the first one. Where are those reports?"

Marya was well aware of what Victoria and Diana were working on, so she and Brock made sure Tyler was busy and wouldn't interfere.

Brock had made quite a dent in breaking down the moving boxes and organizing the garage tools. He had Tyler help him load the drawers in the tool bench and put labels on the drawers. After Brock broke the tape on the moving boxes, he would have Tyler flatten them down and stomp them flat. Then he would have Tyler add the flattened box to a stack. Marya was down to the last dozen boxes that needed to be emptied and busied herself putting things away.

Diana and Victoria worked in the area set up as an office with Diana going through the computer file printouts given to Victoria at the office. Victoria sat on the floor next to her desk, going through the scanned copies of the handwritten messages.

Several hours had passed, and they took a break to have dinner with everyone, then put Tyler to bed. Victoria's eyes were getting blurry, and she suggested to Diana they call it a night.

Victoria's mobile phone rang, and she jumped up to get it off the side table. She immediately recognized the caller ID number.

It was the detective, advising her contact was finally made at the Barkley house but was told Brandon wasn't there, and it was unknown where he was at the time. Brandon had missed contacting his parole officer for his weekly check-in the previous week. Messages were left, directing him to contact his parole officer immediately Monday morning, and if he didn't, they would have to take additional action to bring him in for questioning, including issuing a warrant.

The detective asked if anything out of the ordinary had happened, and Victoria told him everything was status quo. The move went fine, no one noticed anything strange, and the patrols had been observed at both her mother's home and her home. The detective promised after he heard from Brandon's parole officer, he would give her an update. Victoria relayed the information to Diana, Marya, and Brock.

'Victoria, do you want me to stay the night? I really don't have anywhere to go tomorrow," Diana inquired.

"No, with the police patrol and the security system, I feel safe. And tomorrow morning, I'm going into my office after I drop Tyler off at school."

"Is Travis in Chicago by now?"

"I'm pretty sure he is. I told him I would talk to him tomorrow. I didn't think I could handle talking with him tonight," she said as she was sitting back down on the floor.

"I get it. I really do. I'm just sorry we haven't found anything yet in these reports."

"Me too."

Victoria looked at the stack of reports on the corner of the desk, and as she reached up to pick up one of the reports, her hand brushed against the pile, causing several to fall to the floor. She picked up one and was about to tell Diana she should just forget about it when Victoria's hand froze, and Diana heard her gasp.

"Victoria, what is it?"

Victoria handed the packet marked "October 2013" to Diana. In the center of the scanned messages was a phone number from a 561 area code in Florida with the caller's name listed as Drew Anderson, requesting Victoria Hart contact him immediately. Victoria felt the color drain from her face and her hands trembling.

"Oh my God! He was telling the truth. He didn't lie." Victoria sat on the floor, placing her hands on each side of her face, her heart beating like a drum in a tribal war dance. She could feel the blood surging through her veins, and she had to lean forward and press her hands to the floor to steady herself.

Marya must have sensed something was amiss and walked into the office. Victoria raised her face, and Marya watched as the tears streamed down Victoria's face. Marya guessed what Victoria found and hurt for her daughter.

A while later, Victoria sat at the kitchen table. Marya had made her some tea, and she had her hands wrapped around the cup as if it was a lifeline.

Reaching out and gently taking Victoria's wrist in her hand, Marya calmly said, "Victoria, you've had a shock to your system. You need to give yourself time to come to terms with this. Don't make any decisions on how to handle things right now. Please, Honey, it's for your own good to give it some time."

"Your mom is right, Victoria. I've had to deal with circumstances that shook my own world and counseled others who had as well. Making a rash judgment could be detrimental, not just to your wellbeing but also Tyler's. You really need to think this through. Take your time. Step back a bit and weigh all the facts, including the emotional ones," Diana added.

Brock had been standing in the background but now came forward. "Victoria, I'm not your dad, and from what I hear he was a remarkable man, but if you were my daughter, I would tell you this has totally knocked you for a loop, and you need to cut yourself some slack. The dust needs to settle on this. Once you can look at it with a clear, calm mind, I know you will make a good decision about what to do."

Victoria was still numb but heard everything they were saying, taking it all in. She felt totally drained.

"My offer still stands, Victoria. I can stay the night if you want," Diana offered.

"No. I really just need to get to bed. I'm still planning to go into the office after I drop off Tyler."

"Okay. Well, I'm going home then. If you need anything, just call me, okay?" Diana said, picking up her purse and giving Victoria a hug.

"I will. Be careful on the way home," Victoria told Diana as she walked to the door.

Soon after Diana left, Marya approached Victoria and asked if she needed her to stay.

"No, Mom, you head home. I'm sure you both are pretty tired too. It's been a long week."

Marya gave Victoria a hug and left with Brock. She didn't think any amount of ice cream would help Victoria tonight.

Victoria locked up the house and set the security. As she passed by one of the front windows, she saw one of the police cruisers drive by slowly. She knew she had to deal with one issue at a time, but right now, Brandon Barkley was not first and foremost in her mind.

Exhausted mentally, emotionally and physically, Victoria fell into a deeply troubled sleep, only to awake halfway through the night to retrieve the pillow Travis slept on from the guest room, falling back asleep with her arms embracing its softness, inhaling his scent.

CHAPTER 36

Victoria's alarm buzzed at six on Monday morning. As she rose from the bed, she felt like she hadn't slept at all and zombie-walked to the bathroom. She made a beeline for the shower while shimmying out of her tank top and lady boxers. She increased the spray on the multiple fixtures to a pulsating jet and worked her neck around to her shoulders and lower back with the streams. After washing her hair, she flipped the temperature lever to cool, not realizing she moved it a bit too far and the shock of cold water certainly caused her to quickly come out of her sleepy stupor.

She was wrapped in a robe and drying her hair when Tyler moseyed into her bathroom. She teased him, aiming the dryer in his direction, and he laughed when he looked in the mirror to see his dark chocolate colored hair standing up.

Oh, the simple things that make a child happy.

She wondered if and how her discovery of last evening would affect him.

After giving Tyler breakfast and making herself a protein fruit smoothie, Victoria put together his snack box. The preschool supplied a noon meal, but they had a snack break mid-morning and one in the afternoon.

Then she went and laid out his school clothes. While Tyler was getting dressed, Victoria finished getting ready for work. Just before leaving the house, she phoned her mom, and they agreed her mom would pick Tyler up at preschool, take him to her house, and wait for Victoria to pick him up.

Victoria had picked out a navy-blue pencil skirt, burnished copper silk blouse, and navy heels. Looking in the mirror, she noticed the color of the blouse reminded her of Travis' hair and fond thoughts of him invaded her mind.

At just after eight o'clock, Victoria pulled out of her garage, noting the police cruiser passing by on patrol. She dropped Tyler off at school and headed to her office.

She remembered everything Travis told her about checking her surroundings, when getting into her car to be careful, and see if she could get someone to walk with her to her car. She had taken other precautions as well. There was no question about it—she had to do what she could.

Traffic was normal, and found herself mimicking Travis by checking her mirrors. She arrived at the parking garage for her office building a little after nine. Several other building tenants were arriving, and she walked with a group of them to the elevator and was grateful several had offices on the same floor. She entered her suite of offices and was enthusiastically greeted by Abby.

"Hey, Victoria, welcome back! We sure missed your smiling face around here."

Victoria was happy she was able to hide the stress she was feeling.

"You have a visitor already, and when he told me he was your friend from high school, I brought him to your office to wait."

Without saying a word, Victoria rushed down the hallway.

Did Travis miss his flight... or maybe he decided to stay after all?

Her heart was racing.

She came around the corner and dashed through the doorway. "Travis, I'm so happy you..."

Victoria stopped dead in her tracks, dropping her briefcase.

The dark hair and scent of a certain cologne.

Drew was standing, facing the window, and as he turned, he held a picture frame in his hand—the picture of Tyler and her. The framed picture Victoria had sitting on the credenza behind her chair. She could see Drew's jaw clenching, his espresso-colored eyes flashing anger, shock, and so much more.

He raked her with his eyes, then in a calm but rigid voice, asked, "Victoria, who is this?" while turning the framed picture toward her.

Victoria felt the blood draining from her face but knew she had to go on the offensive.

"What's it to you, Drew? And what are you doing here?" she asked angrily as she picked up her briefcase from the floor and set it on her desk, along with her purse. She purposely had her back to him so he wouldn't see her face.

"You tell me, Victoria! What is it to me? Or should I ask, who is this to me?"

Abby, unaware of what was happening, innocently and cheerfully bounced into the office and asked if she could get anyone anything.

Both Victoria and Drew gave a resounding "NO!" Abby looked at both of them and quietly left, closing the door behind her.

Victoria cringed. "I shouldn't have yelled like that at her. I better go apologize." Moving toward the door, Drew raced her to it and reached out, placing his hand flat on the door, preventing her from opening it.

"You're not going anywhere right now. Sit down, Victoria. Now!"

She remained standing. She knew he knew. He figured it out when he saw the photo—Tyler was Drew in every way possible, a perfect clone.

"Are you going to tell me, or do I need to lay it all out for you, Victoria?"

Her offensive plan didn't work, so she decided to keep quiet.

Just then her intercom buzzed. It was Abby.

"Victoria, I know you're busy, but there is a Detective Casey with the police department on the line, and he's insisting on talking to you. He said it's vital he speak with you."

Victoria said urgently, "Put him through and hold all my calls, Abby, unless it's family or until I tell you otherwise. And, Abby, I'm sorry I yelled at you."

"No problem, Victoria. I'll put the call through now."

"I have to take this, Drew." Without waiting for his response, she answered the line and tapped the speaker button.

"Yes, Detective, what's going on?"

"I'm afraid the news isn't good. Brandon Barkley has disappeared. He hasn't reported to his parole officer, his father denies knowing where he is, and his mother isn't anywhere to be found either. It's also come to our attention, after speaking with several of his buddies who he reconnected with since he was released from prison, he's been talking trash about you, your family, and your friend Diana to the point, he's made outright threats to your life. He told them he was going to make you pay for what happened to him. We're positive now he was behind the car accident and the attack on you while cycling."

Drew was taking it all in, concern and incredulity on his face as he drew his brows together.

Victoria had her hands clasped, and it was evident tremors were running through her body.

Victoria stammered, "Until now, I had hoped the incidents were just a fluke. Tell me, Detective Casey, what I need to do."

"First off, you need to make sure you don't put yourself in a defenseless position. I realize you're at your office now, and there is staff around you, but make sure you have someone with you at all times and alert your staff, in case Brandon attempts to make contact with you at your office. The more people who are aware of the situation, the better. Make sure you let your mother and your friend Diana know as well and advise them to take precautions. I've sent an extra patrol over to your son's preschool as well. We have an APB out on Brandon Barkley and are doing the best we can to find him and bring him in. The fact he didn't report into his parole officer, coupled with his threats, it's clear he has violated his parole and will be immediately locked back up once we find him. We'll beef up the patrols at your home as well as your mother's and your friend Diana's. As long as we haven't caught him, please stay as safe as possible."

"I will. I'll call my mother and Diana now."

"If we have any new information, I'll contact you immediately."

"Thank you. I really appreciate everything you're doing."

After she clicked the phone button to disconnect, her face drained of color, and she fell into her chair in stunned silence. Drew watched in dismay with creased brows and jaw clenching. Victoria brought her hands up and covered her face.

A few moments later she took a deep breath, reached for the phone, and called her mother's mobile number. She knew she would be at the V.A. Rehab Center by now and had hoped she could answer her phone.

Fortunately, Marya picked it up immediately, and Victoria put her on speaker.

"Mom, the detective called. They have an APB out on Brandon. He violated his parole, and he's been making threats against me, you, and Diana." Victoria then went on to relay what the detective had told her.

"Hold on, Honey."

Victoria could hear her talking to someone nearby, then Marya came back to the phone.

"Brock is here, and he's going to drive me to pick up Tyler at school, then take us to his place. Brock is texting you his address right now. Victoria, please make sure someone is with you wherever you go. Is anyone there now who can help you?"

"As a matter of fact... yes. Drew is here."

There was silence on the other end of the phone.

Drew moved around the desk near Victoria and motioned he wanted to say something.

"Mrs. Hart, this is Drew Anderson. Rest assured, I won't let anything happen to Victoria. Just make sure you and Tyler are safe and secure. Victoria and I will stay in touch and let you know where we are at all times."

After a slight pause, Marya responded, "Thank you, Drew, for... being there for her. Brock and I are going to leave now to pick up Tyler."

Victoria leaned near the phone, "Mom, I love you. And please tell Tyler I love him."

"I will, Honey. And we love you. Just be safe. We'll see you soon."

Victoria ended the call. She felt disconnected as if she was being pulled apart and away from those she loved. A dread came over her, and it was clearly apparent from the look on her face, especially the fear in her eyes. She felt a chill run through her and wrapped her arms around herself.

"Victoria, what are you thinking?" Drew asked.

"I'm afraid. Afraid of something happening to me or those I love, and I won't see them again. I don't have any control over this, it's all in the hands of the police right now."

"No, it isn't, Victoria. You do have control. You just have to make sure you don't expose yourself to a dangerous situation. I'm sure the police have a handle on this, and they're out there right now looking for this piece of crap, so he doesn't hurt you or anyone else. Plus, I'm here. I promise you, Victoria, as long as I have a breath in me, I will protect you."

Victoria could only nod.

"I need to call, Diana," she said, reaching for the phone again.

Diana's phone rang only twice when it was picked up, and Victoria put her on speaker.

"Victoria, so glad you called. All of a sudden there are police cruisers up and down my street in front of my condo and officers on foot around the sides. Did you hear anything?"

"Yes, I just got off the phone with the detective. Brandon is on the loose and has made threats against you, me, and my family. There's an APB out on him."

"I'm going to stay put. I have a friend from the crisis center who I know will come over and stay with me or take me to a safehouse. You'll be able to reach me on my mobile phone no matter where I'll be. What are you going to do?"

"Brock is taking my mom to pick up Tyler, then they're going to Brock's place. I thought about heading to Brock's, but if Brandon is out there watching me, the last thing I want to do is lead him to where my family is. I might just head home. I've got the security in place, and the patrols are more than likely beefed up at my house as well."

"Wait, you can't go by yourself. Look what happened on the road going home or when you were cycling. He could try to do something then."

Looking at Drew, Victoria responded, "I won't be alone."

"Who...?" Diana asked.

Drew answered for Victoria, "Me..."

"Travis, is that you... you stayed! Oh, I'm so glad!"

"No, this is Drew... Drew Anderson."

Dead silence. Drew's eyes focused on Victoria's, and his telltale jaw clenching made its presence known again.

"From the halt in conversation, you must have heard my name mentioned before," Drew stated calmly.

"Ah... well, yes, your name has been brought up on occasion.

Victoria, are you okay with this? I mean if you would prefer my friend and I come get you, we can."

"I'm fine with it, Diana. I'm in good hands. And I trust Drew... in more ways than one. I know he'll watch out for me," Victoria said, slowly rising from her chair and walking over to the edge of her desk.

"Okay, then. You've got my number. Call any time."

"You take care, Diana. Please, be careful," Victoria said.

After Victoria reached over the desk and disconnected the call, Drew moved over to stand beside her, his eyes no longer angry but warm and caring.

"What now, My Queen?" he asked gently. "Where do we go from here?"

The question was double-barreled.

Victoria walked over to the window and closed her eyes. She felt Drew come up behind her, the scent of his telltale cologne had already enveloping her. His proximity brought emotions to the forefront. Memories of the past—their past.

Priorities, Victoria, priorities!

"I... we... can't go to Brock's. Brandon could be out there right now, watching every move I make, and as I said earlier, I don't want to expose my family to his sick vendetta by leading him to them. It would be much safer for me to go home. At least there, I would have security, the police patrols, and if need be, other forms of protection."

Drew raised his brows at that last bit of information.

"I need to call a meeting of the department managers here and advise them of what's going on. I certainly don't want a workplace incident to occur because of me and someone who has a grudge."

Drew placed his hands on her shoulders and turned her to face him.

"Victoria, this is not a grudge. This is outright insanity on Brandon's part. In your phone conversations, the detective and your friend Diana both alluded to prior incidents... or attacks as they should be called. Brandon has obviously gone off the deep end and is totally irrational. More than likely from his drug abuse."

Victoria was quiet with her head down, but Drew could tell her mind was going a mile a minute. With his left hand on her shoulder, his right hand lifted her chin up.

"I promise you, Victoria, I'll do whatever it takes to protect you. You'll be alright. We'll be alright," he solemnly vowed.

He pulled her to his chest and cupped the back of her head with his hand. Wracking sobs bubbled up from her. She tried desperately to hold it in, but the waves of fear for the lives of those she loved overwhelmed her.

She raised her face to his, crying, "I'm so scared, Drew. I'm so scared for my family."

He hugged her tighter and let her release the pent-up emotions.

After her crying had subsided, he reached into his pocket and handed her his handkerchief.

As she wiped the tears, she said, "I'm sorry. It's just so—"

Drew cut her off. "Nothing to be sorry about, Victoria. This jerk put you through hell years ago, and now he's doing it again. I can't even imagine the anxiety you've been going through. You're one tough lady, and I don't know how you've managed to keep it together."

"I have to get myself together a lot more before I talk to the staff. Just give me a couple of minutes." After looking at the time on the wall clock, Victoria went back to her desk and buzzed Abby at the front desk.

"Abby, I need you to have all the executive staff and senior accountants meet with me in the larger conference room in twenty minutes, including yourself."

"Sure thing, Victoria. Can I get you anything?" Abby kindly inquired.

"No, I'm good. Thank you, Abby."

CHAPTER 37

Victoria sat in her chair, placed her elbows on her desk, and covered her face with her hands. Drew sat in an armchair across the desk and watched her closely. He wanted to fix this for her. He wanted to make sure no one ever harmed her. She didn't deserve this. Even with what transpired between them, she certainly didn't merit what Brandon had done and planned to do.

Victoria swiveled around in her chair and opened the mini-fridge in the credenza, pulling out two chilled bottles of water. She turned back and handed one to Drew.

"Nothing stronger," Drew teased.

"I wish... but unfortunately not."

Victoria took a towelette from a package in her bottom desk drawer and dabbed at her face. It did little to remove the vestiges of her crying, but at least the smeared mascara was gone. She still had Drew's handkerchief and looked at it. She looked up at him, and he smiled.

"It's washable, don't worry. Besides, I have dozens of them."

Victoria's desk phone rang, and she could see Abby had put it directly through to her. It must be either the police or family.

She tapped the speaker button, "Hello."

"Victoria, it's Mom. We picked up Tyler, and we'll be at Brock's soon. Just in case, Jamie and Riley are going to be there as well. We told Tyler you had a meeting and since you might be late, he would stay with us for a bit. Have you heard anything more from the detective?"

"No... nothing more. I'm going to meet with the staff shortly and give them a heads up about what's happening. It's only right I make them aware. I'd feel terrible if something were to happen here I could have prevented. Then I'm... we're going to head to my house."

"Why aren't you coming here?"

"Mom, more than likely, Brandon is out there, watching my every move, and I don't want him following me to you and Tyler. I'll make sure the detective knows when we leave and where we're going."

"Okay," Marya said hesitantly, "Just please be safe. And Drew... is he...?

"Yes, he's right here. I doubt very much he'll let me out of his sight, especially now."

From across the desk, Drew nodded, raising a brow, and gave a quirky smile.

Victoria's intercom buzzed, and Abby told her everyone had assembled in the conference room.

"Mom, I need to go now... I love you. Give Ty a hug and kiss for me."

"Will do, Honey. I love you, too."

After Victoria hung up the phone, she pushed back from the desk.

"Come with me, Drew, please."

"I was planning on it," he said, rising. He put his arm across her back as they exited her office and walked down the hallway.

When they came to the reception area, Abby already had one of the administrative assistants monitoring the front desk and the main door. Victoria instructed her to set the security so no one could enter their company offices unless they were buzzed in, and it would require Victoria's approval prior to admittance.

Victoria entered the conference room with Drew closely behind her, then Abby, who closed the door.

Victoria looked around the room and saw the faces of people who had become friends over the years. She wasn't sure exactly how she would tell them, but with a somewhat shaky voice, she persevered. She didn't go into the sordid details of the events of over ten years prior, but she spoke about Brandon, his incarceration, and his recent subsequent release. She told them there were incidents the police believe to have been instigated by Brandon, the threats he was making, and there was an APB out on him and an arrest warrant.

"I completely understand if you wish to leave work today and head home to be safe. I'm going to be leaving shortly as well. Please inform your staff about what is happening. It's my hope Brandon Barkley is caught quickly and won't be a danger to anyone anymore. I'll be in touch with Abby who will use the email blast and text notification to update you. She can do it remotely from her laptop, so she won't need to be here. I know this may cause some issues with your client appointments, so if you need to meet with a client, please do it away from here for the time being. I really don't know what else to say, except be safe."

Charles, one of the other senior partners, came forward and took Victoria's hands.

"Victoria, we're all family here. What affects you, affects us. I'm sure I speak for everyone here, we only want the best for you, and that is for you and your family to be safe. All of our clients have our mobile phone numbers, and the direct lines ring through to those numbers. It's no hardship for us to work remotely, and if we need to meet with clients, it's not an issue. We all have access to the computer file system, so everything can be done out of the office. Just take care of yourself."

"Thank you, Charles," Victoria said as she gave him a hug.

Charles teasingly asked as he nodded to Drew, "Is this gentleman your bodyguard?"

"Charles, this is my... dear friend, Drew."

Drew reached out and shook hands with Charles.

"Well, he certainly looks strong enough to be a bodyguard. Take care of her, please. She means a lot to us here."

"I know what you mean, and you can count on it, Charles," Drew responded.

Everyone filed out of the conference room and went to their respective offices. As each left, they either clasped Victoria's hand or gave her a hug. Drew was awestruck by the camaraderie everyone had with Victoria. To her credit, she was the epitome of a successful businesswoman, combined with the heart of a mother lion. They loved her... he loved her—of that he was certain.

As Victoria and Drew left the conference room, she turned to Abby. "Abby, please..."

"I've got this, Victoria, don't worry. I know what to do. Just do what you have to do and keep me in the loop." Abby gave Victoria a hug and headed to the reception desk.

After Victoria and Drew entered her office, she picked up her purse, checking its contents and glanced over at the coat rack where she kept a knee-length sweater coat for days when the weather turned chilly.

"There are restrooms in our office suite at the end of this hallway to the right should you need one. I'm going to walk down there now before we leave."

Drew shook his head but had a strange feeling Victoria had something on her mind.

"I'll be right back." Victoria grabbed her sweater coat and her purse and left her office.

Five minutes later, Victoria walked back into her office with her sweater coat on and her purse strap slung across her shoulder. Picking up her briefcase, she said, "I'm ready if you are."

Drew emphatically told her, "We're taking my rental car. Brandon obviously knows your car, but he doesn't know mine. We can get yours later or have the police patrol it while it's here."

"Okay, but I need to get my garage door opener out of it. It's on a key fob in the center console. I'll disengage the automatic opener from the vehicle system too."

As they were leaving the office suite, members of her staff were exiting as well. Instead of distancing themselves from her, they actually crowded around her, almost acting as a shield, each one of them giving her a smile. Their actions didn't go unnoticed by Drew.

He walked with his right arm around her shoulders and his left hand holding her left hand, giving her a gentle squeeze to let her know he was there for her. Drew's protective stance gave Victoria a sense of security and an emotion she felt she'd lost a long time ago.

"I'll call the detective and my mom from your car and let them know we've left the office and are headed to my house," Victoria whispered.

Drew nodded.

As they exited the elevator on the floor of the parking garage, people hung closely to Victoria and Drew until they had to head to their own vehicles.

Victoria pointed out her vehicle in the reserved section. Drew had his rental car parked across the aisle in the visitor's section.

Pulling away from Drew, Victoria said, "I'll just be a minute to get the opener and disengage the system. Here, take my briefcase for me."

"Victoria! Wait!" Drew called out as he gripped the briefcase, but Victoria was already halfway to her car.

Drew hurried to his car, tossed her briefcase onto the back seat, and started the car. As he was backing out to pull next to the back end of Victoria's car, he heard her scream. He stopped and jumped out of his car.

When Victoria had released the door lock on her car and was reaching into the center console, she had been grabbed from behind, and she screamed. A hooded figure threw her to the ground next to her car. She knew it was Brandon. She scrambled to get to her feet, but she took a pistol whip to her head and was knocked down. Dazed, she tried to reach into her coat pocket.

Victoria heard someone shout her name. It was Drew.

Brandon attempted to throw a kick to Victoria's side just as Drew launched himself at Brandon and caught him off guard, stopping him cold. They both rolled to the pavement beside Victoria's car.

In a haze from the blood streaming from her head, she could see Drew struggling to get the gun away from the Brandon.

Then the sharp report of a gun firing, then another one.

Victoria could hear the echoing screams and shouts of people in the parking garage. She rolled to her side and tried to get up.

So dizzy. She looked over and saw Drew and Brandon motionless on the pavement. She could see blood oozing out onto the cement and started crawling to Drew's prone body.

"Drew... Drew... I'm here..." Victoria struggled.

Sirens... yes, sirens... "Help is coming, Drew, hang on."

As she finally reached Drew's lifeless body, she extended her arm and with a trembling hand stroked his face, her fingers touching his hairline at the temple. It was sticky with blood.

"Oh no, Drew... no... you can't leave me now. Please, don't leave me. We have a son. A beautiful son who needs you. I need you."

"Well, isn't this just a pretty picture," came a screeching voice.

Claudine Barkley! She was dressed in an outfit similar to Brandon's with a hooded sweatshirt, her eyes bulging with a look of sheer madness.

Waving a gun back and forth at Victoria, she hissed, "You destroyed our lives. We lost everything because of you. And now your friend here took my son."

A low moan came from Drew, and Victoria huddled closer to him.

Claudine Barkley cackled, "I want you to watch as I make sure he's dead. I want it to be the last thing you remember before I kill you."

As Claudine maneuvered around her son's body, Victoria reached deep into her coat pocket.

Claudine smiled at Victoria and said in a shrill voice, "Say goodbye to your friend, Victoria. You're next!"

Claudine raised and leveled her gun at Drew. Victoria swung her hand up and pulled the trigger on her gun just as Claudine was tugging the trigger on hers. The impact from Victoria's bullet hit Claudine square in the chest, causing her shot to go wide, ricocheting off the pavement. Claudine clutched her chest, and with horrified eyes, fell to the pavement next to her son, her blood pooling on the cement with her son's.

Office workers, who had crouched behind their vehicles when the shooting started and witnessed everything, came forward just as the police and paramedics arrived.

Everything seemed like it was in slow motion, and what only took less than two minutes seemed like longer.

Several paramedics worked on Drew while two others tended to Victoria. All she could see was Drew being loaded into the ambulance and the paramedics working feverishly on him.

Victoria had wanted to go with Drew as they rushed him to the hospital, but they told her she had to go separately.

She murmured a prayer, "Please God, please save him. Please let him be okay."

The detective arrived at the scene just as they were loading Victoria into an ambulance and jumped in as they left for the hospital.

"I'm sorry we weren't able to get him before he got to you. We had no idea his mother was his accomplice. We located her vehicle parked around the corner, and there's damage to the front end from when she tried to run you down while you were cycling. However, the tampering of your car was definitely Brandon. He bragged about it to people at a bar he was frequenting."

"How did you know he was..."

"Her car... we had it on alert, and it was spotted. As soon as we confirmed it was hers, we called all the district units in, not knowing what we would run into.

"From what the officers first on the scene reported, there are numerous witnesses coming forward, stating Brandon attacked you, then your unarmed friend Drew stopped him from killing you. During the struggle, Brandon was killed by his own gun, and Brandon's mother fired a shot, hitting your friend. We have his name as Drew Anderson from his wallet ID. If you hadn't done what you did, there's no telling how many more people would have been killed by that crazy woman. There were quite a few people in the parking garage, and they're all grateful to you. I know right now everything is a blur, and they need to attend to you at the hospital, so I'll stop by later and get a statement."

"Could you please call my mom and call Diana and let them know?" Victoria asked while trying to keep her eyes open.

She felt cold, very cold. By the time they reached the hospital, the paramedics had her hooked up to an IV and had stopped the bleeding from her head wound.

CHAPTER 38

It was Tuesday, and twenty-four hours had passed since the attack in the parking garage, and Victoria was finally able to open her eyes without pain. Several times over those hours, she awoke and asked about her family, asked about Drew, then she would drift off.

Due to her severe head injury, she was kept in ICU, and her mother was allowed to visit with her. Marya informed her she told Tyler his mommy was on a business trip and would be home soon. She also told her she brought Tyler back to her house and would keep him there until Victoria could go home. She wanted things to be as normal as possible for him.

The doctor advised Victoria she was out of the woods. They would be moving her to a regular room on the same floor, and she'd be able to have more visitors if she wished. Victoria didn't think it wise to have Tyler see her at the hospital, especially since she still had her head bandaged, so she decided to wait until she was released.

The only information she could get on Drew was he was alive, but in a medically induced coma in the CCU area of the hospital. She so wanted to see him, but only family could visit. Drew had no family, well, just one, but he didn't know him—yet.

Diana came by to visit and told Victoria she was helping Marya out with Tyler, keeping him occupied.

"Victoria, I called Travis. He'd left several messages, wondering what was going on since he couldn't reach you. I filled him in on what happened. I hope you don't mind."

"Mind? Why would I mind? Travis is a dear friend, and he did so much for me during the move and with the Brandon issue."

"But... Drew? He asked why Drew was here. I told him I didn't know. You and I had just found out about Drew's call less than twelve hours before he showed up. Did you...?"

"No! No way. I have no clue why Drew came to Phoenix. It was a shock to me when I walked into my office and saw him standing there. He had seen the picture of Tyler, and I could tell he pieced it all together. There really wasn't any sense in denying it, so I just didn't say anything... until...."

"Victoria? Until what? Diana asked.

"The parking garage. Drew was lying there wounded, and when I crawled to him, blood was seeping from the side of his head..." Victoria shuddered.

"Then what?"

"He was unconscious and dying as I watched his life flowing out of his body. I told him I needed him, and he couldn't leave me. I told him we had a son, and his son needed him."

"From what I've heard of Drew's injury, I doubt he heard you. But I do agree with you, he probably figured it out when he was in your office. The fact you didn't just come right out and tell Drew he had a son doesn't change that."

"I know. It's still touch-and-go for Drew. I can't do anything about it until he pulls through. And I know in my heart he will."

"They still won't let you see him?"

Victoria shook her head.

"How much longer do you think they'll keep you here?"

"The soonest Thursday but more likely Friday. They want to make sure there aren't any complications. This is the second time I've had head trauma. Brandon's doing both times."

"Glad that issue is over with. I'm going to get going now. By the way, I have an interview tomorrow morning with Travis' firm. Wish me luck!"

"Hey, great. Thanks for helping out with Tyler, Diana. I'm truly blessed to have you as a friend. You're more like a sister, actually."

"Okay, Sis!" Diana said, giving Victoria a hug.

Victoria laid back on her pillow. It didn't take much to feel exhausted and sleep came immediately.

WEDNESDAY MORNING, the doctor ordered up an additional head scan on Victoria to make a comparison to the one from Monday to determine any further issues.

As they were wheeling Victoria down the hallway, she noticed the secure area marked CCU. She knew Drew was just a short distance away, probably still fighting for his life. She so wanted to see him if just to hold his hand.

After being returned to her room with the scan completed, Victoria awaited the report from the doctor. Marya peeked her head in the doorway.

"Are you up for visitors?"

"Always for you, Mom. Come on in."

Marya stepped in, followed closely by Brock.

"Wow, I get a twofer," Victoria exclaimed with a smile. But Marya noticed Victoria's smile was lacking in its sincerity.

"What's up, Honey? That wasn't a real smile, and you know it."

Victoria hesitated, knowing her mom could read her like a book, and whatever she said had better be truthful.

"I still don't know what's happening with Drew. I only get little pieces of information, and what I do know is he's still in CCU. Hence, only family can visit, and he has no family... sort of. He saved my life, Mom. I wouldn't be alive today if he hadn't stopped Brandon." Tears started to fall down her cheeks, and Marya rushed to hug her.

Brock quietly left the room unnoticed.

Marya sat on the edge of the hospital bed, holding her daughter and listening to her sobs.

Ten minutes later the doctor came in and gave Victoria the good news she would probably be released the following day. The doctor said he would check her in the morning, and by noon she should be on her way home with any prescriptions and home care instructions.

Victoria was delighted, especially since she would be able to see

Tyler and allay any fears he may have had about her absence. Victoria realized some scrapes and bruises would still be noticeable and planned on covering them up with makeup.

She knew Tyler was very astute for his age and probably had questions as to what really was going on. Fortunately, Marya had called Victoria at the hospital, and they pretended she was on a business trip out of state, so Tyler was able to talk to her on the phone.

The doctor didn't look to be in a hurry to leave and was exchanging glances with Brock who stood silently in the corner of the room.

"Victoria, I understand your friend, Drew Anderson, is in CCU, and he was instrumental in saving your life. Seeing Mr. Anderson has no relatives, I think it entirely reasonable to give authorization for you to visit him. I believe it not only would be in his best interest but also your own. Emotional and mental attitudes play a significant role in healing. He's in a medically induced coma, but it's believed even though he's 'asleep,' we're sure he'll be able to sense your presence. And if you speak to him, he may subconsciously hear you."

Victoria's heart was pounding. "How soon can I see him?"

"Is now too soon?" The doctor was rewarded with one of Victoria's genuine smiles.

"I'll have the orderly bring a wheelchair for you, that's the one stipulation. I don't want to have to extend your stay here if you get too emotional and fall over."

"Thank you, Doctor."

The doctor turned to leave and gave Brock a nod. Victoria knew then and there, Brock had something to do with it.

Just over five minutes later, an orderly pushed a wheelchair into Victoria's room. Victoria had taken her hair down from the ponytail and put on some lip gloss, thinking there really wasn't more she could do with her banged up face and head or the scrapes on her arms and legs, but it would have to do.

Her mother teased, since Drew was in a coma, he wouldn't be able to see her. It was then Marya realized Victoria was fixing herself up more for herself than for Drew. Victoria needed this—another beginning.

"Victoria, do you want us to wait here until you get back? Tyler is with Diana at my house and time isn't a factor."

"If you don't mind waiting."

Brock answered, "We'll be here." Leaning in to whisper in Victoria's ear, he said, "If possible touch him, hold his hand. He'll sense it."

Victoria looked at Brock and mouthed, "Thank you."

As the orderly pushed Victoria in the wheelchair through the security doors of the CCU, her heart raced. The lighting in the CCU was different, very muted and it was very quiet. All the room units were walled on three sides, and the wall facing the nurses' station was made of glass with a wide, automatic sliding glass door.

Victoria noticed the nurses' station had huge monitors, one for each unit, gathering ongoing medical information on the patient.

They came to a stop in front of one of the units, the orderly pushed a button, and the sliding door opened with an almost inaudible swoosh.

Victoria could see a bed almost entirely surrounded by equipment and monitors. The beeps normally heard on such monitors were silenced, confirming the information transmitted directly to the nurses' station. The orderly wheeled Victoria around the maze of equipment to the side of the bed.

Victoria gasped as she laid her eyes on Drew's motionless form. His head was wrapped in bandages with a small tube coming out of one area.

The orderly told Victoria he would be right outside the door and excused himself.

The area around Drew's eyes was dark and soft stubble covered his chin and cheeks. No matter what, he was just as handsome as ever, and he took her breath away. There was no telltale smell of his cologne, however, only the sterile smell of the hospital. He was on oxygen and had an IV with several lines being fed into it.

She wanted so much to touch his face but held back. Instead, she raised her hand and held his. She could feel his pulse.

She remembered what the doctor had told her. She tried to speak, but her mouth was dry. She tried again.

"Drew," she said hoarsely, "I'm here. It's Victoria. I don't know if you can hear me. I hope somehow you can." She paused waiting to see if there was a response. There was none.

"I'm not giving up on you, Drew Anderson. Not by a long shot. And I don't want you to give up. Yes, Drew, we have a son. You have a son. And I know you will love him as much as I do, and he will love you right back. He's got your beautiful dark eyes and wonderful dark chocolate hair, and his smile... his smile lights up my world just like yours did. I know he's going to rock someone's world when he gets older. I want to get him a bike for Christmas, and I want you to teach him how to ride it, so you have to get better. You have to."

Victoria choked back the sob in her throat.

"Tyler loves story time before he goes to bed. Sometimes, I put the book aside and make up stories to tell him. He likes those the most. And he loves ice cream... he tells everyone it's his favorite food. Just like his Dad."

Victoria found herself gently squeezing his hand and hoped she didn't hurt him. She looked down at his hand while she held it in her long slender fingers. Drew had teased her about her long slender fingers, and she smiled.

"Oh, we've wasted so many years. Years we could have been together. I'm so sorry, Drew. I didn't know. I didn't know until the day before you came to Phoenix that you did call and try to reach me. I didn't know."

Victoria stroked Drew's exposed arm with her other hand, enjoying the feel of the dark hairs under her fingers.

"I wonder if you know how many times I relived our time together in my mind. It was often... very often. What I wouldn't give to go back, but I know it's impossible. But... maybe we can move forward. That's why it's important you get better."

Victoria didn't know what she was hoping for while talking to Drew. Maybe a sign he had heard her. Any kind of movement. But nothing came. She had intently watched his face—no sign of recognition he heard her—the only movement the rise and fall of his chest as he breathed.

Sighing deeply and closing her eyes, she prayed, "Dear God, please hear my prayer. Please bring Drew back to me. Bring him back to meet his son."

Victoria leaned forward and placed a lingering kiss on his hand, hoping in some way to convey she was there, and he was loved. A tear fell on his hand. Then she gave his hand another gentle squeeze and released it.

Victoria backed her wheelchair up slightly and motioned to the orderly outside the room. As the orderly came in and turned Victoria's wheelchair toward the door, they missed seeing the movement of Drew's hand reaching out.

CHAPTER 39

Arriving back in her hospital room, Marya and Brock noticed immediately the happy and hopeful face Victoria wore when she left to see Drew was now tired and drawn. It obviously did not go as she hoped. The orderly asked Victoria if she wished to stay in the wheelchair or move to her bed or to the chair beside her bed.

"I really would like to get up and walk around. They had me walking the hall a bit with a nurse early this morning, and since I'm getting released tomorrow, I really need to get my legs steady. I have a munchkin at home to run after."

Brock and Marya knew Victoria well enough to know this was a diversionary tactic to not talk about her time with Drew.

The orderly nodded, helped Victoria out of the wheelchair, and removed it from the room as Marya and Brock each took a side and walked with her. They were a good distance down the hallway when Victoria spoke.

"He looks so fragile, lying there, hooked up to all those monitors. I talked to him, and I prayed for him. I have to be realistic, he may never recover."

"But Victoria, what if he does? I know you and Drew will have things to work out. But Tyler will have his father. The fact he put your life before his own tells me a lot about him," Marya said.

Brock interjected, "Victoria, you need to get yourself well, especially for Tyler. He's been very inquisitive the past couple of days. He's very intuitive... just like your mother."

"I know. I told Drew how Tyler lights up my world."

After making a couple of rounds down the hallways, they returned to Victoria's room, and the doctor poked his head in.

"So, how did it go when you went to see Drew?"

"I talked to him and held his hand, but no response," Victoria said sadly.

"Hmmm... interesting."

"How so?" Victoria asked.

"It seems after your visit, there was movement. It was detected on the monitors. It wasn't a muscle or nerve reaction to the injury. It was an actual brain-directed motion. Enough so they are going to wean him off the drugs used for the induced coma. They should know by tomorrow morning. If all goes well, they might move him to the ICU."

Victoria knew she had tears in her eyes and silently prayed this was a sign Drew would get better.

Brock and Marya left shortly afterward, and Victoria slept for a while.

Mealtime rolled around, and Victoria could hear the rattle of the food carts holding the patients' trays of food. She was hungry, and her stomach growled at the aromas coming from the hallway. An orderly brought her a tray as she sat up in bed and moved the hospital bed tray in front of her. After the tray was in place, she lifted the lid on the plate... and grimaced.

Just then Diana walked in, bearing flowers and a small thermo-bag.

"Diana, please tell me you have real food in that bag."

Smiling at Victoria and waggling her brows, Diana opened the bag and pulled out a Chicago style hotdog from one of Victoria's favorite restaurants.

"Oh, my God! I love you. ... And fries too!" Victoria exclaimed.

Diana had yet another bag and pulled out a chocolate malt.

"I figured hospitals do try to notch up their meals, but you deserve something special for all you've gone through. I hope this isn't going to screw up your hospital menu. Your mom told me it would be okay. I guess she checked your chart when she was here today."

Leave it to Mom to know.

"While Marya and Brock were here, I took Tyler to the Desert Ridge Marketplace, and we had ice cream, then he wanted to go into the bookstore. He had his eye on a couple of storybooks, and I couldn't help myself. You now have two more books in his collection."

"Oh, Diana, you're so sweet, and thanks again for helping to look after him."

"No problem. He's a fun kid. Besides, who knows, maybe someday I'll have a kid or two, and this gives me good practice."

In between bites of her hot dog, Victoria asked her how the job interview went, and Diana told her she really had a good feeling about it. The location and position were perfect. If she got it, she would be working in Travis' department once he relocated.

"Speaking of Travis, he asked for me to give him an update each day. He truly cares about you and Tyler."

"I know, and I truly care about him, so does Tyler, but right now, everything is still in limbo. When I saw Drew lying there in the CCU, the connection I felt years ago was still there. And it's not just because we had a child together. It's something more. I think that's what held me back from Travis. I have a connection with Travis, but it's different from what I feel with Drew. I keep trying to find a word to describe it, but I just can't."

"Your mom and Brock filled me in on Drew, your visit with him today, and what happened afterward. Any more updates?"

"No, nothing. It's a wait-and-see. Supposedly, they'll know more tomorrow, especially if and how Drew reacts to the change in medication."

"What about the detective? Have you heard anything more?"

"He came by, took more statements. I still have an eerie feeling. And I still can't believe Brandon's mother helped him."

"You're not regretting what happened, are you?"

"No. I know it was a situation of life and death, and I had to do whatever it took. She made it quite clear she was going to shoot to kill. The detective had a list of witnesses to the fact it was self-defense."

The rest of Diana's visit was spent discussing Tyler and what Victoria's plans were when she was released.

"When I see Tyler, I'm going to hug and kiss him until he or I drop!"

Diana looked around the room and saw all the bouquets of flowers.

"You're going to need a truck for all these," she said, waving her hand at the flower arrangements.

"No, I had my Mom take pictures of all of them with their cards, then removed the cards so I could send out thank you notes. I'm going to ask the nurses to disperse the arrangements to other patients and leave some at the nurses' stations. They've been awesome."

Diana cleaned up the empty food wrappers, tossed them in a trash can, and moved the hospital tray table away from Victoria. Diana could tell Victoria was tired and told her she was leaving and would see her sometime the next day. She knew Brock and Marya would be picking Victoria at the hospital and taking her home, so she would more than likely take care of Tyler at Victoria's house and await her arrival there.

After Diana left, she laid back on her bed. An orderly came in and retrieved the food tray. He noticed the food wrappers in the trash, nodded, and whispered, "Good choice!" and left. A nurse came in, checked Victoria's vitals, and gave her the prescribed medications.

Before Victoria drifted off, all she could think about was Drew and hoping somehow tomorrow there would be a miracle.

THE SOUNDS of activity in the hospital hallway Thursday morning brought Victoria out of a deep sleep. She remembered once during the night, a nurse came in to check on her. Victoria had needed to use the bathroom, so the nurse stood by as Victoria walked by herself to the bathroom and waited for Victoria to return to her bed.

Daylight was now streaming in through the windows of her room. A different nurse came in and asked Victoria if she would prefer to have breakfast first or to shower. Victoria jumped at the chance to shower, but then realized she didn't have any street clothes to wear when she was released.

The nurse told her not to worry, she could just wear a clean hospital gown, and when her mom came to get her with her own clothes, she could change.

When Victoria was first admitted, Marya had gotten Victoria's purse from the detective. Once Victoria was put into a regular room, she gave it to Victoria who had it stored in the cabinet next to the hospital bed. After showering and getting into a fresh gown, Victoria retrieved her purse and dug into it, looking for a hairbrush, a hair band, and her makeup bag. She found them along with a single small plastic bag holding her watch and her pearl stud earrings she'd worn on Monday. She didn't remember removing them at the hospital, so she surmised one of the nurses must have.

She allowed her hair to air dry a bit before running the brush through it and pulling it back into a ponytail. She kept her earrings in the plastic bag but put her watch on. She was surprised it wasn't damaged. She looked into the mirror above the bathroom sink and knew she had to perform a miracle of her own. After applying some moisturizer and dabbing on makeup in an attempt to cover the scrapes and bruises, she brushed on some blush and slid lip gloss on her lips.

Looking back into the mirror, she said to herself, "Well it'll have to do."

An orderly brought in her breakfast. This time, it smelled and looked good, and she was ravenous. The nurse came in and took her vitals, and the doctor came in shortly after and gave her the news she indeed was going home.

Victoria hesitated to ask him if he knew how Drew was doing. The doctor sensed it and told her Drew had opened his eyes for a little while. He wasn't very coherent as yet, but neurological tests were all very good.

"What do you mean he wasn't coherent? Victoria asked.

"The nurse thought he said he wanted ice cream of all things. Can you imagine that?"

"Yes, I can... indeed I can," answered Victoria, smiling.

Brock and Marya arrived at just after ten o'clock as Victoria was finishing filling out and signing her discharge paperwork. Marya had a small overnight bag with her and opened it up.

"Hope you're okay with what I brought."

"More than okay, Mom, anything to get out of this drafty hospital gown. I keep thinking I'm flashing someone."

Victoria picked up her favorite turquoise warmup pants and jacket, a bra and panties, and headed into the bathroom. Five minutes later, she exited the bathroom and slipped on a pair of bootie socks and her sneakers.

An orderly arrived with a wheelchair as was the procedure when discharging patients.

Looking at Brock and Marya, she asked, "I really would like to make a stop before we leave the hospital."

Brock spoke quietly and briefly to the orderly, and the orderly nodded.

Brock and Marya totally understood and suggested they load the car and bring it around to the front entrance.

The orderly wheeled Victoria to the CCU. When they got there, Drew wasn't in the room. As a matter of fact, the now-vacant room had been totally cleaned up. Victoria asked the station nurse where he was, and she motioned to the ICU just down the hallway.

Once Victoria was directed into Drew's room, the orderly wheeled her next to his bed and went outside.

There were fewer pieces of apparatus around him. He still had an IV and a nasal cannula to administer oxygen. There were other things stuck to him to monitor his heart rate and blood pressure, and he was still very pale. They had removed quite a few of the head bandages, and the drainage tube was gone.

She leaned closer, took his hand in hers, kissed it, then pulled back and looked up to see his eyes open and staring at her, a slight smile on his lips. Victoria was sure her heart had just jumped out of her chest and was doing backflips around the room.

His hand clenched hers. Even though verbal communication was basically non-existent, so much passed between them as they stared into one another eyes. The lump in Victoria's throat prevented her from talking, and it took several moments before she was able to intelligibly form words.

"Ice cream? Really, Drew? That's all you could think of to ask for?" she teased. She was rewarded with a smirk and a wink.

She knew it was difficult for him to talk and brought her index finger to her lips to let him know he needn't speak.

"I don't know how much they've told you. I'm being discharged today, but I'll be back very, very soon. I'd stay, but I want to get home to my... to our son. I've missed him so much. You're going to love him, Drew, and he's going to love you. We have a lot of catching up to do. So, hurry up and get better soon."

Drew smiled again, this time motioning with his other hand to come closer.

She knew she was supposed to stay in the wheelchair, but she got up, anyway and leaned close to his face.

His hoarse whisper was barely audible, "I love you, Victoria, always have and always will."

There were tears on his cheek, and she wasn't sure if they were hers or his.

"And I love you, Drew Anderson."

VICTORIA HAD BEEN home for several days and was able to stay in touch with the hospital about Drew's status. It was obvious to the doctors and staff she had a positive influence in his recovery, allowing her to communicate directly with them, especially after Drew voiced his approval. He had been moved to a private room and had been healing rapidly. There was no determination as yet when Drew would be released, but Brock had made arrangements for Drew to stay in the guest room at his condo when it happened.

Victoria had stopped in to see Drew several times. It was during one of those visits she found out why he had come to Arizona. It was to finalize a deal expanding his security company into the Phoenix market area.

His investment partner flew to Arizona once Drew was out of the woods and completed the transaction as well as signing a lease on the premises they would use for their offices. The fact Drew would pick the Phoenix area to develop business for his company, instead of anywhere else, told her he hadn't given up on her or them.

Victoria's injuries had faded to the point where they were almost indiscernible. She had returned to work, and Tyler was back in preschool, already talking about the Christmas holidays and getting the decorations up.

Travis had come to town and called Victoria, asking to see her. When he arrived at her house, she greeted him with a hug. Tyler ran down the hallway and welcomed "Travis the Tree" back.

After catching up with Tyler on the Lego situation and giving him yet another new Lego playset, Travis asked Victoria if they could go out on the patio to talk. Victoria told Tyler it would be nice if he went back in the play area of his room and built some special to show Travis. He took off running.

Victoria and Travis walked out to the patio and sat on the sofa.

"I'm glad the Brandon issue is over."

"As well as I. The forensic reports confirmed it was self-defense on my part. When Drew struggled with Brandon to get the gun away from him and blocked him from getting to me, Brandon's own gun fired, killing him instantly. Claudine Barkley fired almost at the same time, striking Drew on the side of the head. The bullet didn't penetrate his skull but caused internal bleeding and trauma to his brain. I cringe thinking what might have happened if I didn't have my gun or if I had missed. I thank you for taking me to the range and helping me with my target practice."

It got quiet, and neither spoke for a few moments.

"Victoria, I want you to know something. I do care very deeply for you. And I know you have feelings for me, but not like mine for you. I also know in my heart, you and Drew have something extremely special between you. Loving someone is making sure they are as happy as they can be. It's what I want for you. I'll always be your friend, and if you ever need me, I'll be there for you. I just want you to be happy in your life. You deserve it."

Victoria gave him a hug, and he responded in kind.

Later, as she stood at her door waving goodbye to Travis, she knew he would always be her friend.

Everything was back to the normal routine at both the Hart households.

EPILOGUE

The most recent reports from the doctors indicated Drew was in good health, considering what had happened, but he seemed increasingly antsy to get out of the hospital, and signs of depression were setting in. The doctors were hoping to release Drew in a day or two.

It was the next morning when Victoria drove to the hospital. She peeked her head around the corner in Drew's room and was happy to see him sitting in a chair, looking out the window, appearing deep in thought.

"Good morning, Drew!"

His head turned, his eyes lit up, and he greeted her with a smile.

"Hey, you just made my day, Victoria!"

"I did? Well, I'm going to make it so much better," she said cryptically.

Drew cocked his head, drawing his brows together, questioning her comment.

Victoria opened the door wider, and Tyler walked in.

A gasp could be heard from Drew. He pursed his lips together, and Victoria could see his eyes start to glisten over.

"Tyler, this is my friend I told you about. His name is Drew Anderson," Victoria said, trying to ignore the lump in her throat.

Tyler, being the precocious child he was, walked over to Drew and put out his hand to shake it.

"Hi, Mr. Anderson, I'm Tyler."

Drew had gathered his thoughts, shaking Tyler's small hand.

"Hi, Tyler. You can call me Drew if you'd like."

Tyler nodded.

"Mommy told me about your accident, so I drew some pictures for you to make you feel better and smile," Tyler said, waving several sheets of paper in his fist.

Victoria stood off to the side of the room, watching the interaction between Drew and Tyler... father and son, trying desperately not to break down.

Drew asked Tyler to jump up in his lap and show him his pictures, which Tyler was more than happy to do.

"This one is of Mommy and me when we went to see the wild horses at the river. And this one is me and Gramma and her friend Brock at his fire station. He let me sit in the fire engine and everything!

"This picture is me and some other children at school on the playground. See the swings! Do you have children, Drew?" Tyler inquired, looking innocently up at Drew.

Drew took a deep breath and answered, "I hope someday I'll have several children," carefully phrasing his response and purposely arching an eyebrow at Victoria, causing her to blush.

"Then I can play with them. Okay?"

"I'm sure you will, Tyler," Drew said, nodding.

Tyler continued with his presentation, "And this picture is you in a hospital bed. I didn't know what you looked like, but Mommy told me I look just like you... and you look like me... you really do," Tyler said, cocking his head to one side.

"And this last one is of a Christmas tree like the one we're going to put up in our new house. Are you going to come see it, Drew? Christmas is only a week from now. If you're all better, you can come spend Christmas with us. Can you?" he asked innocently.

Drew glanced over to Victoria, standing off to the side, who was wiping away a barrage of tears and smiling. The look they shared between them was profound. The fire had never gone out between them.

"Yes, Tyler, I'll be there... for this Christmas and for many Christmases to come."

Victoria walked over and knelt beside Drew's chair and put her arms around both Drew and Tyler. The circle was completed. And the word that could only describe what was between them—MAGIC!

The End

COMING SOON!

Hearts Healing
Book 2 in The Phoenix Rising Series

Follow along with the next book in the series as Victoria and Drew continue with their love story and Diana and Travis start their own. Brock and Marya's bond grows stronger with the adversities they face.

SPECIAL THANKS

Special heartfelt thanks to...

My family, especially Paul, Kim and Karen for your incredible love and support throughout my roller coaster life, especially during my writing...

My husband Richard for putting up with my mood swings, middle-of-the-night writing, being there with a shoulder to cry on and to wipe the happy and sad tears from my face...

My dear friends Peggy, Grace, Margaret, and Lynnette, who always listen to my rants and raves with loving hearts and open minds....

My fantastically talented personal team of Byron and Sylvia Medina, Tonia Miller, and Jeanine Coleman...

My awesome publishing team at Dragonfly Ink Publishing... Dakota Willink, Sandy Ebel, Cheryl Maddox, and Antonette Santillo; there are no words to fully convey how fabulous you all are. You've held my hand throughout the entire process. Your care and concern, your talents, and your encouragement are purely overwhelming.

You have all "risen above and beyond!"
Penelope

ABOUT THE AUTHOR

Penelope Bell was born and raised in the suburbs of Chicago. Her love of reading and writing took hold at a very young age—you would always see her with a book or a pen and paper in her hands. She loved mysteries and stories about horses or dogs or tales of knights in shining armor. As she grew older, romance stories intrigued her, especially if they were historical and took place in foreign countries.

When she was 20 years old, she went on a three-week road trip with her parents, traveling through the Rocky Mountain states, down the west coast, then throughout the southwest. The memories were long-lasting and impressionable, and over the following years, she made several trips to the southwest, savoring the atmosphere, varied terrain, and climate. The snow-capped mountains of northern Arizona, the Ponderosa pine forests, the Grand Canyon, and the high and low desert regions beckoned her. Her parents had retired and moved to Arizona, and when an opportunity presented itself to her, as a divorced mother of two, she relocated to the greater Phoenix area, traveling cross-country with her teenaged children, two affectionate cats, and a silly but protective Irish Setter.

Caring for her children and her aging parents and working a full time job didn't allow for much reading or writing time, but somehow, she managed to squeeze some of it in to her life. It brought her happiness and serenity.

Writing is her passion with photography coming in as a close second. Penelope self-published several "coffee table" photography books, one of which included her poetry and short stories. Her family has always been supportive of her writing and encouraged her to publish her novels.

Penelope's stories have been a catharsis for her. She writes what she knows. Lead characters deal with events and situations very familiar to her. In many ways, she feels it has liberated her from her own past traumas and taken her from being broken to being made whole again.

Music is vital to her, and she always has it as a background while writing. She affirms it gets the creative juices flowing and the imagination soaring.

Her advocacy for the protection of wild horses is near and dear to her, and you will more than likely find the struggle to prevent the extinction of those majestic creatures within her books.

Penelope met her "forever" in 2007 and lives in Scottsdale, Arizona with her husband. In the summer, time is spent at their cabin up in the northern Arizona forests. Maintaining her heritage and traditions and spending time with family is very important to her. She and her husband both love to travel and have done so extensively, including most of North America, the Caribbean, and Europe, savoring the histories, cultures, and geography of those places, yet they cherish those quiet times at home, sharing each other's thoughts and dreams.

Please visit www.PenelopeBellAuthor.com to learn more about Penelope and future works.

 facebook.com/PenelopeBellAuthor

Made in the USA
Columbia, SC
08 February 2020